August Descending

by Paul Bentley

July 10, 2013

To my brother Frank,
Hopefully there are some laughs here
for you. And a few remember-when
classroom moments ☺!

Paul

Any resemblance to actual persons, living or dead, is purely coincidental.

Cover design by Virgil Wong, based on his painting *Alchemy* (virgilwong.com)

ISBN-13: 978-1490375908
ISBN-10: 1490375902

About The Author

Paul Bentley is a retired teacher, a freelance writer, and the author of Sh*t A Teacher Thinks (and sometimes says). He lives in the Northeast with his wife and cat.

To my Mother & Father

The First Writers In The Family

August Descending

by Paul Bentley

Prologue
Summer Nocturne

Surf City: There is no blue book value on summer or on the lazy hazy days of living off the work grid. If only I could prolong it, stretch out these remaining September hours into some type of Stephen Hawking elongated worm hole and blast my corporeal self through to an alternate universe, a different destiny. But the first day of school is tomorrow and no amount of gin cradling or swirling the ice to dilute the little that's left will stop that reality.

A derelict stumbles past me from the other end of the bar. He's on his way out the door, pulls up short, turns around, squints, stares intently at me like I'm Hitler reincarnated. Then shambles over. His army fatigue jacket is cross-hatched with dirt and splayed with motorcycle patches. His beard is unkempt, still wet with beer. He smells like damp basement, old socks. His hair a tangle of weathered baling wire.

- I know you, he says, slurring his words badly. You're what's-his-name, that prick I had for English. . . He sways sideways and grabs the back of my bar chair to steady himself. August! he finally says. Mr. August! You know, he drools, you were a son-of-a-bitch. Remember me?

- No, I say. I had lots of assholes over the years. Apparently one of them hasn't changed.

- Ahhh, haha, I get it, he says. Very funny. My name's Jimmy Klein. Remember me *now*?

- Yeah, I say, I remember you, and think, Jimmy Klein, the punk from 20 years ago. The one who told the class they were suckers to work since it was just easier to flunk for 36 weeks and go to summer school and pass in

1

5. Jimmy Klein, the trouble maker who was suspended twice because I reported him. Jimmy Klein, the weasel who stole my Schwinn back in the day. Cut the lock and weeks later left the 10-speed in a demolished heap in my parking spot. Nothing proven, but the skulking skinny shit did it.

- Aren't you going to ask me what I'm doing these days?

- I can   see. Drinking till you can barely stand. Probably stalking on Craigslist too.

He backs away from my chair, sways more, and starts a swing. I lean back. Grab his slow one-cylinder punch. Pull him down. Headfirst into the bar. He hits with a thud and slumps to the floor. Moaning. Vinnie the bartender, a fat tough little guy, is around like a shot. He bends over the slightly moving schmo. Slaps him on the cheeks. Tosses a glass of water in his face like this is some wild west saloon and the bartender has to clean up before the sheriff arrives.

Together we get Klein to his feet.

- You want to press charges, Mike? Vinnie asks. I should call the cops anyway. Maybe an ambulance.

- Nahh, I say. Don't do it for me.   He's a harmless lunk. Not worth a phone call unless you want to cover your own liabilities. . . I think to myself that Klein and I never liked each other and while that is sad for a teacher to admit, in this case it was true then. And it's true now. It occurs to me that I just evened the score with Klein for trashing my bike, as if the universe needs balance despite any arbitrary passing of years. I also think of Carl Jung and his ideas on synchronicity. Klein and I. Together again. Clashing again. Causally related? Meaningful in any present or future way? And are we even?. . . The thoughts have no inertia and I leave them. I'm all out with this kid, and was years ago.

Klein is suddenly struggling. Shaking off the both of us like a rising zombie apocalypse. He says, Get your fucking hands off me and leave me alone, you cocksuckers!

- You're a real sweetheart, Vinnie says to him. Look pal, get your ass out of here and stay out.

- You don't need to worry about that! He lunges out the door and we watch as he crosses the street and stumbles off into the void.

And just like that summer comes to an end.

Chapter 1
Initiating Countdown - 9 weeks
Paper Cut Empire

Daydream Believer: It could be worse. I could be in a combat zone getting my nuts shot off. Or working in a core-melted nuclear reactor cleaning up radioactive waste. Hauling giant steel cages onto storm-tossed decks while frigid Arctic waters numb my ass and behemoth Alaskan king crabs threaten to de-groin me. If the pitching deck doesn't toss me overboard first.

But I'm doing none of that.

I pass out the papers and tell the students they have 10 minutes to fill out this office survey. It's an extended first period and about half of the seniors immediately put their wrists to it. The rest are looking around, yawning, sneaking peeks at cell phones, reapplying makeup, rearranging hairdos, chomping gum, messaging in pantomime, etc. It's a dead zone. The work sensitive, intelligence fallow, low resolution academia that administrators call homeroom

Thank god we only have it once a month.

I settle in for a quick 10 minute zone-out myself when some gum snapping, harrumphing, wide-eyed first rower gets my attention.

- Excuse me, Mr. August, so like, do we *have* to fill these forms out? the hayseed blond asks. There's like no place for names. . . Her large hoop earrings clang like a cruising ice cream truck.

- Well, if you were paying attention, which apparently you weren't, I said this was an anonymous survey. You know what that means, *right*? . . . I smile to buff out the sarcasm.

- I guess so. So we *don't* have to put our names on them, right?

I nod my head.

- What's the penalty if we don't do them? asks a dim-witted, tight tee-shirted mesomorph. He's adrift in an air of stale cigarette smoke and hair mousse. Jersey Shore type.

- You won't be allowed to take the SAT's, get final grades, or graduate.

- Seriously? . . . This comes from Marcus Schmidt, a corner-seated slit-eye who until seconds ago was staring out the window in a 7:35 a.m. daze.

His drab mono-word tone is reflective, rote. I doubt he's even fully aware of what he's saying. I *do* know I have to stop this dialogue right now or we are going to be totally gone on this fucking diversionary tangent.

- No, not seriously. . . I smile wider and stand up. Standing up is always a good show stopper unless you're a midget. Maybe even then . . . Listen, do the survey, don't do the survey. But the chitchat and noise stop *now*.

I'm trying to project confidence and establish a tone for the year. The seniors go quiet. Could be suppressed laughter. I catch a few, What's up with this guy? glances. Makes me wonder if my old-fashioned strong-armed tactics are relevant anymore. Am I? Teaching methods change, education theories change – this survey is proof of that. But what teaching changes are in me? Probably none. Sad to say. I used to think I was a pretty damn good teacher. Now after 2 years of marginal evaluations I'm not so sure.

I continue standing – a muted alpha male posturing. Ten minutes later I collect all the papers. Only a few are blank. Most have at least some doodling. I tell them to take a quiet study hall for 20 minutes.

- But Mr. August. . . Marcus the somnolent dweeb is now awake. . . my guidance counselor told me about this survey. She said after we finished we were going to discuss it.

- Do I look like a survey teacher?. . . I hold out my arms wide. . . The answer is no, so just follow directions. Get out a book or go back to sleep. . . What I don't say is that this homeroom bullshit period and arse patting survey was foisted on us by an administration determined to turn mainstream academic teachers like me into some sort of social worker. A head patting, heart massaging, jerk around therapist. I put in a lot of time on school work. Evenings, weekends, vacations. These peripheral surveys about post grad life are a distraction. And nothing I'm equipped by training or personality to handle. We need this time for academics. Piling on learning, returning basics, keeper-of-the-chalk stuff.

- Mr. August . . . the former daydreamer is still not done and looks around to rally his already mentally departing classmates. . . I'd like to discuss it. I mean, I took the time to do it and–

- Discuss it with your guidance counselor. I believe that she is qualified.

- But–

- Sorry, *BUT* one more word and you're gone. . . I raise my eyebrows.

- That's not fair. We should–

- *You* should discuss it with Guidance . . . I take out a piece of paper . . . Here's a pass Marcus. I'll see you in class.

I might be overreacting, engaging in what playwright Terence Rattigan called a reflex action of the spirit. But it's only the first day of school. Too soon to let the inmates run the asylum or to tacitly endorse this attempt at teacher-student oneness. I'm going to comply with the directions, just not fully. Not open rebellion. Not even a one-room coup d'état. Just flexing a personal crotchet that classroom is classroom, psychology is psychology, and bullshit is bullshit.

Marcus Schmidt: *WTF!? I can't ask questions? I think August believes I'm a smartass and maybe I am. But I DID the survey and if we don't discuss it now I know it'll just get trash-canned like all those forms you fill out and never get back. August expects us to follow directions but he doesn't follow them himself. WTF. I know some students who think that gray-haired old man needs payback. The only reason he's gotten a pass so far is because we were here when his wife was sick and died. Still, if he doesn't lighten up. . .*

Windmills Of Your MInd: Maybe if Amanda hadn't died. Or I was younger. Or this chair not so ass-numbing hard, the day shorter, this over-perfumed, 200 pound–

- Mike, are you with me?

gorilla of a principal not as boring as shit. Or as committed to SOP, the old bump and grind like some veteran gangbanger, I could enjoy my free period.

- Mike?

I stare back. I don't say the obvious, that I drifted off. I *am* tempted to tell her she's hemorrhaging stupidity. Logrolling the clichés. Hoopte-foking-doodle.

Her eyes narrow. She's staring at me like maybe she's discovered the existence of an alien probe. And is it fight or flight? . . While she's staring I'm wondering to myself when I got so negative. Filled myself with cusses, faux swears. Saw everything in blacks and grays. . . Guess it was after my wife Amanda died and the world turned to shit. . . I remind myself now that I *am* a literary person. Have better words. Deeper thoughts. Brighter instincts. Somewhere. But where?. . . I never was a pontoon of sweetness. But it *is* worse since Amanda died.

- As I was saying we need to get your objectives for the year in writing and agree on an action plan and means of assessment. . . She smiles broader. Wiggles her fat caboose forward. Tits swaying. Her wide sculptured coiffure doesn't budge under the lacquered phyllo layers of hairspray. Her plus-size dress is high and tight, more Vegas showgirl than school chieftain. It could be my imagination but she seems to be radiating some serious Suddenly XXX vibes.

She segues into the usual educational cant about district objectives, dovetailing, needs assessments, while I rip off a brain fart and look around the room. A few plants on the counter. Framed private college diplomas on the wall. The usual menagerie of framed-to-impress photos ringing her desk. One is of a younger Nunberg, a twenty-something biker straddling a large Harley. I'm not quite impressed, but I am forced to consider that perhaps this 45ish hyper-bureaucrat *did* have a life once. On the wild side?

- So what do you think? Do you have anything in writing, any thoughts?

- Frankly Ms. Nunberg . . . and I stress out the zzz sound . . . my only real objective this year is the same basic one I have every year. To maintain discipline and to know my subject well enough to generate interest and learning. Beyond that I thought I might do something with my Film class. Incorporate some of the new digital editing programs. . . The thought and my boredom trail off. I'm thinking this whole thing is getting fucking painful. It is definitely too lengthy. I could be doing real school work now instead of engaging in this yearly parboiled blandness. And I'm thinking that maybe I should have just blown off this conference and claimed a senior moment – that's the way I roll Toots. Or maybe, and this is a fey thought, come in actually prepared with at least a soupçon of objective. But it's only the second day of school. Weeks early from the usual month-in meeting on objectives. Nunberg's request to meet today caught me by surprise.

No big deal.

The objective game is old. Meet it, don't meet it. Fabricate numbers, tweak statistics, all for what? And for who? Emerson said, Let a man then know his worth and keep things under his feet, i.e. can the BS. I drop into more introspection that this quintessential desk jockey was once a biker and pretty high achiever. The last thing I hear before the image and smell of dad's wet diaper intrudes is, Let me propose an objective that just might help you and. . .

Bernadette Nunberg: *It is obvious that Mike August is not really with us today. His gray hair needs combing, a closer more recent shave would be nice. I don't care about a tie, but a clean ironed shirt should not be an anathema to a true professional. . . I know he's had many personal problems in the last few years, at least according to his personnel folder and the superintendent. I've been here for less than half a year myself and don't really know Mike. . . The superintendent tasked me to knuckle down with the teachers. Objectives, we all have them. In Mike's case I think I came up with a good fit. It will not be an easy goal, but maybe Mike doesn't deserve easy after 2 years of poor evaluations. And missing as many days as he has missed. I don't like playing hardball with him but there are pressures on me that he just would not understand. . . A former colleague told me that trying to reform senior staffers is like trying to polish turds. It's a gross and very inappropriate simile. Though it might be a good fit for Mike.*

Blowin' In The Wind: The class is watching a movie while I'm sitting in the back trying to figure out exactly what-the-hell this objective means. Nunberg wants me to mentor and conference with six 12th graders for the rest of the year. Regular meetings right up to graduation. Like I am some kind of surrogate parent, big brother, ersatz guidance counselor. She was clear that these would be students I never had. Thought starting fresh was important. Said there would be input from guidance, the school psychologist, and others on who exactly the 6 would be. But that the final decision would be hers. Mentioned diversity was key, along with choosing 6 who would benefit from one-to-one faculty guidance. . . What exactly she wants me to accomplish with them is vague. Said I should support them, be a listener. Beyond that I should try to improve them in any social or academic way I see fit. It should be measurable. But that we could work that out later. Admits that it *is* an unusual and unprecedented target. Said something about it being a pilot program, like I'm an aviator and not a fucking teacher.

I Walk The Line: Hudson's is our neighborhood watering hole. It's flush in an area of two-and-three family homes, just off the industrial and art deco center. Customers were allowed to smoke up to this year, and if you were born during-or-after disco you probably don't know any of the jukebox songs. It feels right to me. Maybe because I am a factory town kid at heart. Weaned on the smell of booze, machine oil, and foundry soot. Maybe because it really *is* a place where everyone knows my name.

My friend George waves me over.

- So amigo, what's up? he asks and points to Vinnie that this one is on him. You look hassled. I thought you developed a thick and impermeable idiot callous long ago?

- I thought so too. But. . . I tell him about today's conference and the Big Brother gauntlet being tossed in front of me. He doesn't say anything, holds up one finger, and goes to the head. I check out the baseball game on tv and the new shapely waitress. She smiles back. Two retirees are rolling dice at the other end of the bar. The pool is over a grand and there's excitement with each toss.

George is a former high school and small college basketball star. Has the calmness common to big men. He's smart, well read. A man who seldom wastes words and seldom talks without thinking first. I'm confiding in him because he's a friend. And he's listening because he's a friend. Sometimes life *is* that simple.

He returns and gets right to it.

- This is something you should do, he says. Other high schools have it, or versions of it. It's where education is going. It's what yesterday's homeroom period was all about. You'd be a sort of test case for us, a pilot program that could have a real and lasting impact.

- What about the fact that I don't want to do it?

- If you were *that* sure you wouldn't be talking about it. Besides, it's not like you have a lot of choice. You and I both know that you need a good evaluation this year. You're overdue. And if Nunberg wants you to do this objective, then your chances of getting a good eval are better.

- Probably true, I say. . . I do a face palm and rub my sore eyes. . . But it frosts my ass, I continue, to be nurtured by that middle-aged cuntlet. She reminds me of a burlesque queen.

- It's not like you have another objective. . . I tell the students I counsel that our lives are defined by opportunities, even the ones we miss. You'd be helping yourself, helping a half dozen kids who need it. And who knows? You may even have a little fun in the process. God knows you could use some fun.

I take a long pull on the gin and stare at the pressed tin ceiling. We stand in silence thinking, drinking, watching the game. It's comfortable after sitting all day to stand on the sawdust, one foot up on the floor rail. The bar is smooth with only slight pitting in the polyurethane. Very relaxing to lean on. I think of all those generations of factory and foundry workers who drank away their paychecks and would have given their right nut to have my choice. I don't feel guilty about it. But it does make me think.

George Raven: *I feel sorry that Mike's forced to deal another radical change in his life and I tell him that. He thinks life has become one big SNAFU, and I guess it has for him. But I tell him shit happens. More shit happens the longer we live. And he needs to suck it up. Like the former soldier he is. He counters I'm not some goddamn, tv-ready, pop-psychologist. But an over-the-hill schmaltzy guidance counselor who drives a luxury gas-guzzler too big for his garage. But a damn perfect ego fit. . . Mike can be funny as hell and we have a good laugh. That's when I know he's OK. Mike's been my friend for years, and he's a great teacher. But Mike will do what Mike wants. Always has, always will. He listens to me. But isn't much on hearing.*

My Back Pages: I dream of riding bulls at some dung-and-fried-pizza-dough country fair and wake up tired and disconnected from the bright morning sunshine.

I stand in front of the mirror. Splash water on my face. See a man whose features have filled out since he turned 48. Cheekbones and chin line still visible but lack the sharp definition of the running and basketball years. The expansion with age before the shrinkage of death. The hair gray and thin on top, longer on the sides. The forehead splitting into horizontal seams like the clapboard on the house. The eye corners shooting out radial lines like a sunburst or my cracked tires. A small scar under my left eye. A white island in a brown sea – reminder of a long ago piece of shrapnel that took off the skin below the pigmentation. The pores on my nose seem bigger. Uglier. Blood vessels starting to break on the sides. Roseate spotches on my sun-drenched neck. Dark liver spots dot arms and hands.

I start to trim my nasal hair and note for the first time that fine white cilia-like hair with dusty wax is trumpeting from the ears. I slam the mirror with a wet hand and crack it. Tears well up. I'm pretty damn emotional for a cold-sober morning. Could be age. Ratcheting up sentimentality even as it's stealing looks. Puerile behavior in the face of mortality's rot. Damn.

The Dipsy Doodle: After lunch I check my mailbox. There's a letter with no return address. Local postmark. I open it. Inside is a full sheet of paper. Centered, neatly typed, are 4 capitalized words: OUT OF MANY, FEW. . . What the hell? I stuff it into my briefcase, then drop in on Nunberg and sign off on my new Doctor Freud, au pair objective. She's quiet, undemonstrative. Which surprises me. Thought she'd be thrilled. Gush as if I just volunteered to be the guinea pig for a revolutionary vaccine. Like maybe if only this prototype is successful the U.S. will regain the world's education lead.

I go to class wondering what-the-hell I just got myself into.

Chapter 2

Tap Dance Faster

The Air That I Breath: The high school sits on the edge of the urban downtown and suburbs. There's a winding drive past a manmade pond, a copse of hardwoods heavy with leaves not yet autumned. All a prelude to three large horizontal pods of glass and steel in early sixties architecture. Cinder block attachments for the auditorium, gym, and pool. A brick and glass superintendent's wing attached as if by afterthought to the back. I've always thought the external impression pleasant. The internal one has changed with the years. Continued immigrant waves, a rainbow coalition befitting the 21st century. Not quite big city but certainly different than the demographics of the surrounding colonial-striated towns and villages.

It's time to deal with some of the diversity.

The Girl With The Dragon Tattoo: This is a period I normally monitor a study hall. But I've been released from duty for the rest of the year to sit in the English office and do this.

I'm staring at a 17-year-old emo girl with tangerine-streaked hair that frames a face heavy on mascara. Her lips and eyelids are studded with silver piercing. Her pink frilly blouse overlaps a hole-dappled denim skirt. I have no memory of ever seeing her before. Do not recognize the name. And other than the cursory overview George gave me, I know nothing about her. Dark on the rock, a mucked out mind.

- Czarina Koppel, is that right?

- Zoe.

- Zoe then. My name's Mr. August. Do you know why you're here?

14

- Something about you're going to be my mentor, a faculty listening post. My go-to psychic guru. . . She says it straight-faced and fast.

- Where did you hear all that?

- Word gets around.

- I see. Well, I don't see myself as playing all those roles. We need to keep this professional–

- Like I'm in the confessional, or on the couch. . . Her face is as unemotional as the wall. She shifts her position. Crosses one leg over the other and her skirt rides up high above the knees. I haven't seen so much skin since cheerleader tryouts.

- I'm not a priest, rabbi, or psychologist, I say and try not to stare. Listen, I know you don't want to be here–

- Do *you* want to be here?. . . She suddenly smiles. It looks forced, emotes artificiality. Her heavy gothic air overrides the slightly upturned corners of her mouth.

- Ha. Well no. . . Yes. . . I'm not sure.

- You're not? she says in a tone that's more teasing than challenging. Except that it's not very well performed. . . Listen Mr. August, she abruptly says, if I can be frank. You don't exactly have the reputation for this sort of personal bonding shit. Can I say shit? Anyway, you don't. I don't either so let's just admit that this isn't going to work. You can say whatever you want on whatever forms you have to fill out. I'll go back to study and you can correct papers, or whatever. Unless you really *do* want me to stay.

Her legs are still crossed. She's leaning back now, which causes her skirt to ride up even higher. If I shifted position I could probably see all the way up the V, panties and all. If she's wearing any. Of course I don't. I *do* silently debate about mentioning the school dress code. But then we'd be in a discussion over her clothes. Or lack of them. That is not a tangent I

15

want right now. . . If I didn't know better I would swear she was coming on to me.

Are they all going to be like Little Miss, I wonder and glance at the name again. . . Zoe? If so it IS probably going to be one big fucking waste of everyone's time. I can feel a headache starting, my temples start to pulse. If it goes to the eye twitch it'll be a definite physiological sign I should bailout. If I still can. If Nunberg agrees. Might do these kids more harm than good being subjected to me in this open trench coat way. To borrow an inappropriate phrase.

I ask her a few questions using a generic form George Raven gave me. Determine she loves art. Knows how to kickbox. Lives with her mother and brother. Wants to go to New York when she graduates. And could not care less about clubs, teams, sororities, do-rag gangs, mall rats, clicksters, hoes, heavies, dudes, duhs, stoners, slackers, preps, or nerds. . . I call her Lisbeth Salander. She's smart, and smart enough to not care what I or anyone else thinks. A cosmopolitan intelligence. Fuck you self-confidence bundled in pink and denim. George knew who Zoe is. Said she has no rays. I disagree. It's just dark energy. Pessimistic, to the max. A mind-your-own-fucking-business attitude that doesn't care enough to care much at all. I'm surprised she even talks. And I'm surprised she flirted with me. If that's what it was. Which I now doubt. It just does not fit her hermetic styled independence.

Zoe Koppel: *This isn't a conference I want but it isn't too painful. Probably around the squirm two level of a tattoo. I try to hit August fast with a lot of words and hope that it will cave him. End his talking. Not the conference. Ending these conferences early is not in my best interests. I know what I hope to accomplish but I can't imagine August does. I wonder if he's*

16

imagining I'm going to roll up on him and give him a lap dance he'll never forget? I hope so. . . He didn't say a word about my flashing, even when I gave him an opening. Of course It's only our first meeting. Today was Institutional Psych 101. But one of these days he's going to try to play psychological nursemaid to me because that's what Nunberg's directed him to do. If that's the case he's rehearsing for a play that is definitely not going to happen. . . Talk, talk, talk. Shit. Life isn't a library. I'm not a fucking open book. We need to keep on meeting but with a whole lot less talk.

He Ain't Heavy: Thomas Jefferson Sato saunters in swaying from side-to-side as if there is an earthquake and the floor fluid. His open-laced army boots thud heavily. His peach basket sized baseball cap is sideways, his cargo pants have enough extra room for a small car. He bounces his head in my general direction and he drops heavily into the open seat.

- So what's up Mister. . . His eyebrows go up over large brown eyes and a wide oval face. . . Mister?. . . His eyes are translucent like frosted glass. His brain momentarily opaque.

- August, I say. Mr. August. Like the month. Or august as in eminent.

- Huh?

- Nothing. So Thomas–

- People call me TJ.

- TJ it is. So TJ, tell me a little about yourself. What do you like to do, what don't you like? What do you want to accomplish this year, hope to do after graduation?

- You want to know those things? . . . He's puzzled but not upset . . . I mean, Why? I don't even know you, Mr . . . August. You're not my new guidance counselor, are you?

- No. I'm an English teacher. The principal thought it would be a good idea if students had someone on the faculty they could talk to in a personal way. Sort of like a grownup friend. We're hear to discuss anything you want to discuss. I'm here to support you. Not judge, grade, or discipline. . . Even as I mouth the words I'm trying to sound sincere, look sincere, be sincere. Offer a little of myself but not too much, i.e. the Goldilocks strategy. Not too *this*, not too *that*, just right. I sense this is a good kid. It'd be nice if I could do the right thing by him. I'm not sure I can. I'm not sure I care enough to try.

- Cool.

It takes a lot of prodding over the next 15 minutes to find out he's a Sansei. And he's proud of that. Considers himself a fair student, works a lot of hours bussing tables. Has a girlfriend named Phoebe who waitresses. I know from George Raven that TJ lives with his mother and that the father died young. That TJ has had at least one juvenile brush with the law. TJ tells me he'd like to join the army after graduation, qualify for the GI Bill (my family can't afford college, Mr. August), and maybe someday go to the Culinary Institute. . . Evelyn Waugh in Brideshead Revisited talked about the languor of youth. Doesn't sound like TJ's had much.

TJ Sato: *Mr. August turns out to be OK. Kind of like a flash crowd, I mean he just shows up. One minute I'm in the middle of class, then there's this teacher. He wants me to talk but I really don't feel a lot like talking. He seems OK with what I tell him. When I mention the army he says he was in the army too a long time ago. That's all he says about it. Maybe he'll tell me some good army stories the next time we meet. . . He tells me our time is up. Then says something weird. Not to look back cause I'm not going that way. . . I don't know what I said, or what he heard. It doesn't mean* *anything. I saw him looking at his wristwatch a couple of times so I guess he was probably bored and just talking because he has to.*

It's A Small World: While I wait for my third and final conference of the day I look around this pukey cream-colored English office. I never spend any time in here and wouldn't be here now except that my room is being used for sign language class. A few of the younger teachers in the department use this space for lunch. Some use it as a time-out cell i.e. I don't want to send this teen arm pit to the office and have admin think I can't control my students. But I don't want the snot-hair disrupting class anymore either. . . It's not a bad space as far as time capsules go. There are two older Macs, stacks of lined paper, post-McGuffey pre-digital out-of-print books, dried out magic markers, broken tipped pencils. In the corner are catacomb files holding yellowed curriculum. Centered above the computers is a framed photo of a shag-haired decades-gone department chair.

Overture from Aida: There's a knock and a statuesque girl with short layered black hair stands framed in the open door. She favors one leg which cocks a well-turned hip to the side. Mr. August? she brusquely asks. I nod. She enters quickly, does not look around. Drops her luggage-sized pocketbook on the table and sits down as if time is money and this meeting is no platinum card. She looks familiar, is definite classier more stylish than the school's usual tee-shirted-jeaned undergrad. Impression is Beyoncé on the runway.

- You're Destiny Gibson?
- Yes.
- I'm Mr. August. You never were in one of my classes, were you?

- No.

- Do you know why you're here? . . . Her eyes flash maturity. The same perceptive steadiness that Zoe Koppel showed.

- I believe so.

- I have a form here–

- What would you like to know?

- Care to fill it out yourself? . . . I push the form and a pen across. . . It will probably save time.

- No problem.

She writes quickly with little or no thought and I study her. Teen haute couture. The top is a silky blue-black abstract leopard pattern over black slacks and short leather heels. Around her neck is an ebony bead choker with emerald stone. Earrings match, the silver rings on both hands are deeply etched. Her Nubian skin is almost coffee but a shade lighter as if tempered with one small container of cream.

- There, she says and pushes it back. Anything else?

- Would you mind waiting a minute while I read this?. . . I'm not trying to give her a hard time, though a lesson in patience appears much needed. But if she's in such a hurry and is as truly independent and with-it as she appears, she probably doesn't need much help. We should establish that now, i.e. it's not like my own time is toilet residue.

She glances at her thin flat wristwatch, shrugs, and says, If we could tie this up fast I would appreciate it.

- No problem . . . I scan her answers fast like I am a veteran CSI-FBI profiler. Her goal this year is to be valedictorian. Wants the Ivy. Wants to run a publishing house someday. Ultimately would like to become a U.S. ambassador. Is fluent in Spanish and likes Spanish writers. Volunteers at the soup kitchen and senior center.

20

- I see you're not involved in any school activities except for National Honor Society?

- I leave that stuff for my sister. I'm not looking to pad my résumé. It'd only be a distraction. Graduating number one is the only goal I have. I set it before I even got here, and nothing, no one is going to prevent that.

- But you say you want to go into publishing and you're not even on the school newspaper?

- And write drivel about the food in the cafeteria or the no-cell phone policy?

- Then why do you volunteer at the soup kitchen and senior center?

- That's real world. I make a difference.

I smile. Think that maybe we should switch places. Outwardly she's a helluva lot better dressed and inwardly seems the better adjusted. If there's any chink in her armor I don't see it. Even setting her future trajectory to blaze across the heavens seems realistic and within reach. . . But still waters run deep and how could there *not* be some problem in her 17-year-old world? There always is or why would Nunberg have assigned her to me? Still, I have my serious doubts that I can be of any help. Or that I even if I care to try. She seems like a bit of a prima donna, a holistic princess. A front-loaded, brain heavy patrician.

I sign her pass and she leaves for class.

Destiny Gibson: *I'm happy August keeps it short. He said we are mandated to meet and apologized. Which I appreciate. He also said that in the future he would work around my schedule. I was tempted to tell him it is my sister Asia he should be trying to help. That business about not standing for the Pledge Of Allegiance because of centuries of injustice. Or that incident the other day insisting the cafeteria offer a more culturally* *diverse menu. I'm all for Afrocentricity, but. . . August seems intelligent. If only he were about 20 years younger and definitely more stylish I might actually like to give him a try. Sort of a reverse on that old European idea of young men losing their virginity to an older whore. I know it would be an eeech thought for most of my immature classmates. But not for me. I'm not ready for that kind of distraction yet. And certainly never with this middle-aged man. But I wouldn't mind losing my virginity this year to some older stud as long as it doesn't get in the way of my graduating #1.*

Those Were The Days: Hudson's is not crowded and I'm talking to Deirdre the new waitress. Turns out she is a former August student. I initially go robocall on the name, and get nothing. Too many years, too many students, too many cell-and-synapse killing beers and gins. Then. . . it's vague. . . Good student, skinny teen. But no more. Leggy, full-faced, full-breasted, long brunette hair. A full wattage personality. Looks like Jennifer Lawrence plus a decade. . . It's probably the subtle tow of my first drink but it seems like she is laying on the old bunga bunga. Or maybe she is just naturally friendly, helped along by 20% tip considerations. Or heard about Amanda and is into rescuing the perishing – Saroyan's phrase. In any case I haven't had sex since Amanda, and I have no interest in it now. If she does. Which on second thought I doubt. Mercy fucks never were in vogue.

George steps alongside me and says to the bartender. A very very dry martini here for MIkey. No vermouth–

- three olives, Vinnie says.

- You're doing a helluva job, I tell Vinnie. . . I can feel the gin working its cool exuberant way into my voice. I make a conscious effort to tone it down. Not that I care about what these regulars think. But someone might insist on taking my car keys and I need to get to my father's.

I swirl the ice around while I fill in George on the three conferences. I mention how different the three students are. Tell him I'm not certain that I can really accomplish anything. I don't give a lot of specifics. He works everyday in other people's personal crap and doesn't need more now. . . He quotes from somewhere and says, Uncertainty is an uncomfortable position but certainty is an absurd one. Adds, Pick a goal that's important to *them*. Better still let *them* pick it. Something that really tweaks their loins. Something they really feel.

I clink his glass and add, The young naturally *feel* what's best for them just as they naturally feel the hardness of a hard-on or the wetness of a snatch. . . I say it to shock. I am in that kind of mood after a mind numbing, scrotum tightening day. It doesn't work. George smiles and clinks my glass again.

This time I laugh and George looks at me. Eyes holding me hard. Mike, he says, I have a feeling you'd better do a good job at meeting your objective. . . Why? I ask. Nunberg said I could keep it loose. Gave me the impression it was all just a smoke-and-mirror show. . . I'm not so sure, George counters. I should know more in a few days but if I were you. . . Don't mean to tie you to the post without a the firing squad in sight old buddy, he says.

- Christ, George. You talked me into this!

- I know . . . Furrows appear on his brow extending well onto the bushy knoll. . . This is where I expect him to say, Well partly. I mean, you had the final say. In any case I'm here for you. . . He doesn't say any of that. Instead merely warns, Don't panic.

Fuck. Don't panic? One minute I'm enjoying a drink, feeling that life's a grooved track. The next that life is living me. Damn, and f-it! . . . Civilization, the idea of an intelligent universe – a big delusion. Life's a fecking primordial swamp oozing muck. A sucking quagmire with blood-draining leeches. Paleozoic predators. And a viperous low-crawling principal.

There is laughter at the other end of the bar. Deirdre catches my eye and gives me the big coruscating smile. I sober up fast. The lightness as gone as the ice. I smile back weakly. Down the drink. Order another.

Takin' It To The Streets: There is nothing like the sound of a car crash, the metal-on-metal crumbling and tearing, to cut a scar into your memory.

The evening is a wavery bluish-green blur. Like I'm wide-eyed under-water with no goggles. Hudson's five drinks back, drowsiness settling in. On a well lit street I take a corner too fast. The rear end comes around. Tires scream. I steer into the slide, reflexes a nightmarish mishmash autopilot. The back tires jump the curb with a thud, A traffic sign flashes past. Ripping. Metal-on-metal. The car rights itself. I hit the brakes hard and come to a rubber-leaving stop in front of a wooded park entrance.

I look around. Check my rear views. The street is quiet. Empty. I start to get out. Want to inspect the damage. Then decide to get going. The GMC is driving fine. The last thing I need is for a cop to come along. Don't think I could pass a field sobriety test. Walk the heel-toe even with training wheels. . . The speed limit sign in the distance is still up. Only slightly out of plumb. Are they ever a true 90?

Jan and Dean do a Dead Man's Curve refrain in my head. My hands are shaking, my foot thumping like it's working a drum pedal. I roll down the window, take a few deep breaths, and drive off into the fading light and spectral quietude.

Chapter 3

Once More Unto the Breach

Hit The Road Jack: I'm a hungover thunderclap, which is not good for a school day. I hit the shower and get ready trying to remember the ride home last night. The metallic screech stands out and I wince at the memory. It's as grating to my sensitized nerves as it was at the moment of impact. I make a mental pledge to start drinking less. Even as I'm thinking a Bloody Mary would hit the spot.

When I finally check out the car it's not bad. Back bumper scraped and creased. But attached. Rear license plate missing. Ripped right off the bolts. I move the front plate to the back and replace the front one with one of Amanda's old ones. I'm now running mismatched plates, but who's going to check?

I drive to school slowly via last night's route. No license plate along the way. Not at the crash site either. Who knows where the metal tag flew off to. I'll apply for a new one at motor vehicle when I get the chance. Just another little errand on life's unending to-do list.

Ber Mire Bist Du Schoen: George takes one look at me in the faculty room, laughs, and says, You're beautiful, kid. . . I gulp some coffee and tell him it's going to be a long day. He says, At last you won't have to worry about Nunberg. She's out on a personal day. Adds that it's something about her dog.

Green, Green Grass Of Home: The house sits comfortably on an old-growth street under lines of Piranesi wires. In a neighborhood of modest Roaring Twenties bungalows. Front porch gliders, wind chimes, and welcome mats. Lawns neatly clipped. Houses years outside of needing repainting.

This is where I grew up. I remember the shortcuts, most of the older trees. The fire alarm box we pulled once. The storm drain where the raccoons retreated after raiding backyard garbage cans. There was a bathtub crypt in Coogan's front yard surrounded by a sea of perennials where Jesus raised a paint-crazed finger with the tip broken off. The garage hoops, the flagpoles, the treehouse – all rusted or rotted. Or as gone as the night a 40-pound meteorite hit old man Grotowsky's house and smashed through the roof, the bedroom, and living room. Shattered in the basement.

Nostalgic benchmarks, grounding memories. But not quite enough to sustain me in these diurnal visits. The reality keeps me up nights.

I don't bother to knock but enter through the back breezeway. Push through the clutter and find the old man sitting at the kitchen table eating chicken. There's a heavy frying smell, a pan smoking on the burner. I take out the last cutlet, drop it on his plate, and turn off the gas. He doesn't look up but laughs.

- What's so funny, Dad? . . . I notice that his shirt and pants are pressed and that his shoes are polished.

- Ernie said something funny. Told me he's seen better looking chicken shit. Ha. That guy couldn't boil water. Ernie! my father says and spears the last cutlet and shakes it at the refrigerator, you are one funny Polack. Even dead. Now, why don't you go haunt your wife? You never said diddly to her when you were both alive, so maybe it's time. I want to talk with Mike.

- Ernie isn't here, Dad. It's just you, me, and the cat. Wherever she is.

- Really? You don't know squat. . . Max looks around. . . Well, Ernie *was* here. I guess you scared him off.

Six months ago these phantom conversations scared the bejesus out of me. But repetition breeds numbness. Sadness when I remember what a vibrant man he was. Stallion DNA. Maximilian was a science and math prodigy. A whiz kid who loved Erector and chemistry sets. Graduated college at 19. Then a few years ago financial downturn, mom's death. Recently this onslaught of the crazies.

- You look good Dad. I see you ironed your clothes. . . My father is a sharp looking guy for an octogenarian. The years have stolen a couple of inches of height but he's still ramrod straight. Has a lean crevassed face that's burnished brown from gardening and golf. Body is solid. More wiry than generic 80ish. His hair is long and combed straight back. A Leyendecker model or Mafia don.

- Which is a lot more than I can say for you, he says. You look like you've been cluster humping a commune.

- You're right, I say and think, No use in denying it. I force a smile. Max seldom pulls his punches and it will be a long evening if I counter. Jab, jab. It's where I get my dust off mouth. That mouthy Oscar Levant, Don Rickles, Ricky Gervais attitude that substitutes wisecracking for substance, sarcasm for deliberation. . . Amanda stopped all that. With her I could really talk. Conversations that were heartfelt not just cerebral claptrap. And never, or seldom, resort to a punchline. A putdown. I was a better man when Amanda was alive, just as Dad was when Mom was still here. But with Amanda and Bernice gone it's been an age of regression for us both.

27

Verbal acupuncture, cock-of-the-walk stuff. Old warriors who circle and count in units of psychic blood. At least that's the way it was until recently. For the last couple of weeks Dad's talked less-and-less. Sometimes not at all.

- Damn right I'm right. Ernie thinks you look like a guy who climbs into Salvation Army bins for his wardrobe.

- Ernie said that?

- He said you looked like a bum.

Two months ago Ernie entered the picture. At first I thought Max had overdone his nightcap or medication. Which still does not make talking to yourself OK, but does explain it. He was severely depressed when Bernice died a few years ago. They'd been together nearly 60 years. He was lonely. Jimmy Stewart had Harvey, Max has Ernie. Or so I rationalized. When I mentioned the parallel Max said, There's a *big* difference between talking to a *goddamn* rabbit and a human. Said if I didn't get that, I didn't get anything. Psychologically anemic.

- Have you been drinking? Max asks. I smell booze. Ratty clothes and gin breath. Great combination.

- I had a couple at Hudson's, I tell him. Don't mention it's part of my morning pledge to drink less. . . Dad, I'm going to check out a few things, I say. Just keep eating.

I start a load of clothes, go into the bathroom and clean out the litter box. Turn off the tv, empty the cheroot butts. Smooth over the bed, pick up some spilled pills. Come back into the kitchen. Find the clothes iron in the refrigerator, and start washing dishes. Through all this my father is as silent as the radio. He regards me with no more interest than he gives the cat rubbing up against his leg.

I put out new cat food and water, throw the clothes in the dryer, and check the thermostat and stove one last time. I'm helping him take his blood pressure and cholesterol medicine and a dark stain is spreading across the front of his chinos. I escort him into the bathroom. Help him change his diaper. Together we get him into his brushed twill cotton pj's and bed. I kiss him on top of the head and tell him I'll be back tomorrow to vacuum. He nods almost imperceptibly. I leave him lying on his side. I'm exhausted, a little drunk, and sweating.

Maximilan August: *Mike's a good kid, I couldn't ask for a better son. . . I know I'm gradually losing it. It's not painful. More like drifting in-and-out of a dream. Life's the dream now, and it's with me less-and-less. I don't want to be a burden to anyone. Certainly not Mike. What parent does? I know I have some dementia, and Alzheimer's is probably the cause. I'm not stupid. I read, I analyze. But that doesn't mean I want to talk about it, though I guess I'm going to have to. One thing – Ernie is not a figment of my imagination. I might be an engineer, but I always believed in ghosts. My mother was with me briefly after she died. And now Ernie. He was here even before this senility crept in. I just didn't talk to him. Didn't see much point. We were never that close. Actually he was pretty much of an idiot. But now. . . Some writer – I don't remember who – said we all have a myth and we live by that myth. If it turns out Ernie is my myth I guess I'll never know.*

The Tide Is High: Early the next day I get Max an appointment with his GP. I call Max's next door neighbor and tell her about the appointment. She pops in on Dad every morning and maybe she can warm him to the idea. I

29

also mention the frying pan and stove. I should probably get the gas turned off. And soon.

I'm making these calls from my room between periods. There's overlap but not too much and foke it anyway. This is important. A helluva lot more exigent than collecting homework that was likely plagiarized or just blown off. The class is talking quietly for a change. Perhaps catching the words *dementia* and *Alzheimer's* and sensing that in the riffle and purl of life, their own struggles are pretty foking gnomic.

Chapter 4

T- Minus 8 Weeks

Fragments From the Edge

Ghost Riders In The Sky: An angry parent once asked me why I ever became a teacher. Like maybe I should have been a chicken de-boner or shopping cart wrangler. It certainly wasn't for the money or lack of other opportunities. I was good in other fields. Not for summers off. Or short hours. Or any altruistic reason unless *gut feeling* is the new altruistic.

For me it just felt right. My raison d'être. Sort of what economists call *value added* as in Edgar Cayce, Shirley MacLaine, New Age stuff.

At least it felt right all those bright-eyed years ago with large operatic emotion and wellsprings of energy. Then generations of students, endless mountains of paperwork, till yadayadayada I am as psychologically gone as ejected sperm. But still plugging away, still determined to do a good job even if I *am* registering high on the human pH scale.

This goal, this objective thing – I don't need any administrative droid trying to kiss me off. Benihana me on the school butcher block. I will go when I am good and ready. And not a second, not a goddamn downbeat sooner. The hell with objectives and any administrator who uses them to harass and RIF a good educator.

That's my attitude in theory.

When I am pissed off.

In practice it's not that simple.

When Amanda was diagnosed with cancer and started treatments, I started missing more-and-more school. She was never a strong person.

Needed a lot of emotional and physical support. There was no one else to give it but me. And then Max started to slip away too. . . My school evaluator was sympathetic but honest. Gave me 2 years of back-to-back supine evaluations. In most school systems mediocre reports still would not leave me in bad shape. But here teacher positions in the event of a reduction-in-force, are determined by performance, *not* seniority. I need a good-to-outstanding evaluation this year to secure my position in the event of a downsizing. And I need to keep this job. The world is not crying out for English teachers.

Smoke From A Distant Fire: Jack Kaufman walks in soundlessly on soft suede shoes down at the heels and an air that is as inconspicuous as Manischewitz at Passover. I am not even aware he's here until the chair grates across the tiles. The only heads-up from George is that Kaufman considers himself a throwback to the Beats. His red plaid wool shirt is open. Underneath is a tee emblazoned with the world **BELIEVE** in bold Helvetica, the *LIE* in script.

   He sits down without acknowledging me. Leans back with arms crossed, and waits. The hat is tilted back. One of those urban lumberjack models, probably a Filson. Heavy and quilted. Not cheap.

   - Jack Kaufman?

   - Mr. August. . . The voice is cigarette baritone.

   I push the form across with a pen and say, If you don't mind.

   He writes quickly without apparent thought in a tight neat print. Some of these students have filled out so many forms it's become a faux undergrad major. A métier without any real world carryover. . . I feel sorry for the young myrmidons. Poor Walter Mitty fucks.

I eyeball the answers. Push back in the chair. Smile at him. He smiles back. Unless young Kaufman is one mordant son of a bitch, even beyond me, I'm not sure I shouldn't show this to the school shrink.

- You're serious? You want to channel Jack Kerouac's spirit?

- Just his literary voice. I like how he melds jazz and prose. The impromptu riff structure of the narrative.

- Your biggest goal between now and graduation is to party with Allen Ginsberg and to one day write a book in the style of *On The Road*?

- Kidding on Ginsberg, though it would be very cool. I'll use the old Route 66, or what's left of it for my book.

- You want blaze like a meteor – live fast, flash bright. Not languish like an old dwarf star. Sounds like Jack London.

- The literary figures I admire lived high and wide.

- And you want to go to Columbia.

- If it doesn't get in the way, why not? New York is a moonshot. One of the great lumens of light and true hellraising.

I stare into his eyes. Look for any sign of put-on. Mention that he does know, *don't you?* that the Beats were heavily into drugs. Kaufman says he is not into self-destruction for the sake of the blaze factor of self-immolation. Avoids acknowledging drug use himself. In which case I'm supposed to report him. Says he would like to win an open mike contest this year. That the best artists and writers all have a bit of crazy in them. Quotes Burroughs' the only possible ethic is to do what one wants to do. States it would be a helluva lot of fun to buy a school bus, fill it with a bunch of Merry Pranksters, and replay the cross-country trip of Cassady and Kesey.

I push back. Take a breather. Have to admit he's smart – Columbia just might be in his future. And to confess I find him entertaining as hell. Even if

33

it is all grand bullshit. Smartass with a dash of Norman Bates schizophrenia. . . I don't ask him about his fascination with the hep ones of the fifties. I tell him that I enjoy his non-uber p.c. And honesty. If it is indeed honesty and not just some droll, tongue-in-cheek put-on. Mention that I've had other dry jokesters over the years. That I hope at least some of it *is* joking at my expense – no hard feelings. I don't tell him that I see a bit of me in him. Ha. The poor shit. . . I'm sure he'd love to share a reefer now and we could listen to some bongos and flute improvs while snapping our fingers and sipping expressos. But it's time to get on getting on. I tell him I'll be in touch.

Jack Kaufman: *August is not quite hip but he's no 4 x 90 square either. I know he doesn't dig all the message but he seems smart enough to separate the steak from the lunchmeat. . . I'm not worried about any profiling he's doing. The parking lot is empty, the gas pumps dry, the store fronts abandoned. The old man cruising in reverse. He's trying to focus on the future and the now me. But he doesn't realize that now never is. It's as gone as soon as it happens, if it ever happened, because even as it's entering the stream it's gone. But let him keep cruising. . . I suppose my parents will like it if they think this school is being proactive, trying to normalize me. William Burroughs said, How I hate those who are dedicated to producing conformity. That's an idea I can really dig. I mean, fuck normal, fuck the overseers of jackboot lockstep. . . I downplay the drugs. Don't know what side of the Mason-Dixon he's on. Burroughs said, Anything that can be done chemically can be done by other means. Of course W.B. was the wrong cat to be spouting that soapbox jive. I mean, he had his spaced-out years. Me, I'm pretty cool with any highway a cat's* *cruising as long as his h-rod ain't looking to push me off the road. Dig that and you dig me.*

Little Miss Sunshine soundtrack: I'm spinning a pen on the table and looking at a school poster on the office bulletin board. DO YOU HAVE HOT LIPS? It features a blowup of ruby red puckered lips and has my attention until a head appears in the door followed by a forward leaning body. The impression is that the girl is slightly out-of-kilter, that gravity has her in tow. I immediately stand and become a bleaching klieg light.

- You must be Audrey. . . I smile broadly at the girl. . . Come right in. Here, have a seat.

I pull out the chair and wave her in. I received an emailed attachment on Audrey from the Planning and Placement Team yesterday, i.e. the iMe has been briefed. She's Special Ed. Mostly self-contained classrooms but mainstreamed for 2 of our lower level courses. The overall analysis: She has language and processing difficulties, mild dyslexia, some fine motor problems. But is a dedicated learner and determined to fit in and succeed. Works well above ability. . . I have no idea why she's part of Team August but I do know that any goals I set for her will have to be in accordance with her IEP – Individual Education Program. And cleared with her people.

She looks nervous. Sits down. A well scrubbed naturalism. Rebecca Of Sunnybrook Farm missing only the parasol. Her eyes are flitting in my general direction but not quite on me.

- Audrey, great to meet you. I'm Mr. August. . . I hold out my hand. She looks at it. Breaks into a glacier-melting grin and enthusiastically shakes.

- Hi Mr. August! . . . Her voice is loud, the timbre down-home friendly. It takes me back. I cannot remember that last time anyone was so happy to see me including my cat and dog.

- Audrey, do you know why you're here?

- You're going to be my sort of friend this year . . . Her brown eyes are wide like clay pigeons and if she smiles any wider I wouldn't be surprised to see her skull pop out.

- Haha. Yes I am.

Her smile, that seconds ago was lighting up the room, drops like dirty hair. She looks puzzled, almost hurt.

- Did I say something funny? she asks.

Oh shit, I think. Forgot that her IEP said she is very literal. Hyper-aware. As quick to smile as to frown. Moods freely hinged. . . I suddenly realize I'm not ready for this glacial outpouring of friendliness or sudden turnabout. It's too fucking intense. Too needy, too complicated. I'm not a pair of crutches. This seems like the high road to hell.

- I laughed, I say, because I thought of something funny one of my students said this morning.

- What? Her look is honest curiosity.

- She said that my head. . . was. . . like. . . a. . . fuzzy. . . coconut.

Audrey laughs from the gut, Hahaha, even as her eyes narrow and features twist.

- I'm happy you liked that. How about if I ask you some questions, you tell me some answers. OK?

Over the next quarter hour I learn she wants to be in the autumn musical. Go to college. Likes the Narnia series and any story with romance. Would like a boyfriend. Has older twin brothers who are lawyers. Loves animals and ice cream.

At one point a hyperburble of shouting comes from the hall. Audrey is briefly panicked but I motion for her to stay seated. And as quickly as the,

I'LL KICK YOUR FAT ASS! starts, the student resource officer has it under control.

By the end of our meeting I'm still undecided if I will take her on. I never considered myself especially good with special needs students, and I would hate like hell to have my job depend on success with such a needy one. I'm thinking I can get out of this if I want. If those SPED people even a nanosecond could read the now negative bubble over my head, they'd pull Audrey so fast her already puffed out sweater would blossom like a parachute.

Seems almost unfair that Nunberg has even assigned her to me. Amateur counseling and extreme needs, not a good educational mix. I know jettisoning a student is not a noble thought. But I'm not going to like myself either if I lose my job because of an inability to help this girl.

I remember Kierkegaard's encouraging a leap to faith. Old man Wallenda still walking the wire at 73. Of course he fell and died, though I don't think he leaped. Point is, don't transition to some quirky static drone. Like I'm being with these thoughts of dropping Audrey. . .

I think of Molière's saying that life is a play with a badly written third act. Lately mine has been the pits. To succeed with her would be to really succeed. Trouble is, finding a way to help Audrey would be like flying by roadmap. Not quite impossible, but damn hard. And with lots of risk.

And there is the girl herself. Sticky, emotional velcro. But likable and charming.

I once heard a tv evangelist say that there are angels who come to earth in the form of needy people. Here to help us by letting *us* help them. . . I have never met a saint or angel before. Or if I did I probably dropped a quarter in the instrument case and kept going. Still if there was ever a heavenly avatar it *could be* Audrey Clover. Could be. Not every cherubic face with dimpled chin has godliness at her core. I don't think she's a Lizzy Borden. But who knows?

Audrey Clover: *I like Mr. August. He talks nice. He's not my teacher but I wish he was. Maybe he can help me with my writing. I'm not a good writer but I want to be. I like to write about animals and my family. I bet Mr. August is a good writer. He said he has a dog and cat just like I do. He also likes ice cream. We have a lot in common. I like how he likes my sneakers and dress. He said he thought he taught my older brothers but he could not remember their names. Rodney and Stuart. When I told him I wanted to go to college he said there is a school for everyone. He's nice.*

Send In The Clowns: My last interviewee is late. I step into the hall. It's deserted other than a pair of freshmen going at it like two street urchins in an alley. I'm supposed to break it up but they're so sex-washed and I am so preoccupied with conference concerns I give it the go-by. The urchins hit the locker and the harsh metallic rattle brings a teacher from around the corner. There's a warning. They move slowly off down the corridor. Awash in libido lustalis. Hands hooked under each other's belt in a friendly booty grab. Stuck together like a skin graft.

With five minutes left Jorge Espinoza steps in. He looks at me, I look at him. Nothing is said.

- You want to see me? he finally asks and remains standing comfortably in his black and neon cross-trainers. He's tall – about 6'2", maybe 190. An inverted granite triangle in a retro-Brooklyn sweatshirt.

- I did fifteen minutes ago. Where have you been?

38

He puts a pass on the table, and I check the time and signature. . . This was signed 2 minutes ago, I say. Why didn't you leave on time?

- I forgot, he says and adds, I already have a counselor. Why's it matter if I show up on time, or if I show up at all?. . . His frustration matches mine. Mitigated a slash by the fact he's still a student, I'm still the teacher, and this is still a goddamn caring school.

People do forget, I think and for a second I'm tempted to let the lateness go. He doesn't want to be here, I don't want to be here. . . Instead I say, It obviously doesn't matter to you. But that isn't the point. The point is that the principal wants this thing to happen. So it's going to. And on time. Comprende?

He doesn't react. I know I am pushing it with the *comprende* crack, but there are times when even a mini-rant has a momentum all its own. I almost rein this one in, but not foking quite.

- Listen, I say sounding perturbed though it's more tiredness than annoyance, there's not time to do this now. But here's a pass for tomorrow, same period. If you're late again you're getting a detention. And we can do this warm-fuzzy soothe-atron thing after school . . . I'm still overacting. Actually all this is more ironic and funny to me than irritating i.e. the fact that I'm taking this me-you tango semi-seriously and he's not. The after school line is BS. No way I am punching OT to do this. I raise a half-smile to belay any return posturing. It has an immediate effect.

- Yeah. OK. Sorry.

Sorry? Did he say sorry? I can't remember the last time a student used that word. And like he meant it. We're not ready to be hoisting beers at the bodega yet. But it is a good sign.

- OK, I say. See you tomorrow.

The Sun Ain't Gonna Shine Anymore: I don't go to Hudson's after school. I do check on Max and do a little grocery shopping. My butt is dragging. I'm exhausted. I always thought that life was supposed to get easier once you were toilet trained and weaned. And maybe it does for awhile in the early years. But not when you're approaching fifty and a triple care giver. Right now I'd like to implement the psychological tool called Cosmic Rage. Fuck you, fuck YOU, FUCK YOU! Yell it at the top of my lungs like a Howard Beale devotee. But I keep it in check. Fight off the tremors of neurosis. Try to stay calm in a life of increasing nip-shit. It doesn't help that my briefcase is filled with compositions. . . I'm adrift in a sea of work and stress. Clinging to a chunk of waterlogged driftwood with my tea pinkie. Everything, everyone needs to back off. It is about me. I'm walking here. I'm foking walking here!

I pour four fingers of gin, unpack the groceries, and let the dog out. He's waiting with the patience of the old, the canine old anyway. I microwave a slab of frozen lasagna and eat in the kitchen watching the news. Later I sit in the living room with a pile of film critiques. In the old days Amanda would come in, rub my neck, and we would massage the day away. It might finish with a bare-ass tumble, it might not. But there was always the thrill of expectation in the blood – that youthful sense that Remarque talks about – that unites the young with the course of their days.

I fall asleep and wake up around 10. Papers on the floor, the cat in my lap, the dog at my feet, ink on my fingers. I remind myself that no man is alone who is loved by his cat and dog.

Chapter 5

Moving To the Music

Jesus Won't You Come Back Here: Months after Amanda died my well intentioned evaluator told me I had to snap out of it. I could fuck up my classes. Try to enjoy the present, she said, Seize the day. The Essence: Carpe diem and all that shit. I told her I'm not built like that. That the past *is* my life. That those were the best years and nothing now compares. . . It hurt to confront that then. And it hurts now to feel soul-deep that there is only monochrome ahead. I hope it's not true. Hope I can shake myself out of what feels like the clinically depressed doldrums. A life that is quickly deconstructing August.

But fuck up my classes? Hard to believe they could get any worse.

Baby The Rain Must Fall: I'm passing back film critiques. The senior class is pushing the decibels. I stayed up late to finish grading these compositions. A cardinal rule of mine has always been to get papers passed back within a week. You had a week to write the papers, I tell them, I have a week to grade them. Fair is fair. Some students want same day delivery. Not likely, I tell the knuckle draggers.

- Mr. August, Giselle the hayseed blonde taps the paper as if calling for another card, so like I can't read this comment.

I go over, glance at it. Inwardly sigh. I'm tired, not up to explanations. I pause and finally say, It says, Directions. . . I tap the word which is printed boldly and legibly. . . And this is a question mark after it, I say and tap again.

- What does *that* mean?

- It means you didn't follow directions. . . I'm trying to keep it simple. No lengthy screeds. Pacing myself for the long day.

She stares hard at the paper, turns to page two, then flips back. What directions? she finally says as if this is Find Waldo and I intentionally left out the little red-striped foker.

- The ones on your checklist, I say. The ones we went over.

She mulls this over while most of the students drift away into their own lala lands. A few listen closely. Probably hoping that Giselle's argument budges me. And opens the door for their own plea bargains.

- So even if I wrote a good composition, she says, I can't get a good grade because I didn't follow directions? I only got a C.

- Are you sure you want to have this conversation now? I ask. . . I like Giselle. She's always out of herself and forces you to be too. The type who always has another question, another comment. A natural kick starter, though she's tiring me out today.

- It's OK now, she says.

- If you say so. . . I take a deep breath. . . The bottom line is that your composition isn't good. It's fair. You barely make the minimum length and mainly reiterate a lot of what we said in class with no original points of your own. . . I try to keep my voice pleasant, factual. Off the plane of meanness.

- That's not so bad.

- You're right, it's not bad. But it *is* average. Your prose is bland. No good use of vocabulary, figurative language. Not even any quotes from the movie itself. I went over what I wanted when I went over the checklist. And when I read an example of a good review.

I don't feel good about taking Giselle on this perp walk but at least there is no press or flashbulbs. Not many students following our see saw either.

- Fine, she says and with an airy shrug stuffs the now folded comp into her backpack.

She has no further reaction and I think of a long ago teacher telling me that the first person to talk is usually the one with the least to say.

- Any other questions? I ask half-heartedly. Anyone else need something clarified?

I notice that the morning sun is centered in the window now, light hitting the white walls squarely. There's a radiance, a whitewashing, a sanitizing of the class that lends an almost spiritual aura to the room. To them. Excluding the knuckle cracker, the nose picker, and the one trying to covertly to scratch his teenhood. Sanitized, but no nimbuses. I see Marcus looking my way and talking to the soccer-shirted girl next to him. She raises her hand.

- Madison?

- This assignment *sucked!*

Her energetic bluntness and the word take me back. But only momentarily.

- Really? And what kind of compositions did you think you'd be writing when you signed up for *Film*?. . . She's giving jockettes a bad name.

She looks at Marcus, back at me, and she says, I don't know, but this one *sucked*.

- Well then, I say, embrace the suck. . . Opps, I think. Know instantly that I'm kicking it up. Drastically. The dialogue so far has been SOP. Embrace the suck is new. The connotations and definitions multiple. Some sexual. Shoot, *I* think, and damn. I always avoid the sexual. But this slipped. . . Most civilians would consider *embrace the suck* as harmless blow-away dust. But they never worked in public education. I suddenly feel like my fly is open. That I bent over and my pants split. That a phhht little

43

fart ripped off unexpectedly. . . I could apologize but that would only bring more attention. I keep the Rue Morgue deadpan.

- What? she says. . . Faces look up all around the room.

- Embrace the suck, I sa y again with no choice and think, Get off this!. . . I pivot and add, Or it's not too late to drop the course. Not a lot of choices here. . . Am I on the exit ramp? I wonder.

The students are alert now. Most are looking back-and-forth between Madison and me waiting for the next round. But I seem to have landed a haymaker. She trades words with Marcus, then faces me. Mute button pressed.

- Well then, I say turning away from her rondeur anger and laser glare, let's talk about our next film. . .

Madison Murphy: *Drop the course? That guy stands a prayer. I'm sure he knows adding and dropping isn't so easy for seniors. Right now most of my schedule depends on having this Film course early. What an jerk. Film is supposed to be easy and August assigns reading and this written review the second week like we have nothing better to do. Like most of us don't play sports. Or have part-time jobs. Like most of us aren't trying to line up college applications, visitations, taking the SAT's again. The only reason he'd like me and probably a whole lot of others to drop is so he can do even less than he does now. Marcus and I figure that August is betting if he assigns enough work early we'll quit. And how he treated Giselle! I didn't read her composition but Marcus said his friend did and he said it was worth at least a B. Embrace the suck. Effing hell.*

The Daring Young Man On The Flying Trapeze: Jorge Espinoza shows up not only on time but a couple of minutes early. I am impressed and immediately push to mend fences.

- Listen Jorge, I say, I think we got off on the wrong foot yesterday. I know you apologized but I'm sorry too. I understand your wondering what the point of all this is. . . I hold out my hands, palms up flexing the good shepherd, my people posture. . . Frankly, I'm not sure that there is a point. Time will tell.

- You don't have to apologize to me Mr. August. I was the late one. I was wrong.

- Nice of you to say it . . . I offer to shake hands and there is no hesitation on his part. He smiles and as we shake he takes off his hat. This is a good kid.

For the next 15 minutes I learn he doesn't play school sports though he looks like Michelangelo's David on steroids. Says he did in middle school but discovered he didn't like the team thing. He weightlifts, confesses someday he would like to enter a bodybuilding contest. I know it's self-centered, he says, but my parents say a person has to have pride. He and his parents came from Ecuador when he was 13. Mom and Dad run a small two-room restaurant. Jorge helps out. He says his only real goal now is to graduate. Thinks it's a reasonable ambition, though he knows it isn't very lofty. I quote Browning, Ah that a man's reach should exceed his grasp or what's a heaven for? He asks me what Browning said about money and keeping a business going.

Jorge is another squared away student like Destiny. If there is any way I'm going to affect change in his life, I'm not seeing it. Might as well be offering oil to Shell. Or trying to talk Nunberg out of this objective.

Jorge Espinoza: *I heard Mr. August is not really into the personal stuff, which is why I came in late the first time. But he's friendly now and acts interested. Though it could be an act. I did catch him looking out the window a few times. He seems to think I'm a natural athlete just because I weightlift. I have to explain there's a big difference between hitting a baseball and hitting the dumbbells. I also tell him I would have played football but. . . I don't want to tell him there are too many jerks on that team. And that I prefer putting my faith in myself and not depending on teammates. . . Even if I only graduate from high school I'll be the first in my family. That's not so bad.*

Lean On Me: I'm sitting in George's small sun-curdled office and the bedrock quiet is soothing. Nice to have your own semi-retreat off the beaten path. I'm hemmed in by hot house plants, bleached family photos, a yearbook board of UV faded head shots, and dried out felt pennants hinting there is a land of milk and honey just beyond these walls. I've always been envious of this retreat. Maybe even a little resentful. Doesn't seem fair we are on the same pay scale. Or that guidance is exempt from all teacher duties, then given these oases too.

The PA clicks on announcing the deadline sign up for Do You Have Hot Lips. Outside in the Guidance wing I hear beetle-like movement, muted voices, the sound of a microwave beeping. It's life in strobe light motion, swaddled in heavenly ether gauze.

- Mikey my friend, what can I do for you? George barges in sling loading a stack of student files and munching on what looks like a chicken burrito.

- Nunberg. You told me not to panic and I'm not redlining yet. But what's new?

- Funny you should ask . . . He drops his corduroy ass into his vintage Steelcase swivel and offers to cut the burrito in half. I shake my head and he says, I was just talking to one of the secretaries. The closet QT is. . .

He says there's a lot of pressure to cut next year's budget and staff. Not brain-ripping news, I think. George says, No buyout, just make life tough for anyone not up to speed. He adds, You gave Nunberg a great opening by agreeing to that objective. My guess is that when you meet with her to finalize it, she's going to play hardball. Maybe not plant punji sticks in your path. But not help much either. . . He takes a bite of the burrito and says while chewing, Then, who knows. Redo the objective next year? Get assigned lots of behaviorally-impaired troglodytes? Multi-rooms spread out around the school?

- She can also dump all the worst duties on me, I say. And the union can't do shiz about it. All within the contract. She can also start observing me everyday. Nitpick me to death. And in the end hand out a crappy evaluation anyway.

George says, Yeah she can. But seriously, when you signed off on the objective without any idea how you were going to meet and assess it, what were you thinking?

I'm tempted to remind him that he's at least partly to blame. But I don't. Reiterate that Nunberg said we would keep it loose for now but that one day before the end of first marking period we'd finalize things. I didn't think anything about it, I say. She seemed laid-back. PMS free. My bullshit detector never registered.

- Well, don't panic yet, George says and starts sorting through the student files while working the burrito. You'll think of some way of meeting it. Or I will.

- I'm trying to stay calm. But it's tough knowing she can push me out the door if there's a cutback in staff and I don't get a good evaluation this year. You know I'm not in any financial shape to lose this job.

- I know, George says and keeps his head buried in those damn student files.

A lightbulb clicks on and I reach into my briefcase, rumble around, and find the crumpled letter. OUT OF MANY, FEW. I show it to George. He glances at it and says, What is it? I explain how it was in my school mailbox the second day of school. He says someone's playing a joke. But not him. He goes back to the files.

- I wonder how I ever got these particular 6 anyway? I ask trying to keep him in the conversation. And maybe elicit some pity, or a new strategy. I sure-as-hell hope Nunberg didn't choose 6 that she thought could *not* be improved, I say. She said guidance would be involved.

- I never heard anything about it, George says absentmindedly. By-the-way, the squawk on the street is that you're doing OK with them. Not quite Love Daddy Of The Year. But not the antichrist either.

- Good to hear, I say. By the way, what the hell is Do You Have Hot Lips?

George laughs. Nearly spits out the burrito. The phone rings. The bushwah's over.

George Raven: *I don't blame Mike for being worried. The breaks haven't gone his way. Amanda had a good corporate job. But they burned through money like dot-com hedonists. Saved nothing. Then the company moved overseas. MIke didn't want to relocate. Fortune 500 lifestyle gone. No health insurance. Mike had dropped his own when we went to a larger co-pay. Around 3 years ago Amanda was diagnosed with Stage IV pancreatic* *cancer. Mike couldn't pass the physical to get them back onto the school policy. Still hasn't, though I don't think he cares anymore. They went into a lot of debt. If he were to get the ax now, he'd be up shit creek.*

Bristol Stomp: I'm using a corridor that skirts the edge of the caf to get back to my room and reminding myself to play it cool with this objective thing. The worst that Nunberg can do is not much in the grand scheme. Not compared to the hand Amanda and Max drew. I feel good about George's compliment. Maybe like Captain Jack I really do need to let my crew, those half-dozen, take me to the horizon.

I'm just outside the cafeteria when I see Zoe and Nunberg up ahead. They're about 30 feet this side of the caf doors and are standing close talking, Nunberg leaning in. I stop and step off to the side so as not to get crushed by the surging wave of just arriving first lunchers. It's a reflex action. Standing on my tiptoes and doing a bob-and-weave to keep Zoe and Nunberg in focus is not. . . They appear to be arguing, a real bitch stomp. Nunberg is subdued but red like an unripened peach. Zoe's face is cobwebbed with darkness, helped along by the usual overlay of mascara. Nunberg points a finger at her. Zoe throws something down on the floor, turns on heel, and moves off slip streaming through the student mass. I blend with the crowd and move to where they just were as Nunberg herself click-clacks off in the opposite direction.

Up against the wall is a crumbled piece of paper. Hungry students are crowding close, bumping, pushing like a drift of pigs towards the feed trough. I spread my elbows wide, nudge out a space, and pick up the paper. I push back against the flow till I'm in open space. The paper is a memo on Nunberg's stationery. In a tight cursive is the simple edict, See me at your earliest convenience. . . I flip it over but that's it. See me. . . Not

49

much. What the hell does it mean? Why would Nunberg want to see Zoe? Is it about me? How do they know each other? They must or why would Nunberg have assigned Zoe to me?. . . See me. . . Hardly implicating like the Zimmerman telegram or Wikileaks. But interesting. Or is it? Maybe it's just a small nothing in search of a big problem.

If I Had A Hammer: Many in the first wave of diners are seated and already eating. There are airborne edibles, bodies jostling, a cacophony of strident yelling and unvarnished laughter a.k.a. normal lunch interaction. The teachers on duty are clustered together in a far back corner sipping coffee, eating while standing, laughing amongst themselves possibly over the idea that they really *do* have control. A phantasmagoria of shadow.

I do not miss caf duty.

I'm at the opposite end and nearly through when a singular voice says, Would you like to sign my petition? The voice is loud, the energy unidirectional. I stop. A lone black girl who I have never seen before is standing in front of a dining table pushed close to the wall. A mylar balloon with a picture of Malcolm X is floating from one corner.

- What's it for? . . . I walk over.

- I'm trying to get enough signatures to force the administration into implementing an African-American field of studies. We have one history course, one English course but that's nowhere near enough. . . She steps closer to me, holds out a pen, and smiles. No sign of nervousness or solicitation. While trying not to stare I cannot help noticing that she's talking Angela Davis while looking Rihanna. Her short-sleeved sports jacket with slightly raised shoulders is a strikingly deep royal purple. A burnt-orange crewneck shell with a silkscreened pic of Malcolm X pops it more. The jacket is open over a tall slender figure. The voice fluid bravura. The eyes ship-side portals.

The click-clack of leather soles on tile turns my head towards the main corridor. Nunberg walks by with Superintendent Hoxley. She's practically fused to his side. Doesn't give me a glance.

- Sure, where do I sign? . . . I take the pen, bend over the petition, scan the names and notice I'm the first faculty member. . . I'm signing big and bold, really John Hancocking it, when a handful of peanuts hits the wall and ricochets onto the table.

- Hey Asia! Why don't you go back to Africa if you don't like it here? . . . It's a male voice. Loud, forceful. Rank with humus and base rust. There's laughter from different directions.

I straighten up. Asia picks a lone peanut out of her hair. Nearby a table of multi-hued faces. Amusement mixes with slight surprise that a teacher is so suddenly present. And not looking too foking pleased.

- Knock it off asshole, she tells the towheaded boy in the middle. Underhandedly tosses the peanut onto his table.

- What did you call me? Ass–. . . His belligerent tone is ratcheted down when he sees me. Come on, he says to her emoting innocence. We're just having some fun. . . He's smirking while overtly looking at me as if to say, WHAT! You gonna make a federal case out of some peanuts?

I recognize him as a football player, one of this year's schlock tribe. I have nothing against football players. I helped coach the team years ago and I have had many fine pigskin students over the years. It's not the case with this particular stumpy schlub. His name is Curt Moseby. I had him sophomore year and it's only through the grace of flex scheduling and perhaps some random mainframe quirks that I'm spared the dunce-packer this year. Moseby stacks denseness, cantilevers petty meanness. A thought retardant bully whose main redeeming feature is that he's an only child.

- Take your act where the sun don't shine, Asia tells him. She steps closer and says, But first sign this petition. . . She waves it in his face. . . I can't promise you there'll be picture books and crayons in any new courses, she says. But maybe with enough help from your football demented jock scrapers. . . she looks from one-droll-face-to-the-next. . . you can understand more than the page numbers.

The football tribe is not laughing. Moseby's pit bull genes rise to the surface. He slaps the petition aside and stands up. I jump in. Ease Asia back. Tell Moseby to either sit back down. Or we're taking a walk to the office, I warn.

- What about her, August? She started it.

- That's MISTER August to you. And no, she did NOT start it. Those nuts you threw came awfully close to hitting me.

- Who said I threw them? Don't you think if I did throw them and was trying to hit you I could?

- Not from what I've seen on the football field.

Students from surrounding tables break into raucous laughter and there is general pointing and gag reflexing. I hear someone say, I'll vouch that Moseby threw those peanuts. Another chimes in, Me too. What a flaming dork. . . It's intended that Moseby hear the backup and he does. His defiant look drops the length of his beard stubble. But he's still standing. Fists clench and unclench. I see Jorge Espinoza and TJ Sato in the background. The on-duty teachers are pushing through.

- What's it going to be? I ask. Getting your butt back on that formica or taking a walk? . . . The hypothalamus kicks in. Some long ago camo testosterone supercharges. Adrenaline races. Nerve endings spark. . . The

52

soldier wants Moseby to take a swing. Infantryman is ready for the swing. He's already playing it out. Sidestepping, grabbing Moseby's wrist and elbow. Leading his momentum facefirst into that lally column. It's all fleeting. An effervescent urge. A primordial Cormac McCarthy bloodlust. Cannot hit students. Cannot touch students. Certainly cannot use excessive force even for defense. Knock him on his ass, says the id. Brute force is not the answer, says the super-ego. My hands rise slightly. Weight shifts onto trail leg.

As if sensing a potential violence even greater than this own, Moseby dials it back. He turns his head, sticks his ass out, and sits down in slo-mo. Once seated he resumes glaring at me and Asia. But the flash point has passed. Weasel, not warrior.

- You can still sign the petition, Asia says to him.

- Go to–

- OK Asia, I say, enough. . . Army is in retreat, the middle-aged teacher stepping up. . . Go back to your own table, I tell her. And the rest of you. . . The student body that has been gaining ground now retreats in the face of encroaching teachers and the swift demise of peanut wars.

- Hey! Wait a minute, everyone! . . . Asia is waving her petition at the receding tide. . . It's not too late to help yourselves and your school.

Asia Gibson: *Trouble is nothing new with me and this school though it usually comes from the main office. I'm grateful for that teacher who helped me. I think I had it in control, but you never know with those locker room homies. Phys-ed has wrecked more minds than drugs. Push drugs not iron would be a good mantra for them. In any case the signature sheets are filling up. I doubt it'll have any effect on admin but you never know. Pressure from the press would help. School officials hate bad press and* *coming from me would make it lots worse. Many white faces would not be happy.*

Don't Think Twice It's All Right: Even as I am stepping over a broken Rickenbacker in the breezeway next to the trash can I'm replaying the cafeteria scene. Outwardly I think I appeared in control. In psychological terms there was challenge stress, but no panicky threat stress. Moseby sat down because he picked up on the unspoken. Maybe some micro-body language. Possibly he can read minds like a dog in-tune with humans. I doubt it was because he respected my authority. Maybe he was afraid of losing his football eligibility. . . I know now, even as I knew then, that I would never be the first to strike. Cold cock the little porcine bastard. A peremptory strike would mean my job. Arrest, humiliation. Getting my sperm tanks twisted publicly like some animal balloon. Plus it's just not me. I'm not a chest-thumping primordial. . . Max never punched or slapped me, though as a peanut I got my bare bottom whaled a few times. Condign punishment. I don't think I'm any the worse for it. I might be a little better. Max imprinted a rolled magazine, not a way-of-life.

The Human Comedy: Max, Dad, I'm here! I yell. . . On the kitchen table are the remains of the day. A cold cup of coffee, a partly spilled bowl of tomato soup with crumbled Saltines. A large sausage link stripped of the skin but uncooked. This kitchen was once steam-softened. Redolent with the pleasant odors of cabbage, dumplings, potato pancakes, pierogis, chicken soup, goulash, beef stew, noodles, koilitch, apple pie. Now it smells stale. . . Nostalgic Loss Aversion: I generally don't like to think about what once was here. Objects in the rearview mirror may appear close. But they are as gone as yesterday's sex.

I walk into the living room. Max is sitting in his recliner. Television is on but the picture is frozen. A cigar is burning in the ashtray. Half a glass of scotch is within easy reach.

- Hey Dad. Why's this old movie paused?

Max raises a hand in acknowledgment that his only child is here. Then puts a finger across his lips omitting the soft shhh susurration. I sit down and pet the cat. After half a minute he says, It's amazing. That young lady is the spitting image of your mother when we got married. . . On the screen is a black-and-white low-def headshot of a dark beauty. Her wavy hair is swept back over one ear exposing an elegant neck and is held in place by an ornate barrette. Her eyes spell danger. I grab the remote, hit the Info button, and say, It's Jane Greer. I don't remember mom ever looking like that. You putz, Max says, what baby remembers what his mother looked like? She doesn't look like that in the pictures we have either, I protest. She does in *my* mind, Max says and takes a drink.

- Dad, why is there an uncooked sausage on the table?

- Because the stove isn't working. Goddamn cheap child-labor foreign crap . . . He's pulling on the cigar now, still staring at the screen. He suddenly says to the cat, Anyone expecting the worst won't be disappointed.

- No Dad, your stove works. I turned off the gas. Don't you remember I told you? You still have heat and hot water so you'll be fine for now.

- You turned the gas off?

- Just for the stove. And don't be turning it on again or I'll have it shut off for the entire house and you can pack up and move into the assisted living facility we talked about.

- Like bloody hell I will, he says and mumbles, I'm getting fucked with my pants on.

- How did my old guitar get broken?

- That tone-deaf Polack Ernie said I should give him the guitar since you never play it anymore. I asked him, What's a spirit going to do with a guitar anyway? Play with Elvis? He called me a cheap Jew and I swung. Damn near threw out my back.

- What was my guitar doing in the kitchen?

- I brought it down so you could play me a song like you used to.

- You never liked my music.

- Bernice did. And it's about time you cleaned out your room.

- I know. I will.

For the next half hour I do the usual household chores until his place is cleaner than mine. I'm checking windows when an idea comes to me and I yell into the other room, Dad how would you feel about. . .

Before Sunset: I grab the Rickenbacker on my way out and scarcely notice the knot of teens half a block up as I drive by. They give me a double take but from my POV they're just part of the same busy wallpaper I see all day long. Twilight is morphing into dusk. The streetlights are on. It's a comfortable street, at a comfortable time, in comfortable symmetry. The luminous colors are fading but the streetscape is still glowing. A glazed acrylic mural. A feeling of electricity. Of Maxfield Parrish. Technicolor on acid.

The feeling holds till I turn east and put the sunset behind me. Suddenly I can't wait to take off the shoes, clothes, and soak under a long hot shower. It's been a long day. Another one. I need a drink.

Moonwalk: The rest of the week is uneventful except for a few risible marks. A teacher screams at the top of his lungs during a faculty meeting when a department of education official tells us we need to work harder to meet state mandates. . . A student says to me, Me obtaining an A+ in English is hyperbole, right or wrong? I think, Fecking-ultra-hyper-right. But tell him, Only in this world . . . Another student tells me she has a short losing memory. I say, Is that like a short-term memory? She says, No, maybe, I don't know. . . Early on the morning of my birthday before students arrive I'm walking towards my room when one of our 30-ish science teachers yells, Hey August! He's standing at the far end of the hall, looks both ways, then pulls down his pants and moons me. Big fat white buns. It only lasts a few seconds but it gives me a good laugh.

I see my mentees only in passing. Audrey gives out an enthusiastic, Hi Mr. August! in the hall. A real oversized spanglement. . . I'm buried with the academics of my 5 classes. Nunberg can give me a bad evaluation just as easily for neglecting my classes as she can for failing my objective. I feel like Sisyphus. But instead of trying to push a round boulder up the hill, it's a pyramid-sized building block. Square, foking huge. Not budging.

Chapter 6

Countdown = 7 Weeks To The Horizon
South Of Righteous

Mercy, Mercy Me: I'm sitting in the English department office thinking this conference thing has been a big waste of time. Boring, unproductive, unremarkable in any way. Conversations have been polite, but no ah-ha moments. Education as speed dating. Bodies in, bodies out. Echolalia.

It's not how I want to be spending my time even if it is necessary for keeping my job. I know in the news and some fiction that dedicated teachers living for their job is the fossilized standard. As if we are all Mr. Chips or Miss Jean Brodie. Archetypal teachers. But we're not. For me teaching has always been important. But it was never the be-all, end-all. There's a big world outside these walls that I've made time to enjoy.

At least in the old days.

Today I'm feeling down. Remind myself that lots of people in most jobs do things they don't want to do. But have to do.

Life is a strange business when you're not in charge. Strange, but not funny.

The Threepenny Opera: Zoe Koppel says she's with no group, never has been. This is in response to my asking, Do I know any of your friends? I ask her about a boyfriend and she says, No time. Must be spending too much contemplating new body piercings, I think. I probably should not bring it up but I say, Why do nice looking girls such as yourself make pin cushions out of their bodies? Canvasses out of their skin?. . . For a second she looks pissed. Her voice backs it down to, You're showing your age. . . It's hard not to, I say and add, Could it be that like the Japanese philosopher Suzuki you feel you're an artist at living? Your life *is* your work of art? Body too?. . . She looks tired, stifles a yawn, then yawns. Says, No, I create real art. . . I tack and ask, So what's filling your time?. . . She says, Painting. Some sculpting . . Not jewelry? I ask thinking of all she's wearing. . . No, not really, she says. . . *This is going nowhere*, I think. There are openings but it never gets beyond mono-question, mono-response. I need to cut through the PTO chitchat. Jaws-of-life away the whole-psyche hum job.

Maybe the place to start is how she's dressed.

Zoe's wearing black lace tights under a hip-hugging mini. Her low cut, sleeveless top is exposing the tops of her breasts and seems molded to her figure. There's little left to the imagination, outside the brand. The cloth-to-flesh ratio low. The effect sexual exhibitionism à la street walker. When she leans back flashing me even more I decide to call her on it. This has been going on for the last 5 minutes.

- Excuse me Zoe, I say. You're not exactly within the school dress code, are you?. . . It's not the first time a female student has shown me more than her naked intellect. But that sort of exhibitionism usually happened when I was a younger teacher and not snow-dusted.

She pauses and shrugs.

- You can't be in school dressed like this. . . I don't mention she certainly cannot be in a one-to-one conference with a male teacher dressed like this. She's smart enough to know it. . . I add, We'll forget it this time.

Her eyes are not hard but they aren't intimidated either. She is part of the bulimic botoxed generation which regards looks and the apotheosis of youth second only to breathing. She knows exactly how she's dressed.

But I don't want to overreact. It's not like she's in a g-string and pasties.

I try to lighten the mood and say, Isn't that a new hair color? Wasn't your hair red before?. . . Hair seems like an OK neutral topic, though it's still keeping the conversation mundane and on the physical. . . Not unless you think apples are oranges, she says and pushes back her chair. Are we done here? she asks bored. I really need to catch some study time. . . Yeah OK, I say, but just one last quick thing. Is everything OK between you and Principal Nunberg? You two seemed to be having quite an argument the other day outside the cafeteria.

This time Zoe's face drops. Her eyes ablaze. She freezes in mid-step. No benign indifference. It dawns on me we have finally moved out of the realm of conversational vapidity. It's only a feeling. But I trust gut.

Zoe says, We were negotiating the price of one of my paintings.

- Is that why she wanted to see you?. . . I hand her the note.

She looks at it and says, You picked this up off the floor?

- Someone else did. They gave it to me. Thought it might be important. Is it?. . . My voice is friendly, my eyes serious.

- Not unless you want to get into a bidding war over the painting. . . Zoe is back to being unflappable.

- Maybe I would. Where can I see it?. . . I don't know where I'm going with this. But I read the subconscious mind processes millions of neural impulses a second while the conscious mind handles less than 50. Accessing the instinctive is important. And it's telling me something is out of whack.

- The principal saw it hanging in the art room.

I say, Well, good luck selling it. See you next week. By the way, your hair, it's a pretty cool green. Lime?

She rolls her eyes and is gone.

Go Your Own Way: I continue sitting a few minutes after she leaves. I made the last comment about her hair to distract her from our Nunberg discussion. If there's anything really there I don't want her thinking I locked onto it. . . I meant to ask her earlier if I know her parents. There's something familiar about her face. But I forgot, maybe because I was thinking of Nunberg. Or maybe because there was the definite smell of marijuana on her, a fact that's just now sinking in. I try to remember. Were her eyes bloodshot? Did she have that far-off lotus-eater look? Drug use wouldn't surprise me. *No* drug use would.

I like Zoe. She just might be the most interesting of my 6 mentees. On one hand she's an artist which by definition causes her to interact with society. On the other she seems wholly independent. I like her, but I'm not sure I trust her. I certainly don't trust Nunberg. For now I'll give Zoe the benefit of the doubt, as I would any teen. I don't like not trusting students.

Zoe Koppel: *I'm surprised August mentioned my clothes. I'm not dressed any more inappropriately than I was for our first meeting. Perhaps my charm is wearing off. He checked me out pretty close but I have a feeling he'll never do more than look no matter how much I show him. . . I was taken back when he mentioned Nunberg. I know we were in the hall and in public view but I never saw him. I warned the stupid bitch the hall wasn't the place but she was pretty pissed off when I didn't get right back to her. No matter. . . Another total waste of time here with August. Ass-numbing Telemundo tv in HD. . . He sure is noisy. Wanted to know about my pins, rings, and tats as if he really cares. Actually, he's not so bad. Bit of a righteous dude. And I suppose I could talk more. But what'd be the point? It's not like he'll ever be any real help.*

Your Cheating Heart: The History Of Film class is looking over the reviews I just passed back. There's plenty of resentment over the fact they had to do another one so soon but it's leaving under the tsunami of good marks. Giselle seems thrilled with her B-. Or at least she's not a whorl of complaints.

- Mr. August, what does this grade mean? Madison asks without a hand raised. Marcus is talking to her so who knows if she's doing this on her own.

But it's anticipated.

I knew her grade within the first 2 paragraphs. Foresaw a battle. Looks like it's here. Apparently stupid and nervy are free today. I walk over to keep things as private as possible in a room where everyone knows everyone else's business.

- That's a zero, I say pointing to the red number, and that's a P next to it. Which stands for plagiarism. It's all explained if you read the comments.

- You're claiming I cheated? she says in a surprised voice.

- It's not hypothetical. Are you sure you want to have this conversation now?

I silently register surprise at her surprise. Why is it that students think they can pass off professional work as their own? As if teachers who earn a living with words cannot recognize the difference. As if we read their papers while sleeping, or picking dingleberries off the cat's butt . . . Maybe some teachers do. Shortcut assessments all to hell. It's easy to fudge a close reading. But I don't. Not on major papers. And Madison should know that. . . Madison is a ballsy girl who I knew would become even ballsier when confronted with a zero. There was no way around it short of approaching her privately before class. Which there was little time for. And no desire. I gave her an academic middle finger and she's not going to take it.

- It's a *fact*?. . . Running true to her competitive nature she's body checking. It occurs to me that one-upmanship may be great on the soccer field. But it sucks here.

- It is. If you want to discuss it now, step up to my computer. Bring your paper.

She stands up. Flips up the hood on her school sweatshirt. Doesn't acknowledge her fan club except for having her game face on. I motion for her to stand behind me and hit the bookmark tab. I created a Madison folder for this paper. It's time to use it. Her paper consists of six paragraphs. See your second paragraph? I ask. She nods. Well, I say, look at this. . . I'm pointing to a NY Times review and the section that matches her composition word-for-word. I do this for the next three paragraphs in her main body. Each one from a different periodical. Each one lifted verbatim.

I lean back and let the evidence speak for itself. . . . Case against this bunco artist complete.

- But, she finally says, some of it was my own.

- True, I say. You had a very short introduction and an even shorter closing that were yours. Maybe six sentences total. The other 90% of this paper was plagiarized.

- But I researched. That took time. And effort. Don't I get any credit for that? And my beginning and ending?

- No, you don't. Professional writing is professional writing. Your writing is your writing. The two should not be mixed except for short quoted sections where you give credit to the author.

- You never told us that.

63

- Plagiarism and what it entails are covered in my course expectations. Which I went over. Not even to mention that you're a senior and have been taught since elementary school *not to copy!*

- They never taught us that.

I spin full around and look long and hard at her. Look, I finally say, your grade is a zero. . . In the background the class is getting restless. A wad of paper sails under the neon, a student is panhandling in the aisles for lunch money, a girl tries to sneak in late. The conversations are loud enough that I hear an individual request for a BJ. . . See me after class or after school, I tell Madison, if you have anything more to add.

She's slightly flushed but not with victory. There will be no World Cup ripping off the shirt to reveal the sports bra. She's blind with anger. Cannot see the screen for the pixels. But it's not my problem now. Class maintenance is.

- OK in here. Sit down and quiet down! Maya, where's your late pass? . . . This class would be classified as barbarian if I could raise it that high.

Leaving On A Jet Plane: I check my mailbox during lunch and one of the school nurses corners me in the main office. Are you taking your Film class on your annual fall field trip to New York? she wants to know. . . Maybe, I say, maybe not. It's not the kind of class right now that I want to be seen with in public.

- Well just in case you decide to go, take this.

- What is it?

- It's a medical alert sheet for 14 of your 30 students. I was going to put it in your mailbox but here you are. If you go on the trip you need to stop by my office first and pick up all the prescription medicine for those 14.

I glance over the list. Everything from irritable bowel movement and la-tex and peanut allergies, to migraines, diabetes, and asthma.

- You want me to carry the medicines for all this? I ask almost laughing. Can't 17 and 18-year-olds be responsible for carrying their own pharmacy? I never had to do this before.

- It's a new policy. We went over it at the first faculty meeting.

- I must have been in the lav, I say sounding very student.

- It's still the policy. Certain medicines cannot be carried by them be-cause some prescriptions might be used to get them relaxed or high. Also, medicines that are out of your control can be shared. You could wind up with a flipped-out group.

- They're spacey anyway. . . . And can't students get their freak on regardless of who has their stash?

Around us seniors with late arrival-early dismissal privileges are signing in and signing out.

- I'm only telling you the policy and what has to be done, she says.

- Listen, the students have time on their own, I say no longer amused. They wander, sightsee, eat, shop. What if I have all the medicine and someone needs his or her fix? How are we supposed to get together?

- Don't they have cell phones? Don't *you*?

- Sure. But sometimes we get separated by a mile, maybe more.

- You need to carry the medicines, she says. And if anything goes wrong and doesn't get acted on, you're liable.

- Ha. Liable? You're kidding?

- No. This is not a joking matter.

65

- Well, it's pretty funny to me, I say. I'm damned if *they* carry the medicine and get in trouble. And I'm damned if *I* carry it and don't get it to them. . . This is like Catch-22, I think. Yossarian did not want to fly anymore. I don't give a flying fuck anymore. At least not about field trips. . . I say to Nurse Ratched, Here's my answer. Forget the field trip. Keep your alert sheet. No hard feelings. Have a nice day.

I walk off smiling. What-the-hell. One less thing to strain the brain about. One less distraction to meeting my objective.

School Nurse Betty: *No one seems to understand that I have a job to do too. Some teachers act as if I am the enemy and not a co-partner in education. They don't realize I'm looking out for the students' best medical interests as I have to do. I try to play fair by the teachers too. I anticipated that Mike would give me a hard time. Guess maybe I should have just left the sheet in his mailbox like I planned. . . It's a shame if he doesn't wind up going on the trip. It will be a real loss for the students. But it will be his loss too. Even if he doesn't see it that way.*

Octopus's Garden: I'm alone in my room at the end of the day and Madison comes in bent forward under the weight of her high-riding backpack and gym bag. She doesn't look angry or contrite. Doesn't look anything. I glance over her shoulder to be sure the door is open. SOP, CYA. Male teacher, female student. Calm vs god-knows-what.

- Mr. August, she says, I know I copied some of my paper. But I really thought it was OK. Lots of students do exactly what I did.

- And if I catch them, which I frequently do, I give them a zero too. I'm not picking on you. Plagiarism equals zero is the equation in every school I know.

- Would it be OK if I redid the paper? My average really can't afford a zero.

- No. Sorry. Papers are a one-shot deal. You did it. I evaluated it. It's history. Remember though, it's a long marking period. Isn't over till November. There'll be a lot more assignments, many more opportunities to raise your average. . . I remind myself to stick to pussyball. No hard hits. Know that this is a conversation I've had many times. Best to stick to the script, as I'm doing. Honest, harmless, time-proven discourse. A verbal form letter. No sense twisting her uterus.

- Can I do extra credit? Something to erase the zero? . . . Madison is getting exasperated fast.

- There's no extra credit at this time. I may offer it before the end of the marking period. But there's nothing now.

- So there's nothing I can do? . . . Her mouth is tight, the anger barely controlled.

- Have a good practice, enjoy yourself. Your final average has a long ways to go.

- I might be sending out college applications before the end of the semester. This quarter's grade will be on the transcript, but not the final grade. Right?

- I don't know. You'll have to ask your guidance counselor about that.

Madison's head nods almost imperceptibly. She doesn't say anything more. Looks out the window. Briefly. Then leaves. No tears, and surprisingly no histrionics for someone I perceive as a bit of a drama queen.

Madison Murphy: *I should have known August would not cut me a break. You'd think he would know enough to back off on first semester seniors* *after all the years he's taught. The course is supposed to be a gut, and he's turning it into a marathon run. That old fart needs to get a heart and common sense. . . I don't like the way he talks to me either. Like a parrot. Like he's bored. Too bad I can't get him on the soccer field. I'd like to show him what it feels like to get kicked in the privates like he did to me. And have to keep playing. I don't know if it's too late to switch sections to another teacher. Or if there's even another section that lines up with my schedule. But I'm sure as hell going to look into it.*

Chapter 7

Outrunning the Darkness

Non, Je Regrette Rien: I'm sitting in my classroom the next morning before first period and for some reason Madison crosses my mind again. I don't think it's guilt over blowing an important communication. Went well from my vantage, even if it was all rote. Maybe it's caution now. I'm sensing that it's not over. That the pigheaded Madisons of the world do not just go gently into that good night and accept what they perceive as defeat. I'll probably be getting a phone call soon from mom. It's usually mom. Though there are bitch enabler dads too. A tough, but not unfair judgment in my reamed out experience.

I don't feel bad about how the me-her pissing contest went. Not good either. Trouble is, even if I want to cut Madison a break I have to be fair to the majority who did the assignment correctly the first time. Guess maybe I should have explained that to her. Not that it would have made any difference. Madison is tunneled-visioned. Her grade, her grade. Doubt she's interested in examining the bigger picture. My gut is that it's the teen in her. But there are plenty of adults the same way. Self-centered corn shuck souls.

The beat writer William Burroughs said, Be just. If you can't be just, be arbitrary. . . Kaufman used that line with me. . . I think I was just with Madison. And *just* fotching right.

You've Got Your Troubles (I've Got Mine): Becky Capello, a first year English teacher and my unofficial mentee and study buddy, walks into my empty room. She's practically in tears. Sits down at a desk in front of me and says, I was observed yesterday. My evaluator is saying the class was too contrived.

- Damn. That's tough, I say looking at the 22-year-old and thinking, Who wouldn't love this lady? Smart, chic. The fresh looks of a younger Mila Kunis. Brains of Jodie Foster, wit of Tina Fey, poise of Anne Hathaway. Which may be hyperbole, but she's still topnotch. And still a female teacher the senior teen boys dream of dating. And fucking. And the girls begrudgingly emulate. . . Who's your evaluator? I ask.

- Nunberg.

- Yeah, she's mine too. Like she would know what teaching a class is all about. Understand her classroom background is zilch. That she was a speech therapist.

- I heard that too.

- Guess she thinks that working with stutterers, lispers, and illiterates qualifies her to stick her fat patootie into an American Lit course.

- I know. . . She wants me to record a class within the next two days. Watch it. Evaluate myself. Then get together with her for a conference. . . I thought I wanted to be a teacher, that I loved it. . . Becky's face goes long, fishboned with tiny crinkles. . . But I'm not so sure anymore.

- You're a great teacher, I say. Your students love you. I've heard nothing but good.

- Thanks, she says. I needed that.

I pause and think about some of the young teachers we've lost in recent years to retail, the insurance and travel industries, to tech and research firms. One twenty-something even decided she'd rather be a dog groomer than subject herself to our daily bullshit quotient. The non-organic pressures.

- What's needed here, I finally say, is for Nunberg to back off. I'm not sure exactly how we can accomplish that. But we need to try. I'm going to think hard about it. Here's my own new unofficial goal. By half year she's totally off your case. Mine too. Her super-ooga-booga BS gone.

I smile in an attempt to lift both our spirits. It's big talk. Much bigger than I'm feeling.

- I'll buy you a drink at Hudson's if you can pull it off, Becky says and pats my hand.

- And maybe cook me some real lasagna like only a real Italian can make?

- You got it, she says. Meatballs too and salad. Just get that nasty woman off my case. . . She tucks a long brunette strand behind her ear, gives me a wink, and is gone.

I get up and start erasing the board. Was she just kicking up her usual ingenue persona to casual flirt? Like it might be added incentive for me to actually do something?. . . Ha. No. More likely it's just youthful exuberance misinterpreted by a middle-aged myopic like me. The usual case of age thinking he still has it. The grand delusion, the mirror, mirror on the wall appeal that fools only frail egos or dreamers.

I think of Charlie Chaplin telling Albert Einstein, Nothing, it means nothing, when the physicist asked him about the cheering throngs that surrounded them in NYC.

The bell rings. It's time for nothing.

Bridge Over Troubled Water: The English office is not improving with age. Dust is building up on the counters, blinds, and floor. White motes of autumn pollen float brilliantly in the air. Moisture streaks the large windows

71

like contrails across the blue. The floor is marred with long black scuff marks as if some budding street artist is using his heel as a rubber brush to create an abstract drag strip. The feng shui is dirty locker room, maybe even funerary. I'd much prefer a Japanese rock and water garden with hibiscus blossoms and maidens in brightly flowered sarongs. I'd also prefer having a different objective this year but part of mine is sitting directly across from me. Eyes bright, voice eager. Excited like he just got his first snatch.

- Mr. August, TJ Sato says, I saw you in the caf the other day.

Oh oh, I think and immediately know I need to downplay. Do not need a shart storm from a simple school walkabout.

- Were you going to hit Curt? TJ wants to know and adds, It looked like you were.

- It was just my Mister Teacher pose, I say. Most fights can be avoided by strong posturing. They're won before the first punch is ever thrown.

- Really? Gosh. Curt Moseby is a pretty tough dude. But you could have taken him, right?

What to say? This is Joey questioning Shane . . . Western Theory: Sometimes it doesn't hurt to reinforce the notion that justice *is* on the side of the right. That good *does* triumph. Ideas that can help the young through the tough puzzling years ahead.

- Yeah TJ, I could have. . . I give a half smile like tough guy Alan Ladd.

- I thought so. I know Curt. He lives in my neighborhood.

- That so? I say losing interest fast . . . I think to myself that I do not really want to talk about that brainless jock cup. But if it helps steer TJ right I'm willing to stay with it a bit longer. But not much.

- We had a fight in third grade and he kicked my butt good, TJ says. Curt used to have his own gang in the neighborhood. I was in it for awhile.

Freshman year I got in trouble. I didn't mean to shoplift so much stuff from that store. It just got out of control. Now I try to keep away from him. And gangs.

- So things are OK now?

- Pretty much.

TJ says it slowly as if it's not totally true. . . I realize that like most teens TJ is caught between the kid and adult worlds in what can be a hazy time of inertness. He needs to move on. It also occurs to me that with his fixation on things military, his expertise on shoot-em-up video games and weaponry in general, he might be a kid tailor-made for school violence. It's always the outsiders. The geeks. The weirdoes that turn schools into shooting galleries. . . Does TJ have that in him? Is he just enough of blighted soul?. . . I don't think so, but you never know. It's certainly possible. And something never far from my mind when I deal with the fringers.

- What neighborhood do you live in? I ask trying gently to sidetrack.

- Mill Pond.

- That's the neighborhood I grew up in. My dad still lives there . . . Diversion time, I think.

- Really? Wow.

TJ smiles like I just announced I'm his long departed father and just like that the caf incident is forgotten. . . It's for the best. Especially TJ's best. He's already told me he wants to enlist. We've talked about the army. Maybe too much. He probably dreams of glory. Of medals and ribbons. Marching in the Memorial Day parade. Maybe getting a homecoming fuck from a local teen queen. . . I don't want it on my conscience if he comes home in a body bag or on a stretcher. Nor do I need him succumbing to the dark side and becoming a school shooter. . . I just don't need to be elevating kicking Moseby's can to plinth status or talking military every conference.

I reminisce for awhile about the old neighborhood. TJ is fascinated by the night Grotowsky's was hit by the meteorite and I expand it. Dramatically coloring the part about how the whole family was out in the front yard. Police and fire sirens wailing. Searchlights scanning the sky. Teenage daughters in their nighties. Rumors circulating about an impending alien invasion. . . I'm exaggerating, frequently lying, but sometimes dealing from the top. It's great theatre. He seems to appreciate the performance. Ivan Grotowsky gave my father one of the meteorite fragments, I tell TJ and hold up my fist to indicate the size. I say. . . Can I see it? TJ immediately wants to know. Sure, I say, I'll bring it in next time we meet. Think it would be OK if I hold it too? TJ asks. I don't see why not, I magnanimously offer. It's not like it's kryptonite or uranium.

As we talk I'm happily aware that my soft-pedaling the caf incident worked. That whatever special op warrior TJ was casting me as is gone. I'm relieved.

TJ Sato: *That's something about Mr. August and me being from the same neighborhood. . . I don't blame him if he doesn't like Curt. Not too many adults do. Not a lot of kids in this school either. Curt is a pretty hellacious troublemaker. I heard that him and his friends want to get back at Mr. August. They're trying to come up with a plan. I'm not saying anything today because I don't want to worry Mr. A. And I don't want to be a stoolie either. . . I can't wait to see that meteor.*

Do That To Me One More Time: See me at your earliest convenience. You have the right to bring union representation, the email says. It's from Nunberg. Doesn't mention why and that pisses me off. Big tomatoes like to do this. Email you with no subject line, equally vague text. See me. Well dumpster dump her headfirst. Who would want to see those squash legs and Mars Attacks mile-wide bouffant? Not me. . . But union representation? Shit. Looks as if I'll be getting written up. Again. It's happened before. Years ago when I used the school copier for union business. Another time when I grabbed a student's arm too hard and left marks. Still more times when I. . .

Kung Fu Fighting: Hahaha, the laughter comes from the hall along with the sound of a scuffle. I get up and go to the door. A bunch of girls are riding piggy-back, grabbing at each other's arms and shirts. Their male wheelmen are maneuvering and attempting to kick out each other's legs. A chicken fight sans swimming pool. Lots of yelling. Laughing.

Just a high school hallway and another day.

I start to protest, then stop. It *is* funny. Institutional comedy. The wavery behavior of teens being teens.

Two couples go down. Another slams into the lockers. I'm laughing myself. Try to imagine what Nunberg would do. If she would do anything but spin on her heel. It briefly crosses my mind to get Becky and enter the fray. The couple that whammed the lockers is down. One pair left standing. Teachers appear. Yelling. Name taking. Words like detention and suspension. Protests that it's someone's birthday. Teachers retreat. Celebrants plunge on down the hall. Laughing. Poking each other.

Both Sides Now: I go back to the computer. I'd like to email the principal that I can't meet today, or tomorrow. But anytime after that. My room or hers. No mention of a no-sweat attitude. But I'd be hoping it shows. Meet whenever, about whatever, wherever. . . Maybe it would be childish tweaking her badonkadonk. Maybe not. Old military doctrine: The one left holding the field of battle is the victor. I held this field before Nunberg got here. And I plan on holding it long after she's gone.

That's what I would *like* to email. And maybe I would if I did not have 2 years of mediocrity on record with the real possibility of a third and being shown the door. For the first time since I got tenure I feel uncertainty. That breeds caution. And damn nervousness. Fuck! Who likes getting written up – and over what this time?. . . I need to shoot off a minimally invasive answer. Not hostile, condescending, or bumptious. But not toady either. I type out that I will see her tomorrow during my free period. Simple and direct. I only hope the meeting is.

Splish Splash: The bullet hole in the ceiling above the backbar is part of Hudson's appeal. It was put there by a drunk construction worker who got tee'd on payday when he'd gone through most of his paycheck and Huddie himself shut him off. The scar cutting perpendicular across the bar near the taps was cut there by an angry unemployed logger pissed off about not being allowed to add to his tab. Went out to his car. Came back with a Stihl with the 32" bar. He was low on gas and only got about halfway through before the chainsaw conked out. And someone conked him.

The welcoming succor of my friendly neighborhood tavern. Almost as entertaining as school when the jerks are in attendance. But not fucking quite.

76

- What can I get for you? Deirdre bounces up and pushes a coaster in front of me. . . The usual?. . . Her eyes lock on mine and I'm thinking her life is sunshine with a core of the hots.

- Why not. Gin in, stupidity out. It'll give me something to blame between now and bedtime if anything more goes wrong today.

- Bad day?

- Not in terms of nuclear holocaust or our sun going super nova. Huge compared to a bad gin-vermouth ratio.

She laughs and is back in no time with a tumbler filled to the brim. You know Mike, she says as she wipes up a few leftover burger crumbs, you were always funny. Always my favorite teacher. . . She fixes a loose earring and rubs her neck.

- Thanks Deirdre . Of course the competition back then wasn't too strong. A bunch of old dotties left over from the JFK years. Guys who would fart in the middle of a sentence and kick the dog. Or would have if one were around. . . The joke is old, Deirdre laughs politely. I ask, So how's it going for *you*?

She says she goes to the university branch part-time and is studying history. Would like to become a lawyer. Is divorced. Lived for awhile in Arizona but didn't like the heat and bugs. I hate spiders! she says dramatically. . . Spots and splashes of fear? I'm surprised. The Victorian bug-mouse phobia doesn't fit the kind of person she projects. Could it be an act? Casting call for a fearless man? Or is that *me* projecting the kind of woman I want? And need?

She says she likes working at Hudson's. The tips are good, she says, but being on my feet for 8 hours or more is tough. Adds she would not mind a clerical job, ideally something in the paralegal field. . . I ask her about the logistics and finances of working and going to school and she admits it's tough. I'd like to cut back on my work hours, she dreams aloud. But what with tuition, books, car payments, gas, rent, utilities, food, trying to save a little is impossible.

Suddenly I'm hit with one of those riptide eureka moments not alien when I'm drinking. She pours me another and I say, Let me run a little idea past you. . . I talk slowly as it germinates. . . Add, You don't have to give me your answer right now. But. . .

We finally shake on a deal, her hand lingering a tad longer than Ms. Manners would advise. Then she leaves to service some mighty thirsty customers who have been tapping fingers and spinning glasses.

Deirdre Good: *I'm really happy with the deal Mike offered. I know he's mainly looking out for his father but there are other ways he can get part-time caregiving without involving me. I know damn well I'm flirting when I lean in close and practically toss my hair in his face. But it's just fun. I'm long past the crush I had on him when I was a student. Typical schoolgirl fantasy. I suppose it still could happen but I doubt it would be on his incentive. He seems complacent, resigned to his daily routine. . . We read Madame Bovary in his class and I haven't forgotten how he looked at me and said, Great personalties have great passions, there's nothing wrong with that. At least I thought Mike was talking to me. That probably WAS a schoolgirl fantasy. His wife was living then and I doubt he fooled around. Plus I was no Lolita. . . He's not quite sloppy these days but. . . Wood, especially older wood, always looks better polished. He should go easier on the gin too.*

Up, Up And Away: I'm finishing my third for this Happy Hour thinking about the deal with Deirdre when Jimmy Klein stumbles in. He's lurching for the men's room and spots me. Shit, I think, here we go again. I look around. Vinnie's not to be seen. I keep one eye on the kitchen door, another on the scrotum sack approaching.

- Hey asshole, Klein pulls up short. Don't think I've forgot what you did to me. . . He rubs his head.

- What you did to yourself, I correct him.

Klein goes grim. He's swaying but his voice is surprisingly steady. Ha, yeah, he says. Figures you'd say that. Never wrong, always the teacher. So how's your school year going?. . . I don't say anything and Klein adds, Rumor is there's going to be cutbacks. . . He tilts like a out-of-plumb barstool and takes a step sideways to right himself. I stay silent and the drunknik leans in. Close. Halitosis of wine and empty stomach. Says, You're not worried about that, are you pal?

I lift my glass in a mock toast. A voice over my shoulder says, I want you to leave now, Klein. And I don't want you back in here. Ever!

- I was just going to piss.

- Piss in your pants for all I care. But get going.

Klein stares blankly into Vinnie's face as if his temporal lobe might have seized. Turns without another word and heads out. Gets through the door. Turns to yell *fuck you*. Misses the step. Crashes to the pavement. Someone says, The drunker they are, the harder they. . . I start to rise but Vinnie checks me and says, The poor bastard can't walk and talk. Let's see if he can shut up and stand.

Someone offers 2-to-1 on a ten spot that Klein won't be on his feet within a minute. The wagering starts, the time's noted. All eyes focus on the crumbled phoenix. . . The douchetard is slow. Makes it to his feet in stages. There is some dispute if he made the 60 seconds. He's looking back at us through the window. Catches my eye and gives me the finger. Vinnie waves him off.

- Maybe Huddie put up with that bullshit, Vinnie says when all heads are bent back over glasses. But he's dead and I don't need it.

- You think he's all right? I ask jerking my thumb towards the street.

- Sure. I've seen him worse. Heard one time he jumped through a plate glass window when the bar maid shut him off. Pretty tough guy. Or he was way-back. Klein's been in-and-out of here over the years. Doesn't drive, walks from somewhere not far away. But I can tell you one thing. . . Vinnie pauses like he's Rick and I am Captain Renault police prefect of Casablanca and I just told him I'm shocked, SHOCKED to find that there are drunks in here. Got that, Deirdre? he says. Klein is banned for life. We don't need that drug pushing meth-head around here.

MacArthur Park: I'm not a quarter mile past Hudson's when I spot a figure half-in a street hugging hedge row. I pull the GMC over and get out. . . Klein's groggy, the front of his pants wet. His face is a kaboodle of scrapes and cuts. I probably should call 911 but my cell lives in the glove compartment and is dead. And I'm not sure I'm under the .08 DUI limit anyway. Police are not an option.

I cover the seat with an old blanket and hope the battered palooka. doesn't soak it through. He's skin-and-bones. Not much trouble getting him in and seat belted. He remembers his address though he's not really coming around. He reeks of urine, cigarettes, and marijuana. A drug toned day. I'm hoping he doesn't piss again. Or throw up. Or take a swing.

He slumps sideways and is fast asleep and snoring before I can say craptastic. In five minutes we're at his house. I get him partially awake and out of car when he turns and kicks at me. Misses and dents the passenger side door. He slumps into my arms. I ring the front bell. Knock a few times.

When the door opens I almost drop my human sack.

It's Zoe Koppel.

Chapter 8

When Hell Calls

Chitty Chitty Bang Bang: The class comes in. Pushing at underarm books. Grabbing hats. Laughing. Asking about tonight. Stepping over chairs. An ever increasing crescendo. . . Some have no idea why they're here other than it's where the busses dropped them.

- Get out your homework, I say.

Fumbling. More laughing. Half have it. A quarter know they're missing it. A quarter hear glossolalia. Damn fart welts. I think of Emerson's vision of natural polarities. The universe and all things balanced by opposites. Light by dark, teacher by student, instruction by bafflement. Robinson Crusoe spent 15 years alone on a desert island and when he discovered a single human footprint on the beach he went crazy anticipating the complications of interpersonal interaction. He eventually did well against the cannibals. Don't know how he would have fared with this bunch.

I'm going through the motions of collecting the homework. The class is antsy. Yesterday afternoon keeps intruding till it's all I'm thinking about.

A lock turns, a deadbolt is thrown back. She looks as surprised as I feel. Bring him in, she finally says and stands back. I've got one arm hooked around Jimmy Klein's waist, his arm is draped over my shoulder. I follow Zoe Koppel. We walk through a small Goodwill living room with a couple of Ikea pieces. I deposit Klein in a one-bed flop off the kitchen. The walls are covered with b&w photos. High quality. Nightscapes. Candid character studies. Some risqué Annie Leibovitz-like blowups. . . Klein rolls onto his side, knocks a framed photo off the nightstand, and laughs as if he's a mad scientist. I pick it up. Am surprised to see Klein as a cool Brando type straddling a Harley. . . He's snoring before I hit the door.

On the stove a pot threatens to boil over. A pre-teen buttoned-down boy does homework at the kitchen table. When I say hi the Tiny Tim raises a hand in silence without looking up. The over-aroma is tangy beef and slow-cooked vegetables. The under a room and house fumigated with cigarette smoke and pot. A calendar and a Felix the Cat clock decorate the kitchen wall. Some chocolate chip cookies sit under plastic wrap on the counter. In the living room are more b&w enlargements and several original oil portraits and nudes in the style of a budding Lucian Freud.

At the front door Zoe avoids eye contact. I want to tell her not to worry. It's not like the family secret is The Tell-Tale Heart or The Cask Of Amontillado. Lurking death, a dismembered body, a 50 year walled up victim. . . It's only dad – a drugged-out, liver-wrecking, rancid piece of booze-besotted waste. Requiescat In Pace!. . . I'm out on the stoop, the door closing, scraping against the floor, when I say, He should be all right. Small lump on his forehead. Drunk, pretty gone.

Zoe nods.

- I found him in a hedge on Wilson Street–

- Mr. August you don't have to say anything more. I really don't want to know the details.

- Is Jimmy Klein is your father? I ask. When she reluctantly nods I say, Are you and your brother going to be all right? Where's your mother?

- She works at the nursing home. We'll be fine. If you don't mind I've got work to do.

- OK, I say. . . By the way, someone is a really good artist.

She frowns, nods. A twisting scarf of emotion. . . The door closes with a thud. Locks snap back into place.

As I drive away I feel of twinge of sadness wondering what kind of life they have that's minus a working mother, and plus a fugzilla father. Latchkey, for sure. Abusive?. . . Of course Zoe's mother could be a basket case. Mommie Dearest, Serial Mom, Lady Macbeth . . . I really do hope things will be all right.

I finish collecting the homework. One of the unprepared chimes in with, I didn't do it because I didn't understand the assignment. So is it still a zero?

I don't respond to the spiked-haired Goth. I've crossed the fed-up chalk line. Most of these students have it so much better than Zoe and her brother. And yet they still can't manage their 1.5 bath, 3 bedroom time. Get their lives as orderly as their Netflix queues. The girl is already turned around laughing, drawing attention to her new pink do. Mission Accomplished. It's a shade that reminds me of a flamingo, penis, or a raw vulva. Maybe a strawberry margarita.

I do a mental hiccup and funnel my thoughts to next period and a bigger papoose.

Eye In The Sky: Principal Nunberg has her hands folded in front of her and I can't help noticing there's no wedding band. No husband type either in the plethora of photos on her desk. I can't resist and ask, Sons and daughter? Point to a good looking trio of young adults in front of a classic stone building. No, she says, relatives. I'm so proud of them, she says with an unconvincing toss away brevity. . . I notice that they don't share her form-hugging clothes or the lacquered sense of Madame Tussaud style. Many heavy woman are attractive or appealing in a Rubenesque way. Not

Nunberg. Too oogah-boogah phony. To me. Might be a hit with the S&M crowd.

I suppose my questioning her about the pictures was my pathetic ding-dong attempt at sympatico diplomacy. But her face is now freeze-framed seriousness. I get a sinking feeling. Wish I had brought union representation.

- So Mike, she says and glances at a sheet of paper in front of her, I asked you to meet with me to discuss a few concerns that I, and others, have.

I instantly vow to say as little as possible. Silence is often the best strategy.

- The first concern that has been raised, and these are in no particular order, is the incident in the cafeteria the other day, she says. Some people thought you were a bit over zealous in gaining control of the situation. . . She pauses but I don't step in. Her voice takes on a deeply grave tone as if she is saying Kaddish for me. . . It was mentioned that you seemed more threatening than the student, she says. That you assumed an almost martial posture. There was a definite in-your-face attitude.

She leans back and waits. I say nothing. I'm trying to keep my face blank. Like a mortician's. She finally asks if I have any comment. Not really, I say, though I'm betting Asia Gibson wasn't the one complaining about my behavior and quelling an otherwise explosive situation.

- You exaggerate, she says and purses her lips. But let us move on. There was also concern about your handling, or *not* handling, of a chicken fight in the hallway outside your classroom. Students were loud, physically out-of-control, and you merely stood by observing. Even laughing. . . Her voice trails off and this time I take the opening.

85

- Those were some of the best students and athletes in this school, I say. They were in control though it might appear to the untrained nonathletic eye that it was a pell-mell donnybrook. It wasn't. It was good-natured fun. They were loud because it was a birthday celebration. We were still between periods so classes were *not* being interrupted. . . Even as I attempt to justify myself to her, I know that I should have stopped the ruckus. And would have at any other time in my career. I'm still not sure why I didn't other than it really *did* look like fun. But she doesn't have to know that. And I remind myself to stop talking so much. Any defense looks like guilt over matters that were, and still are, highly subjective.

- The way I see it, she says, is that you overreacted regarding literally some peanuts. And underreacted where physical injury was imminent. . . The cadence of her words is hesitant, her face nervous, off balance. Am I imagining it or is there a reluctance on her part? Uncomfortable in the educational zeitgeist of playing the tough administrator?

I'm tempted to tell her that I've been in the tiled trenches for 23 years. Have had many of the worst students. Have prevented or broken up many physical altercations. And never once had a single complaint lodged against me. I would then ask her when the last time was that *she* got physically between 2 red-eyed bow-wows in the pit. Or the last time she stepped into the cafeteria to supervise. . . But I bite my lip. I'd be flirting with insubordination. Dafuq. Why push it for this marionette. Give her more fodder for a possible negative evaluation on me.

- Anything else? I ask and force a smile. Like maybe I'm about to break into a treacly glissando and tip-toe off through the tulips.

- You cancelled your annual field trip because you did not want to be bothered carrying student medicines.

86

Since it's a declarative independent clause and not interrogative I don't say anything.

- Well? she says.

- Well what? I ask hyperaware. You haven't asked a question.

- You know what I mean, she says with a definite edge. Why would you cancel a trip you take every year over a medical necessity?

- I didn't cancel anything. The class is not doing the work and does not deserve a field trip. If their work improves, the class knows a field trip is still possible.

This is not a total lie. But even so I don't like stacking up half-truths. I feel in need of an ablution of mind and spirit. . . If she wants to wring my thigh warmers she should at least have the decency to pull down my pants. I'm guessing she has a lot of experience in that department. . . She has to know that I've broken nothing in the contract, in the teacher rules of employment, or in the everyman book of common sense. She doesn't have a legal leg to stand on. And while she can bust my ass regardless I doubt she has the testosterone or chest hair to give me a formal written reprimand.

- I also heard you failed to discuss the homeroom survey the first day of school. I thought I made it perfectly clear that a group discussion was to be held.

Her voice is calm, reasoned. Which is even more infuriating. I force myself to remain equally prozaced.

- I did not feel qualified to be answering questions on vocational matters and future personal plans, I say calmly. Any more than I feel qualified to be mentoring those 6 students you assigned me. But I'm trying.

- You need to try harder.

I pause. Then show my vulnerable side. I'm giving all my free time for class preparation and correcting papers, I say. My father has Alzheimer's. My mother died a few years ago. My wife last year. After suffering a long time. I'm still recovering from all that. My house is falling apart. My cat and dog need grooming. I'm in terrible financial shape. Just as bad physical shape. I have no medical insurance. And on top of everything you want me to be all things to all students. Some kind of omniscient student whisperer. Needless to say, I'm totally stressed out.

I exhale. Sad for my circumstances. Sadder that I confessed it all. Stripped myself naked and prostrated myself before her. A supplicant before the shrine of Nunberg.

- I'm sorry for all that, she says, and looks and sounds sincere. In a surprise confession she says, We all have our problems. My dog was killed a little while ago. Hit-and-run motorist. . . Before I can say anything the wind sock comes about and funnels a cool breeze. Nunberg says, But anything not school related is not our problem here. . . She taps her desk and slams me with, You need to get your educational act together.

WHAT? Fuck you! I think. Stuck on stupidity, hemorrhaging callousness. A natural born hard ass. Exhibition-quality bitch. . . I look at my watch. Force myself to get tough. I say, The period's nearly over. If there's nothing more I have a class coming in. . . I stand and grab my briefcase. . . Even as I do so I'm wondering if I'm suicidal. Today's Stupid Mistake #1: Don't intentionally provoke your enemy by walking out.

A blush rises across her doughy features. Her internal igniter no doubt sparking. But she remains sitting as if modeling correct professional behavior. Her voice unforced calm.

- Before you leave, she says, sign this. . . She pushes two typed sheets across her desk. It is what we just discussed, the twat stain adds. Naturally you have the right to respond in writing and have that response added to your file. Keep one copy for yourself.

A formal written reprimand.

She did have the hair.

Fuck her. I sign with a quick flourish thinking I just peed on an electric fence and here's the jolt. Though getting zapped was going to happen anyway. . . She takes her copy and asks, When am I getting the final paperwork on your objective?

- I believe we agreed at the end of first marking period, I say easily trying for Top Gun cool. My stomach takes a flop.

- I will see you then, she says. And dots it with a firm, Don't be late.

I start to leave, stop, and for some unfathomable reason ask, Did you ever agree on a price for Zoe's painting?. . . Cue eerie music. The surprise on her face is unmistakable. She says merely, What are you talking about? The tone forced lightheartedness, almost girlish. I hold her eyes, then say, Never mind. I was thinking of someone else. Give my best to your family. And to your husband. . . I don't wait for a response but I'm out the door thinking my last crack was petty. And not giving a shitarooski. Today's Stupid Mistake #2: Don't give your boss a bunghole whack because the retaliatory job bonk will hurt you a lot lot more.

Zoe's painting and Nunberg playing dumb about it. What the hell is going on? And what was that about her dog being killed?

Bernadette Nunberg: *Mike no doubt feels I am being unduly tough on him and maybe I am. But I have pressures on me he would not understand. . . It is perfectly clear that he doesn't regard anything he did as amounting to a hill of beans. Isolated, none of it is. But taken together they show the definite pattern of an educator grown cynical and not always acting in the* *best interests of the students. All that is in the reprimand he signed. I would have explained it to him if he did not abruptly walk out. Administrators say when a conference is over, not teachers. I can see that he doesn't want to play pretty. . . I am shocked he mentioned a husband as if there is any indication I'm married. And why would he ever bring up Zoe Koppel's painting? I wonder if he thinks he knows something?. . . Mike reminds me of a glass of stale beer. Flat, but still can make you crazy. I doubt the carbonation can be put back in.*

Lady Sings The Blues: Destiny Gibson is resplendent as usual in a Diane von Fürstenberg style wrap dress. Short in length, long in leg. Curvy ballerina-length gams wrapped in sheer black hose under the tight-fitting puffy-sleeved tan dress. I'm no fashion maven but the low V neckline seems just a little too V-ish. Would undoubtedly pop flashbulbs on the red carpet. But I don't think I should be seeing as much skin and boob as I'm seeing. Not in school.

I raise my eyes as if they were never down there. Females dress this way because they *want* people to look. Of course. For some old cronies Destiny's appearance would fall under the category of good-reason-to-keep-living. But it can't be that way for me. Any checking out of the goods I do has to be terse and along the lines of are-you-within-the-school-dress-code? Undress code, in this case. I briefly wonder how she ever got through this much of the day without any teacher or administrator calling her on what's obviously a d.c. violation. And now it falls into my lap. So to speak.

She's tight-lipped this morning. Face pinched off in a pique. She offers no greeting other than sitting down, legs akimbo, mouthing a sotto voce,

Damn. . . Destiny's had little patience for these meetings from the first. And I've been trying to keep them as painlessly short as possible. . . Maybe she's picked up on the fact I don't really want to be playing the ornamental jabberwocky. So she's now pulling back too. Electroshock or colon hydrotherapy less painful. . . Well fuck her, and fuck Nunberg if that's the case. I'm fed up with it all.

We sit for a quiet minute. It occurs to me it's not like her to swear. Even a mild *damn*. Her vocabulary the far side of thesaurus i.e. she has Choice, capital **C**.

- Something bothering you today, Destiny? I ask not really expecting an emotional strip tease. Her reply surprises me.

- I'm worried about an AP English assignment. . . Says she has to write an original letter from the point of view of any character in Freedom. Elaborates that it has to reveal the personality – the fears, prejudices, likes, dislikes, motivations, ways of dealing with conflict, etc.

- Franzen, I say. I've read Freedom, The Corrections too. So what's your problem with the assignment?

- Anything involving creativity like this letter has never been my strong point. It's going to be a long course if there are many more assignments like this. It could wreck my average. Keep me from being valedictorian.

She curls up her legs under the chair. Mind spinning like a hard drive.

- It's been a long time since I taught AP, I say. But I can give you this advice. In order to write creatively you have to read fiction. And eventually you'll *think* creatively. . . Live poetry, write prose.

There's a squawk of static, a chime, and Nunberg's voice comes over the PA. She announces the deadline for audition signups for the autumn play. Reminds everyone about the big football game next Friday night. The school fight song blares briefly. Nunberg wishes everyone the best of luck.

There's a squelch of white noise. The PA clicks off . . I think, *Hoo-fotching-rah.*

I smile at Destiny and repeat, Live poetry, write prose.

- I read nonfiction, she says.

- Have you ever noticed that the best nonfiction writers write creatively? Laura Hillenbrand, Hampton Sides, Carl Sagan, Doris Kearns Goodwin, Susan Sontag, Joan Didion, David Halberstam, and others. There's really no such thing as nonfiction. It's all fiction to varying degrees.

- That's good advice. Live poetry, write prose. . . She opens up her laptop and asks, Would you be willing to read my rough draft? Edit, make suggestions? The draft is done. I'm sure you have plenty of compositions from your own classes. But you did offer to help me if I ever needed it.

Her legs are now crossed. The dress riding high. Don't know if she's deigning to sneak me a look as a potential reward for helping her out. Or if she's just a clueless twit who goes around exposing her fleshy shanks and bare buttus as part of a Destiny-centric life.

- Sure, I say getting my eyes back where they belong. You can drop off the rough draft on my desk or in my main office mailbox. Probably the mailbox is easiest, I say thinking that maybe we don't need contact again so soon.

- Sounds fine, she says. If I have any questions I'll email you or stop by.

There's not a lot more to say. There was a point when I was going to tell her that anyone with her runway sense of fashion is already loaded with more than enough creativity to master an AP assignment. Just need to rechannel. Earlier than that I was going to point out that she needed to dress appropriately for school. Another Zoe. Rah-rah-fucking-lower-the-skirt. . . One thing I never was going to bring up was that poster on the wall. Do You Have Hot Lips. What does that goddamn thing mean anyway?

She leaves, the bell rings, students pour into the halls. Off-and-effing-running again.

Destiny Gibson: *On one hand I hate to ask Mr. August to help me out. On the other hand isn't that the point of all this? I know I need to loosen up my concrete-sequential side. Get more abstract-random according to an online article I read. When I pick up the pen or my fingers touch the keyboard my right hemisphere locks down. I tried dictating a composition and typing it from the recording. But it still wasn't very good. . . I know I am flashing Mr. A more than is usual for teacher-student but it's not like there's anything to it. At least on my side. I like looking good. And I like others liking it too. . . I'll give him the rough draft and I hope he truly is able to provide some quality editing. It's going to be key to my year, though I have my doubts he'll be able to help much. On one side is the uncreative me. On the other is the over-the-hill Mr. August who teaches the general kids because he either can't or doesn't want to deal with the higher levels.*

Looking For An Echo: It's a beautiful day. Indian summer. The warmth opening windows and spirits. I decide to take part of my free period outside in the courtyard. Just sit in the open sunshine. Enjoy the blue unfiltered sky. Breath some nonrecycled air. Clear my mind. Float. August TM. Hope nature can power me down.

I'm turning a hall corner, preoccupied, cutting it a bit too sharply when I practically run into Zoe. Sorry, I say as I sidestep and pause. But she keeps going. Moving fast. Her pink, ochre, and purple outfit with yellow waist scarf a pop of color against the denim and stone washed crowd. I don't think I have ever seen her dressed so flashy, so trendy. But it occurs to me I know nothing whatsoever about woman's fashion. Even less about Zoe.

Outside I sit on a bench reserved for faculty. It's flush in the sun, unoccupied, and set off to the side of the student area. Only seniors and staff allowed out here. There are   picnic benches, carefully pruned white birches starting to give up their leaves, a drinking fountain, a battery of raised solar panels, pathways of scored concrete stained in the school colors of maroon and white. A couple dozen twelfth graders sit around just talking. Several others throw a frisbee, 5 or 6 play cards. Card games are not allowed but it's too nice to bust them. And me. Just one more thing for Nunberg to write me up over if she finds out I let it go.

Nunberg. Her office is straight ahead in the corner behind the large rhododendrons. The shrubs were originally planted in an irregularly spaced cluster. These many years later they've grown together. Branches intertwined and overlapping. They reach the top of her windows. I noticed earlier that the effect inside is private and dark, the shrubs an effective awning and blind. Probably too late to prune them back. If Nunberg wanted. Which I doubt.

I'm staring at the bushes, thinking that the principal's privacy is almost total, when a flash of pink, ochre, purple, and yellow pierces the green. It's just a glint. A sudden madras flare. But could it be Zoe? I suddenly forget the azure sky. The crispness of the fall scented air. Know I need to get closer.

I mosey over trying to remember exactly where Nunberg's desk and chairs are. Try to orient myself. Avoid whatever little sightline she might have. Her chair does not face the windows. People generally sit across from her. I get to an angle where I should be towards the back of the totem's head if she's seated. The rhododendrons are thick. I'm catching only the faintest glimpses of color that could be Zoe.

I need to get into the bush. And I need a reason if Nunberg calls me on it later.

The senior boys are still tossing the frisbee. I back off and yell to them. At first they don't understand but I start running. Hold up my hand. A former student smiles and lets go. It sails towards me chest high. Spinning like a anti-gravitational UFO. Perfect. Would hit me in the numbers if I were in uniform. But I don't want that. I stumble. The disk flies past.

I regain my balance. Laugh. Wave the boys off. I delicately pull back branches and pick my way in. The plastic plate hasn't penetrated far. But far enough. I see Zoe's dark face in partial profile. She shakes her head and a strand of bright hair falls across her forehead. Nunberg stands and reaches across the desk to brush the hair back. Zoe leans back out-of-reach. Nunberg sits down.

I grab the frisbee and a dry branch cracks. The snap freezes me and for a second I think the jig is up. But neither looks my way. I get out faster than I went in.

- Hey Mr. August, the student yells, you're not very good.

- No I'm not. . . I smile and toss it back. He jumps in a futile grab.

I sit back down and try to make sense of what I just saw. Are they still negotiating the price of a painting? Doesn't seem likely. Do principals touch students and is it OK when it's female-to-female? Maybe just some polite grooming?. . . I realize that I'm no closer to knowing anything. But that there most certainly *is* something to know. . . I briefly marvel how life works out. The influence of chance. If I had not decided to take some sun. If I had not cut the hall corner close and noticed how Zoe is dressed. If I had not caught a flash of color through the shrubs. . . If. If. If. . . It's a strange little melodrama the 2 of them are now playing out. I just need to know what the hell it means.

Paradise Lost: The cemetery is peaceful this mid-September afternoon. I drive its narrow bowered lanes. The overhead trees reflecting off the windshield. The sun darting in through the leafy hardwoods. Pastel shades of yellow and red. Warm pools of soft light. I pass a white Bobcat with russet rims that's backfilling a grave. I give the operator a wave. The baseball-capped head nodding back. Park alongside a fieldstone wall of cambered granite with green patches of lichen and moss. A wire trash barrel overflowing with dead summer flowers.

No one else is around.

A garden of stone.

I fill the watering can from a brass spigot in a gray vertical slab and walk the downslope to the grave. Avoid a large fallen branch and flush sets of markers. I don't think there's a rule you can't step on someone's tombstone. It just seems proper.

The ground is soft and spongy. Thick neglected grass. The first fallen leaves. I look around. It's an old section of the graveyard. So many engraved monuments, so many corpses. The visitors come-and-go. Not the full timers. Longfellow referred to a Jewish cemetery at Newport as the groaning earth. He pointed out that dead nations never rise again, implying that the stiffs will. . . How many of these interred once believed that? And yet here they lie a-moldering. . . Who here had a reputation for being smart, cute, athletic? Who was known as a saint, a bastard, an easy lay, a tough sell, a quick temper? Was any a murderer or wife beater? An ordained priest, minister, or rabbi given to pedophilia or dipping into the holy coffers? Doesn't matter now. Death doesn't care. They are all equally decomposing. Dust-to-dust.

So many family names I know. Over there is the Kilner obelisk, several generations of newspaper people and writers. The old man once did an article on Max. . . The   Weeks mausoleum huddled in the curve of the stone wall. A family of dry goods merchants, later bankers. If I had any savings they'd be paying the interest. White bird deposits dot the main stone. . . The oversized rough cut granite monument under the pruned cherry. Fyler, a philanthropic family back when industrialists were the movers and shakers in our valley. Amanda's father, my bastard-in-law is friendly with a couple of the descendants. Berries stain the rough surface.

At Amanda's simple headstone I water the pot of mums and remove some dead petals. I pull out intruding grass blades that are running over the stone's face and brush away broken acorn shells. A single gray squirrel leaps overhead. More acorns fall.

I rub my fingers over Amanda's engraved name and can almost see her walking towards me, like she frequently does in my dreams. I talk low and tell her about the latest antics of the cat and dog. Remind her our anniversary is coming up but that she doesn't need to get me anything. Though an appearance or some sign that you're OK would be nice, I say. There's a slight rustling of branches. I get a little teary-eyed and force myself back to the present. Tell her I don't deserve what Nunberg is doing to me and say, But you probably know that.

There's a sound of honking. I look up and outlined against the blue barely visible through the branches is a V wedge of Canadian geese flying south. Moving fast. I lean into a better position. Where in god's name are they going? And why? Aren't they at home in the cold?. . . I love Canadian

97

geese, Amanda did too. Called them stretched ducks and marveled at their regal bearing. I was impressed that they mate for life. Both of us found it hard to believe there are asshole hunters that blast them out of the sky just for the sport of it. Like there's a sheen to downing flesh with a flurry of steel pellets. Or maybe the peckerwood marksmen are just pissed off about all the crap the geese leave behind. That would at least make a little sense. I know what a mess they make around the small pond at the high school. The ground wicks the shit into the water, which pollutes it. I'm surprised Nunberg isn't out there blasting away.

The din fades, the geese are gone.

I return my thoughts to Amanda's grave and her. I start in a low tenor All Of Me. I played the Dinah Washington version many times when Amanda was dying. It was our song long before that.

I sing it slow. Dragging out the words while the squirrels chatter overhead and the leaves fall. Till the song is finished. And I'm cried out.

I leave a small pebble on the marker.

Chapter 9

6 Weeks and Counting

Tectonic Shifts

This Door Swings Both Ways: I decide to eat my lunch in the faculty room. Have not done this in a long time. Can see some of the new teachers looking at me like I just wandered in from the street. I hear one actually whisper, Who is that guy? Students have cliques, teachers do too. I'm long past being part of any lunch group. Most of the ones I used to eat with have long since retired. And as of late I have not been exactly Mr. Warm Fuzzy with the new or older teachers. More of an observer than a participant in the faculty scene.

I pop a leftover fillet of scrod into the microwave, sit down, and look over the newspaper. I can feel eyes on me, and a voice at my side says, Darn Mike, why don't you just set off a stink bomb? I look up at a smiling Becky Capello. . . I shrug and don't bother to tell her about the old days when I would sometimes brown paperbag pickled herring and onions, liver and bacon, Korean kimchi, or French bread with roasted garlic. This scrod is nothing. Practically Chanel No. 5.

- Anything new with Nunberg? she asks and remains standing. Nothing, but I'm working on it, I say. Work faster, she says, then she leans closer and whispers, *Italian dining*. I laugh and she goes back to her table.

- Mike, long time no see. . . Manny and Howard, two old-timers from the math department are suddenly sitting down opposite me. The last of the clean shaven, shirt and tie, ditzy whiz brain anachronisms. For some reason they have always reminded me of Beldar Conehead. Though they look more like Penn & Teller.

- Hi boys, I say. Good to see you too.

- What do you know about the superintendent wanting to stick it to the older staff? Howard asks. We heard he wants us gone. . . Howard is the Penn lookalike, though not as cool. His neatly clipped hair with slightly tapered sides reminds me of the barber shops I grew up with.

- Yeah, I   say,   I heard that too . . . I tell them how I got written up yesterday and their faces grow dark while offering sympathy.

- We're talking to the union, Manny suddenly says. Mentions strength in numbers. Setting the example for the younger teachers. They know nothing about how hard we fought, he says. How it's taken years to get to the current working conditions. . . While he's talking it occurs to me that Manny looks like Teller who in turn looks like the sad old film comedian Harry Langdon. My mind's drifting. I force myself to concentrate on Howard's high piping voice. Howard mentions last resort strategies. Sickouts, slowdowns, coming and going at the bell. Dropping the non-mandated like writing recommendations. Job actions. Aging like a fine bottle of water.

I smile, though the topic is making me uneasy. Aren't I in deep enough shit with the admin as is? I tell them I have the same concerns. Mention that I've been written up before, that it never amounts to anything. Don't mention that this time if feels different.   I stay mum on the anonymous letter.

- Sure you can count on me, I say. Just like in the old days when we negotiated the contract. Then I get silly to mask the swamp malaise that's settling in. Add, Well, well, we meet again Professor Moriarty. . . Manny and Howard look puzzled. I say, I'm referring to Superintendent Hoxley.

The game is on. . . Right, they say in unison and depart. I go back to my fish wondering why Nunberg is not on their cases too. And hope crazily she's going alphabetically.

Who'll Stop The Rain: My juniors are antsy this afternoon. Not unusual right after lunch. They're suffering from sugar overload and having their hormones stoked. They do everything during lunch. Eat, make dates, break up, play grabby-gropey, gossip, copy homework, share test answers pro bono. Everything to get the juices flowing.

- Mr. August, can I go to the bathroom? There's a single hand flapping in the air, a voice fraught with wet panty syndrome.

Everything but go to the lav.

- I don't know, Charlene. *Can* you? . . . It's the same response my teachers used on me. I know she's in a hurry but English classrooms are the last bastion between the street jivers and grave. English according to Fowler's. Grammar way station. That's the way I foking roll.

Charlene looks puzzled. Presses her lips together. Then pushes them out in one of those duckbill face pouts. There's some kibitzing. She reloads and egged on by her classmates asks, May I go?

- Go!. . . I sweep my arm towards the door, finger points the way.

She grabs her pocketbook. Is out the door faster than I can say wee piddle diddle. And now predictably Maybelle has her hand in the air.

- Mr. August, *may* I go to the lav? Maybelle knows the routine.

- No, I say and go to the podium ready to intro The Road. The would-be pisser is not deterred and comes back with, Why not?. . . Because you go everyday Maybelle, I say and for some reason I notice her black cornrows give her head a pleasing symmetry. Very aerodynamic. . . But you let

Charlene go, Maybelle says with the straight logic of a gravity toilet. . . Charlene never asks to go, I point out. Today was her first time. You ask everyday. . . But I really have to go, Maybelle pleads. Says, *Really!* as if she's already dripping water. . . Fine, I say, you *may* go. But in the future, do it during lunch or bring in a doctor's note explaining your bladder problem and leave the note with the school nurse. . . Seriously? she says. . . Seriously, I say.

Urinator meets terminator.

Another Q&A that uses up class time but generates nothing linked to the curriculum. Oh well, I think, actual teaching is not part of my objective. Though if I don't teach, and teach well, Nunberg will probably find out about it. It all seems to come back to her these days. Every time I go teacher, or don't go teacher. A big sister world. Omnipresent surveillance. Could she have spies in here?

I confiscate a misused laser pointer and am about to nab a hacky sack when I hear, Mr. August?

A figure walks in.

It's Destiny.

I motion her to my desk and she hands me a rough draft. Just thought the sooner the better, she says and looks over my class as if she has stumbled into a wasteland. She smiles at me and says, No rush. Then is gone in a cloud of musk and ponytail sway.

Destiny. Charlene. Maybelle. Some of the continental drift between me and contract renewal.

I'm Forever Blowing Bubbles: Audrey Clover is telling me about how her dog took a dump on her bed (went potty, Mr. August) but says it's OK because, He's a really old dog Mr. August. You have to forgive really old dogs when they mess up.

I'm happy she doesn't see any human parallels.

I'm still not sure I want to work with her. It's counter intuitive to my gut that says any meaningful help she can get would have to come from her own SPED people. Maybe family.

Suddenly she says, People should forgive old people too when they mess up. Their brains don't work right. Sometimes they don't recognize people. Sometimes my grandfather calls me Martha. I'm not Martha. That was my grandma's name. He gets real confused. My dad wants to put grandpa in a home. Rodney and Stuart are helping. They call it a home but it's not grandpa's home. It's like a hospital but nice. I saw it. It smells funny. Grandpa does not want to go but they say he has to. It makes him sad. It makes me sad too. I love Grandpa Clark.

- Well Audrey, I say, that's the way life is sometimes. We have to take care of those who can no longer take care of themselves. Do whatever it takes. . . I pull out all the clichés and tell her most people work and simply do not have the time and energy to take care of aged loved ones who get – I start to say funny, but switch to *confused*. I emphasize that I understand her concern. Mention King Lear also questioned if it was too much to ask to be loved and taken care of after a life of giving.

- Who's King Lear? she asks with those twisted-up features that are so much a part of her overt honesty and transparency. . . I like that in her.

- A man Shakespeare wrote about.

- Was he real?

- No, though there's a bit of Lear in us all. Lear is us, we are Lear. . . I say this knowing she won't really get my point, whatever it is. . . I'm thinking of Lear now, and Max and Clark. How fortune and inheritance are

103

frequently kept from the young. And health and the ability to enjoy the money kept from the old. . . I drift away from Audrey. Think of the sanctity of family in generations past and my father's family Ashkenazi. How despite physical and mental hardships they did their own caregiving. Took in the aged members. Cleaned up the snot, drool, crap, piss. And eventually buried them. A cycle to be replayed with their own lives. . . But in Max's?. . . Certainly not my own.

- Mr. August, Audrey says, what would you do with Grandpa Clark?

- That's a difficult question Audrey. I don't know. I do know that whatever your family decides if it's done with love it's never wrong. That's the only answer I have. . . Shoot, I think, really promoting the obvious today. 1-800-HUG-A-BOO. . . So Audrey, I say tacking away from the grave, I heard an announcement on the PA for the play audition. Didn't you say you wanted to be in it?

It's a good way to close out the conference and she gets excited. Starts jabbering away like I am the avatar of Busby Berkeley and Bob Fosse casting the gala. She's a cute kid, and with her long plaid skirt, button up sweater, and loafers just might be right for a part.

It occurs to me that maybe, just maybe I can help her. And should.

Audrey Clover: *I like talking about Grandpa Clark. It makes me happy. Mr. August and grandpa would get along good. . . Mr. August asks me if I'm going to try out for the play and it makes me excited and nervous. Some of the students like High School Musical. But I like Grease. I know a lot of the songs. Mr. August asks me what my favorite song is and I say Summer Nights. He asks me to sing a little. At first I'm too shy. But he says if I want to be in the play I will have to sing in front of lots of people. He tells me Grandpa Clark will be very proud of me. I start to sing Summer Nights and* *he asks me to stand up. He says it will be that way at the tryout. I stand up and move my head like Olivia Newton John does. He asks me to dance around a little too while I sing. When I finish Mr. August claps and says I did really good. I am going to sign up for the tryout now.*

Looking For Love In All The Wrong Places: I'm coming down a back set of stairs and I hear what sounds like moaning. Like a lusty sex mash-up. The stairs are almost empty, the last students disappearing top-and-bottom into the thinning corridors.

At the bottom I pause, listen, then curl around the stairwell noiselessly on my rubber-soled mocs. Under the stairs are a young freshman couple pressed together in a passionate lip-lock. Tongues wiggling down throats, hands saying I Love You in an orgy of duo-grab delight. Bacchanalian revelers without the wine, needing only youth and a quiet lonesome place. Well lit is fine. Her ring-studded hand is pressed against his crotch giving johnny a little squeeze. One of his hands is doing her butt crack. The other is up under her flimsy blouse in a circular massage. I'm taken back for a second. It's the most hall porn I've caught since that unzipped couple near the elevator shaft last spring.

As if they sense my presence the XXX wannabes freeze. Heads break nose-length apart and turn towards me. I say, Time to be moving on. Get to class!. . . They open up more space between them. Slow, like two wartime lovers reluctantly parting for what may be the last time. It'd be easier and faster to separate siamese twins joined at the head.

They start to walk away. Slowly. Still arm-in-arm. Still in the throes of on-ly slightly diminished carnality. Hands resting comfortably on each other's crack. As they pass, the girl with her messed-up do and blotchy red skin turns and says, Did you get a good look? Her defiance temporarily overriding her non-climaxed passion. G-spot on hold. Her angular paramour with the lupine features of Wile Coyote, mohawk haircut, and Skeletor tee nods. . . The question does not surprise me. Other teachers over the years have been fed it. The perennial youth vs. age tension. Hands-on teen vs. senior-age voyeurism. At least the way they see it.

- Didn't see anything worth seeing, I say. Certainly not from a couple of bumbling amateurs like you two. . . I'm aware that even in my current monastic days I'm not envious of these two. Their pathetic my-penis-will-break-your-heart attempt in broad daylight. In a concrete, steel, and glass public cubbyhole. And now I'm wondering what he was planning on doing about wet, jissom stained pants if she climaxed him. Probably not planning at all. Strong-willed enough to prevent ejaculation? Would she be sex-savvy enough to get him close but not all the way? Is he sheathed in a condon or a diaper like Max?

I almost laugh out loud, but remain stern. Show only teacher-esque.

They are by me. Have not sped up at all. Without turning she says in one of those low and throaty, the breathless-side-of-Marlene Dietrich voices, a word that sounds like *asshole*. It's meant to be audible. But not quite discernible. . . Minor teen rebellion. Not open in-your-face insurrection. . . I could fall into her little trap and belch, *WHAT* did you say? In which case she would deny saying anything. Or claim she was talking to her butthole hanger friend. . . I let it go and the two-car Love Train moves off down the track. People all over the world joining hands, getting laid. Just not around this old stuffy fart.

Tower Of Song: I like Jack Kaufman and hang the moniker The Kid on him. He makes me smile even if he is a phony. Holden Caulfied caliber. Makes me a little envious too. Takes guts to be this flamboyant.

He's sitting slouched back in a tatty Harris weave sport coat, black tee, what looks like a Barbour moleskin cap, ratty jeans, and down-at-the-heels brogans. True to character the flat tan cap is *not* on backwards and there's an old yellowed paperback sticking out of the jacket pocket. His eyes are shaded by black rectangular sunglasses. Like he was time-warped here from Ferlinghetti's bookstore in Frisco in the middle of an author interview.

But he wasn't.

He's just a high school kid. Directly impacting my future.

- Jack, I say, interesting outfit. Another cool riff would be an eyepatch and European beret.

- That'd be OK for the Hollywood beats, he says, but you'd never catch Kerouac in that getup.

- By the way, you know you're *not* supposed to be wearing shades in school, right?

- It helps me relax. Puts the zen in my con-*zen*-tration.

- Fine. As long as we're in this office. . . Listen. I'm going to ask you a straight-up question.

- Ask away. All things are one dust.

- Ha. Yeah. Well, here it is. What's with you and the '50's retro?

- It feels real to me. . . Like I'm connected. Tendrils of time roping me back.

- It was a cool time. But it was also Ozzie and Harriet, three-part Mr. Sandman harmony, hula hoops, bubblegum cards.

- I ignore all that. I'm reaching for the universal truths.

- How do free love, drugs, and a dearth of responsibility fit into universal truths?

- Love is the great consciousness of life. All the rest is a wink. Besides what's so great about the present world or the future that I wouldn't want to reshape either into a more easy-bake feel?

And just like that we're off on one of those teacher-student philosophical jaunts. Plato in the agora. Nietzsche at Leipzig. Freud at university or in his Vienna apartment. Except that this is just August in the English office. Thinking this air-moving circuitous jaunt just a big pelvic thrust. But hoping it will take us somewhere new that's objective worthy.

The Kid mentions his love for jazz and his vintage vinyl. Satchmo, Shearing, Thelonious, Mahalia, Anita O'Day, and a bunch I don't know. I keep a straight face and ask him if he's so into fifties music why he's not auditioning for Grease. . . Grease! he laughs and leans so far back he nearly capsizes. Man, Grease, he says, is Rebel Without A Cause for squares. The sapless energy of saplessness. They sing and hangout out at the malt shop! You have *got* to be kidding, he says.

He's still smiling when I ask if he's ever been in a play. A couple of classroom shows, he says and adds, I was a frog once. Had to croak a lot. . . Ever perform in a real production? I ask not sure where I'm going. . . No, he says, a few piano recitals for family. . . What about the open mike competitions? I ask. Didn't you say you wanted to win one?. . . Right-o, he says and the smiling attitude is suddenly as gone as Charlie Parker. If you really want to know the reason I haven't entered any yet, he says, it's because. . .

He hesitates and says, Tell you what. You tell me something about yourself that's revealing. And I'll answer your question. . . Something about myself, I echo. Some deep, dark secret? I ask. . . Doesn't have to be deep or dark, he says. But if you want *me* to reveal something that no one else knows, *you* should be willing to do it too. . . Like   we're signing the Declaration, I say, entrusting our lives and fortunes to the other. . . More like a trust game, he says. I fall backward, you catch me. You fall backwards, ditto. . . Shouldn't you go first as the student? I ask. . . Hey man, you set the wheels in motion, he says. If you want to chock the tires now, no problem.

- OK, let me think. I look out the window. What to confess? Don't want to shake The Kid's neutrons too much. . . OK, I say, here's what I got. I shouldn't admit this to a student. But I probably drink more than I should.

- Me too. I think people probably know that about both of us. Something else. Didn't I hear you were in the army? Ever kill anyone?

Kill anyone? Wow. Takes me back. Not so much the question. Students have asked me that for years. More like how casually he asked it. The Kid has balls. . . And what do I tell him? The truth? Capital blood-and-guts? And am I ready for that strong a nexus with this particular teen if I do? Skull and Bones bonds?. . . My gut is to say nothing. Beyond that it's to feed him a plausible canard. My FU is to lay a whopper down. But then what – more lies?. . . One of Cormac McCarthy's characters says that he has no faith in men to act wisely in their own behalf. For some inchoate reason I'm thinking I should just fess up. That it's in my best behalf.

- Yes I did, I say suddenly and add, and that's all you're getting. No details. That fact in itself Is a very big deal. No other student knows it, not many adults. I trust you will keep it absolutely confidential. . . Why I tell him – damned if I know. It just feels true. Occam's Razor: The simplest explanation is usually the right one.

- Wow, he says, that *is* a very big deal. Guess it's my turn. Here it is. I'm shy around people. The thought of performing in front of an unknown

109

crowd turns my knees to jello. My voice sounds like it's been microwaved. I know most people think I'm a natural actor but. . .

I'm surprised, but *not* surprised. His schtick is all a big overcompensation. Fact is, I think to myself, the Kid is a phony but a very vulnerable, very likable one. I briefly consider telling him about Demosthenes. I assume The Kid knows the common strategies to overcome stage freight. . . He loves music. Poetry is music.

- You play the piano, I say. What about accompanying yourself for the poetry? Music calms the nerves. Sets a tempo.

- Piano is not the right instrument for my verse. And I don't want to both play *and* speak. I don't think I could. A flute would be good. Maybe even an acoustic guitar. I've thought of music before. But there's no one I can ask. The help wagon is empty, the anguished bawls of children rent the night.

- What about an acoustic Rickenbacker?

- You know someone?

I hesitant. Finally tell him I know a pretty good player who's a little rusty. A lot rusty. We talk. He expresses doubt he really wants to publicly perform even with backup. The bell rings. He leaves.

I'm getting up, thinking I don't really want to perform either when I see something under his chair. I pick it up. Look closely. Are my eyes deceiving me? I stuff it into my pocket and smile. It's a bag of grass. Haven't seen one in a long time. I look around. Laugh. Feel like the Pope Of Dope. Even though it's only a nickel bag and I'm not exactly Cheech.

Jack Kaufman: *I'm pretty damn floored to learn August plays acoustic guitar. Says he started on electric as part of a rock band in high school. Then switched and formed a 3 person folk group with two girls. Says they didn't play-for-pay a lot but were popular when they did. Mentions* *something about his old man using his Rickenbacker as a baseball bat. But he's pretty sure he can get it fixed. . . Not sure how I feel about all this. I mean it's cool how he confided in me. August a killer. Guess I'm not surprised. Screaming bullets in the rain, whiskerless faces hunkered down in the bush. . . But us as a music team? People will probably think I'm King Suck Up. But he's not my real teacher so. . . I don't figure we're going to make music or poetry history. But we might be good if I can get up the nerve. Sedate the nerves. And he's not Mr. Spastic Fingers. Just hope we aren't a bummed-out-ocalypse. I have my doubts he'll go through with it. He seemed pretty maybe . . Let the Delphi oracle speak. Let us pluck the lyre, blow the panflute, and hearken to the message.*

A Hard Day's Night: The late night house is dark. I'm winding down, a cold drink in hand. Papers are done. The cat and dog helping me fight off an early autumn chill. End-of-day ennui. . . Night noises amplify. Metronome regularity punctuates the little domestic tranquility I get these days. A background track of creaking boards, snoring dog, purring cat, ticking mantle clock, whirring antique Frigidaire. Speeding midnight drivers, motors running hot. Headlights sweeping the room. Heading god-knows-where.

Where am I going?

There's that maybe rendezvous at an open mike. Tickle me with a belt sander. Whatever made me volunteer for that? The Kid's entertaining claptrap blinding me to the fact that I *never* volunteer for anything remotely school related. And now I have to remix fingers more in tune these days with picking olives out of gin glasses than picking strings. Of course I didn't say *absolutely* I would, so it's not too late to pull a reversal. Say I couldn't get the guitar fixed, though it should be repaired before Jimi Hendrix is slush. Then of course we'll rehearse. Maybe become a juggernaut duo. Maybe so totally suck that Jack Kerouac himself rises from the grave to kick us senseless with his meatless tibia. Could also fall somewhere in the middle. Milquetoast talent, lukewarm reception. For sure it would be a helluva lot easier to just not do it.

Don't know how I feel about The Kid knowing I killed someone. Late at night like this with a drink I tend to say no sweat. But it does bother me. At least I was semi-puckered and didn't tell him the details. With his imagination he's probably thinking I'm Bourne or some human P&W engine sucking bodies in, spitting entrails out. . . I'm not proud of it. But it was war, a long time ago. I've made peace with the guilt and with a god who lets young people do that to each other. . . I don't blame god. But since then I've lowered my expectations of him. And raised them for people.

My school objective. If it was not for that I wouldn't have been talking to Kaufman in the first place. And where am I now with that bababooey improvement thing?. . . Audrey might be getting in the school play, though that's a mighty big *might*. Spoiler Alert: She's not that good. . . Kaufman at the open mike. But he depends on me and I depend on, what? Gin pickled skills?. . . Koppel is an enigma wrapped in a riddle. . . Destiny. A formaldehyde brain. Spoiler Alert #2: She flat lines the creative writing index. . . While Sato and Espinoza?

Perhaps a group goal. One thing for all 6. Hot wax, strip, peel, and voilà! New teens, different people. . . But *do* they have a common thread I can work with? Right now I'm seeing them as diverse, dissonant, dweeb independents. Polytonal, polyrhythmic.

The Big Q: Is it really OK to transform people into what my vision is? Or what Nunberg wants? Like some Henry Higgins understudy?

112

Far Out Thought: Suppose she picked these protégés because she thought they really could *not* be helped? Maybe that's why she was talking to Zoe. Setting me up to fail. Damn! It would certainly go along with the fact she wrote me up over a bunch of minor meltdowns. . . But what the fuh did I ever do to Nunberg aside from laughing inwardly at her? Could she be some spurned person from my past? An old fleeting lay on some drunken college night? Seems unlikely with Amanda always in the picture. . . Far Far Out Thought: Her dog was killed. Hit-and-run. Around the same time I hit that speed limit sign. Was that *thud* more than jumping the curb? There was nothing in the street when I checked my rear views. Of course it was getting dark. Could she have my license plate now? Be silently committed to evening the score for killing her mutt?. . . More likely she's just a tiger principal out to gut and disembowel her way to the top.

I take a long drink and pull out the letter. OUT OF MANY, FEW. Is it a joke like George thought? Nunberg's doing? Our local taxpayers group which is pretty damn militant? Jimmy Klein or some other P.O.'d former student? My father-in-law the banker, the king prick? A guy who resented a poor teacher Jew marrying his daughter and essentially cut off Amanda because of it.

Kaufman's weed might stir some insight. Been a long time since I smoked. And what did I do with it? Bust me now. School. I put it into my desk drawer then locked it. I think.

I pet the cat and it kneads its paws pulling my flimsy bathrobe into little scudding waves. Nicking the hell out of me. I down the gin, shoo away the cat. I give myself a low level scratch. Then really massage myself. It feels good.

As I'm walking up the stairs it occurs to me that if Amanda and I had children, I'd have someone now to lean on. And in my old age. I would not have to always be alone. Nuzzling myself in a dark empty house. . . Max has me, I have no one. Damn. I'm winding up a fucked up mess. Like an old sorry horse from Animal House destined for the glue factory.

Dead Man's Curve: The rest of the week doesn't move me any closer to meeting my objective. Hudson's helps the stress though I really can't afford it. Knowing Deirdre is with Max helps more. Within the school there's little this week that's calming. One of our older female teachers gets between 2 fighting males, takes a roundhouse to the side of her head, and goes down for the count. . . A veteran science teacher leaves his class to go to the lav and in the interim one student hits another in the eye with the proverbial elastic band. The teacher gets called on the carpet. . . The world language coordinator who's getting divorced gets a formal reprimand by Hoxley for living off-hours in the department office. . . A health teacher who chews gum is ordered to stop because it's bothering an anorexic student.

The center is loosening, morale throughout the school spinning outward. There's an increase of vandalism in the lavs and locker areas. Teachers are increasingly calling in sick leading to a shortage of subs. The local newspaper runs an article on our budget woes and prints an editorial with the headline, High School Is Low School.

Things are on hold with Nunberg till we meet again. Hopefully not till the end of the quarter in 5 weeks. Why go looking for negative feedback when that's all I'm sure I'd get. Kingsley Amis said a bad review might spoil your breakfast, but you should not allow it to spoil your lunch.

It's nearly the midpoint in the quarter. Lunchtime.

Chapter 10

Tick Tock - 5 Weeks
Life By Dying

The Abba Dabba Honeymoon: The October 1 email is from the assistant principal. The subject line says, Meeting Tomorrow. . . I do a mental yawn. There are always meetings. Someone left the toilet seat up. The superintendent is constipated. Little Lord Fauntleroy failed a quiz. So-and-so's third uncle twice removed on the fifth cousin's side has an opinion he would like to share.

It's always some sad dookie blues.

I open it and start reading. What? There's a sexual harassment complaint against me? From who? I reread it several times. It says only that there's a meeting tomorrow in the assistant's office. All involved will be there including the girl's parents. I wrack my brain. Has to be that little leg spreader yesterday. The one under the stairwell. The one who was heavy on the mascara and eyeliner, light on the crotch. The one imitating Lil Hot Teen Mama.

What exactly did I say to her? I think I called them both amateurs but how is that sexual harassment?. . . Damn! Is this year's stomping of August ever going to end?   More importantly, will I wind up with another written reprimand on my record?

The Cell Block Tango: As I'm puzzling over all this some up-noise from the back of the junior class breaks through and turns my head away from the computer. I ask, What's going on back there?. . . It sounds like

Maybelle and Charlene. But no one's asking to go to the lav. Things are getting passed around. There's enough excitement that I figure someone is either getting naked or giving birth.

I stand up.

Chloe, a taupe-haired budding anorexia nervosa candidate asks, Mr. August, do you think I was cute? . . . She holds up what appears to be a wallet size headshot.

- What's that? I ask.

- It's me when I was 6. Do you think I was cute?

I'm not getting the happy vibe.

She hands me the 3½ x 2½ with matte finish and I stare at a fairy-like little blond head. Ivory-scrubbed. Bright-eyed. One of those kids who if they had a brain-warped parent might be made over as a midget glamour doll. Pedophile fodder. Except this one is still as fresh and wholesome as Pollyanna. The top of a red flowered pinafore showing, a pink silk bow tied around a white collar. It's like a Valentine's card.

- Yes you were, I say.

Suddenly more photos are waving in my face. Hands reaching out to me like I'm the long awaited teen Messiah. A child beauty pageant judge. One-by-one I look at them all. See more little Vienna sausage noses than Disney. Repeat the *cute* verdict ad nauseam. Keep it all an orgy of positive physical reinforcement.

Chloe is looking less-and-less pleased. When I ask about it she says, I like the way I looked then. . . Her face is dark.

- And you don't now?. . . I finish her thought in a deepening vacuum of chilling vibes.

- No.

I Hear You Knocking: What to say? I'm not the school psychologist. Probably cannot even match the insight of a fortune cookie. Student mental health is usually taboo for me lest I worsen things. There have been a few teen suicides since I've been here. Though I doubt Chloe is at that point.

- Most kids are cuties, I say, and you certainly *were* a cute kindergartner. When you think of yourself now, is your old photo still the way you see yourself?

- Yes, Chloe says.

- I totally understand. In my own mind's eye I picture myself when I was around 30. I had more hair, a lot fewer wrinkles. No gut. . . I pat it for added effect and the class laughs. Make yourself into a genetic mutation and they love it.

It suddenly pops into my head where to take this psycho-babble. I tell the class about the time I told my wife she was cute and wife shot me back one of those voodoo type looks. The kind of unspoken curse that means do your own laundry, buy lots of frozen dinners if you plan on eating. I say, Thought I was giving her a compliment, but it turns out that women as they get older do not want to be thought of as *cute*. They want to be attractive. Glamorous. Sexy. Fly. At least my wife did. She had no problem with me calling the dog and cat cute. But her? She wanted to be exotic, mysterious. A dangerous woman. A lot of which can be accomplished with hair, fashion, and style. Don't have to have the looks, capital L.

I should also mention that beauty is in the eye of the beholder and tell them to believe in themselves. But those lessons are another sidebar, another day. There's only so much time.

I finish with, Cute certainly has its time and place. But it's time to be moving on. The Road. Get your books out.

Moaning and groaning. They could stay off-task forever. But the school is not paying me to be Vidal Sassoon. As we start going over the reading, it occurs to me I never did find out what was with all the elementary pictures.

Chloe Manhoff: *It's pretty obvious that Mr. August is only talking to make me feel better. All the other kids know it too. I mean he's acting like he's talking to us all but if it weren't for me it wouldn't be happening. Teachers do that all the time. Make like it's a group thing when it's one person and very personal. This whole cute lecture is sooo lame and embarrassing. Normally I would be angry. But I like Mr. August and I know he means well. He does have some good points about cute not being the go-to look as you get older. Think I'll try a new haircut and coloring job tonight. Maybe blond and straight. And a new outfit. When in doubt, change. Rad if necessary. I am feeling a little better.*

Wilbury Twist: I stop by George's office to see if he knows anything about the sexual harassment meeting. He's surprised as hell to learn about it. Says he can't remember the last time anyone – teacher *or* student – made sexual peccadilloes an issue. I describe the bump-and-grind girl. Mention I don't know anything about her. He asks about her hands. Her hands? I say. Yeah, he says, you can tell a lot about a woman by her hands. If they're placed around your throat or baby makers she's probably upset. He laughs and I do too, though there's not a damn thing funny about it. He tells me not to panic.

Didn't I Blow Your MInd This Time: I'm walking down the hall from guidance. Sudden movement through the glass of a closed door and the sound of two familiar raised voices. I stutter step. Walk past, then slink back. The antagonists come into view. It's Zoe and Nunberg. Again. This time in the back corner of an empty social studies room. Both suffering from a shortage of estrogen. Voices tense. Clipped. They remind me of a couple of gamecocks set to go at it.

I turn my back to the door, wave at some students, and with my hand behind me turn the knob, crack the door. Students pass by me in waves, their noise and chatter ebbing and flowing. Interrupting the inside dialogue. I'm catching only bits-and-pieces. Nunberg says, I'll get (noise) job. But I don't want you involved. You need to stop (noise, noise, noise). . . My tin ear is having a difficult time separating the main track from the background squelch. . . Zoe retorts, You don't tell me what to do. I'm not (noise, noise). It's money and you're not getting (noise, noise, noise, noise). . . Nunberg tries to pacify. Says, Just leave (noise) alone. I'll (noise) him, I promise. But you don't need to (noise, noise, noise). . . Zoe says, Drop dead.

It doesn't seem that they're negotiating the price of a painting. Body language is Amazon gladiator. Zoe keeps trying to leave, Nunberg keeps cutting her off. They're working their way towards the door. Nunberg suddenly grabs her arm and turns Zoe around. Zoe breaks the grip and stimulates slapping Nunberg across the face. Stops her short. They freeze.

At that moment one of my students goes by and gives a stentorian, Hey Mr. August!. . . I put my finger to my lips to shush her, and I glance back into the room.

Zoe starts to turn towards me. I bound half a dozen steps down the hall, spin and walk nonchalantly back. Several students sweep by and give me amused but clueless glances. . . I'm almost to the door when Zoe flies out. Sees me. Passes without a word. Her eyes are dark. Crystalline fury. I wait till she turns the corner and look back into the room. Nunberg is sitting with

119

her face in her hands. Tears? I can't tell. Didn't think she had tears in her. Her body isn't wracked with sobs. I wait. She just sits there. Finally takes out a silver compact. Opens it. Says a few inaudible sentences to her reflection. Sighs.

My mind is racing. What the hell is going on? Nunberg sentient?. . . And the 2 dueling Amazons. Practically bloody. Over a painting? School related? Could it be me? Job was mentioned.

I'm getting a headache. And acute paranoia. Maybe that's the price of eavesdropping and not, as Wordsworth said, embracing the self-sufficing power of solitude.

Solitude? Shit. Not much of that in a school.

Don't Cry For Me Argentina: I ask Jorge Espinoza what's new since the last time we met and he looks thoughtful. I'm not expecting much so I'm surprised when he says, Our restaurant is in trouble. Business is really down.

So far these conferences have revealed he's going to shave his head soon because he thinks it's a better look for body builders. He can run a 100 meters in under 11 seconds. His favorite food is mole chicken burritos. And a few other trivial sundries. The most personal thing he's said before is that his grandfather has not been well.

- I'm sorry to hear that, I say. Where's your family's restaurant anyway? I've been meaning to stop by for dinner . . I think to myself that there is no way I could begin to support all the businesses my students' parents have been affiliated with over the years. But this really is one I want to try. Just hope Ecuadorian food is not ass-burning hot and hemorrhoid stimulating.

- We're three blocks west of the theatre, he says. It's called El America Ecuatoriano.

- I know exactly where it is. I'll stop by tonight, I say and wonder how many people have even noticed it. Small strip of handsome but older brick buildings in need of mortar pointing and paint. Metered street parking. Neighborhood that's seen better days since the railroad depot closed and the nearby cemetery turned into a haven for drug loonies, homeless vagabonds, and the restless ghosts of hookers-past. Some of my former students in the mix no doubt.

My thoughts now go to flesh-pot whores in skin-tight yoga pants and K-Mart sequined satin blouses. Penis-eating mouths, wine breath, hair caught high with those plastic turquoise clamps. And just like that the sexual harassment complaint is back in the forefront of my mind.

Because tomorrow's meeting really *is* bothering me. And maybe because Jorge shared his personal with me. But mostly because life seems to be spinning out of its established orbit I ask if he's heard anything about me lately. . . No, he says, I don't think so. Like what?. . . Oh, something along the lines of sexual harassment. . . Sexual harassment Mr. August? he asks dumbfounded. You? No. Never. I don't think the students think you *have* a sex life. Sorry. . . It's OK, I say and add, if you hear anything let me know, OK?. . . Sure, he says. I got your back.

Got my back? When has a student ever said that to me?

The low octane thought starts pumping that unless *all* my six start relating personally to me like this I am never going to meet my objective. Job here, job gone. A vaporous vapidity rolling in. Twenty-three years down the drain. Leeching in the septic field.

Jorge Espinoza: *I'm not surprised Mr. August has never been to my family's restaurant. I've never seen any teacher from this school there. . . I'm definitely surprised Mr. A asks me if I heard anything about him and sexual harassment. It's just not the type of question I'd expect from any teacher. Guess it shows he considers me an adult. It's a good feeling. I graduate this year so why shouldn't I be treated like a grownup?. . . He asks me how my grandfather is doing and I tell him he is old, has cancer, and worrying about the business doesn't help. He looks at me funny and I get the impression he's going to try to help out. Hope it's not my imagination. A break from god wouldn't hurt either. My mother and father are always praying for it. My grandfather says god doesn't endorse restaurants, Zagat does. He's a smart man. Cynical like Mr. August.*

That's Entertainment: Before leaving school for the day I swing by the music wing. Kids are everywhere. Stretching, singing, putting on their dance moves. Gettin' jiggy with it. An eyeful of noise like a scene from Fame or Glee. . . It's a section of the school I'm seldom in. Too far off the beaten path. Stairway to teaching paradise. . . The noise is at raucous levels, the decibels shaking every molecule. They let it all out here, and in the caf, gym, and stairwell. Good to have release points or it would all be shuttled into the classrooms. Of course some of it shows up there anyway. No kill switch on fun.

- Anyone know where Miss Arbuckle is? I say to no one in particular.

A girl in a ballet tutu looking more like Swan Lake than Grease does a series of pirouettes in front of me as if we are dancing the grand pas de deux and I'm now supposed to pull a Balanchine. It's a pretty mesmerizing sight this close up.

She comes to a sudden stop. Does not waver or fall on her skinny arse. Says, Miss Arbuckle is in the back office. The girl is slightly out-of-breath. Looks me up-and-down like she's the casting director. I say, I'm here to audition for the part of Teen Angel. Honestly? she says and adds, I thought maybe Coach Calhoun. . . I'm tempted to be a smartass and ask her if she's spring loaded and needs a windup every day.

I tell her, Thanks.

Sophia Arbuckle is alone, her back to me. In that instant I decide to pad in soundlessly like some deviant stalker. I'm suddenly playful. Decide it might be fun to sneak up, cover her eyes, and give it the old corny, Guess who?. . . If I can keep my nerve. . . She's holding a clipboard and looking over what are probably lists of today's auditioners. Her hair is in a bun. She's dressed in black leotards with a white cable-knit cardigan. Legs are shapely, WNBA length. Great tush, better tatas. One of the best Roman faces I have ever seen. Age to her is mink. Looks every bit the actress and dancer she once was. . . I used to have a mild crush on her but never did anything about it except moon-eye her at faculty meetings. Me, and half the male staff. Those once-upon-a-penis feelings. Short of sexmageddon urges. Evaporated with time. And as the platonic-ascetic relationship developed between us.

She rises, turns, and here I am. Three feet away. Startled. Then animate. Mike! she exclaims like she means it. Like maybe there really is something in play.

- Hi Sophia. . . I make a move to hug her and we embrace in a contact that's only slightly more intimate than a Facebook poke.

What little is left of the romantic in me would like to think we're in sympatico. In-sync libidos. Nothing wrong with a little bit of middle-aged ego stroking. Reinforcement of the yawning maw of fantasized sex. . . But I can feel in her physical tenseness it's not like that anymore for her. If it ever was. Which I doubt. And I do not want to get all hopping end-of-day crazy here. I remind myself to keep it cool. Daniel Craig savoir faire, teacher edition.

- Mike! It's *so* good to see you. I can't remember the last time you came to our music wing.

- It was when you performed at the Faculty Talent Contest. You were great. I can still hear you singing Think Of Me from Phantom.

- You're sweet to say it. That was 20 years ago. Maybe more.

- Guess I'm overdue.

- You are. But I'm really busy now with the auditions. Is there anything I can do for you.

- Auditions are why I'm here.

- You want to audition? . . . She pauses, laughs, puts her hand on my arm . . . We couldn't even get you to sing in the faculty chorus for that talent show. And now you want to audition for Grease?

- Not me. One of my students. Audrey Clover. . . It occurs to me Sophia did not mention my *age* as an audition factor and for that my life of sometimes total illusion is grateful.

- The name rings a bell, she says.

Sophia checks her lists and tells me Audrey auditioned yesterday. When I ask how she did, Sophia says, I've seen worse, though not this year. . . So there's no way she makes the cut? I ask. . . Mike, Sophia says, Audrey can't sing, her dancing is even worse. If she were a boy, maybe. Boys I need. Girls, as you can see out there, are more plentiful than polka dot dresses around here. . . I'd like to ask a really huge favor of you, I say and see her eyes go up. Put Audrey in the play. Any part. Even a walk-on, walk-off role. . . I could put her in the crew, Sophia offers. She could paint scenery. Maybe help out with costumes, sell ads – those sorts of things. . . Could she do some of that anyway, I say, and *still* have a bit part. A teeny-weeny one? Anything?

- Why are you so concerned with this girl? Sophia asks. Never mind, I don't have time to hear about your conversion. OK, I'll find something for her.

- On stage, in a part?. . . I'm looking and thinking Sophia reminds me a lot of Coco Chanel both in looks and attitude. Chanel said she rode horseback like she had a pair of balls. Sophia has got them, or whatever it is that gives a person gumption. Designer spunk with gemstones.

- She'll have a part. And, by-the-way, you owe me big time for this one.

- And I shall make restitution. Mike August balances all his accounts. By the way, what's with that little Tasmanian Devil whirling around out there? The one in the tutu. Music box dancer.

- You mean Desdemona? Audrey can't do anything but she's sweet, Desdemona thinks she can do everything, and she's a bitch. I'll take Audrey.

Look Homeward Angel: As I'm leaving I stop at the far end of the hall and look back. Students are standing in a large circle around Sophia and a couple of other adults. Parent volunteers? Assistants? I have no idea and again marvel at how little I know about what goes on around this school. . . Schools do not function at a high level because of teachers like me. I suppose I should feel guilty that I'm a straight academic these days. But I don't. I had my years of coaching, chaperoning dances, mentoring beginning teachers, wiping the principal's ass, etc. It's what is expected of young staff members. Except that here's Sophia doing it and she's old enough to remember rotary dial phones and when Madonna had pointy cone tits. . . In the Jung school of thought there are universal archetypes and I guess I'm the Father, maybe Grandfather figure now. My paternal role is clear, at least to me. I should provide sage advice, model psychological ease, provide a stabile learning environment. Bridge the past and present. And like Tennyson's Ulysses remember that it is not too late to seek a newer world . . . to push off. . . and smite the sounding furrows.

And not get my sorry keister fired.

Sophia Arbuckle: *I'm surprised that Mike's here. Floored that he's asking me for a favor like this one. The only time I see him these days is at meetings. There was a time when we ate lunch together regularly in the faculty room. Years when we went out for drinks after school on Friday with a bunch of the teachers. It never went beyond that. We were both very much married. . . Putting Audrey in the play is a big deal. I'm going to cut some performers who are pretty good, just not good enough. So there's the fairness issue. Then there's the idea of favors given, favors owed. Mike is a good man, fundamentally a nice guy. But I played enough Tennessee Williams to know good people can be monsters. . . I need to be ready to justify keeping Audrey if it becomes a controversy. Guess I could always plead affirmative action or whatever the SPED equivalent of that is. I'm assuming she's SPED. . . Mike still looks good though he seems stressed. Tired. He's lost weight too. Hope everything's OK.*

Chapter 11

Blinkers In the Night

They Shoot Horses, Don't They?: Today's sexual harassment soirée is on my mind but I'm trying to novocaine the hell out of worry till we meet. Right now I have Film class so I have to lead like the Greeks are not at the gate ready to tear down the walls over some dame.

The class is in the middle of the WWII documentary Victory At Sea. The Americans are hitting the D-Day beaches, the off-shore bombardment is deafening. I say over the blasts and soaring Richard Rogers score, This is the same action sequence as in Saving Private Ryan. . . I say this in an attempt to give them a point of reference.

- Why don't we watch Saving Private Ryan instead? Marcus Schmidt asks with no hesitation. That's a good movie, not like this black and white old crap.

I hit the Pause button on the data projector's remote. Freeze frame a casualty in the sand getting a transfusion. Marcus looks at Madison. I can't tell if he's recruiting for pop-the-teacher time or he wants some appreciative applause for highlighting his microeducation. It's a twilight in here. Their faces shades beyond the pale.

- How many of you have seen Saving Private Ryan? I ask the class. . . Almost every hand goes up. . . I look at Marcus and say, That's why.

- Why? . . . He's sincerely puzzled.

- Because you're not here to see movies you've already seen. You're here to experience new films. Get a sense of a film's place in the evolutionary process.

- But *you've* seen it many times, Marcus says. So how's it helping you? Shouldn't *you* be learning too?

It's not a bad point, I think. If he were serious. . . Marcus is a sniper, there's one in most classes. Get teacher in crosshairs and snipe away. Thwat, thwat, thwat. Peashooter comments, death by a thousand BS nicks. Probably already has a vision of my chalk outline on the floor. . . I suddenly wonder if he was put up to this. Administration controlled? A designated spirit fracker?. . . Not likely. Better odds I really *am* turning into a bipolar grand marque of schizophrenia. I need to stop. Can't be seeing little Nunbergs everywhere.

Madison says to him, Good point! unnecessarily loud, and I see a few others nodding in agreement.

- I am learning, I say to him and think, Learning that the name Schmidt is another way of saying human de-evolution. But your parents are paying me the big bucks primarily *to teach,* I say looking directly at him. To *teach!* So if there are no further questions, let us continue. . . I hit the Play button and hope the blood and gore hold them till the bell.

Marcus Schmidt: *It's pretty fun to jerk some teachers around. I call it payback in August's case. Yeah, I know I'm being a wiseass but I'm not like this with everyone. August just rubs me the wrong way. Normally I'm live and let live. Maybe if he eased up on Madison and the class I'd ease up on him. One thing's for sure. In about 30 minutes he's gonna get a big shock. Don't figure he sees this one coming. Maybe I'll jerk him around just one more time when the period ends. Build a case for maybe me getting out of here too.*

The class is leaving and Marcus stops at my desk. Mr. August, he says, could you meet with me now to go over your new rubric for the latest film review?. . . Can't do it now Marcus, I say, I'm tied up. After school, for sure. . . That's OK, he says and smirks as if he is just busting my chops anyway. Poor bastard. I'd like to tell him he's going through life like a pole vaulter – ass always preceding his head. But I don't. He wouldn't get it.

Theme From Psycho: The secretary tells me to go right in so I open the door to the cubbyhole office and I'm immediately confronted with the assistant principal. A bearded Ernest Hemingway lookalike. Fairly intelligent, quick to pacify, quicker to cover his own heinie. Has a fat man's steadiness. He's wearing a gray herringbone jacket with a red and blue tie, pink shirt with a blue pinstripe. Sitting opposite are Madison Murphy and two adults. The resemblance is Darwinian, they can only be her parents. I'm not quite shocked. But I feel like a idiot. Only dumber. Cannot believe I didn't see this coming. Not Ms. Stairwell Hustler at all. But Madison. Damn!

- Mike, good of you to join us, John Higham says.

As if I had a foking choice, I think and almost say, You can't hold the execution without the guest of honor. . . But the jaundiced professional nods and says, My pleasure.

Higham makes the introductions. Hands are shaken with emotionless civility. Their first names forgotten by me as quickly as they're said. . . Madison has some concerns, he says, so I thought it would be good if we could all meet and air them out. Madison, he turns to her and says in a voice that is insulin coma calm, I'm going to paraphrase your statement.

129

- The statement essentially states, Higham says, that on the second or third week of school — she can't remember exactly — Mr. August inappropriately used the word *suck* several times. The sexual meanings of the word are clear, Madison writes. Everyone knows what they are. She also notes that everyone in the class heard suck used. She wants an immediate apology and a transfer to a different section of Film. One with another teacher.

I'm thunderstruck but also a little relieved. She's upset over the word suck? Well fuck suck. . . I realize this is making a damn mountain out of a piss-ant hill. But it's still going to have to be played out. Ruffled egos soothed. Hemorrhoids packed back in.

- I only vaguely recall the incident, I say. Madison. . . I turn to face her. . . what exactly do you purport I said?

- I complained about the assignment and you said for me to, Embrace the suck! Those were your exact words. I didn't even know what that meant. I still don't. I think it sounds dirty.

- I said, Embrace the suck?

- Yes.

- What were your exact words when you complained about the assignment?

- I said something like I didn't think the assignment was fair.

- OK, it's coming back to me now . . . I sit bolt upright and address the parents. Your daughter told me in front of the class that the composition assignment *sucked!* She used the word first and used it very forcefully. I believe the word *suck* has come etymologically to mean displeasing, bad, poor quality. We can check that right now with an on-line slang dictionary if you like. But I'm sure we're all aware of that popular usage. Of course the word has many connotations. Suck can also mean fellatio. But that was clearly not the intent when Madison used it.

Madison starts to protest that she did *not* use it first and Higham interrupts. Tells her it would be a very simple matter for him to call in class members right now to verify or contradict Mr. August's account. But is that really necessary? he asks. She starts to mention Marcus Schmidt, then grows quiet.

- First off, I say turning back to the parents, I've been teaching here for many years and have never had a sexual harassment complaint lodged against me. I keep the door open when I'm alone with a female student and always give them plenty of personal space. . . I explain to the parents that these students are young enough to be my own children, even grandchildren. And I do *not* hit on them, I say. Emphasize that it would never even occur to me to do that.

Dad is looking even keel, his face rings a bell. Mom is sitting with her hands folded. Long painted nails looking vampirish. . . I say, When Madison told me the assignment sucked and I said to embrace the suck, I meant to embrace the challenge of doing a difficult assignment. I was vaguely thinking of the advice a soccer coach might give, knowing that Madison is one of our soccer stars.

There is dead air. No one is sure who should talk next.

Finally the father mentions that even in that slang context he does not approve of the word being used in school. Especially by an English teacher. I tell him he's absolutely right and that even as I was saying it I knew I wasn't using my best judgment.

I'm honest. It shows. Faces soften. In the interim I notice he's wearing a dress shirt under a lined nylon windbreaker with Murphy Construction stenciled over the heart. He looks old school. Thick-necked, butch exterior.

Skin weathered burgundy. . . He says that English teachers aren't coaches. That things said on the athletic field are usually not fit for the classroom. I tell him that I agree totally. Apologize to Madison, then apologize to the parents for all this trouble. Apologizing is usually a defuser and I've apologized more times than I can remember. But never to placate. Did it because I was in the wrong and knew it. That's what a man, a good teacher does.

I settle back. I don't feel good. Do feel tired. Headache rising . . . I did the macho-crotcho, manning-up bit and expressed sincere contriteness. But the stress takes a lot out of you.

Something still does not seem finished. It takes Higham to say, This incident was a long time ago by semester standards. I'm a little surprised Madison took this much time to bring it to our attention. He looks at her, eyes asking for more, as if he is on the verge of slapping the polygraph on her and wants her to confess to 9-11 or global climate change.

When she doesn't answer I say, Madison, you wanted an apology from me. You got it. Do you still want the transfer? Yes, she says almost too fast. Why? I say. I get the feeling you don't like me. But I assure you that the feeling is *not* mutual.

She looks at her father. He tells her to speak up but instead she clams up. . . Is that the reason? Higham steps back in. You don't like Mr. August? You are past the add-drop period. We don't transfer a student at this point for anything other than a serious reason. . . He does not have to mention her using the sexual harassment complaint as a ruse. We all get it.

When she continues t o keep the Mute button pressed I say, Madison, did you ever tell your parents you got a zero for plagiarizing a paper?

- What! Mom is suddenly all pepped up. Madison, is that true?

I scarcely hear the rest of the conference. Slip into telemetric feedback, fortressed in my psychic pneumatic suit. . . Madison charged me with sexual harassment in the simple-minded attempt to get out of my class. And all because of a zero. A zero on her importance scale was ironically anything but. . . Don't suppose there's a chance in hell that she will give *me* an apology for behaving like a goddamn shitonian teen beech. . . I should be max pissed. Not only at Madison but Higham too. He never verified Madison's assertion with any other students in the class? Or asked me about any of it before calling me in front of this 3-panel FU-FU-FU inquisition?

This has been a total waste of time and worry. A 100% suckfest, suck-adelic, suckalicious, sucky piece of suckshitski.

Maybe I am exonerated. And it went down easily and by the book. Like I clicked my heels 3 times and returned home. But I'm tired with a full blown headache. Postcoital letdown after a fuck, or near fuck. And of course there is still a pissed off Madison to deal with back in the classroom. She's lost again in her mind. Will probably blame me. Again. Spritz even more of her tetchiness around in Film.

Sometimes when you win it's not really a victory.

Madison Murphy: *So I'm stuck with August. That fat retard Higham won't approve a transfer and my parents back him. My father says right in front of everyone that it's up to me and Mr. August to try to get along. Says that's the way it is in the real world. You don't always like your boss or think he's fair, but life goes on anyway. . . I suppose he's right but it's not easy. Even if my grades went with me I was so counting on a new class and starting over. I feel like I'm on a roller coaster and the tracks just ended in space. . . My mother says I owe Mr. August an apology. I tell her I'll think about it. . . I* *should have known nothing good was going to happen when my dad said he had August for a teacher years ago and that he was a good guy. Life sucks.*

Chapter 12

Do the Good Life

Peace In The Valley: It's the weekend. The low October sun is pushing through the sheers and pooling the bed in white luminescence. Guess I forgot to close the blinds last night. Too many gins have that routine busting effect. The cat is stirring above my head, dog already heading for the door.

The digital clock beside the bed is black. I vaguely recall pulling out the cord thinking it was the easiest way to insure the alarm didn't go off. Head hurts. Tongue parched. Bathroom calling.

Nothing compared to the pain of that meeting yesterday. Higham. The poor man's Poirot. Played it like he just cracked the Jack the Ripper case. And Mrs. Murphy. What about when she said, Whom is fooling whom, Madison? Ha. Must think she's Joan Crawford playing Mildred Pierce, or wherever that pretentious line comes from. . . The mister seemed OK. Even to my gelid eye. . . And then there's Madison. Not quite the spawn of Satan but not one of Alcott's Little Women either. Not intimidated, totally unrepentant. Looking for an apology in her would be like searching for Sugar Man.

Madison, she *is* just a kid. Though kids have power. A lot in the 21st century. . . Kid or not she ought to be severely punished, the son-of-a-bitch side of me says. The New Age, Grand Master of universal vibration realizes it's just her hyperthyroid energies run amok. . . There's no doubt she was crag-fast, an apropos climbing term. Couldn't go forward, couldn't retreat either. On a mountain she would have died. In school she gets to return to my class. Ha. Bet she wishes her ass were on a mountain.

It's nice lying in bed like this. The Scottish poet Alastair Reid said that a writer should cultivate leisure. That there's no such thing as wasted time. . . Damn, my head hurts. The cat tapping it is not helping. My cat. I love my cat. She definitely cultivates leisure. Switch on, switch mostly off. Life at its basic. Counts in units of sleep.

Guess it's time for me to get up and charm the hell out-of-the-day.

Working For The Man: I park behind a green fungoid Honda in Max's driveway. There's a dent in the rear quarter panel, a faded sticker for a spay/neuter clinic on the back window. A college parking permit on the front windshield, rust on the rims, several strips of duct tape under the headlights.

This early day of October could not be warmer. I remember when I was a kid this neighborhood would be filled with people out raking on the weekend. No leaf blowers or lawn vacs then. Later the smell of burning leaves and somewhere in-between jumping into varicolored piles. Not enough leaves are down yet to work up a sweat. But it'll be happening soon.

I yell, Good morning! as I enter the breezeway. The smell of coffee is heavy, the litter and trash gone. A look of unflappable cleanliness tethered to the inside. Max is sitting at the kitchen table cradling a cup listening to the radio. There are the remains of pancakes and sausage on his plate. He's dressed in black trousers and a blue cotton shirt. Looks ready to go somewhere. But where?

- Hi Dad, I say. I walk over and give his shoulder a hug. . . He looks at me slowly. Smiles. Lifts his cup. . . How's everything? Where's Deirdre? . . . I'm faintly cognizant of a distant vacuum going. The radio is loud.

- Who?

- Deirdre. The girl who's staying here. The one who cooked those pancakes. They smell good.

- I think she's in the basement. Who is she?

- Dad, we went over all this. She's a former student of mine and a waitress.

- You shouldn't be fooling around with your students. I agree with Ernie on that. . . He stares off as if fascinated with a raised shelf holding an Aunt Jemima cookie jar, a small spice rack, and a butcher block knife set.

- She's not my student anymore. And we're not fooling around Dad.

- You will be . . . He takes a sip of coffee and adds, If you can't keep it in your pants be sure to wear a rubber. No bareback. No glove, no love. Or have her take the precautions. Ernie says women have plenty they can do these days. Not like when your mother and I hit the sack.

- Shit Dad, enough. . . I look at him and can't tell if he's serious or just smart-mouthing. Scavenging one-liners from some distant stag party. Or maybe trying to finally give me The Talk. Some belated paternal instinct kicking in.

- OK, OK, just trying to be helpful, he says. Ernie just said to keep your schlong where it belongs. That's pretty good advice unless you're a eunuch. Then I guess it doesn't matter.

Max tells me this as if it is advice I can't do without. Then goes silent. A tamped-down tapped-out old man. Exhausted by the simple effort of talking to his son.

I sigh. Take his plate and utensils to the sink and wash them . . . Watching Max go in-and-out like this reminds me of Dr. Jekyll and Norman Bates except that Max is not violent. . . I think of Dr. Manette, Ophelia,

137

Winston Smith, and Annie Wilkes. Literary characters who were also out-there. Only one ever came back.

I place my hand on his and say, It'll be OK Dad. When he doesn't respond I cut off my own sadness and ask him if he remembers what became of the meteorite chunk that old man Grotowsky gave him. . . He doesn't answer so I say, I think you kept it in a box. I used to take it out and think, Wow! Like it just flew in from The Twilight Zone.

- It's in the basement, he says suddenly and with authority.

Amazing, I think. Must be Jewish dementia where you forget everything but where the precious stones are. It's a line he himself once used.

Do You Believe In Magic: The basement just a week ago was a mildewy dingy jungle. Tangles of cobwebs, cardboard boxes soft with moisture, dusty holiday decorations, a rusted weight bench, seized-up treadmill, bundles of mice gnawed newspapers and magazines. Mountains of hardcovers heavy with foxing and booklice. A push mower missing a wheel, broken furniture, flat-tired bikes painted with corrosion. A warped ping pong table. . . Show me a man's junk I'll tell you about the man. The only reason in recent years to come down here was to use the washer and dryer, or workbench.

It's been cleared out. The few remaining boxes neatly stacked. Anything not gone resting against the foundation walls. The floor swept, a dehumidifier going. Even the light bulbs have been changed to a higher wattage.

Deirdre is standing on a step ladder vacuuming cobwebs from the overhead floor joists. The wet-dry vac deafening. She's backlit against the fluorescent light of the workbench and I watch her for a minute. She leans and stretches, her body an elongated sine wave.

138

I move forward and turn off the unit.

- Damn! she says and immediately climbs down. When she sees me she's instant smile. . . I thought the cord pulled out again, she says. Pulls out some makeshift earplugs.

- Great job, I say. But you didn't have to do all this. Home improvement wasn't part of the deal. . . I notice that her hair is covered with cobwebs but even knowing how much she hates spiders I'm not about to reach out and brush them off.

- I know. But I just couldn't stand to come down here and do laundry. . . She runs her fingers through her hair, snaps the cobwebs to the floor with a look of disgust, and says, It was creepy-crawly. Nothing dead, but plenty of mice pellets. I asked Max and he told me to go ahead and use my best judgment. Throw out anything but his tools. . .   She tells me there's a lot more she could do but thinks it's good enough for now. I tell her it would pass any city inspection.

- Out with the old–

- in with the new, I finish the thought and instantly regret it. Almost as annoying as correctly someone's grammar. A habit I broke myself of with Amanda's help. . . Maybe I'm now trying to reestablish the old comfortable teacher-student distance. Maybe it's because I'm nervous. We're alone. Max not even a noise above our heads.

- Something like that, she says. I saved anything that looked important.

- Most of the important stuff is in the attic crawl space and closets, I say, though the value of even that is garage sale, not auction. Mostly five-and-dime, dollar store junk. . . I look around again and say, I'm sorry I wasn't here to help you. . . She tells me it's OK.

I wonder briefly if she's OCD. Cleans a lot, and well. Tidier here than when we used to play table tennis. . . It's obvious she's established her

139

domestic side. I'm keenly aware that clever woman do not generally do anything without some personal gain in mind. George Bernard Shaw said that clever and attractive women are willing to let men govern as long as they can govern men. . . I don't think Deirdre wants to govern me or anyone. It's the insecure assholes of the world like Nunberg who need to govern. Deirdre has a fine mind, a striking face, curvaceous body, and can probably hit the curve ball. She doesn't need power. Or a man. Especially an old lounge act like me.

- I don't suppose you came across a rock about the size of a fist, maybe smaller, in all those boxes? I ask.

She says she did. Has been using it for a paperweight. Marvels when I tell her what it is. Laughs when I recount the night the meteorite hit. Says *no problem* when I ask her if I can have it back.

When I ask about Max she says he doesn't need professional round-the-clock care yet. In her opinion. Admits the little she knows about Alzheimer's she got from on line articles and blogs. As if reading my mind she tells me our neighbor still pops in when Max is alone. . . Says she sees a lot of him in me. That Max is a handsome man.

Out of everything she says it's the *handsome* comment that sticks. . . I wonder, Is it possible she's a gold digger? An Anna Nicole Smith type out for Max's money? I suddenly get an image of his head buried in her tits and her cuddling him like a man toy. I can easily imagine his head shoved between her legs, though it's not an image I want to hold. . . Wonder if she knows he's as broke as Bernie Madoff? She's broke too, but probably broker. . . I'm not giving it another thought.

- Before you leave, she says, I have one question. I hope you don't take this the wrong way. Is Max Jewish?

I laugh and say, He has the heritage and pessimism. But not the reli-
gion. I mention my mother was Greek Orthodox. Toss in that none of us
ever went to church or synagogue while I was growing up. . . Max and I still
don't, I say. I believe in belief, and maybe in the life improving properties of
good gin.

Deirdre smiles and says. Good beliefs. I believe in those too.

I'm physically retreating, she's following. We pause at the base of the
stairs. I can feel the old third leg stirring. My breathing tightening. Know
that if I stay much longer. . . I'm thinking we could wind up like that young
stairwell couple in school. Layers of cheap thrills, sex big, romance and
love nowhere. And above it all the stairs. An apparent aphrodisiac. . . I
remind myself to cool it. There's been no verbal or non-verbal look or body
language that Deirdre's given me to show she feels anything but gratitude
for this roof over her head. Still, I wouldn't mind swinging on her nipple
rings. If she had them.

Time goes on holiday. We stare uneasily at each other. It takes the
flushing of an upstairs toilet and the waste water starting on its 3" pipe race
overhead to snap us back to basement and safe conversation.

- Why do you want to know if Max is Jewish? I ask.

- It's that Aunt Jemima cookie jar. Isn't it a symbol of stereotyping and
oppression? So why would a Jewish person have it?

- If a Jewish person wouldn't have it, what makes you think he is?

- He was listening to news the other day. They were talking about the
Middle East and he said *we* should have never returned to Palestine. Or
declared independence in '48. It was the way he said *we*.

I laugh and tell her Max keeps the cookie jar because it was a joke
between my mother and him. I say, She used to kid him about his gloom-
and-doom. She said if Aunt Jemima could smile so could he. He'd kid her

back and say a true Jew when confronted with 2 bad choices chooses both. He chose her and unhappiness. He loved her a lot.

Deirdre Good: *Our agreement is that in exchange for room and board I have to run the house. I cook and clean, make sure Max is dry and presentable, and of course there's the cat. So far it's been easy. Cleaning out this basement has been the biggest physical challenge but it was my choice and I like cleaning. It relaxes me, lets me think about school and things. It's also a fitness center I can afford. . . Max is a sweetheart. I don't mind that he drifts off. It gives me time to do homework undisturbed. When he's lucid he's funny as hell. Dry like his Shredded Wheat. . . Mike is a special kind of guy. I hope we can get to know each other better. I don't think it will ever go beyond talk and friendship. I really don't want it to. He's too set, I'm too unsettled. Still, talking to him like this I can imagine a life of supermarket flowers; the missionary position; dinner at the Elks or Moose. Maybe satellite radio with presets on the oldies.*

Upstairs I grab the rock and show it to Max. He smiles, we talk. I tell him I'll be over tomorrow to take him out for lunch. He says, Worries go down better with soup than without. . . Then in a surprising move he kisses my cheek, pats my hand, and says, I understand. . . I ask, What do you understand Dad? But he just smiles and keeps patting my hand.

Open A New Window: I'm able to find a parking spot on the street about a half block from El America Ecuatoriano. I'd come here with Max tomorrow for lunch, but Max is beyond the years or mind set for experimentation. He prefers the same restaurant, the same meal, and early dining. I've taken him out to eat once a week for the last year but it's not like he's had 52 meals. More like 1 meal 52 times.

It's a well worn but handsome flat-topped building. The 3-color brick-work laid in an English bond. Arched over the windows, dentils along the roofline. The sign tan with green lettering and small hand-painted American and Ecuadorian flags on each end. The windows latticed, the door center-paneled glass. Several 3-foot plants in heavy earthenware containers fronting the windows. It's welcoming. Looks about half full.

Sitting by a window at a small cafe style table I read over the menu and check out the specials board. I ask the middle-aged waitress to explain guaraches, lengua asada in salsa verdes, chilaquiles with shrimp, and mole poblano. Teachers tell students that the only dumb questions are the ones not asked. I'd be pretty intel-challenged not to ask about something that could potentially make my innards a blazing inferno. All while paying for the privilege.

Lots of strange looking dishes around me.

The graying lady is helpful. Though none of what I ask about is whetting my appetite. Especially the tongue roasted green. I ask how the cactus avocado tomato quesadillas are, and she says very popular. I settle on the whole red snapper grilled with just a touch of lemon jalapeno sauce. I ask that it not be too hot. She suggests a Modelo Especial as a good beer.

The small room has a dozen tables. Stools and counter service when you enter. The stools are empty. A vision-dominating upright cooler at the far end. The glass doors showcase designer soft drinks, imported beers from south of the border, chilled wines. A few nondescript wall hangings including a Madonna. Viney plants, the stems and branches encouraged by wires to follow the ceiling. . . There's soft guitar music playing. . . The

143

floor is glazed terra-cotta. Tan and red, 13x13 tiles, laid in a straight grid. . . I don't know what dining in Quito, Ecuador is like. But unless I stow aboard Aero Express Del Ecuador I'm thinking this is about as close as I'll come anytime soon.

The beer is cold, invigorating. I stare out the window at the sparse sidewalk traffic and think of the space rock. Yes that's the chunk old man Grotowsky gave me, Max confirmed. Could be from a meteorite, he said, but who knows. Max confessed he never said anything to me but the Grotowskys had a dirt floor in the basement. Said that Ray Grotowsky was a foundry worker who used to bring home factory slag and laid it down in the cellar to keep down the dust. That meteorite, Max said, might be nothing more than foundry waste. . . I said oh crap, and Max said that most meteorites will attract a magnet because of their iron-nickel. This one doesn't, he said, but it still could be the real thing. . . I told him about TJ Sato and how excited he was at the thought of holding a real interplanetary specimen. Now, I said, I don't know what to do. . . I expected Max the scientist and engineer to tell me to level with the little bastard. Something like, Don't perpetuate a lifelong fraud on the already delusional sprout. It's not like you're hiding alien carnivores in Area 51. . . Instead he said, Keep the magic. . . That's when I kissed him goodbye.

Let's Hear It For The Boy: The waitress returns with a glass of water and a plate of nachos, salsa, and sour cream. She says my meal won't be long. Asks if there is anything else. I tell her to say hi to Jorge for me. That I work at the school.

- Oh my god, she says with a lilting Spanish accent. You're not Mr. August are you?. . . When I say I am she's suddenly excited like here is Javier Bardem or George Lopez in her place. Penélope Cruz in drag.

Maybe Tito Puente come back from the grave to headline this table. Viva la España! . . . Just a minute, she says practically breathless. I'll be right back.

Within minutes the whole family sans grandpa and Jorge are standing around me. Hundred watt beams. Whipped cream voices. . . I've heard that teachers are respected in some parts of the world. But never expected deification beyond rock star. The whole place is looking at me. It's embarrassing. My face is getting warm.

I tell them that I love the look and smell of their restaurant. That it reminds me of a Galápagos eatery I pass all the time in New York. Add that every dish I see looks right out of Bon Appetit.

I'm laying it on heavy. But these are nice people who deserve a break . . . Edgar the father and cook says the fish is fresh and that they use locally grown produce whenever possible. Then they excuse themselves and I'm left with my beer and a warm afterglow. It reminds me just how important my job is and I suddenly feel guilty over the moments in recent weeks when I was not at my best. Or even at my better or good. I make a quick resolve to up my teaching level and to overall suppress any ingrained sarcastic remarks. I also wonder how long the resolve will last.

By the time my meal comes the nachos are totally gone and my ravenous appetite has been downgraded to hungry. . . The fish is orgiastic good. The rice and beans a tangy complement. The sauce just the right amount of twitchy syncopation. The overall impact – I could hit the cemetery down the street and die happy.

Marie clears. I order coffee and tres leches cake. She lingers and asks how Jorge is doing. It flashes through my mind that it's always conference time for teachers. Sometimes even years after bambino is grown and filing for unemployment. I explain I'm not his classroom teacher. But she nods as if a teacher-is-a-teacher and any opinions I have are from on-high. I give her my overwhelmingly positive thoughts. Stop short of comparing him to Simón Bolívar. She says she is so happy he's doing well. That it's important if he's ever going to become the Spanish teacher he dreams of. . . I'm surprised. Jorge never told me about wanting to be a Spanish teacher. But I say nothing other than, Your son has all the makings of becoming a fine teacher.

Teacher? Jorge? Could be important. I wonder if I've just moved closer to meeting my objective. Keeping my job. . .

Chapter 13

Time Pitching - 4 Weeks To Game's End

Walk Away Renée: Film projects are due at the end of the semester, I say. . . The project is 20% of the course grade so I'm being careful to clarify the written requirements with plenty of verbal elaboration. I'm at the podium, going over the multiple-page directions showing examples, answering questions when there is a loud, Mr. August!

- Marcus?

- I need to leave now. I have a doctor's appointment. . . His hat is on sideways. A real Goofy festival. I know it's partly an act. Motivation = jerking me around. Would love now for me to say exactly what he thinks I'm thinking i.e. take off your hat and stop the foking goonball act. . . I tell him only to take off his hat and I smile and wait till the hat is off before I reply.

- Let me see your pass. . . He brings it up and I examine the crumpled square like maybe he's a master forger trying to pass a Benjamin. . . It says here you're being dismissed at 9, I say. That's 15 minutes from now.

- I have to go to my locker first.

I'm tempting to say, Fine. Then wave him off with a dismissive, Go . . . Get rid this psychogenic pain. *That* would be the expedient and easy thing to do. . . Instead I say, Senior lockers are in this hall, maybe 30 seconds away.

- I need to go to the lav too and get a drink, he counters.

- Three minutes f or the first, 10 seconds for the hydrating, I say. Maybe 5 minutes total. Add another minute to get outside and you still have around 9 minutes to go. . . I guess I'm hassling Marcus because I really *don't* like him. Am a little tired and irritable. And would prefer not to open my veins and bleed out professionally just yet. I'm doing what I'm supposed to be doing i.e. running a tight classroom. Nunberg always a consideration.

- I'd rather be early than late.

- I'll let you go in 8 minutes. This is important material I'm covering. If you foul it up you're going to blame me and I would rather *not* have that happen. In any case take your pass and sit down, please. . . I sound very reasonable.

- I need to go now.

- Sit down. . . It's succinct and authoritative. The Diamond Principle: To cut something hard, use something harder.

The wheels are turning. Marcus finally says, I'm leaving . . . He goes back to his desk, grabs his back pack, slaps the hat on – backwards this time. And heads for the exit.

I'm on my feet before I can think. Strides ahead of him. Frame myself in the doorway. An immovable object.

Marcus slows. Stops a few feet away. Shifts his backpack to the other shoulder. For long seconds he doesn't know what to do. What to make of my 5'11", 185 pounds blocking his way. I don't either. And I don't know what I'm going to do if he attempts to push past or squeeze by.

Finally he says, I'm leaving. . . Sit down, I repeat and I am reminded of my earlier head-to-head with Moseby in the caf. Moseby sat down. Marcus is nowhere near as tough. But he's a bit crazy along the lines of unpredictable. And probably would not want to lose face with his classmates who already think he's a bit of a loser. My perception. The class is intently watching our Napoleonic standoff. . . I'm leaving, he says again and adds, I have to go. I have a pass. You can't stop me.

Can't stop you? I think. Shit and go blind. I can knock you on your ass right now. And probably should. If there was ever a student who would benefit from a good old fashioned ass whooping it's you, Marcus. I picture him down and out. And me being led away in cuffs.

He looks ready to physically challenge me. If he touches me first I have the right to defend myself. Maybe charge him with assault. At least breach of peace by threat if he assumes a fighting stance or verbalizes intent to mix it up.

He does none of that. With slight hesitation he moves slowly forward as if walking on ice. I put out my hand in a reflexive stop-action. Leave it out there, fingers splayed as if I am about to push against his chest.

He keeps coming. If we make contact things will escalate. Fast. And not for the better. I retract my arm only at the last second. Stand aside. He shuffles past. Gives me a side smirk as he clears the door. I want to grab him by the scruff of the neck and yank him back in. But don't.

- Do what you have to do, I say to his departing back. And I'll do what I have to do. . . He called my bluff, if that's what it totally was. Is now accelerating down the hall. Technically skipping class. The unartful dodger.

I slam the door. Several students jump. I go to the desk, take out a discipline form as reminder to write him up later. The class is a dead zone. I felt like Snake Plissken sans eye patch during the standoff. Now I feel like a loser. Even if standing aside was the right thing to do. Not getting bodily in the way in the first place was the better thing. I have never blocked a student from leaving class before, and a few have cut out in the past. You just go on with the lesson and write them up later. Did I really want Marcus to stay that badly? Do I really want to write him up now and maybe have Nunberg find out about my human barricade? She didn't like the one with Moseby. I put the form back into the drawer.

Maybe I really am losing it. Why would I risk everything for Marcus?

I half expect Madison to come running to his defense now, but she says nothing. Sits there waiting to resume her note taking. . . I have to give her credit. Since her transfer failure she's been decent in here. Conscientious. Not quite Teddy Bear huggable. But good enough.

Mac The Knife: I no sooner resume going over the film projects then another hand raises like a periscope. Whitney? I ask hoping she doesn't have a dismissal pass too.

- Mr. August, do you hate us?

Hate us? The question takes me back. Why would she ask that? Am I giving that impression? Sure Marcus is a pain-in-the-arse. But there are plenty good students in here too. Did I give him *too* hard a time?

- I don't hate you, I say then instead of shutting up I add, Hate is too strong a word. . . I think to myself that this is not going anywhere I want. I'm off the academic track. Heading down a path that is definitely not academic. Or student friendly.

- Do you dislike us?. . . Whitney is not going to let it drop.

- No, I say. Even that would take too much emotion . . . Whew, and I think, What the *hell* are you doing August?

- So you don't care about us?

- I care about you academically. But even then, only if you do. If you don't, why should I? I finished high school years ago. Now it's your turn. And remember, you're old enough to vote, enlist, work, get married. You're not kids anymore.

The class goes silent. In my heart of hearts I know I blew it. And don't know why. I really *do* care about them. Especially the more diligent, friendly, soulful ones. But how do I say that? Yeah, I care about the good kids in here, but not you lunkheads and pud-whacks. . . I'm aware that I'm coming off as an inhuman lump who cries glycerine tears and emotes hologrammed feelings. But I hope, and think, that the more sensitive can see beyond my detached shtick and maybe catch the human.

In any case, tempus fugit. Education, objective, education. It's time to get back to assigning the film project. I hit the data projector and page 1 of a former student's script illuminates the screen. Here we have, I say, forcing some enthusiasm and blocking out my f-ups, is what I consider to be an excellent. . .

Whitney Dutson: *I don't mean to make a big deal out of what Mr. A says because I don't think it is. I think he likes us a lot more than he admits. At least a bunch of us. Some of the students give him a hard time and they know who they are. So does everyone else. This course is considered a gimme. Even though August assigns homework it's all easy. This isn't AP Physics. That's why there are so many douche bags in here. They want to cruise senior year. They think an A is just going automagically appear and they're P.O.'d because it doesn't. I honestly don't know how Mr. A puts up with it. How all the teachers put up with it. . . I'm not sure why I want to go to college but I know it's not to become a teacher.*

Still The Same: I check my email and there's one from Nunberg reminding all teachers that objectives have to be finalized and approved by the end of the quarter. That gives me a few more weeks to hi-res something that right now is in soft focus. More realistically like a cataract blur. What my final paperwork will look like – I confess *is* getting to me. Though I'm trying not to internalize it too much. Worry leads to stress, stress leads to brain lockage. . . I need an objective breakthrough. A new idea to pop before I'm forced to consign it all to a ouija board or tarot card reader. Sort of like some of my students who don't study, don't do the homework, but hope and pray that somehow, someway the paper, test, quiz will write itself. Divine voices whispering the answers. . . Hail Mary, full of grace, pray for us academic slackers.

Coming Round Again: I eat my lunch in the faculty room. Haven't been here since the blood brother ritual with Manny and Howard. . . I hit 80 seconds on the microwave for my leftover red snapper and wait. Yucks and dirty looks rise again from the culinary philistines. Funny. Back in the years that smoking was allowed here, this place was a toxic white cloud. Created by some of these same people who now are grimacing over this littoral smell. They never considered the feelings, lungs, or noses of us non-smokers then. So let them stick a finger up the nostril now. It occurs to me that most of the time I come here I stink it up. Coincidence or low rent humor?

The red snapper was good enough Saturday that I went home, typed out a restaurant review on spec, and emailed it to the local daily. Never wrote a food column before, but used to do a lot of freelance writing for the paper. I didn't see it in today's paper but was told it would run soon.

I lift a forkful and Manny and Howard appear over the tines. Again. What's new men? I ask while chewing. Howard says, That fish isn't. Manny adds, We heard you had a meeting with Nunberg which wasn't too pleasant. . . Not since I told you she wrote me up, I say popping a can of tomato juice. I have a feeling, I continue, that what's between her and me has got little to do with me finalizing my objective. It might have something to do with documenting incompetence. You know, don't let the screen door hit you. . . They both look worried and Howard says, Christ. Manny adds, So it starts.

They want to know if I talked to the union yet and I say no. Manny tells me Nunberg is in solid contract compliance so far. I observe that dinosaur turds are solid too. They ask about my objective and I say, It's a mentor-mentee goal. Add, I don't know how I'm going to meet it. . . Manny nods in sympathy and asks how I ever got roped into *that*. I steal a line from Will Rogers and say that stupidity got me in, and stupidity will have to get me out. I confess to being worried. Admit to doubt, seclusion. Say, I'd feel better we were all in the same boat. You getting written up too. Misery loves. . .

They pale. Admit their worst fear is that they'll wind up transferred to the middle school. I'd rather retire, Howard says, than teach lower math to a bunch of wet-nose kids. Manny adds that neither of them is ready for retirement. But we're not ready for that teaming thing either, he says.

I give them a little Cormac McCarthy and say, Let's not hold the funeral till there's someone to bury. Remind them that they've outlasted dozens of administrators, several RIFs. Tell them to rest easy, no one is going anywhere. My words ooze calm, my demeanor is girded round with nonchalance. Calm - I'm feeling anything but. . . I point to the Do You Have Hot Lips poster on the wall and ask if they know what the hell it means. I never even noticed it, Manny says. We're math teachers, not cruise directors, Howard adds. Well boys, I say, that's the essence of the problem. We're all clueless as to what's going on around here. Expendable shitz. Our day has come. And maybe it's gone.

Slip Slidin' Away: The cafeteria is jumping and I stop to talk to Asia who's still gathering signatures. This time she wants a Spike Lee film series to be shown during Black History Month. She's wearing a *Malcolm X* snapback from the movie and a *Do the Right Thing* sweatshirt. Her large mouth reminds me of Nicki Minaj but without the sense of putting people on, that life's one big glitz show. Did you get enough signatures for the new African-American field of studies? I ask. She tells me she got 300 but doesn't know if there's a magic number administration needs. They won't commit either way, she says and adds, it's frustrating.

I sympathize, sign her new petition, and wish her luck. Think she's probably a savvy enough crusader to know that trying to change anything in education is like trying for a foothold in zero gravity.

I'm halfway to the far end when I see Curt Moseby and his cohorts stand up from their table. They're laughing, distracted, start walking. Directly towards me. Taking up the whole aisle. Underclassmen jumping out of the way. Moseby looks surprised when he sees me. No one moves over. No one slows down.

We're 15 feet apart. Suddenly Jorge Espinoza is at my side. Opposite Moseby. Intentional maneuvering on his part? There's no time to wonder. Dynamics shift. The two lines almost stop. I pick up the pace. Say, Excuse me. The two jocks in front of me part. Wisely. Fortunately.

I turn around. Espinoza and Moseby are toe-to-toe. The Ecuadorian standing half-a-head over him. Break it up! I say. Moseby, you and your gang get going!. . . The 2 antagonists slide sideways, shoulders locking for an instant before Jorge gives a jerk that sends Moseby fighting for balance. A rather nice bon voyage sendoff, I think, even if it is borderline rules violation. . . I'm not going to pretend Tag Team August doesn't feel good. It does. An air-bridged alliance.

Curt Moseby: *That goddamn August. It's always something with that guy. Why doesn't he just admit he doesn't like me? My father accused him of that a couple of years ago when I was failing his course and he denied it like the coward he is. . . First he takes the black bitch's side. We were just fooling around, having some fun. Like peanuts are a big deal. Like maybe they would've gave her a concussion. He's like, Let's go. I'll kick your ass. He thinks he's bad. But he's just a old dog with fleas. Now it's the spic. Espinoza shoves me and August says nothing. Does nothing. You can bet your ass I'd be suspended if it was the other way around. . . That's 2 strikes against him. . . I hear TJ is his good buddy now. TJ the chink, Espinoza the spic, Asia the monkey. What's up with that?*

It's A Heartache: I hand TJ Sato the meteorite and don't say a word. He's holding it like it's Waterford crystal. What a difference between this beta male and those dork-knockers in the cafeteria.

- Wow! he says. This is really cool.

I remind him of the backstory. Tell him about my own sense of wonderment and how I used to make up Rod Serling plots. While he's studying it nose-to-craters I ask how life is going these October days.

- They're letting me go at work, he says still keeping the stone close. My boss said they need someone who can work full-time. And my girlfriend told me she needs her freedom but hopes we can still be friends. . . He tries to sound like it's no big deal. Like maybe his goldfish died. But his face is long, his voice resin and sap.

- That's rough, I say . . . I start to drift off to my own troubles. But his droopy eyes yank me back. I can tell he's trying to man-up around a teacher and being in school. I look away to give him a little recoup time.

Decide I'll try to give him the little comfort that lies within me. I vaguely wonder if this is mentoring. Or just being human.

- I know how you feel, I say. I liked this girl a real lot in high school. We dated for almost a year. Then one day she dumped me like I was the creature from the Black Lagoon, with cooties. I never saw it coming. Never thought I'd get over it. I ran away to New York for a week. Thought about suicide. Almost stepped on the third rail.

Of course I'm fabricating some heavy duty bullshit. Amanda and I dated for most of high school and did not part until her death. But TJ doesn't need to know that. I briefly wonder why I'm bothering to empathize or give advice at all. Remind myself that I am no school psych. Not a role model for anyone. And that objective aside TJ and I are only together because of some temporary warp in the education-fad-du-jour continuum. . . I feel sorry for him, sure. But I feel sorry for myself too. Is it that I feel *more* sorry for him? Really *do* want to make a difference? Or simply that I want to keep my job and TJ coming round is part of the teen means to that adult end?. . . Many reasons I guess. Life isn't always clear cut.

Really Mr. August? Wow. That sounds a lot like how I feel, he says then grows quiet again. No doubt mulling over the strange fortuitousness of life.

The sun pours in through the large uncurtained windows. The room is tomb silent.

The familiar click-clack of leather soles on tile turns my head towards the door. Nunberg walks by with Superintendent Hoxley. She's practically fused to his side. Doesn't give TJ or me a glance. She passes. The hall goes back to being a mute colorless scrim.

The moment expands as TJ delves deeper into the age-old interactions of male-female love. The mysterious and transitory nature of most copulations. Undoubtedly weighing the pleasurable amorous benefits against the long-odds of anything real outlasting coitus.

He finally asks, How did you ever get over her?

I look out the window. Some landscapers are digging around a dead rhododendron alongside the science wing. They're laughing and kidding each other in Spanish. A chain is hooked at the 5" base close to the ground. The other end secured to the axle of a pickup. The dirt, sweat, and guffaws are flying. I'm surprised they are working so close to the science building *and* during class. If the work has to be now, the department that should be getting George Lopez'ed should be foreign language.

I look at TJ and he's waiting with the patience of that meteorite. . . How *did* I get over Amanda? Simple answer: I never did. . . Can't tell TJ that. Hell, I didn't even tell him the rock he's worshipping like some monolith from Kubrick's 2001 might be nothing more than solidified industrial sludge. A factory ejectamenta. A grand shat on us all. . . Guess I'll hit him with the standard clichés. Time heals all, look for the silver lining. Keep busy, buy a dog, invest in Prozac–

- Hi Mr. August!. . . Audrey Clover is standing in the doorway, waving at me, casing the room. Her enthusiasm is instant shock therapy.

- Hi Audrey. Got a minute? I wave her in and she springs forward like her knees are jointed with springs. . . Congratulations! I heard you made the cast of Grease.

- I did! she says. . . She swings side-to-side, her gold gingham circle skirt moving like an eggbeater around her. She's flushed, roiling with excitement. Moves in like she wants a hug. Despite my reservations about physical contact with female students I make an exception. Keep it fast with plenty of space.

TJ Sato is looking at her wide-eyed like he's never seen an actress before and maybe would not mind meeting a bona fide Grease legend. High school red carpet glitter. Twelfth grade A list. The glitzy music-drama wing yin to his dirty dishes yang. . . For the first time I notice he's dressed in a button-down white poplin shirt and pleated black trousers. Probably his restaurant uniform. And superb timing. Almost prom ready.

- That is so great Audrey, I say. I am very proud of you. By the way, do you know TJ Sato?

I introduce them, give quick background sketches, ask Audrey if she wants to join us. They look at each other. No smiles or talking. Steamy interest? The marriage of true mimes?. . . I think of an old couplet: Ah, come to me my sex-starved pet/I'm hotter than a crêpe suzette. . . I ask if she has to get to class and she nods. She's still looking at him as she leaves. Like his mug has been making the evening news under Person Of Interest.

Who would have guessed?

I wait till she's totally gone and he's settled back into a more apt teen reverie. The sexogenesis settling out. Here TJ, I say and hand him the meteorite. I want you to have this. To keep. This stone is good luck for whoever owns it. Sort of like King Arthur's Excalibur, Bilbo Baggins' ring, Dumbo's feather. . . I know it brought me a lot of good fortune over the years, I say. And now it's time to pass it on.

He's holding the meteorite. Barely looking at it. Light years away. . . I'm suddenly doubtful the universe will reboot. Might have just wasted a rather nice rock specimen, whatever it is. . . Can't say I blame him. Of *course* the thought of screwing Audrey in his mind is a helluva lot more appealing than owning a pitted stone. Or popping bubble wrap. Or whatever the hell it is he does for kicks. . . He's in the throes of love. And some ball-grabbing, randy, itch-to-twitch, love-slathered horniness.

TJ Sato: *I think her name is Audrey. I didn't hear Mr. August too good when he said it. I never heard that name before. I don't remember ever seeing her before. She's a senior like me but I don't think we have the same classes. . . I've never been to a school play but I think I'll go to this one. Her skirt was pretty amazing and she looks great in it. . . I wonder if Mr. August would mind finding out what Audrey thinks of me. I hope she doesn't think I'm some kind of pervert. I mean I never even said a word. Just stared.*

Audrey Clover: *That boy is nice. He has a really nice shirt and pants on. Cool. He looks like he could be in a band. He's sexy. I wonder if he would like to be my boyfriend. I never had one before. Harold liked me in kindergarten but we never kissed. We held hands once. I think that boy's name is BJ. I hope not. That's a bad word. Maybe if he's my boyfriend he'll come to the play and clap for me. That would be really nice.*

Rhapsody In Blue: My last conference today is with Zoe. She's been on my mind lately, inextricably coupled with Nunberg. It's not unusual for a student to get on the wrong side of a principal. That could explain their confrontations. But there's something about the 2 of them together that is definitely beyond the usual educational scrum. And why isn't Zoe suspended for physically threatening to hit her?. . . I haven't talked to the young lady since that day at her house and I briefly consider the notion that this is no way to run mentoring. Or whatever the hell it is I do. But then I tell myself it's not really mentoring. Though it *is* starting to feel like it.

Her hair is pink today with blue streaks. I'm pretty sure it's new since she was an apple and orange before – never lemonade. But I'm not bringing it up. Foke meaningless pitty-pat.

I get right to it.

- Sorry, I say, if I fouled up by bringing your father home. But it seemed like the best thing to do. And of course I had no way of knowing Jimmy Klein is your dad.

- It's no big deal. We choose our friends but not our family.

- Too bad too.

- Klein doesn't like you either. . . She's blunt. It's refreshing.

- Do you think he hates me enough to send a letter?. . . I tell her about OUT OF MANY, FEW. How it could be a reference to staff cutbacks and me being shown the door. I ask her if Klein has a Smith Corona, Underwood, Royal, or Remington. The note was definitely written on a typewriter, I say. She tells me she hasn't seen one but that a mocking threat is certainly within her father's makeup.

Before I drop the topic of Jimmy Klein I ask her why they have different last names, though it's not unusual with students. Zoe brushes it off with a, Koppel is my mother's maiden name.

A distant truck horn beeps twice. I look away towards the sound. It's a brief oasis while I stretch out the seconds before bringing up another biggie.

- So Zoe, I finally say, I noticed the other day after you stormed out of that empty classroom that Principal Nunberg was sitting in there. Alone. And not looking happy. Her face was cradled in her hands.

I half expect Zoe to say, If her face was covered how do you know she was unhappy? But Zoe doesn't say anything. I break the silence with, Guess the negotiations for the painting didn't go well?. . . She says,

Something like that. Her tone and look say that not a single fuck is given either.

The truck air horn that seemed distant before suddenly rips off a series of thunderous blasts. Must be at the cafeteria loading dock, I think. That reminds me of food and though it's only mid-morning my stomach gurgles and grumbles.

Unexpectedly Zoe says, Mr. August, you don't need any help around your house, do you? I mean, now that you're alone. Housekeeping stuff, or whatever. I wouldn't charge much. I really need money. . . She says it seriously but softly, like maybe she's auditioning for cook or upstairs maid. For a second she starts to physically reach out to touch my hand. I draw it back and look at her quizzically. She could be reaching for the pen I'm slowly twirling in my fingers. But I doubt it. I notice there's a flash going on but not as pronounced as the last time she showed me her birthday suit. If this is a come-on it's a pretty damn good one. I *could* use some domestic help, for sure. But not the kind that would land me in jail.

- I already have a cleaning service and home delivered meals, I tell her. Which of course is a lie.

Her hand has retreated. I notice she's wearing false eyelashes, dark eyeliner, blue eye shadow above geranium red lipstick. Which she's now licking. Her face has a full coverage foundation that's not quite bone-white. But is definitely lighter than her normal skin. It pops her eyes and lips. The effect is ghoulish. Physical and psychological shading. A Twilight femme fatale. Like she wants to suck blood. Or cock. I don't think it's my imagination. There's something in her eyes that isn't lust or loving. But *is* a field of sexual energy. Almost like she's a pro sizing up a potential john. Measuring wallet size. Eyes dropping to assess pants bulge, zipper access.

161

I decide to get the conversation off me, and back to Zoe Koppel.

I say, It looked to me the other day that you're already taking on a lot. Cooking, brother-sitting, cleaning, painting, homework. I'd say your schedule is already maxed out.

- Someone has to do the chores. Just because you don't have a lot of money doesn't mean you have to live like pigs.

She is matter-of-fact. With just a swab of sarcasm. The softness gone, the lips still wet. . . The line resonates. Selena Cross used a similar one on Lucas in *Peyton Place*. Doubt Zoe's seen it. She's more of a Fellini-indie bohem.

- I give you a lot of credit, I say. I know what it's like to have others depend on you. Do you still have that dream of going to New York after graduation? I assume you want to join the art scene.

New York. The words are a stimulant to her. LIke I just shoved her off the Chrysler Building or whacked her with a MetroCard.

- It's not a dream. Money is the issue. I may have to work in town after graduation before hopping Amtrak. But I'm going. Leave the crap behind.

I smile and say, Nice if you can. Cormac McCarthy in No Country For Old Men says we can never leave the past. That our lives are made up of yesterdays. And it's made up of nothing else.

- I like McCarthy but he's full of it with that.

- What about a part-time job? I know a few business owners who might be looking to hire. . . I don't reiterate that I am definitely *not* hiring.

- I don't want to bag groceries. Or hand out Happy Meals. Or clean up shit at the nursing home.

- Have you ever considered selling your artwork to someone other than Nunberg? There's a big public out there. . . I let this sink in. Then say, From the little I saw at your house it seems to me you have a real talent. A marketable one. Your paintings remind me of Lucian Freud. Maybe Raphael Soyer. But not quite. Definitely original. You've got a discerning eye for portraiture. I don't know a lot about art but I know what I like. I like your paintings.

She thanks me. Looks away. Not her usual grand aplomb. Appears out-of-kilter like she needs a cigarette or joint. Or handkerchief? Feed the artist praise and you throw her off-balance. Maybe corral the wild beast? Maybe. But my goal isn't that. Maybe the world needs Zoe the bitch, Zoe Frankenstein. PMS can't supply them all.

I mention again the idea of selling her paintings.

Mention the enlarged photographs too. The ones scattered around your house, I say. Very sellable. . . She says the photographs aren't hers. That Jimmy Klein took them. . . Is that what he does for a living? I ask. Thought maybe he was on a disability or unemployment. . . He was a professional lens man, Zoe says. Weddings, news coverage, investigative work. Wanted to be a photographic artist. Never made it. . . Does he still work? I ask. . . You might say that, she says and adds, When the mood strikes.

She lets it drop.

I ask again about the paintings. Zoe tells me her art teachers have always been laudatory. But, she says, they never pushed the commercial aspect. Or offered to help. I tell her I am obviously not an art dealer or purveyor. But I have an idea, I say, that might put some money in your pocket.

At the mention of making money her features notably brighten. We talk and I'm surprised how well it goes. How well this whole session has gone. I didn't call her on using *shit* because she's used it before. And I'm thinking if I expect honest adult conversation then the vocab goes with it. It's not like she called *me* a shit, though if she did she wouldn't be the first. . . I don't push getting the truth on Nunberg and her, or her obvious come-on because I don't think pushing with Zoe would do any good. You push, she pushes back. That's how she's been conditioned. I imagine she's been pushed around plenty over the years by Jimmy Klein, the more conventional students. Probably by most of the adults in this inbred hick town.

There's sudden pandemonium in the hall. Both our heads jerk towards the sounds of hellbent laughter, then running. I go to the door and catch the tail end of a bunch of freshmen turning the corner like they're fleeing the scene of a drive-by. Like they just found out Nurse Betty is handing out free condoms with owners' manuals. . . On the wall is a Do You Have Hot Lips Poster with the breasts and vagina drawn in with red magic marker. I rip it down and toss the crumpled paper into the nearest basket.

When I get back Zoe is laughing.   What's so funny? I ask surprised, aware that I've never seen her laugh before. . . I know what those pillow pokers did out there, she says. They're doing it all over the school and haven't gotten caught yet. . . You think that's funny? I ask. Those hall artists aren't exactly Banksy. . . True, she says, but as an artist myself I appreciate all forms of it. Especially anything that wrecks a Nunberg project.

I notice that her lips are dry. She's not re-moisturizing.

Zoe Koppel: *I feel the best I've felt in a long time. Not just because of Mr. A's compliments and the possibility I might make some serious money. And not by scheming to get it either like I've been doing. More like if anyone actually likes my oils enough to buy them that's a big deal. Painting is hard work. It's nice to be appreciated. My mother does but is usually too tired to* *say anything more than, It's really creative Zoe. . . Jimmy Asshole Klein told me the only reason for artists to create is for money. He's bitter. . . Art is the most important thing in my life. It should be in everyone's. . . I guess I won't be playing up to August anymore, but I don't regret that I did. A person has to do what a person has to do. And screw the people who think this is a Care Bear-Smurf world.*

Chapter 14

Muzzle Velocity

One Flew Over The Cuckoo's Nest: The World Literature class is reviewing Les Misérables prior to writing a final paper. I ask the class, If Jean Valjean lived today what would he be doing?. . . It's open-ended. Fairly mindless on my part. Several hands go up.

In a flurry of answers they toss out: Running a factory just like he did in France and getting fined by the EPA and OSHA. Working for a sanitation department because he was really good in the Paris sewers. Womb Reject #3 offers: Marrying another man since he was obviously gay. Like why else would he sacrifice himself for that dude in court?. . . Womb Reject #2 theorizes: He'd be getting raped in prison because he was probably a pedophile. He was obsessed with Cosette. . . Womb Reject #1 says, Lifting heavy things like maybe a dock worker or UPS delivery man because he was really strong. I immediately ask, Why would he want to lift a dock worker or UPS man? Reject 1 says, Huh?

Just a few years ago these answers would have made me smile. Maybe even chortle. Today they're giving me a headache and validating my theory that we share only oxygen and maybe a straight DNA link to the Paris sewers.

In the midst of all this Destiny picks up her latest rough. I generally don't allow outside students to interrupt class but she didn't ask and the handoff is Olympic relay fast. Usually. I pause the *Les Mis* discussion long enough to compliment her creativity, though it's really no quantum leap in improvement. Thanks for helping me, she says. But even the little creativity

166

I managed seems to have dried up. . . That's OK, I say. There are ways to replenish it.

Just as I say this something that looks like a pop tart or Kotex sails across the room. Destiny heads for the door and I say to the hell-raising red-haired Adrianna, Do you want a detention? This isn't Cape Canaveral. . . Adrianna puts on the all-innocent all-Annie look and says, Why are you picking on me?. . Because I saw your follow-through, I say, so unless you were waving goodbye to Destiny or trying to get my attention for some reason, I'll. . . thank. . . you. . . to. . . stop. I shake a finger in her direction and tsk tsk her. . . I am really holding back. The girl desperately needs a detention.

The one-string banjos laugh. Adrianna hesitates. Shakes her mop top. Then laughs too.

Sometimes I really do miss teaching AP.

The Pink Panther Theme: At the end of the day I pop into the art room on my way out of school. Clouseau on the trail. It's quiet, no teacher in sight. Several students are scattered around working on projects. One putting a piece of pottery into the kiln, another using a putty knife to layer and sculpt inch thick paint. The raised canvass pops 3-dimensionally. The electric colors of Peter Max. I notice the walls are windowed with pastel and charcoal groupings. Lots of originality, but nothing that looks Zoe-ish.

- Can I help you? . . . The voice is behind me. When I turn Christian Maynard says, Oh, it's you Mike.

- Great work your students do, I say and look around.

His eyes join mine in the sweep and he says, Yeah, there are some awfully talented people in my classes.

167

- Would you say Zoe Koppel is one of them?

- Zoe? Yeah. She's probably my best . . . He's talking while watching the girl at the kiln. He excuses himself. Walks over and checks the settings. His white smock is flecked with paint smudges and combined with his wildly mowed hair and 3 day growth, Maynard looks every bit the dedicated and starving artist. Except he's tenured, at the top of the pay scale, and runs a successful custom jewelry business on the side. The irony of municipal salaried boheme.

- Sorry about that, he says when he's back. Have to keep a close eye on them. That kiln is new and expensive . . . So Mike, you were asking about Zoe?

- Have you exhibited any of her paintings this year?

- Zoe? No. Not this year. I just put these up today. Zoe didn't think hers were good enough. She can be very. . . exacting.

- Has Nunberg been in here? Maybe looking over artwork to buy?

- Nunberg? Ha. No. Not that I recall. She's not exactly pro-Maynard. Thinks I should dress in a top hat and tails to teach art. I never got the impression she even cared for these amateur creations.

- Has she contacted you about Zoe's work? Have you seen the 2 of them together?

- No. Never. What's this all about? he asks and excuses himself again.

I wait while he helps a boy get started on the 3-legged electrified pottery wheel. The sophomore looks scared, as if centrifugal forces might spin him off into an alternate universe. Like maybe he saw *Ghost* and is worried about a spirit sneaking up and hugging him. . . I don't know anything about pottery wheels or kilns but teachers who deal with expensive and potentially dangerous equipment have always gotten my respect. In my room the worst that can happen is a paper cut or backpack hernia.

When Maynard breaks loose I tell him simply, I'm the mentor for Zoe.

He nods. Doesn't say anything. Studies me like I am posing for a portrait and he's trying to dellneate bone structure. He gives a student the wait-one-minute finger and says to me, Word is that Nunberg has been on your case.

I smile. The word is correct, I say.

There doesn't seem to be much more to add.

Master Of The House: The next day I'm back with the Les Mis group and they are as antsy as ever. I half expect Destiny to come striding in again, breaking whatever little rhythm the class has. But she doesn't.

It's near the end of the period and I give them the last 15 minutes to brainstorm ideas for a homework paper and to start a lead paragraph.

Most are soon working. Womb Reject # is sleeping with his head down. This student couldn't set a gas pump on fire. Zero for today.

My thoughts go back to yesterday and the fact that Destiny thanked me. This leads to the thought that Zoe didn't. Never expressed a word of gratitude for my offering to help sell her paintings. Not that I offered for the head or arse patting bennies But *thanks* would have been nice. It *was* nice that she finally stopped flashing me, though maybe I should report her. CYA. . . She's a girl of many surprises. There's the small surprise she lied about Nunberg seeing her painting in the art room. A fact Maynard verified yesterday. The minor surprise she tossed out that barb about liking to see a Nunberg project wrecked. Students don't generally bad mouth administrators to teachers. We aren't parents. The bigger surprise that Jimmy Klein is, or was, a photographer. . . I don't know what other surprises Zoe has in her. But nothing I hope that will reverse my polarities and bring on apocalyptic forces. I'm waist deep in shit now and sinking fast.

Some noise interrupts my train of thought. It's Adrianna. She sees me looking and smiles back. . . I pushed it a little with Adrianna yesterday. Probably should not have wagged a finger and tsk tsked her. If she perceives I was embarrassing her. . . While it doesn't seem like much you never know with these feather duster sensitivities. It's 1-in-5 I get a phone call from the parent, 1-in-10 I get called down to Nunberg's and written up. Again. I'd prefer Powerball odds.

The generic 3 notes of an iPhone's tri-tone chime and several students fumble in their pockets. Only one winner. Adrianna clicks off. . . Far Out Thought: Could her little miss hell-comes-calling act be Nunberg directed? Could she be a teen merc intentionally trying to push me to the brink? Like Marcus seems to be doing? It's sometimes difficult to believe that all this open air stupidity is natural. Maybe it's the fluorescent lighting.

More Adrianna noise. Now she's showing the boy behind her something on her cell. They're laughing. . . Fuck me pretty. Though, I guess, it's only the class clown being herself.

Time to check the work anyway.

I grab the hard copy grade book I use for backup and walk over to the red head. The phone disappears.

- You haven't written anything, I say staring down at the white un-blemished paper.

- My mind's not working right now, Adrianna says.

- No prob. Zero for the assignment . . . I make a quick circle in my red book under in-class work. It is flawlessly concentric.

- That's not fair. I can't concentrate in here.

- Brainstorming ideas doesn't take concentration, I say. . . I'm looking down at the top of her head and note that her dark roots are showing through. As I briefly lecture Adrianna I'm aware that other students are writing furiously. That's the problem with not collecting all the papers at once, the last ones get the most time. I take that into account and try to vary where I start my checks. Still my attitude = oh-boo-hoo-the-feck-too-bad.

- But we're also supposed to start the first paragraph, the brain pudge mini-protests.

Well tickle my ear with your tongue, I think and say, I would have cut you some slack it you had a good brainstorming list. But as it is I hope the phone sharing and laugh were worth it.

- They were, she says all smartass.

- Good. I'm reporting you. Plan on serving a detention. And I'll take that phone, now. . . I point to her pocketbook. I'm sarcastic, and overreacting. But I've had it with her. I realize that my fuse is getting shorter these days. I'm not proud of it. I tell myself to calm down. . . She starts to hand me her cell, pulls it back when I reach for it, and puts it on her desk. I probably should also remind her that she needs to touch-up her dye job. But I don't and file it under Extraneous Student Crap I Don't Need To Know Or Remember.

I put the phone in my pocket. Tell her to see Higham tomorrow if she wants it back. I move off and check the rest of the papers barely making the bell. They pile out like gouts of eczema.

Adrianna Cooper: *So I'm getting a zero and a detention. What else is new. I hate to read. It's that simple. My mother and father hate to read too. I mean who reads books anyway? This is like the 20th or 21st century and*

171

August acts like we're supposed to care about what some foreign convict did like 300 years ago. And he's not even real. . . I was lucky to get away tossing that Kotex yesterday. And good thing August didn't see the picture I was just showing. I was wasted. Kissing that girl was pretty freaking outrageous. . . August taking my phone hurts. If he sees some of the pics I have on there like the vodka slamming in the school lav I'm going to be in real trouble. But I don't think they check that stuff. It's not the first time a teacher confiscated it . . I wonder who that black girl is that came in yesterday. Seemed pretty tight with August. Like it's OK for him to talk about stuff that isn't this class with someone who's not even supposed to be here? If he wants to goof off no prob. But then we should be able to too.

Islands In The Stream: The hall traffic is a binary flow moving with the speed of arthritic seniors. I'm standing just outside my door between periods. Some students say hi, others flip a hand in my general direction. Most are too caught up in their own standing-room-only lives. The click-clack of leather soles on tile breaks through. Nunberg walks by with Superintendent Hoxley. She's practically fused to his side. Canoodling? Gives me no more acknowledgement than she gives the students.

I see John Higham buried in the stream. When he sees me he moves to the edge and stops long enough to say, Good meeting the other day with Madison and her parents. You handled yourself well. . . I nod, and he closes with, I appreciate that you kept it professional. Thanks, I say and think, Did you expect dueling pistols? I want to add, You could have saved us *all* a lot of trouble by checking Madison's story first. . . I don't say it. Higham to me is bite-size. A little nosh that I'm not going to waste time on. These 30 seconds are already on the long side.

I wave to some students, and Higham is gone. Toe gunk moving down the hall. Though he's not really a bad guy. At least not in the Nunberg badass sense. . . Nunberg, she's making me crazy. It occurs to me I'd be a *lot* better off if Higham were my evaluator. He seems to respect me. Maybe even likes the kind of concrete sequential teacher I am. Whereas with Nunberg I'm just educational dross who does nothing right.

Friends In Low Places: I'm about to go back into the room when TJ Sato materializes out of nowhere.

- Hi TJ, I say. How's that meteorite treating you?

- Fine, Mr. August. I have it on a shelf in my room. I really like it. . . Then he grows quiet like he's battling the dark side. Finally he says, Remember that girl you introduced to me yesterday? Audrey?

- Sure I remember, and think, Love train arriving. . . What about her? I ask.

- Did she say anything about me? Like maybe what she thinks about me? I acted pretty dumb.

- You were fine. I haven't seen her since you did. But if I'm any judge of women I'm betting she thinks you're pretty cool.

- Really? I wanted to email her but I don't have her address.

- Use her school account. Just keep things calm. Emails are sometimes monitored. Or. . . an idea is quickly forming in my mind. . . how would you like to meet Audrey again? Maybe be around her everyday?

When he asks how, he's excited. His voice palpably raised in maybe the coup de grâce shot to loneliness. I explain my idea. He blinks rapidly, bites his lip, then says OK. I write him a late pass and go in to start the next class. There might be a time-out for love in school, but no schedule change.

The Beat Goes On: The pep assembly is loud. It's in the gym, half a building from here. But it's managing to drown out our rehearsal until I close the door and we move into a small inner room.

Silence. Peace.

We're in a practice warmup space of the music and drama wing. The Kid and I are doing this duet thing for the first time. Practicing for an open mike night called Beatnik Now! It's in a month but our entering it is all a congealed *maybe*. I really do not want to do this stage thing. And won't if we don't get pretty good. Pretty damn fast. I think The Kid feels the same. He seems even more hesitant than me. He's certainly more fidgety.

We're not supposed to be here. Both of us should be at the day-ending assembly. I should be monitoring students who are normally whacked-out nuts, and now are encouraged to go peppy ballistic. I'd rather ride a piece of space debris to earth.

I read The Kid's lyrics. They are good à la the Kerouac world he lives in. He's got 3 pieces that run around 3 minutes each, provided he doesn't go off on an improv. I'm not exactly sure how we're going to do this. Or how it will come out. But the thing is to trust the process and any innate talent. I am not kidding myself on the talent. The Kid's is fresh and appealing. Mine is the before version of Max's basement.

Kaufman starts intoning the lyrics like a smoke-husky Leonard Cohen while I follow along. I'm strumming lightly, trying to figure out some basic rhythmic chords that fit the voice and words. I'm playing behind, keeping it simple, trying to nail down the right triads. The right 1, 2, 3 chords and key. He's starting sad so I'm fooling around in the minor range. . . He's talking about a dog he had as a kid and tying it into lost youth and a simple-pure-love world. He's chorusing about playing with the mutt and using rubato to drag out the thought. Which gives me time to reinforce musically what he is trying for emotionally. Sort of. On my end it isn't going so well. Lacks timing and the close meld of voice and chord. He ends with some Kaufman humor chanting, The bow-wow's gone, the gnarled rubber lost. The pooch house in the dust bowl of memory. If you're looking for the Purina, it's crushed under the tire tracks of Ike. Bow-wow, bow-wow.

I smile. It's good on his end, though the nervousness is still coming through. He's got a subdued but obvious tremble that's drawing attention away from the lyrics. Still, it's a better voice than my backup is.

Kaufman has something, even if it is rough. Young and a hit, can anything be better? A young Bernstein after *West Side Story*. Kerouac after *On The Road*. Justin Bieber after YouTube?. . I doubt The Kid can get there via me or the éclat of open mike. But I am not ready to call it quits yet.

He says he thinks it went fairly well for a first run-through and I know he's being kind. I get a flash of us at Beatnik Now! Tails between our legs. Bow-wow, bow-wow. . . To keep it positive, and maybe defray any immediate criticism headed my way, I tell him that Tom Waits once said that songs are merely interesting things to be doing with the air. Kaufman says he may use that line.

The Dharma Bums: We continue for another 20 minutes till we're near the end of the period and school day. Before I shoot for the door, slinging my guitar cross-back vintage Dylan style, I need to broach a sensitive matter with The Kid.

- Jack, were you missing anything after the last time we met? I say casually.

175

He looks puzzled, then smiles and says, I was wondering where I dropped it.

- School rules and the law aside, you can't be in possession if we're going to meet and rehearse together.

- I dig where you're going. Musicians are feen-heads, smack-heads, slammers, stoners. Guilt through association. August gets taken down with Kerouac.

- I'm dead serious about this.

- Emancipate your worries. I have your army secret on the hush-hush. And I have you covered on this. The sun is not in my eyes. I respect the trees of antiquity.

- I hope so.

- Just so you know. I don't use in school, or ever sell anywhere. That was a freak time I was carrying here.

- Happy to hear it, I say. . . He looks as if he's telling the truth but I ask myself why I didn't turn him in initially. Because partners stick together? I've toked myself? We had a Vulcan mind meld? I know I'm setting myself up for a career ending fall if he screws up. Putting a lot of faith in a 17-year-old like he's a tight-lipped Trappist. The bastard side of me says, Turn him in. It'll be one less worry on the objective. The human side says, If he gets busted it'll probably ruin his chances for Columbia. . . I opt for human, and maybe getting taken down too if he blows it.

The Kid says, I hope you enjoyed whatever it was I lost. Guaranteed to produce enlightenment.

I shake my head and say an emphatic, No. . . I'm not sending a mixed message.

I open the sound-proof door and the proverbial wall of noise slams into us. The school band is blasting away on the school fight song. The tune the Washington and Lee Swing. The lyrics something about keeping the standards high, never saying defeat. I think The Kid and I were better. Certainly quieter.

I'm barely out of the room when Nunberg steps into the wing. Followed by the youngest member of the board of ed. A white-shoed country club assistant pro. She gives my guitar and me a triple-take. Is frozen for long seconds as if someone just keyed the National Anthem. Then she turns on heel like the bearded lady at a barbers convention. Moves off in an undulating wide-ass swag. BOE follows. . . The Kid is behind me and utters a voce alta, Shit. . . What a day ending downer, I think and watch Nunberg's hip-hugging leather shift in retreat, with boy-toy in tow.

Jack Kaufman: *August is not as good on that* Rickenbacker *as I anticipated, though it's obvious he's way out of practice and not used to accompanying a poet. It's that old question of how do you get to Carnegie Hall? The essencehood of us shaking the moths, drawing them in, will be practice. Lots of it. And whether I can stay calm. A-man says he likes my lyrics. Feels confident we'll be money. Doesn't voice the maybeness of laughter in the room. . . I'm a little surprised he doesn't push the Mary Jane bust but he's cool. Wonder what happened to the leaf? Bet he nubbed it out, despite no-no-ing the idea. . . That run-in with Nunberg. I call it Simple Thatness. She hates me. Probably hates August too. I'd hate her if I hated. But I don't. Kesey said, Fascism wants Baptism coast to coast. I think that covers what she's about.*

Un Homme Et Une Femme: I'm almost to the outside door figuring what-the-hell might as well add beating-the-busses to my crimes when a loud,

Mike! halts me. Sophia Arbuckle moves in briskly like she's in the tow of a tractor beam. Maybe invisible pheromone grappling hooks.

- Trying to sneak out early? she asks faux-serious. And what are you doing anyway in this area *again*?. . . Her voice is golden, pollinating. A sexy reminder of bygone fantasies.

- I'm here to see you, I say. At least partly. The sight of Nunberg made me forget.

- Nunberg was here?

- Just for a few seconds. I think I scared her off.

- Good. She's not exactly anyone I'd get the cable fixed to see.

- Ha. I feel the same. By the way do you ever see Nunberg with any BOE members around here?

- Nunberg pops in occasionally. By herself. She wants to start a girls' leader corps. She even offered to be the club advisor.

- Girls' leader corps? What's that? I ask.

- She sees it as promoting the school and girls' issues. Doing fund-raising activities, volunteer work. The girls organizing various events.

- Guess I won't sign up, I say and envision Nunberg surrounded by an army of young, naked, pearl-skinned Brunhildes riding bareback. Swords in hand.

- What's with the guitar? Are you here to sign up for Grease?. . . She smiles and looks beautiful.

- Just doing some quiet practicing. . . I think to myself that in a different time, in different circumstances I might be telling her I'm here to see her. If I ever could get up the nerve. She's not sex appeal that has a lady, but a lady that has sex appeal. It's rare. . . I say, Remember when you said you could use boys in Grease? Is it too late?

- Not yet.

- I have someone for you. Not guaranteeing he'd even make the audition phase of American Idol. But he'll be enthusiastic. And he did check off male on the school form. . . I fill her in on TJ. Let her know there is zero theater experience. Plenty of time since he lost his job. She tells me she can train anyone. Or bury them deep enough in the chorus so as to not trip anyone.

Sunshine Superman: I'm leaving, she's walking me to the door. We keep our distance. The talk is old time Legion Of Decency polite. Would not turn the head of the primmest observer. If one were around. I'm feeling the undercurrent of sexual tension that's only cotton undie deep for me. Fighting to keep my mouth moist, my voice from getting dry and crackly. Though maybe at our age there's little point in pretense. If someone turns you on maybe you should just get to say it.

I open the door and see a cackling underclass throng making for the busses. Laughing, bumping, hollering. Like the pep assembly has gone al fresco.

So close, that angular La Scala face. Without prior thought except on some subconscious remembered sex level I say, Sophia, would you like to go out to dinner with me this Saturday night? I know a little local place. Great food, friendly people. . . I sound pathetic. Nervous. Hunger games for the horny. . . I wonder if they still call it a date?

She looks at me as if it's a surprise but not a shock. I'm thinking the invite was too fast, too dry-tongued when she finally laughs and says, OK. . . And just like that I have my first date with any woman but Amanda since junior high. . . Maybe the earth didn't move. Maybe I wasn't balling the jack. But I did put it out there and who knows what will happen besides a great meal.

Now if only I can get through these damn squirming epidural catheters and beat the busses.

Beer Barrel Polka: It's late afternoon. Tree shadows lengthening, casting the front of Hudson's with a montage of black gnarled branch lines pre-Halloween. It's Friday crowded, many starting the weekend two drinks back. George is finishing a tall whiskey but hits himself with a refresher when he sees me.

- Mikey! he says a tad too surprised and too loud like I'm some mon-signor and stopped in for a bracer before Vespers. . . What's new?

- Everyday, every minute. . . I stand alongside him, motion to Vinnie and have a drink in front of me before I can say, Up the inebriates! I tell whiskey breath I was just with Max, no change. Saw Nunberg, or rather got caught by Nunberg skipping the assembly, I say and take a long pull on the gin. . . Cheez, George says, why don't you just write yourself up again and save her the trouble? Speaking of Nunberg, he says, there are rumors floating around that she's very friendly with Hoxley. Very. Maybe one or two on the board too. . . I say only, Guess she's lonely. Should be with the enemies she's making on our staff. . . Lots of worried people in school these days, George says. Old *and* young alike, though mostly old. The union has called a meeting for next week.

- About time, I say taking a long drink. It's all about money, of course. The BOE trying to weed out the top-earners. Academics be damned.

- I think they feel academics will be elevated. Weed out the ones with the standards of a gas station toilet. By the way, George asks, how's life going with your half-dozen?

- Well, I don't see the tie-in, but there's progress. . . I fill him in.

- Death of a thousand putz. You need to forget these kids for awhile. How about if we go to the game tonight? Neither of us has been for, what — years? Might be fun. The pep assembly got everyone pumped. Yeah the team sucks, but you never know.

Down the other end of the bar there's yelling from some young bachelor teachers tossing dice. TGIF bonhomie. They're here every Friday, a fun loving bunch. Talented, united in their love of drink. Well-lubricated off-hours. Rat Pack, Brat Pack. No guilt. Un-registering penitence.

Watching the men is a winsome lineup of sylphlike nymphs including Becky Capello. I feel a twinge of jealousy. Hell, I feel a kick in the fuzzy jelly beans. Starbursts of emerald green envy. These twenty-somethings have life by its zippity boppity crotch. It's one thing to tell the British Lit students that Wordsworth was right-on with his superior splendor-in-the-grass thoughts. Another to believe it yourself. That the bygone years are source of strength and not an arse-kicking reminder that the best is gone, gone, gone. Pants around the ankles.

I'd go back in a heartbeat if I could. Fancy the pants. And hit the Repeat All button when I hit 30.

- Listen, I say to George, if we're going to the game I need to get home and shower. You need a cup of coffee, and maybe to *not* finish that drink. He laughs and points at my own drink which has just been refilled. It's my turn to laugh. . . Once when George thought I'd had too much he quoted John Barrymore's, You can't drown yourself, you only float. . . I remind myself now that there will be parents and students in the stands. Then I ask myself if I really give a shit. . . George says, And use some mouthwash. I tell him, Get some food in you.

- Did I hear you say you're going to the game? Deirdre Good is suddenly in front of us holding a tray of drinks. . . I'm off duty in an hour. Mind if I tag along? I haven't seen a high school game since I graduated. . . Her rounded twins paps rise and fall with the cadence of yelling to Vinnie, Just a minute.

George coughs, looks down, takes a long pull. I know instantly he doesn't want anything to do with the decision. . . No is not an option. Deirdre's going above-and-beyond with Max. It's a friendly innocent enough request. And why *wouldn't* we want her along? A beautiful young lady making 2 old wormwoods like us look like AARP centerfolds.

Deirdre Good: *I'm a little nervous inviting myself along like this but the guys don't seem to mind. Mike is actually enthusiastic which relieves some of my embarrassment. I don't know what made me do it, it just sort of popped out. Maybe I'm lonelier than I realize. . . I hope he doesn't misinterpret it. I really do want to see the game. I remember years ago in school Mike called Nancy Reagan the only man in the Cabinet. I hope that doesn't mean he's turned off by a modern assertive woman. Maybe it's just that he just doesn't like Nancy types. Republican, West Coast, androgynous, short-haired, flat-chested. I'm none of those. But I'm not going to deny who I am. Or make myself over for anyone.*

Friday Night Lights: Going back to the old high school ritual of poms-poms, rah-rah-rah, fight-team-fight. I think of the short piece In Football Season by John Updike and the excitement and splendor Updike evokes describing a game night he remembers. The way it was when a school and town turned out for the big one.

I'm hoping I am not disappointed.

I'm hoping that it's not binoculars reversed.

I'm hoping that maybe, just maybe, you *can* go home again.

Chapter 15

Weekend Interlude

Be True To Your School: It's a beautiful October evening. The kind of night you remember in the dead of winter when the landscape is a bleak barren white. It's too dark to see the zigzag of autumn color or the browning grass or brambled green creeper hugging the outside fence with the leaves blown up against it. But you know it's there. Just the thought lays down a color palette. There's a dry leaf smell in the air mixing with spackled cigarette smoke and charcoal grilling. A bonfire spirit.

Back in Max's time, or maybe before, raccoon coats, pennants on sticks, hip flasks, muskrat ramblers were part of this scene. I'm sorry I missed that era. Tonight George, Deirdre, and I are in medium weight jackets, no gloves or hats. We're laughing, practically walking arm-in-arm. Probably so cute the students around us could barf.

We pass tailgaters packing up. A former student now parent waves us over and asks if we'd like a burger. He winks and offers me a foamed red cup. Actually it's inviting. I had nothing for supper but cheese and crackers. And a tall gin. I hesitate, then wave him off with a, Thanks but we need to meet someone. . . I generally don't make a practice of socializing with former students, Deirdre aside. Or any parent with active students in the school. Party with the folks, become a student joke.

There is no ticket booth. Just a folding table with a cash box, programs, and tickets for the 50-50 raffle. I pay for the 3 of us, dropping my wallet in the process. There are sideways glances from the booster club parents, and I wonder if my breath mint is working. I avoid eye contact. Try not to talk. George springs for a program. Deirdre opens her pocketbook and buys an arm's length of raffle tickets.

We walk past clusters of socializing students standing with their backs to the field, youngsters who don't give us a glance. . . Amish teens at 16 enter a period called Rumspringa. Their time to sow a few wild oats, socialize, look for a mate. Secular teens, religious teens, these are their days. Adults not wanted.

We continue past a fry shack pushing out grilled hot dogs, burgers sizzling in oil, and fried pizza dough flooded with tomato sauce. I'm inhaling the greasy smoke and my stomach rumbles. Past a couple of sandbagging cops raking in easy OT. Past someone costumed as our mascot. Past the band, cheerleaders, dance team, and Junior ROTC cadets. Uniforms everywhere.

- Hey Mike!. A 50-foot voice from 20 feet away rocks me. Tom a former teammate and classmate gives the big wave. I go over and this once football tackle now a battleship mothball locks me in a bear hug. Cheez, he says, is that liquor I smell? He shoves a brown-papered bottle under my nose. Come on, he says, drink up. You need this.

I wave off the bottle and he asks, How's everything?. . . We do the old long-time-no-see, demi-pal stint. A small enclave of former Jedi teammates form us into a huddle. There's reminiscing but not for long since I see most of these fellows in the course of a year at Hudson's.

George leads us up into the middle section of bleachers. It's open seating. George pushes towards the top where you can lean back against a heavy-gaged wire barrier. The bleachers are packed solid but George practices the belief that there's always room for 2 or 3 more. Rear ends are soft, flex. Have the feline ability to squeeze into any space.

We don't quite make it. Upperclassmen control the top tier. We settle in half-a-dozen rows down next to some grandparent types comfortably ensconced in their portable stadium seats. Blankets across their laps, thermos cups in hand. Deirdre sits between George and me, though the way her leg is pressed up against mine I can't help thinking she's a little more to my side.

I remind myself it *is* crowded.

I look around. Remember when Amanda and I came to these games. Not many but just enough to convince her that high school football was not her Friday night thing. I remember her saying she was amazed that so many people found this a pleasant way to pass an evening after a tough week. . . Deirdre is definitely not of that sorority. She's watching the band and frequently waving to people who give back the big, Hey there Deirdre!

I scan the crowd. Walking past the front of the stands in heels and a full-length fox fur accented with a bright silk scarf is Nunberg. Head tossed back laughing. The BOE golfer bird-dogging her and waving to someone. Looks innocent enough, good school PR. Question: Wonder if his crotcho is bulging under that ¾ length stadium coat? I see George looking too. He winks at me. . . Note To Self: Forget Nunberg for the weekend. Or at least till Sunday night and grading papers. All school related neurological systems need to shut down and abort. . . And I'm thinking this at a school football game? Ha. Must be the gin.

- Anyone want anything? George is suddenly on his feet. I'm going to the food stand. Soda, popcorn, Château Lafite '66?

We tell him no thanks and he's gone. I'm hungry so why I'm opting for food deprivation I have no idea other than I *am* enjoying my liquor buzz. Fun Fact: An 80 proof glow improves anything to do with school. I just have to avoid doing anything stupid like falling down the stairs, passing out on Deirdre, or throwing up.

I'm a million miles away when Deirdre grabs my upper arm, snuggles closer, and says, This is nice. Thanks so much Mike for letting me come along. . . I tell her, *Our* pleasure, stressing the *our*. She put it on me, I shifted it to George and me. What a clever drunk bastard.

Even though she lets go after only a brief cling my sex drive is now hyped. Attached to a spinning well-lubricated flywheel that is going to keep the sperm gun on standby for awhile. Doesn't take much these days.

Deirdre is no fool. I'm sure she knows she is making a high school football game irrelevant by capturing my willy and me. Or am I wrong? Totally misinterpreting platonic friendship for something more? I don't deny that my sense of these things is skewed by Deirdre's physical closeness, and my BAC.

I force myself to focus on football. Try to calm the testosterone high. Remind myself I paid for 3 tickets and at least one of us should get the face value.

You've Got To Be A Football Hero: The teams are running out under the glare of the floodlights and the band is pounding the fight song like this is Super Bowl. Like it's possible to will a team to victory. Even a team that's out-talented, out-experienced, out-of-prayers. . . A coach can't get out, what god didn't put in, says *Chariots Of Fire*. My Thought: Life is not a 1930's serial where invariably against long odds the underdog wins. On a football field he gets the roids kicked out of him. . . The fact that the losing team will be us, the good guys – rah-rah-hoopty-foking-rah.

The cheerleaders are holding up placards with large letters helping us fans spell out the school name. I find myself yelling along with the rest of these phonics-challenged fools. Swept up like this is that song YMCA but a bit more complicated.

George returns with a cardboard tray and hands us each a hotdog and soda and says, What's a game without snackbar pogey? He smiles at the older couple and says to me, You really need to start eating. Regain some weight. Then he wiggles his back end down and starts cheering.

The game quickly settles into a rout. The opposition going through us like we're Pop Warner Peewees. Moseby was laying some serious licks in the first half, a real gladiator against the lions. But now halfway through the third he's just going through the motions. Probably hoping that the mercy rule or a time warp kicks in. He's not the captain but is 3-year varsity starter. When he folds the rest of the second tier athletes don't stand a chance. Shadows pantomiming on a limed field.

- Watch for the pass! Deirdre yells. She's been cheering every play even as the scoreboard unbalances.

There's a play-action, Moseby gets sucked in and recovers too late. His man takes the throw over the shoulder and jets down the sidelines. A 70-yard scoring dagger.

Turn Around, Look At Me: I've seen enough, I say to George and Deirdre and jerk my thumb towards the gate.

They nod in unison though I get the feeling Deirdre would stay till the end. She seems to be really enjoying the people, the game. And keeping my leg warm.

When I stand something bounces off my jacket. I look down and there's a piece of hot dog on my seat. Is it mine, or newly arrived? I look around to see who's looking my way and notice a bunch of top-tier seniors trying hard *not* to look at me. Delinquent half-smiles. Huevos big as mustard seeds. One of them is Marcus Schmidt. Big fucking surprise. I'm amazed he waited this long to pelt me and only mildly surprised he didn't throw something heavier like his dim-witted hair-moussed friend from film who's sitting alongside him.

I could confront him but it would be a waste of time. Once in a similar situation I went and sat down in the middle of ribald dense packers. Some of my former teammates joined me and threatened to toss the young ass clowns over the back grate if they didn't knock off the BS. Big guys full of beer have a way with words.

I smile at Marcus and catch his eye. It's a smile that says now is not my time but it *will* come. Lock and load. . . George instantly catches the situation and stares down the 12th graders. Not a word, just a 6'5" guy who mentally takes names and rips away varsity jackets. George can be pretty foking intimidating when he wants to be. Added to the fact he controls personnel records and there's now a near zero percent chance that there will be any more airborne pork when we walk out.

We start down . I stumble near the bottom, and George catches my arm. Easy there Barrymore, he says. I nod and wonder why the booze is affecting me so late. Has my tolerance gone down with age and stress? Am I a bit light-headed because of Deirdre's closeness? Can horniness metabolize into alcohol? Maybe it's wanting to escape into a more worry-

189

free plane. Mind over liver. I wonder if anyone other than George suspects, or has noticed.

The Night Of The Iguana: We are following the walkway to the lots and pass TJ. standing alongside the perimeter fence near the end zone. Next to him is Audrey Clover and someone who could be Audrey's mother. Audrey and TJ are watching the game and each other. Sweet. Hand holding love under a starry moon-filled sky with the smell of fry shack burgers drifting in. A shame the vaulted heavens are almost totally obliterated by the glare of the stadium lights. A shame too their budding romance is witness to an old fashioned ass thumping on the field. Though I don't think it matters to them. Love, starry-eyed moonglow is the coin of the realm tonight. I can imagine TJ always remembering homecoming, a sweet young girl, and the night he stood next to her with a 2 hour hard-on.

I pass unobserved and belay any impulse to stop. It's time for school to really end.

I almost make it.

- Hey Mike! Tom the Battleship steps away from the fence and holds out the brown paper bag again. I again decline. Ever see a team go so total ass up? Tom asks.

- Yeah, they quit. Played like a bunch of girl scout cookies. . . Even as I say it I have no idea what it means.

- Hahaha, yeah. Girl scout cookies. Tom laughs and Deirdre is smiling like, My name is Deirdre and I approve this banter. More former teammates are turning away from the fence, offering opinions. The band has more guts, our old fullback says. QB adds, Our coach would've pulled the starters.

Not everyone is so critical. A stumpy figure in a school pullover and Ford Ranger hat steps away from the cyclone barrier and tosses in, Figures you losers would be down on the team. I suppose August here blames Curt.

For a second I don't know who-the-hell this is till he mentions Curt. Then it comes back to me. Mr. Moseby. And this is why you don't criticize a team too loudly and never any one player. Parent lightning rods.

- I never mentioned Curt, I say.

- You don't have to. I know what you think of him. He does too. . . Moseby Sr. keeps his distance. But barely. His voice is agitated, patience deregulated.

- Listen mister, Tom says, we meant no disrespect towards your son. Why don't we all go back to watching the game. Or going where we were going.

For long seconds Moseby looks as if he's going to demand pistols at dawn. Tom has maneuvered himself between Moseby and me. Not totally but enough so if Moseby wants to take a crack at my head it'll have to be a roundhouse. . . One day I'm in a standoff with the son, weeks later I'm staring down dad. Pugilistic karma, Mosebys clinging to me like slugs. I suppose I should apologize. Might de-escalate the situation. As my cable repair guy told me, Life can be simple, except when it's not.

- I'm sorry Mr. Moseby, I say, if you took personal offense. I didn't intend it. Curt played a good first half. . . I mouth the words but with bare civility. They're just words. I put out my hand and keep it out. It occurs to me I should not have hedged the apology. But honesty is honesty.

Moseby stares like it's a booby trap. Like this simple resolution is not what the little pug wants at all but would rather carry on the grudge like some poor piece of Faulkner white trash. . . What an inbred jerk, I think and immediately regret offering to shake.

I leave the hand out for long seconds, then say, If that's the way you want it mister, OK. . . I shake my head and retract the hand turning the palm towards him.

- Yeah, that's right, Moseby says. What are you going to do about it?

Do about it? My lightheadedness is gone. Wire taut nerves and the pent up frustration of my recent inimical days push me forward. I've had enough of this dotard. I'm about to say, Clean your clock, when Tom says, I got this Mike. Go ahead. Get the hell out of here. You tried.

I don't turn. Moseby and I have locked eyes. It takes George pulling at my jacket to get me moving.

As the three of us walk away I hear Tom say, We're not losers, mister. Maybe we didn't win a state title but we won the conference and. . .

Ray Moseby: *August pretends he's got nothing against Curt. But Curt, me, and his mother know better. Curt worked hard for August and all he ever got was C's and D's. That's no way to treat a kid who worked so hard. I know Curt can be a pain-in-the-ass but he tells me he behaved for August and I believe him. . . Maybe I'm still carrying a grudge. Why shouldn't I? There's tonight. August picked on Curt in the cafeteria too. Twice. I should go to the superintendent. Maybe get some other parents. . . Wants to shake hands? Like he's got a prayer. The only good news is that he no longer coaches. The team got some bad breaks tonight but Curt played good. He's a good kid.*

Tiny Bubbles: On the ride home I'm up. Still pushing adrenaline. George is not helping. Says he's a little disappointed that I didn't punch out Moseby like Papa Hemingway would have done. Even though he's only egging me on, trying to get a rise, I point out if he wanted a fight he should not have pulled me away. George laughs and I point out Hemingway never was a public school teacher and neither was Mailer or Bukowski. Mailer might have head-butted Gore Vidal, I say, but even those literary brawlers were mostly talkers.

George laughs again and calls me a pussy. It is not the kind of vulgarity that normally leaves his mouth. For a second I'm not sure what I heard. The car goes silent. I hear the intakes and outtakes of Deirdre's breath. Did you just call me a pussy? I ask turning my head. Yeah, I did, George says and keeps his eyes straight ahead. . . Pussy, huh, you stickbean fuck, I say turning my attention back to the road. I was ducking bullets when you were dodging undergrad classes. . . There's no amusement in my voice, no kidding around. I'm hot and not holding back. . . Hey Mike, I was just kidding, he says. It was a bad joke. Sorry. . . Sorry? Listen George, you don't know shit about fighting. Even less about teaching. You sit in that goddamn little private office of yours all day accountable to practically no one. While I bust my hump in the classroom and get shit on by everyone. . . My anger has ruptured. I'm hungover with a headache, and I have taken enough crap for one night. For one semester. I'm tempted to slam on the brakes and punch it out with George here and now. I'm in just enough control not to. But I dredge up the past and let go with, If it weren't for you talking me into that feckless fucking objective I wouldn't be stuck with it now. Goddamn goal that's probably going to get me fired. Pussy? What would a tight cauterized ass like you know about pussy. Fuck off.

- Christ Mike, George says and Deirdre adds, Whoa!

The car goes thunderously quiet. The only sound the engine and the ticking off of my own miserable life.

For awhile it doesn't seem as if anyone will talk. Finally as we near George's house Deirdre says that writers are supposed to cover fights not participate. She says she's proud I offered to shake back at the game, implying she'd be proud now if I offered to patch things up with George.

I pull up to George's colonial. I don't want us to part like this. It's from the heart when I say, Listen amigo. I'm sorry. I was out of line back there. Way out. I'm not myself these days. Nunberg has me on a dead reckoning to Asshole Land. See you in school Monday?. . . Yeah, he says. Forget it. You *are* an asshole. But there are worse things. . . He winks, and is gone. . . Deirdre smiles at me as if she approves this banter too. . . I'm aware that I just resorted to a self-deprecating put down to humanize the asshole me. I hope it worked. George and I have argued a lot over the years, but never to this extent. I'm not blaming him. Asshole seems to be my default position this autumn.

Harvest Home: Deirdre and I ride in silence till she asks me if everything is OK. I say, Sure, thinking she means the run-ins with Moseby and George. She says, I heard what George said earlier. I agree. You look like you have lost weight. Quite a bit. Are you eating?. . . Everything is all right, I say. Just nerves over Nunberg and school. . . We ride in silence again. At one point she drops down the window. Her hair is streaming back over the seat and she laughs as if she is getting tickled or finger massaged in sensitive areas. I don't know what is going through her mind but I can guess. Probably the same thing that's pricking mine.

I turn the corner onto dad's block and half expect to see him wandering down the sidewalk in his PJs. Maybe with the cat following. But the street is quiet, lights twinkling from most windows. Many fronts lit showcases of

Halloween and autumn displays. Artificial cobwebs, pumpkins, dried corn, painted gourds, mums, straw-stuffed figures, spiders, black cats, skulls, skeletons. Lawns of ghoulish tombstones, white-sheeted ghosts and inverted bats hanging from tree branches. A car-sized inflated pumpkin.

Man-made autumn symbols lacking only a victory bonfire and torn-down goalpost.

Aquarius - Let The Sunshine In: I pull up, the GMC idles roughly. A brief moment of awkward silence descends. This is where I half expect Deirdre to ask me if I'd like to come in for coffee or a drink. In the suspended seconds of pause, it all plays out in my under-fucked, over-strained mind. . .

I tell her I'd prefer a drink and we go in. While she's pouring I check on Max. He wasn't wandering the block but who can be sure if he is where he's supposed to be. He   always was a light sleeper.

Max is in the only ground-level bedroom and is snoring away with the complacency of a worry-free worn-out old man. The cat is curled up on the other pillow. In repose and without Ernie he seems like his old self. I close the door tight.

Deirdre is sitting on the couch sipping scotch. She hands me my drink. I can tell even before I put my lips to it that it's my usual. I didn't think Max kept gin, I say. He doesn't, Deirdre says, I bought it. . . We clink glasses. She pats a cushion. I plop down keeping an arm's length away. I need to decide fast if I'm going to make a play. Or just drink. One thing's for sure. I don't feel like a lot of small talk.

As if reading my mind she says, We could go to my room. I think we'd be more comfortable.

We stand. She takes my hand and leads me upstairs. No cock or pussy grab, not even a kiss. Romance in a holding pattern. I cannot think of anything as we climb the stairs but how her booty moves on separate springs. First one bun up-and-down, then the other up-down-and-twist.

Fornicating-only zone approaching.

As soon as we're in the bedroom we're kissing. Her hands unbuttoning my shirt. My hands up-and-under her silky blouse feeling the softness of her breasts, the hardness of her nipples. My shirt is off. I pull her blouse up-and-over her head. She's kissing my chest. One hand is down my pants, the other is pressed against the back of my head drawing me into a deep lingering kiss. . . She's working my stiffy and I am suddenly aware that we need to slow down or this is going to be really embarrassing if I finish before we even get into bed.

I grab her forearm and pull her hand out. I step back and drop my pants and shorts. She steps out of her own, and we tumble into a bed where I used to dream of banging Loni Anderson, Jaclyn Smith, Farrah Fawcett, Raquel Welch, and a host of other pictorial skin queens..

Now it's flesh-to-someone else's delicious flesh. The smell of skin and her muffy muff. The moans and groans of uninhibited carnality. The years of abstinence being swept away by the hurricane 10 force of greedy all-consuming suck face and lust.

She's on top of me and works my boyo into her candy cupboard. . . It's all I can do to say something about a rubber. She shakes her head in a dreamy way and says not to worry. That everything is all right.

Any concerns I have disappear fast.

She starts pelvic inundations like she's riding a slowly rising sea. The waves lifting and dropping her with waltz-like rhythm. I try staring at the vague outline of an old U-2 poster on the wall. Force myself to concentrate

196

on baseball and Willie Mays like Woody Allen once suggested. It's not working. Deirdre is moaning louder. Grinding down hard on me, then giving it a swirl. I try, and try, and try. Finally let go.

We climax together. She falls on top of me. She's breathing heavily into my ear and her still panting excitement is not letting my own heart rate come down. We're slippery and lubricated. I'm thinking we should do this again. Wankie is softening but not much. I roll her off me. We're side-by-side, kissing again. Working each other's body. Things are heating up fast.

I'm scarcely aware of any sound but our own breathing and moaning till the door flies open. Someone is silhouetted in the frame. Deirdre stifles a scream and we break apart. Pull up the covers. Heads peek out.

- Ernie? Max says. What are you doing in here? It's hard to see.

At first I'm not sure if I should respond. Then remember Max is back in the past.

- It's just me Dad. . . I get out of bed. Find my shorts in the semi-darkness and take Max by the arm. . . Why don't you go back to bed, I say. It's late.

- Is there someone else here? he asks trying to see in yellow gray-ness. . . Deirdre and I didn't pull the shades down and the street lamp across the street is fighting through the branches and leaves of the big front maple. It's breaching the window sheers, bathing the room in muted charcoal dimness. Enough to see outlines, not details. An October dreamscape à la Tim Burton and the headless horseman.

- No Dad, there's not. Let me help you downstairs.

I close the door behind us, turn on the hall light, and we descend the stairs slowly without talking. I get him back into bed and he's asleep almost before I pull the blanket up. I kiss the top of his head and turn out the light. I don't think he will remember this in the morning.

Did the creaking of the bed, the moaning, groaning wake him? Maybe trigger long dormant memories of Bernice and him? Will it now provide the basis for some REM sex of his own?. . . I hope it does. Hope Mad Max gets some sort of sex high tonight even if it's only in the sleep stage. Every person should get to release his sperm, vaginal fluids. Realize his or her neon sexuality regardless of age or demons. The more fluids released, the less internal pressure. The less pressure, the healthier the person. Hell it may even be patriotic. Happy contented people, happy contented country. Peace for all.

I go to the bathroom and quickly note that August's Peter Principle is in play i.e. every excited dinky rises beyond its level of easy peeing. Sagging but not as limb as overcooked pasta. Going for a double-header tonight is out. Neither the energy nor the 180+ degree angle.

I grab our drinks and walk back upstairs feeling like Ichabod Drained.

Deirdre is lying in bed but not asleep. I sit down alongside her. Hand her the scotch, prop up a pillow, lean back. I force a good natured laugh and say, What a night!. . . She clinks our glasses and says, It was great. Still is. . . Asks how Max is and I say fine. Tells me her first impulse when she saw someone in the door was that Jimmy Klein trailed us. Says she's seen him around town peeking into windows. And he always gives her the big once-over like he's putting down a deposit. Starts to say she has the knack of attracting— but cuts herself off.

We drink in silence. After a couple of minutes she rubs my leg and kisses my chest. . . The gin is cold and energizing, as is her electric touch. Peter is starting to stir again.

She reaches down and gives him a squeeze. Then starts stroking. She kisses my chest, then rolls half on top of me. She kisses me hard. Her hand is pulling, her tongue exploring. Her fingernails now working with a light airy touch. She moves to my ear and is biting and tugging. I am hard again. Rigid as a joystick.

This time I get on top and pump her with long strokes. Delaying the downbeat, shoving it in hard and deep. She's moaning, swearing, telling me to do it, do it, YES, YES!. . .

The night becomes a bottomless well. Lust-in-the-heart. Rediscovered ecstasy.

What Kind Of Fool Am I?: Thanks for a wonderful evening Mike, Deirdre's voice is soft. Barely breaks through my starlit reverie. I slowly become aware again that the GMC is idling roughly like it might stall. I silently debate for a few long seconds, then decide to go for it. I put my arm around her like some Lover's Lane teen parker. Lean in close. Her eyes are wide, mine closing. Just when I think I might be doing a little tonsil exploration she pulls back. I see her hand outstretched in friendship, her collar pulled high against the night chill that's settling in. I need to get going, she says and adds, long day tomorrow. I had a great time. Thanks again. I really mean it.

We shake. I start to open my car door but she says, No need. It's not a rough neighborhood. . . I watch her walk up the driveway. She turns at the breezeway, gives me a wave, and disappears inside.

I drive away breathing deeply. Wonder if it's possible I just lived the Carl Sagan novel Contact. That I entered a ripple in time-space. Shot through a worm hole. Entered a parallel universe where in fact I did fuck the same, but a different Deirdre. A universe with a different passage of time. And now I'm back, driving away. Recently fucked, but not fucked at all. Pure, virgin-like. But a guy who just got his cock cleaned, his horns dulled. Cognitive time travel.

Too complicated. I need to keep life simple out here. It's complicated enough in school.

Deirdre Good: *When Mike went to kiss me I was a little surprised. But not upset. Maybe if he hadn't been drinking earlier I would have let him. And maybe added a little steam of my own. Though it would not have been good for either of us. I suppose I could have invited him in for coffee or a drink, but I really am tired. Of course it's his family house so he doesn't really need an invitation to come in and maybe check on Max. I am happy he didn't. He might have left with hurt feelings if he thought anything was going to happen like a kitchen kiss, and bedroom fuck.*

Chapter 16

Saturday

Sunrise In the Isles

'S **Wonderful:** Sophia Arbuckle is sitting opposite me in El America Ecuatoriano. Her hair is pulled up in a topknot, and she's wearing a bright floral blouse with black slacks. The black has a slimming effect but she doesn't need help. She is straight, thin, but not shapeless. Breasts jutting out over a flat stomach. Classical pose, body in perfect synch with music from an invisible orchestra. The music that is actually playing is marimba and flute, as easy on the ears as Sophia is on the eyes.

- Mr. August! Marie and Edgar are alongside us almost as soon as we sit down. We are so happy you brought your lady friend. . . Mister and Missus study Sophia like she's a rare tropical bird while I make the introductions. . . You are so pretty, Mrs. Espinoza says. We are happy you have found your way to our modest place.

When we're alone Sophia says she didn't know I was such a celebrity. I tell her little pond, little fish. Point out my review on the wall, two more recent ones from other newspapers, and explain my mentoring status with Jorge. This is a side of you I never knew, she says.

The room is crowded, and loud. We have a table in the back corner of the front window by a large leafy plant. A weeping fig, according to Sophia. It doesn't block my view of the cemetery and my car. The cemetery reminds me of my situation back in school. I turn my head slightly and it disappears. I don't mind seeing my car. Even if it is a junker with dented door, creased bumper, and mismatched plates. It's that kind of neighborhood.

I order the paella, Sophia the lengua asada – roast tongue in tomato sauce. At least that is what I think Marie said. Sophia smiles when I ask for a repeat translation and laughs when I ask if it's anything I should go for. If you have to ask, she says, you can't afford the indigestion. . . On the safer side we're going to split an avocado salad. Safer I think than some of the unpronounceable alternatives. . . Sophia is drinking a short glass of Zhumir Passion Fruit Ecuador, a potent firewater. She's drinking it straight up with a water chaser. I'm having a light Ecuadorian lager.

Sophia is smiling, sipping, looking around. Terrific paintings, she says. Someone's very talented. . . I tell her about Zoe. When I finish she says, If Zoe would like to increase her exposure, a friend of mine runs a small performing arts theater about 70 miles from here. Very upscale clientele. She uses the lobby as an contemporary art gallery and she's always looking to discover new talent.

She looks around at all the paintings and says, Think it would it be OK if I snapped a few pictures?

She takes out her cell, excuses herself to the diners, and works fast. The salad arrives and we start.

I Love You, Alice B. Toklas!: The meal is leisurely. Sophia orders another Zhumir. I laugh and ask if she's feeling anything. I'm not driving, she says, and besides who doesn't want to feel something?. . . A girl after my own heart, I say. . . She says, It's not your heart I am after. . . She's teasing. . . I wonder if it would be too bold to answer the implied? E.B. White said, Be obscure clearly. Sophia isn't obscure. She's clear. Clearly horny. At least I think. . . I don't think she can be scared off by an equally suggestive remark. I take a chance and say, You're welcome to anything from the neck down. I need my head to butt against the wall during school. . . Ha, she says, but didn't you say in the car, No school talk?

The conversation shifts to old times, missed opportunities. Flirts with unrealized love. I'm heating up, she seems to be too. I ask if she is interested in dessert. I am, she says, but only if we have coffee later at my place. . . We order the rice pudding and she starts telling me about her divorce. Theater demands long hours, she says, many nights away from home. . .

Jimmy Crack Corn: She's still talking about the disjointed life theater demands when a pedestrian appears in the window. He doesn't see me. Is blind to anyone, anything, but the paintings. It's Jimmy Fuck You Klein. He's in no hurry. Continues to stare past the diners, some now staring at him. Mrs. Espinoza comes out and shoos him away. He looks at her. Grabs his biceps and rams his forearm straight up, fist pointing to the heavens. He lights a cigarette and walks off towards the cemetery.

- What are you looking at? Sophia asks turning around.

- Zoe's father, I say. That's him looking at my GMC.

Klein is studying the dent on the passenger side door and looks puzzled. He gives the car a walk-around. Looks at the school parking sticker. He's fighting through a fog that's lifting fast. He straightens up and reaches into his pocket. . . I'll be right back, I say and move fast through the chicane of tables. By the time I clear the door he's keyed the length of the green paint and is squatting down next to a rear tire unscrewing the valve cap. I'm running and thinking I'm too old for this Dudley Do-Right shit. My knees aching even as I attempt to lift them higher to gain speed.

- Klein! I shout.

His head jerks up. There's instant recognition but no fast motor skills. He's barely on his feet when I get to him. He punches straight for my eye with the key but he's slow. It's nothing to block the jab and counter with a smashing right to the jaw. He lurches backward into the car, bounces, and crumbles like used toilet paper.

- I saw it all, Sophia is suddenly alongside me. Her breathy voice in my ear. She snaps a pic of the Klein slumped against the car, mouth open.

- Call 911, I   say, even as she's keying it. . . I bend over Klein. He's coming to. This is a scene we've played before and like before I'm thinking even if he is a POS, the value of one square of TP, I should have at least pulled my punch. Foregone the old razzmatazz. Instant regret. Instant wish that our fighting did not have the well established provenance it does.

The Espinozas join the growing circle and in the distance a siren is already screaming open the evening. Sophia is explaining to the Espinozas what happened while a small group listens. I'm watching Klein, asking him if he's OK, telling him not to move. He mouths a barely audible *fuck you*. That's when I know he's all right.

Back In The Saddle Again: At Sophia's house we're in a mutual hurry after wasting so much time waiting around and giving statements. We missed dessert at the restaurant but this final course trumps sweet. . . Her lips are velvet, liquid silk. So soft that at first I am scarcely aware we are kissing. An oral caress. . . She might have been in an equal hurry to get started, but she is in no hurry to finish. She breaks apart several times to look into my eyes and stroke my neck and chest. Sustained slow motion. . . We start in the kitchen, wind up in the bedroom, with stops at way stations in the living room and stairs. . . Each touch, each bite, each nibble lingering slowness. The clock 3 time zones back. My peeter is not totally rigid at first. Not pulsating with the same desire as my psyche. I wonder if it is nerves over school. Over tonight's confrontation with Klein. Over performance now. . . Perhaps I'm losing it from not using it. Or it is just simply age, and the idea that Viagra comes to everyone in the end?

It takes long seconds but with some light feathery tactile help from Sophia, peeter gets there. Sophia's own honeypot is not quite as wet as I remember womenhood being. And my winky gets a little roughed up. Still the sex is great, though the lust-to-fuck ratio is too high and I don't last as long as I would like. I come first, she is right after me.

Then she rolls over. Without a word. And is asleep within seconds. It's pretty damn funny, except that it's not. No slinky fucks tonight that keep coming and coming.

I dress and tiptoe out feeling like I just got used. Drive-by sex. An enriched sense of wham-bam-thank-you-man. Except the wham-bam was in waltz time, and I was not thanked. As if we're a pair of toffs and this is Downton Abbey.

In The Midnight Hour: Riding home I think of how strange it is, but how great to fulfill such a long time fantasy. Unrealized decades, countless moon-eyed faculty meetings. . . Actress Rita Hayworth said, Men fall in love with Gilda but they wake up with me. None of those letdown feelings for me. And I hope none for Sophia. I don't know if I curled her toes. But I did mess her hair and cause a small explosion of moans and sighs. She got me just as pyro-tactile hot.

205

The headlights pierce the night, I pierced her. Rubber humming on the pavement.   Nunberg and school briefly intrude and I flirt with the notion that tonight is a good omen. That regardless of what happens with my 6 and Nunberg I'm not a total loser. I performed pretty well with Sophia. Pretty damn well, and there is solace in that physical fact. Who knew if I even could after so many years? I start to feel a sense of pride when it dawns on me that I'm only dancing on a domed volcano. School won't be dormant much longer. And its effects will be *much* longer lasting than sex with a side of paella and lengua asada breath. Sophia and I used each other tonight, Nunberg is using me. Why and for what end, I have no idea. But I have a strong sense that I have not been in charge of anything. Not tonight, not in school.

Sophia Arbuckle: *I'm awake, it's 3 a.m., and Mike is gone. I'm fine with it. I've slept alone for so many years that I prefer it. Don't mind dining alone either. You can get used to anything. . . Dining with Mike was great, though he seemed distracted at times like he was forcing himself to stay focused on us. Might be my imagination, or his lack of dating. . . He's as charming as I remember from the old days. I thought he might drink too much like he used to sometimes. But he stuck to a couple of beers . . The love making came as no surprise. That's one good thing about getting older – no false modesty. . . Mike was breathing pretty hard after that run. He needs to take better care of himself. I'll be happy to give him a leg up with the sex workouts. Tonight's was good. It's no big deal he needed a little extra help. He's a satisfying partner though I don't see us as becoming exclusive or long term. Maybe years ago if we'd both been free. Maybe not. Missed love* *takes on glamour with the years. . . I hope he's not upset that I fell asleep so fast.*

Chapter 17

Calendar Flip - 3 Weeks
Moving To The Dog

The Day Of The Locust: Classes may fit patterns and stereotypes, just like people. But ultimately each class is a living dynamic organism with its own DNA. The marker of this particular junior group I would call the middle finger. They are nuts, academically alive as dead fish. Care as much about school as they do about world hunger or nuclear waste.

Today a particular uniqueness is that they smell.   Literally. They are radiating noxious malodorous waves of ober-sweet stench that are making my sinuses and nasal passages close up.

And they are hyper. Many turned around. Voices loud, out-of-control.

- What the heck is going on in here? I ask. Quiet DOWN! And what is that smell?

The noise dims and from the back Womb Reject #1 states, It's sort of like when you fart after eating turnips. Womb Reject #2 says, It's Adrianna's perfume Mr. August. She was squirting a bunch of people.. . . I look at Adrianna. She's smiling in that way that says guilty but not embarrassed.

I know she sees herself as class clown. But this time she's gone too far.

- What's going on Adrianna? I ask calmly like the conversation involves 2-ring vs 3-ring notebooks.

- Is something wrong? she asks.

I walk closer until I'm standing alongside her desk. I restrain the urge to pull a dog and sniff her. Or dust her for odorant molecules. It's not necessary. The air around her is powerful enough to down small planes. Bring tears to the heads on Rushmore. Gag me with a spoon, as my former students would have said.

Adrianna   is not a bad sort. Not evil like Veda in Mildred Pierce or demonic like Mary in The Children's Hour. Just a screwball comedienne whose bolts were never fully tightened. At least she's not playing with her iPhone today, though that would be less intrusive.

- Who got squirted? I ask.

Half dozen hands go up. A couple of these students are smiling, the others look P.O.'d like taking a shower with lily-of-the-toilet-cleanser is not too cool. . . It is funny in a Three Stooges farcical way. But I could easily lose it because it's trouble with Adrianna, AGAIN! Damn girl. . . I briefly consider ignoring it. Then remember I got written up the last time I blew off flagrant misbehavior.

I go over to the windows. It's a beautiful sun filled day. I pull up the blinds and throw open the glass. Immediately there are complaints that it's too cold. Can we go to our lockers to get our jackets? a shivering first row girl wants to know. . . Rather than a mass exodus, I say, how about if all those people doused with perfume go to the lav and wash it off. Scrub good, I say. I don't think some of those cheap brands come off with anything less than a sandblasting or acid dip.

- That   perfume   wasn't   cheap, Adrianna protests. Eight dollars for 4 ounces of. . . she looks at the bottle. . . classic eau de *something*.

- Congratulations on your French, I say. Chez Pepé Le Pew.

Adrianna is suddenly on her feet joining the lav diaspora. I jump up and say, Not *you!*. . . She shrugs, sits back down. Goes into an extreme pout. When WR #2 teases her, she sprays him.

I lose it. Kick the plastic wastepaper basket into the wall. It hits with a hollow thud, bounces for a few tumbles, and leaves a wake of discarded paper, hi-energy drink cans, and candy wrappers. Which deadens the class. For prolonged seconds I don't know what to say. I've never vented my anger in such a physical way. Not even when I was an assistant football coach. This girl, this year are making me crazy.

It vaguely occurs to me that Adrianna might be ADHD. No paperwork on her, but she might have slipped under the radar. Would not be the first. I should check with guidance and refer her for testing.

But that's later. For now. . .

I say, Damn it, Adrianna. GIVE ME THAT PERFUME! You are *not* getting a lav break. But you ARE getting another detention. . . There's no protest this time. For some reason I think of my 6 mentees. Cannot imagine any of them behaving like this. There are a lot of qualities they lack. But not manners or respect for school.

I take the perfume and kick the basket again. It tumbles into the corner. I sit down and take a minute to calm down. The remaining students are quiet. Even Adrianna for once. I think about retrieving the basket and scattered trash. Decide to let it all lie. I just sit and stare.

The room is unnaturally quiet. Zip Code 00000. They say women suffer more than men physically because men produce more endogenous opioids, eurochemicals that function as natural anesthetics. I don't know how true that is. Adrianna doesn't seem to be suffering.

The familiar click-clack of leather soles on tile turns my head towards the door. Nunberg walks by with Superintendent Hoxley. She's practically fused to his side. Doesn't give me or the room a glance. Her nose must be stuffed.

I look at the scattered trash and it vaguely occurs to me that I'm developing an anger management problem. Rapidly. I put it out of mind.

Over The Rainbow: I take a breather after class before my first conference. Put Adrianna out of mind. Think of Sophia and how great Saturday night was. The thrill of the unexpected. But hoped for. Definitely takes the edge off Friday night and the finish with Deirdre. . . And where are Sophia and I this morning? Should she have my varsity sweater and class ring?. . . Sophia doesn't seem like the hearts-and-flowers type. Even if she were walking bowlegged with her neck in a brace.

Me, either.

Ditto on Deirdre.

She seemed fine Sunday when I picked up Max. Never mentioned my clumsy car move. Or hinted at it. I invited her along for lunch but she said she was buried in schoolwork. Seemed friendly enough. Asked me a couple of history questions. If there was any sense of lost sex or resentment over my shoulder grab, it didn't show. Hope I didn't leave prints. . . Whether Deirdre and I will screw down the road who can say. Probably not, especially with Sophia in the picture. If she's indeed in it. . . But why say no? Today's no becomes tomorrow's yes when the zippers are in alignment. The more adamant the denial, the more likely the occurrence, says August the fictional lover and the Casanova profiler. . . If we ever do have sex I'll keep it close. Zip the pants and mouth. I'm no tittie-tattler. Never was.

I smile to myself at the bullshit that drifts into my mind. And during school too.

The Impossible Dream: Jorge Espinoza puts a paper bag in front of me and says, My mother wanted you to have this. It's some of our favorite dishes she thought you might like. Don't microwave them. They'll be better reheated in the oven.

- Wow. Tell her thanks, Jorge. I don't know what I did to deserve this but my bachelor bones are greatly appreciative. . . I peek into the bag and say, This looks and smells great. . . Even as I say it I think of the perfumed smells of the morning and immediately put those brain sterilized dim-wahs out of mind. I'm mentally down in the favela now and it's much more pleasant.

- My family is really appreciative for all those paintings you brought in, Mr. August. They get a lot of comments and I think one sold yesterday. And of course your review.

- The review was my pleasure. As far as the paintings go your family is doing Zoe Koppel the big favor. She is very appreciative. . . I wonder to myself how Zoe will react to the impending influx of money. Can you buy happy?

- I really like the paintings, Jorge says. I know who Zoe is. I never knew she was so talented.

- She's like you Jorge. A hidden treasure in this school. . . Jorge is not the kind of kid to emote sentimentality but he looks pleased with the compliment. . . I mention how Sophia Arbuckle and I enjoyed their restaurant Saturday. He says he doesn't know her. Has never been in the theater wing. I tell him about her department, the upcoming play, the meal we had.

It's a pleasant conversation, food and theater. I milk it for awhile enjoying what D.H. Lawrence called the triviality which forms common human intercourse. Then I get serious. Mention how his mom told me he wants to be a Spanish teacher. It's a commendable goal Jorge, I say, I had no idea. You never said a word about it.

He's quiet. Teacher, it's going to be my goal for him. I need to take it slow. Outside in the hall there's the sound of lockers slamming, students running. Never enough time when you're 16.

I smile at Jorge in my best Father Confessor mien and he says, I kept it to myself because it's such a pipe dream. I don't like getting my hopes up. And I didn't want to burden you with my problems.

- It's no burden, I say. Mentoring is why I'm here. . . Remind him that Holden Caulfield in Catcher In the Rye said to never tell anybody anything. But he was pretty screwed up, I say.

I talk about dreams. How they should be the modus operandi in life. Quote John Barrymore's, You're not old till regrets take the place of dreams.

- Mr. August, do you have dreams? Jorge asks awkwardly, unexpectedly.

I'm instantly reminded of The Kid and us sharing the personal. Pretty much avoided it with the others. So far. It'd be an injustice to call it the sharing game as if life is a big LED scoreboard with fireworks if you win. Sharing is more like living full up. With soul. And honesty. Or so my latest mentoring revelation is telling me.

- I have dreams, I say, *and* regrets. . . A regret – I certainly wish I could have done more when my wife Amanda was dying. I've asked myself many

213

times if there was something I missed. Did I make her happy enough? If she had laughed more, would the cancer never have taken hold?

The confession shakes me. I revealed more than I intended. Looks like it shook Jorge a little too. He's probably thinking if he Googles *whacked out* I'll be the first listing. August the grand boulevardier loses the mystique. Alexander Woollcott said some people are successes, some are failures, and only God knows which are which. Nice thought. But I don't think being human = being a failure. We're all winners to some degree. Another revelation this morning.

- Let's talk about your dream of becoming a Spanish teacher, I say. I'm going to assume money is the issue. . . I tell him that his grades are very good and the fact he's Ecuadorian plays to racial diversity. But I'm thinking the best way to go would be an athletic scholarship, I say. Especially combined with those other factors. . . He reminds me he doesn't play school sports. I remind him of his size and say, And if your strength and speed are remotely what you said, I'm confident there's a full ride waiting for you.

I explain how I used to coach. That I still have a few college contacts. Normally I let guidance or the athletic department handle these things, I say, but. . .

We talk about his options. Agree that I'll try to set up an athletic assessment. I emphasize that there are no promises. That my Rolodex is a bit dated. I'll do my best, I say.

It occurs to me that this is going to be a lot of work. Definitely above and beyond. I wonder if this is all about meeting my objective or maybe if some part of it is because I like this kid. I mean, I know I like him but I like my bartender too and so far I haven't offered to wash glasses or clean tap lines for him. . . I think what I'm feeling is a sense of bonding. Something

that hasn't happened in a long time with anyone. Much less a student. . .
Jorge told me he had my back, and proved it. Guess I'm covering his
now. . . I think to myself that maybe Curt's dad is right. Maybe I really *don't*
like his kid and *do* play favorites. But it's hard not to when you have a teen
like this. And a ompaloompa like Curt.

There's abrupt repeated banging on a hall locker just outside the door
and a strident shout, Hey August you ASSHOLE! Followed by the sounds
of fleeing feet.

It's so sudden we're both taken back for a split second before Jorge
jumps up. He's checked only by the lock grip I throw on his wrist. I shake
my head. Half expect him to pull away, which he could easily do. But he
sits back down. . . I shake my head one more time and say, I thank you.
But *don't* do it, OK? I don't want you getting into trouble over this old man.

Destiny appears at the door.

Do The Hustle: Destiny is her usual head-turning self in a body hugging
lace print dress with sheer arm panels and hemline across the upper
thighs. Very tight, very exposing. When Churchill said, Nothing succeeds
like excess, I don't think he was thinking of school fashion. Her curves are
rounded like the Appalachians, her butt crack Great Gorge depth.

I introduce her to Jorge and they act as if they never met. She twists her
head slightly in appraisal. He looks squarely at her. Dark eyes flashing on
both sides. I'm thinking *he's* thinking he'd like to squeeze her like
supermarket fruit. Then he's gone. Suddenly. Like his passport or green
card was revoked.

Jorge Espinoza: *I like Mr. August a lot and don't think it's a stretch to say
my family is never going to be able to repay him. My grandfather is*

215

different. We read Mr. August's review to him and he said, Writing about food is like singing about soccer. One is not the other. . . Grandpa is hard to impress. Says that the only true reviewer is the taste buds. And the only real advertising word-of-mouth. I think the cancer is making him bitter. . . I hope I do well at that athletic assessment. I'm not going to tell my family about it in case I don't. An awful lot hinges on it. Like my entire future. . . I didn't know Mr. August is mentoring Destiny too. She didn't give even one sign she remembered we're in the same graduating class, I guess because we are not in the same league. I'd better concentrate on that sports assessment. And leave the hot smart ladies for college. Or to my wet dreams.

Beyond The Sea: When I'm left with the wistful African violet I say off-handedly, Guess you and Jorge don't know each other. . . Destiny doesn't respond and I toss out, He's another senior I'm mentoring.

- I've seen him around but he has never been in any of my classes, she says patting her hair.

- He's going to be a very successful man someday. A much under-valued stock in this school. . . But let's talk about you. You mentioned the last time we met that your creative well is dry?

- I have the analytical thoughts and structure. Just no fresh ways of expressing them, she says while repositioning a hair pin. Live poetry write prose had a good run. But it's over.

The analog wall clock ticks off the seconds and I take half a minute to construct an answer, while briefly wondering if Destiny's hair is so naturally straight. . . I should have been prepared but time in-and-out of school has been refrigerated.

- Damon Runyon said, All poetry gets written before you take up a pen, I finally say. It's in the dreaming. Have to let go. . . One strategy writers before you have used is simply to copy down good writing. Find a quality poem or a really good lyrical piece you like. Hand write it word-for-word. Maybe more than once. Write slowly. Let the mystical footfalls imprint the brain.

Destiny says she never heard of that strategy.

- Shelby Foote the great Civil War historian wrote his manuscripts with a quill dipped in ink because it forced him to slow down. To blend with his subject matter. Said he did not want anything mechanical between the paper and him. Not a typewriter. Not a pen. Certainly not a computer.

- You're suggesting I write with a quill and ink? Deirdre asks very seriously.

- Ha. No. I don't even know what office supply store or farm sells quills anymore. Even listening to music would be good. Concentrating on the lyrics. Singing along. Letting the words and phrases weave in that way.

As I give her some of my pop and Grammy favorites I can't help noticing she's not flashing me today. Actually has her legs shoved under the table and is not leaning forward to give me the Grand Canyon. Guess that phase of this student-teacher is over. Thank god. . . Maybe she's thinking of Jorge now. It would be a good match. Many similarities. . . Being a dating game host is certainly *not* my job or objective. But this Cupid factotum does add a soap opera dimension that I find entertaining. Don't think Nunberg would find it impressive. Or offer to key the applause track or catch my stage dive. But she's not a romantic.

Destiny is actually using her laptop to take notes on my guru gems. Keyboarding, tapping, clicking. Could not be farther from the quill and ink bottle idea. Which is pretty damn time wastingly ironic. But OK. They're just notes.

While she's typing I wonder to myself just how much you can really improve creativity. Maybe it's like our football team. A mentor can only get out what god. . . Destiny's creativity has improved. A little. Very little. Whether or not it'll be enough to get that valedictorian slot for her, I have my doubts. Which would then leave me with finding another way to improve her. Smile. Shit. That damn objective. It's sad and the stuff of Greek tragedy that my entire career now hinges on the improvement of Destiny and the other five. The high and mighty brought low by. . .

As we wind down the meeting I ask nonchalantly if she saw who was banging on the locker just before she arrived. You mean the one who called you an *asshole*? she asks. I laugh and say, Yes. The one with the limited vocabulary and thoughtful psychoanalysis. . . I don't know the name, she says, but the description is easy. . . She gives me a quick verbal sketch and I'm surprised. I was figuring Adrianna or Marcus. Maybe Madison. But *this*? Almost a smile. Just goes to prove that just because you're paranoid doesn't mean they are *not* out to get you. Even the ones you barely know.

Destiny Gibson: *August's strategies are just unusual enough that they might work. But they sound awfully time consuming and I'm not sure I have that much to spare. . . Asia tells me I will be the first black valedictorian in the school's history if I make it. I normally don't care about such race considerations but I have to admit I would be proud of that. So would my parents. Dad loves to remind me how he grew up in the ghetto and rose to owner of his liquor distribution company through hard work. He tells me I'm lucky I never had his struggles. I guess he's right but I have my own* *struggles here. Asia tells me I use my clothes and looks as a weapon, as if she's a rag doll herself. Maybe she's right, but why not look great if you can?. . . Speaking of looks, Jorge is looking awfully hot today. He's almost too good looking to be straight. I wonder if that was a look of sex interest. Or if he was just checking out my clothes and jewelry?*

Praise The Lord And Pass The Ammunition: The auditorium is not even half filled but that's because it's so cavernous. Not because of lack of interest. The joint is jumping with around 400 professionals. Some ready to give Nunberg, Hoxley, and the board of ed the old Mussolini. The noise is high. Scattered faces twisted in paroxysms of emotion. It's definitely not the usual banal sterility that marks most union gatherings.

I hate staying after school beyond the time we can contractually leave. But this union meeting is key to my year and for most of these other potential Inquisitionees. Despite the palpable passion in the air I doubt if it will come down to even a vote of no confidence. Much less anything radical like a tar-and-feathering.

The ceiling is scalloped. Hollywood Bowl effect. It's lifting and throwing the noise   to every corner. Loud. Backslap Alley. Old reunion times. Teachers from all over the district renewing friendships. Recalling mutual struggles and yesterday's affairs, intercourse, BJ's. Manny and Howard catch my eye and give me the come-hither sign like I am some foking waiter. I smile, wave them off. See Sophia sitting in the middle of a crowded row. This must be serious for you to be missing the Grease rehearsal, I say loudly. She laughs and mouths, *Rescheduled.* I mouth back, *See you soon,* and she flashes the halogen lamp smile.

I find an aisle seat towards the back behind Becky Capello. She turns around and asks, What do you think? I don't figure she's asking about my chances of getting the shag on again with Sophia so I tell her that in the past whenever there were big issues teachers gave impassioned speeches. The union wrote lengthy recommendations. Then the BOE went ahead and did what they were going to do anyway.

We're Not Gonna Take It: The meeting is called to order. The cacophony lowers to a dry buzz. I know it's going to be a hot time when the union president starts right off with, Tyrants conduct monologues above a million solitudes. The U.P. says it's from Albert Camus in The Rebel.

The U.P. is 50-something. Wears a business suit. Looks like what-if Eleanor Roosevelt fucked Jimmy Durante and had a kid. She says she's heard complaints from teachers in every school. Has talked to the superintendent and board chairperson and the outlook is grim.

Says, The bottom line is money and it's just not there. We went over the facts and figures with them. Either we agree to a voluntary pay freeze or we will lose staff. . . She speculates that the board would like to lose the highest wage earners. Though the board denies it, she says. Adds, They also won't agree to a buyout, or any incentive to retire. They deny any negative strategies. They do admit to a lot of pressure from the taxpayers group to keep next year's budget frozen.

There's excited murmuring in the hall. I check out Howard and Manny who are looking as serious as sentries on the DMZ. . . I totally understand that *all* of you would certainly prefer to retire or leave the profession altogether when *you* are ready, she says calmly, and not when the board says it's time.

There is a sign-up list to speak. A dozen people are already in the speaking queue.

The first speaker is an old timer from the tech department who used to teach wood shop and now is handling computer drafting. He's got a lot of words, lots of serpentining points. People are starting to look at wristwatches when he finally hits the bore hole. A productive past is a great past, he says, but it's a shame it doesn't count for anything with this administration. He coughs, looks around at the teachers as if hoping for a sub. Reads the rest from a note card. I've been a teacher for 40 years, he says forcefully. Took refresher courses, went back to go forward. Now that I'm old they want to turn out this gray hair like some old dog. It's wrong.

There's scattered applause. Some head for the toilets. One fervent – Way to go Woody!. . . Becky turns around and under-tones, You'd think he'd *want* to retire!. . . He objects, I say, to how it's happening. . . I understand that, she says, but 40 years! He's been working here almost twice as long as I've been alive! She repeats, Forty years. It's like 2 lifetimes in hell with Nunberg.

People start shushing us and Becky turns around but not before say-ing, Hope you haven't forgotten Project Principal. . . Italian dinner, I say knowing my line. . . I wonder to myself if I can really pull it off. Felt with the belief a child has in Santa or an adult with the Red Sox that somehow, someway, something would open up to get Nunberg's fat tush out of my life. And Becky's. And everyone's. But I'm starting to doubt that now. This assembly isn't helping.

The speakers talk on. Some new and fresh ideas. Others old and schoolworn. Administrators want to play hardball and hold us accountable, but who holds *them* accountable? gets a big round of applause along with,

If we are being asked to sacrifice raises and positions, what is administration sacrificing?

I think to myself that the day is going down with no solution. Which is not surprising. Meetings are group fondles. Usually just a time to blow off steam.

Don't Bore Us, Get To The Chorus: The last speaker finishes and the U.P. asks if there's anyone else.

Against my better judgment I rise. I know this is going to piss off a lot of the tenured old farts. With no gain on my part. But someone needs to state the obvious. Manny gives me a thumbs up, Howard just stares.

I walk to the front of the auditorium, say my name and school into the mike, and hesitate. There's a respective silence. Could be they're anticipating finally getting *the* word. More likely everyone's just tired. And P.O.'d that I'm dragging out this meeting. There's always one, they're thinking.

The bottom line for me is that I don't want to see anyone lose a job, I say into the mike and instantly get a squelch of electronic feedback. Especially our younger staff members, I say pulling back embarrassed. . . I talk about understanding the feelings of the tenured staff especially the ones who fought the good fight, sacrificed contract concessions over decades to get our pay scale up. I say, Some of you may recall I was part of the negotiation team.

There's light applause. They sense I'm building . . . Fact is, I say shift-ing my weight, as much as we want shared sacrifice and it's only fair that everyone do his or her part, we can't force it. We have absolutely no say in administrators' salaries. Or in their numbers. It's a shame, it's not fair. And in a just world they themselves would insist on cuts to their own monies and numbers. It's not going to happen. So, since apparently there's no way around it without losing some of our most valued colleagues, we need to accept a wage freeze for next year. If that's what we have to do, then let's do it.

Someone shouts, That's no guarantee they won't squeeze us anyway. . . True, I say and look around to put a face to the voice. It's tough to be an idealist, I say to the younger middle school teacher. But idealism is why I became a teacher and I am not willing to give that up. Not for people like our bosses who don't appreciate it. Especially not for them.

There's silence in the auditorium. I finish with, Chekhov's characters were always going to Moscow and never getting there. It's time for us to go to Moscow.

I walk back to my seat and can feel some glares and withering looks. There is also a spattering of support. Thin, like gulag borscht. Like whatever it was I hoped to accomplish. I feel washed out. I also feel as if I at least *tried* to do the right thing.

Madame President tries to close the meeting on the thought that nothing needs to be done immediately. Which starts more discussion.

I grab my coat and Becky says, Mike, when I grow up I want to be like you. . . I look into her green eyes and they are twinkling moist. . . I start to thank her when she says, But I'd rather go to Vegas.

I laugh, and I am clear of the parking lot before the crowd hits the doors. Frank Sinatra is singing about autumn winds on the car radio and the wind outside is picking up the brown dried leaves and blowing them across my path.

I'm tired.

Head to Max's.

Becky Capello: *I give Mike a lot of credit for saying what he did. The man has meatballs. Most of the older teachers don't give us newbies the time of day. Much less put their own butts on the line for us. I hardly know most of them, and they don't go out of their way to know me. . . I sure hope that if it comes down to a vote, the older teachers side with Mike and approve a pay freeze. The numbers are in their favor so I'm not getting my hopes up.   . . One oldie who is not doing me any favors is Nunberg. I've complained to our union rep about her. Was told she's within her rights as my evaluator and as an administrator dealing with a non-tenured. . . I'd be smart to start looking for another job. I think Mike would be too, though from what he's told me it might be impossible for him as a top salaried teacher to get rehired. I guess there are advantages to being young and cheap when your ass is on the line.*

Chapter 18

Time Unwinds - 2 Week Window
Atlas Chained

Hello Walls: Tuesday flies by with a few entertaining diversions. One of the cheerleaders is suspended for showing up on her math teacher's doorstep and offering to fuck her way off her academic shoals and past the Pythagorean theorem. . . One of our pregnant special ed teachers who has been out on emergency leave announces she's not coming back but is going to marry a female Republican from New York. . . Guidance holds a college fair and at the height of it someone hacks the PA system to announce an upcoming panty raid and a toga keg party.

Diversions aside it's the last week of October. The showdown with Nunberg and finalizing that objective exactly 2 weeks away. My own sense of imminent disaster is closing fast and I can almost feel her rebar tentacles wrapping my body. Squeezing, squeezing. . .

I don't understand Nunberg, and don't pretend to. In general I have never understood administrators well, but there is more disconnect with her than there was with any of the others. She probably feels the same way.

Beauty School Dropout: There's little worse than starting mid-week before first period with a guidance meeting on a student I don't even have. Teachers have to be in school 15 minutes prior to first period but this meeting backed it up 45. It's the only time the single parent could meet.

- Mr. August, why don't you go first since you're the only one here not involved with academics? LaTisha Korn says.

The heads around the table turn to me. There are 5 classroom teachers, Mrs. Campbell, Jade Campbell, and LaTisha. . . LaTisha is a third year guidance counselor who is normally very effervescent. Uber-smiling like she just got the rabbit-didn't-die test results. But this morning she's projecting a somber gravitas air as if we are a psych board debating on whether or not to commit Jade. . . I'm not sure why I'm here other than to add a dimension that is definitely non-academic.

- Well, I say, I don't know Jade. Never even heard her name until two days ago. . . I do not go into how I know it now and no one asks. These teachers just want me to sprint the hell along and get the hell out so they can too. . . I say, Jade was with her boyfriend Harley and called me an asshole. Actually she yelled it loudly in the hall. I don't know why other than a few weeks ago she and Harley were going at it in a stairwell and I told them to break it up. I believe she called me an asshole at that time too. I did not make an issue of it then since there was some doubt. There's no doubt this time.

- Mr. August, Mrs. Campbell says and looks at her daughter, Jade says she was talking to another student. That nothing was directed at you.

- Jade's exact words were, Hey August you ASSHOLE!. . . I don't see how that could pertain to anyone else.

- That wasn't what I said, Jade protests sullenly, her lip stud barely moving. I was talking to my friend Brigitte and I called her a Masshole because she's from Massachusetts.

I notice that the teen slut bomb lies very well and is not dressed anymore conservatively today than she was when she and Harley were hall raping each other, no roofie necessary. Push-up bra with low V-neck tee. Tits close to spilling out. I can count the moles. Heavy on the eye and face makeup. Skirt barely covering her love hole. . . I have two witnesses, I say, to the actual words. One to the fact it was Jade who said them. The one who ID'ed her is a straight A student with the highest recommendations.

- So you didn't actually see her yell it? mom asks.

- No. But it was Jade's voice. She was very angry the day I stopped Harley and her from engaging in inappropriate school behavior. Yelling, August you ASSHOLE! was payback in her mind.

- That's just your opinion, mom says. Are you aware that Jade has to serve a Saturday detention now because of your accusation?. . . Jade brightens up as mom goes on the attack. A faint smile plays around the corners of her hickey sucking mouth.

I think to myself, WTF? And now I need voice recognition equipment, hall video footage, and scores of eye-witnesses to call a student on a flagrant obscenity? Mom is an asshole enabler, and a hair-dying overly-cosmetic bitch on top of that. Ditto on the daughter. A chip off the old twat.

- No Mrs. Campbell, I say calmly, Jade is *not* serving a detention because of my misguided accusation. She's serving it because she showed poor judgment and has a foul mouth. In my student days I would have been suspended for saying what she did. She's getting off easy.

- You're the one with poor judgment, mom immediately rebuts.

The old not-me-you comeback. I almost laugh and would take a sip of my coffee now. If I had a mug. Which I don't. Admin does not like us eating or drinking at these parent conferences. I chewed gum one time and thought the principal was going to explode like I was endorsing child soldiers or the sex trade.

- It was the assistant principal who gave Jade the detention, I say. Appeal to him if you don't think it's fair. . . It occurs to me I have my own f-you buzz on and need to calm down. Or better still. . . I stand and say to

227

LaTisha, I have nothing more to add. If I think of anything else I'll be in touch.

- Have a good day, she says. Looks around and calls on the social studies teacher.

As I'm leaving I hear #2 on the chopping block say, Jade is failing my course with a 35% average.

Big doppler surprise, I think to myself and close the door behind me. Maybe if we had courses in deep throating or advance skin flute the frosh would be summa cum laude. Or magna cum laude. Something with cum. . . In any case I think I handled that pretty well. There was nothing more to say and walking out when I did prevented any further escalation. Of course I have been wrong before about what constitutes proper handling of a situation. According to Nunberg.

Nunberg. I feel a headache starting.

Jade Campbell: *He's right. I did yell asshole. Did it when I seen him sitting in that room with that wet-back. Harley thought it was as funny too. It's too bad August has to make such a big deal out of one word. It's not even that bad. . . Harley. I'd like to be balling him now instead of sitting in this stupid meeting. I love how Mom got off assistance. She works every day now. She's never home. Harley and me will be getting it on later in my bedroom. I love doing 69 with him. My mom would probably be cool with that. I mean she got knocked up with me when she was 16 so how wrong can it be?. . . I can't take hearing any more about my D's and F's. I don't like school and never will. I want to drop out and have Harley's baby. Harley wants that too.*

228

Itchycoo Park: I'm sitting in the back of Film class fighting sleep. The lights are out and Some Like It Hot is languoring in the yacht scene. I didn't get to bed till midnight last night after correcting papers and cleaning up after the cat. She had the runs and crapped all over herself, the rugs, the bed, my favorite chair. Ugh. I can live with a few dirty dishes, unironed clothes. But diarrhea is hard. No joke. . . Then I had to get up even earlier than usual this morning because of that meeting with honey pot and her talking vagina mother.

I'm looking at the back of Marcus' head, thinking I'd like to bounce a hot dog off it. But then what? He comes in tomorrow flying a Gadsden flag, ammo bandoleers across chest, assault rifle with the drum magazine?. . . I have to shake off these Campbell-induced negative vibes.

Up front the movie screen is filled with Tony Curtis lip-locking Marilyn Monroe. Her mountainous mammaries almost 3-D. Steam heat rising from my male hornies. Thankfully no one is working the crotch. No Jade Campbells.

That meeting with the Campbells. No great secret to find out the couple's names. I asked at our department meeting who knew a young pair – boy sporting a Mohawk and wolfish leer. Joined at the pelvis with a dishwater Courtney Love blond. . . Maybe I was too abrupt with Momma Campbell. But time was at a premium and she was in my face. Though not in my pants as is the family tradition.

That meeting got down to the essence of what being human means. Are we hardwired to dominate or cooperate? Writer and director Tom Shadyac in I Am concludes that life is an egalitarian world right down to the quantum level. Not survival of the fittest. Species cooperate. Even life forms we consider devoid of intelligence. Like Jade and her Mohawk hip hanger. Maybe Marcus.

229

Giselle turns around. Finds me in the twilit back and asks if this is the *real* Marilyn Monroe? Like the one I always hear about? she asks. I tell her it is. I pause the movie and ask if she remembers that during the introduction we went over the bios of the actors. I must have been absent that day, she says totally serious even though it was only 2 days ago and her attendance record is nearly perfect. . . I bite my tongue. Think of Shadyac and his cooperate, collaborate, participate in a loving universe. I say, I'm happy to know you're paying attention Giselle, and being a critical viewer. Very good. . . Giselle beams like I just handed her an Oscar for audience participation. I hit the Play button.

I'd like to be this nice all the time. Make the world better one person, one interaction at a time. My spirit is willing but the tongue weak. And the student and administrative dumbwahs strong.

Giselle Martin: *Mr. August is being so nice today. I expect him to make some wisecrack when I don't know who Marilyn Monroe is. But he just smiles and compliments me on my intelligence. I wonder why he's in such a good mood?. . . Marcus says he'd like to krunkle August. Give him five on the two. I'm not sure what he means but his buddies and Madison laugh whenever he says it. Marcus has been complaining ever since Mr. A would not let him leave early that day. Maybe before that. He was bragging that he hit Mr. A at the football game with a burning cigarette butt. Marcus is such a liar. I think some of his friends really like Mr. A and laugh just to keep Marcus happy.*

The Sound Of Silence: The library is bright and airy. Colorful signs. One sheets with READ! poster taped to the brick and drywall. Green potted plants in the corners. Evenly spaced along the walls, on top of the stacks. A steamer trunk-sized aquarium bursting shimmering streaming bubbles. Wavery oxygen nebules. Tropical fish swimming. Noses bumping glass.

It's tranquil. The media center an oasis for minds battered by stupefying classroom bushwa. I come here when the need arises. There's a little used faculty section in the back. A separate area with a coffee machine, water cooler, cushioned chairs, professional journals, and multiple wireless headphones.

I pass tables of students. Get reminded that a lot has changed over the years. National Geographic replaced by internet porn. Writing notes given way to texting. Not returning books superseded by scarcely recognizing what they are.

The head librarian is in her office. Aids at the computer stations.

Two of our spring athletes toss a baseball. I'm tempted to give them the yer-out sign. But don't. A pair of fuzzheads in desert camouflage are raucously thumbing an ATV mag. They blend in with the light brown veneer of the table and tan back wall and I'm not sure if I'm supposed to see them. I flash a big smile and give an overly loud, Hi guys! What's new? They look at me like I just fell from the sky. I keep going. So much for Shadyac, the petting zoo, all god's creatures great and small.

Pistol Packin' Mama: I pour a cup of coffee and settle into a comfortable chair. Tune the headphones to jazz and get Herbie Mann. I can't see the students, they can't see me, comfort in the womb. I take out a set of compositions and settle in for some uninterrupted grading.

I haven't finished the first composition when a thundercunt of purple walks in.

- Mike, do you have a few minutes? Nunberg is standing in front of me in a color fit for a Roman Catholic bishop. Leather skirt. Chain link belt. She looks around and says, I was talking to an aide when I heard your voice.

I want to say, Poke out my eyes Oedipus. Ever hear the phrase uninterrupted free period? But I just shrug. Take off the headphones and put out a hand towards an empty chair. If she's determined to talk about whatever little mite is biting her ass today might as well get this vagina monologue over with.

She sits down. I stare dispassionately. Don't know where this impromptu meeting is going but I have the feeling I'm not going to be happy when it's over. I only hope she isn't either.

- This should not take long. I can see you are busy. Sometimes I don't know how you English teachers do it. Though, of course, we all have increased paperwork these—

WTF, I think. Trying to relate?. . . I don't say anything. Actually look past her to the wall and notice a Do You Have Hot Lips? poster right above her head. It was paired with Nunberg before. Now with her modeling plus size ecumenical color right under it any salacious thoughts I have are forever wanktus interruptus gonetus.

- Should I have a union rep here? I ask cutting her off. If you're here to chastise me I'm entitled to representation.

- True. I would like to talk briefly about my latest concerns. We can do it now or later in my office.

- OK, no union rep. What's on your mind? I ask cavalierly, though I'm not feeling upbeat. Actually the headache I had earlier is returning.

232

- Mrs. Campbell was just in my office. She was upset. Did not like the fact you called Jade foul mouthed and that you were not willing to remotely consider the possibility that it was not Jade who called you that word.

- Asshole.

- Yes, Nunberg says, that word.

- There was no point in considering it. Jade was lying . . . I don't say anything more. Don't justify my actions like I'm some disconnected sub who can't ID a JD.

- Even if she was, and I am not saying that isn't the case, couldn't you have been a little more empathic with Mrs. Campbell? The mother said you abruptly ended the conference. Something I know you are capable of.

- There was nothing more to explain, to say. Time was short. First period on the horizon.

- Still, it does not look good when we are not willing to give a parent as much time as she requires, Nunberg says evenly. Sometimes they need kid gloves. Time to get used to the idea that their child may not be all they think.

Damn, she sounds logical. Her expression is not hard but one of sympathetic understanding. . . If I didn't know better I'd swear Nunberg really *is* looking out for the best interest of that parent and her sleazy child. And not just looking to blow me back. She could be one of those arbitration lawyers who are not happy unless neither side is totally happy. But that a consensus is reached. Compromise, give-and-take. Let us all just calm the fotch down and be reasonable.

But I know better. It's obvious this fractious bitch is trying to back me into a corner AGAIN. Trying to eviscerate me with her razor tongue and diamond-sharp clitoris.

She crosses her legs and shows more skin. Probably an old biker move. Disarm the male logic. S&M. Strew some leather and chain fantasies. . . Might not have been bad 60 pounds back. I might have even given her a closet poke. If I'd been drunk. Or plumbing the depths of desperation.

Don't think I will say a lot more. Rope-a-dope. Let her punch herself out. Keep my left up. . . I expand the moment. Take a sip, cradle the cup in my hands pensively. I could put the headphones back on but that would be too much of an overt Adam's apple punch even for me.

When she realizes I'm done with the Campbell jag she hesitates. Debating no doubt whether she wants to continue sledgehammering a thumbtack. Or move on. I'm not going to help her. She segues.

- I got a phone call the other day from Mr. Moseby. . . Nunberg rattles on about how she was not going to bring it up as he sounded a little tipsy. But he was also very coherent, she says, and very emotional. Mentioned how you never liked his son and made a disparaging public comment at the homecoming game. . . Says he also accused me of boozing with my former teammates.

I tell her that I don't drink at school functions. Apologized to Moseby for a remark that was not even intended for his son. And offered to sincerely shake hands though I had done nothing wrong. There are plenty of witnesses to this, I say, and to set the record straight I walked away to *avoid* trouble. Mr. Moseby looked as if he might be tossing a haymaker my way.

Now she settles back and we're both sitting in this small room staring at each other. Two animals waiting for the other to pounce. Or retreat. I am not even going to blink. I take a sip using the cup as a time filling prop. A cigar would be better. Blowing smoke her way better still. . . For some

234

reason I think of LBJ calling J. Edgar Hoover a pillar of strength in a city of weak men. I'm no pillar, but I am not a wimp-ass tea pinkie either. Even if my year and career *do* depend on being in Nunberg's good graces.

- Regardless of what actually happened, she finally says, this is another example of issue-after-issue piling up against you. It is almost as if you go searching out trouble. Maybe you need to see someone.

I'm quiet for a few seconds. Surprised but grateful she does not seem to know about the physical confrontation with Marcus, kicking the trash can, or actually punching out a parent - Jimmy Asshole Klein.

- Well, I finally say drawing out the words slowly, there is no such thing as a pile of electrons. Everything you've accused me of since the year began is so infinitesimally tiny as to be invisible to the naked eye. Not one item is a citable offense. Not one in violation of the contract. Or teachers' manual. Not one something other teachers haven't done multiple times. None even violate good common sense, or in loco parentis. . . You see an older teacher who's had a couple of tough years. I see a good teacher who can still make a positive difference. And I resent your saying I may need help. Frankly Ms. Nunberg you are not qualified to make that statement unless you hold a degree in psychology. Which I don't believe most speech therapists have.

- Careful Mike, she says. It is those kinds of headstrong remarks that have me here in the first place.

- Do you hate me, Ms. Nunberg? I ask suddenly. Perhaps on a personal level?. . . I'm thinking to myself of the hit-and-run. It's an out-there thought, but if I did hit her dog, and she has my license plate and traced it. . .

- No. I certainly don't hate you. Why would I?. . . She says it obliquely, as if testing the waters.

Since I'm not about to admit to hitting anything with my car, I go bottom line.

- If I can be honest, Ms. Nunberg, I believe you are here to build a case to get rid of me. . . I tell her about the OUT OF MANY, FEW letter I received and add, This is really all about getting rid of top tier teachers. Cash register education.

- None of that is true. Certainly not your implication that I might have been behind an anonymous letter.

- My   big   point is that your talking to me in this candid manner and refusing to consider my reasoning and feelings is doing exactly what you're excusing me of. I don't see the difference.

Rock Me Gently: Put that away *now!* There's sudden yelling from one of the aides out in the reading room. Laughing. Arguing. . . Nunberg doesn't budge. Suddenly DDB. The nitty-gritty-down-and-dirty part of education not her problem. Not mine either now. We're in beautiful synch. It doesn't last.

- Well, wanting to show you the door is not why I'm here. But you can believe what you want. . . Her ire is up, but her face isn't red. Only involuntary hand rubbing and a slightly elevated tone reveal anything but calm. A practiced controlnik. . . The difference is I am your boss, she says, and I have the right and obligation to use whatever means are at my disposal to do what is educationally best for the students. It is all about them in the end.

Damn educational clichés, I think. If she's going to unleash the cliché battery, and not talk honestly. . . Let the clock do a few cartwheels. . . I know in my heart and every sensorial fiber I don't want to stay. But I'm not walking out again like she's accused me of doing. Not if the Four Horsemen suddenly mount up. Not if she strips and does a naked belly dance. . . Cormac McCarthy in All the Pretty Horses says if a man isn't supposed to be where he is, he would not be there. Guess this is where I am supposed to be. Only wish Nunberg had better legs and a martini shaker.

She finally caves to the black oak silence and asks, How are you coming on finalizing your objective? It's due soon.

So this informal talk has come down to this, I think. Rising action since September culminating now with this no-net moment. Walk off into glory, or fall and get my keister wupped. Or. . . I could put it off. Delay. Wait till she's in a better mood. . . No, too smug. Has an answer for everything. . . I know suddenly I need to end this. . . Bang the drum slowly, play the fife lowly. . .

- My objective is actually done, I say calmly. I need to write it up. But it's all moot now. I was supposed to improve my 6 assigned mentees either academically, socially, or behaviorally. It's done. Four were social introverts. TJ and Audrey are now in the school play thanks to me. Kaufman will be performing with me at open mike. Zoe will be hosting an art premiere that I arranged. Destiny has improved creatively and academically due to my tutoring. Jorge will be going to college on scholarship because of my intervention.

At last the estocada, I think. Bull charges, quick sword thrust, Nunberg down and bleeding. Final Score: August 6, Nunberg 0.

She looks at me like I just ripped off my shirt. And there's a big middle finger painted on my chest. Like I fist fucked her with a boxing glove on. I know I'm pushing the truth. . . But. . . I want the thrill-of-victory moment. Now. For myself. And the bombed-in-New-Haven, no-soup-for-you moment. For her. . . To slap the defibrillator on her arrhythmic goddamn brio and dead chutzpah. . . I have to win, she has to lose, screw all the rest.

She sits there spinning cobwebs. Says, *Interesting* but nothing more till I say, You'll have it all in writing on your desk in the morning. Or I can email you later using the online form. . . I start to rise. She says, Just a minute. Says it firmly, aggressively. Like the fat lady is not singing anytime soon.

- We discussed none of this, she says as she taps her thighs. If you were going to jump right in on fulfilling your objective I should have been informed. . . I have no idea if any change has occurred in any of your six students. No pre-assessment was done or even discussed. No, I am afraid this will not do at all. . . Tells me we need to meet. Discuss. Maybe bring in guidance, SPED, the school psychologist if necessary. Says, You have 7 school days left to have a finalized objective on my desk.

The words are rational. The posture ham-fisted. It occurs to me she could be menopausal and suffering from hot flashes and mood swings. But when has she ever been nice?

- You told me when I agreed to this objective I could keep it loose, I say. Made it sound as if it were all just a romp through the motions. . . Even as I talk about my piloting this program I can see her face hardening with each point. It's no use. She's going to play revisionist history. No way she's letting the dominos fall this easily.

Damn. I can't help but marvel on how easily things are taken from us. Job security. Peace of mind. . . I shut down. Force myself to freeze the wagger. Protest is only feeding her determination. . . The Chinese Finger Trap. I need to stop pulling outward. Relax. S-low-ly extricate myself.

Take Her To Sea, Mr. Murdoch: CRASH! There's an ear-splitting scattering of glass as if multiple stories of windows just pancaked down. Followed by a scream and explosive yelling. I tell Nunberg, I'll be in touch.

I make a fast exit.

In the reading room a crowd has gathered around a shattered aquarium. Water draining like Niagara. The thin rubber-backed wall-to-wall carpet unable to absorb the sudden inundation. A wet baseball rests on the floor. Some teens splashing in the free-flowing streams. The aide I heard yell is standing in the center of them. Bawling her eyes out. The librarian charges out of her office.

I think to myself, Hot damn. Someone should tell her there's no crying in baseball.

I know Nunberg is behind me and will probably chew me out later for professional atrophy. But up hers and this school's.

I walk around the watery fiasco and keep going.

Bernadette Nunberg: *These sessions with Mike are always tiring. Maybe I should not have approached him when he was relaxed and grading. . . I saw him looking at my legs. Men are such easy reads. I'm sure he would love to have sex with me no matter how infuriated he is. Maybe because he is. I agree that sex is better than talk. And angry sex wonderful. But definitely not with him. . . I don't tell him but I am impressed he has done so much with those 6, especially Zoe. I did not think anybody could get to her. But if he did. . . Still, teachers just cannot go off on their own and decide without any administrative input what their objectives will be and how best to meet them. I am curious now what he will come up with. But it had better be good.*

Mother's Little Helper: The busses have left. I'm alone in my room. Still parboiling when George walks in.

- Hey sport, he says, going to Hudson's?

- Foke Hudson's. A pox on people, I say shutting down the computer. I look at him. Haven't seen him since the game. Wonder if he's harboring any bad feelings from our near punch out. Doesn't sound it. . . George isn't one to hold a grudge. But you never know. I don't see any residual anger or resentment. Which means either it's not there. Or he's as good an actor as counselor. Either way it makes me glad. We all need friends. Me especially.

- So I'm going to take a long shot and say it hasn't been a good day, he says with just the right amount of friendliness and concern.

- As good as the Chicago Fire with a side of the Johnstown Flood . . . I tell him about the early morning conference, the dismal state of my objective, and the library water follies. I throw out my arms in frustration and my wedding band flies off. Hits the wall with a metallic clink. I apologize to George for almost pinging him and explain that since I've lost weight nothing fits well.

- Sounds like you need a drink. Come on, go to Hudson's. Better to drink with friends than with the cat and dog. . . I shake my head and he says, No? You're sure? OK. By the way, your Film class will be interrupted next Tuesday. There's going to be a lockdown. A couple of K9 units are going to sweep for drugs. Shouldn't take long. Maybe if you're lucky they'll discover Nunberg is a drug queen.

- Wouldn't that be something, I say and laugh. . . The wheels turn. . . A light appears at the end of the tunnel that doesn't look like the Lower West Side.

Chapter 19

Thursday - Monday

Incremental Steps

I think I'm developing a schizophrenic mindset with a paranoia complex. One side of me says I'm all alone in meeting my objective. A solitary figure in this sink-or-swim phase of my career. The other side says there are forces aligned against me that I don't understand. . . Nunberg is the key, but short of waterboarding how to get answers?

Thursday

Listen To The Rhythm Of The Falling Rain: On a last minute whim I decide to conference with Zoe. I could just drop by her class for this payoff but then I wouldn't get to do any probing.

It's raining. Windy. The bean-sized pellets hitting the English office windows with staccato pinging. Fingernails incessantly drumming on the glass. The type of day it's good to be inside.

Zoe doesn't seem bothered by the fact I pulled her out of class. Or that this is not a scheduled meeting. She plops down and waits. Resigned, or just not caring.

- Zoe, I say I have some good news for you. One of your paintings at the restaurant sold. Here's the money. . . I hold out a couple of hundred dollars in cash. My hand stays out there. She avoids my direct stare. Just when I think that maybe she doesn't want the moolah she takes it. Stashes it in a leather-fringed handbag and resumes her static sitting. I wait but no reaction. No thank you. No, shit this is unexpected.

The rain continues to pelt the window and the sheet of water filming the glass reflects our own images back at us. Two solitary souls. Edward Hopper's late night diners. . . Zoe is not a girl who moves easily out of character. At least that's what I'm thinking till she turns her head, sweeps her hair back, and wipes the eye.

- I have a feeling there's a lot more of that to come, I say. The Espinozas tell me a few more buyers are close. They'll need another painting to hang.

She nods and says, I'll bring one over.

- One good thing about the money, I say slowly. You won't be forced to negotiate with the principal anymore.

- That is a good thing, she says lacklusterly.

- I didn't figure you cared for her, especially after that remark that you appreciated anything that wrecked a Nunberg project.

I'm fishing, but she doesn't bite. Not totally. Says only, Yeah . . . It pops into my mind that maybe Nunberg and Zoe knew each other before Nunberg came here. It's difficult to believe that in the short time Nunberg's been in this school that the two of them could have built up so much animosity. I don't know where Nunberg is from. But it would be easy enough to check, I think.

- So Zoe, I say, it occurs to me I really don't know much about your background. Have you lived in this town your whole life, or some other place?

- Some other place. But I've been here for all of high school.

She gives me the name of a small town around 50 miles from here. I'm not sure where I'm going or where this could lead. But if that town crosschecks with Nunberg it might mean something. Shared secrets, relatives. Common ground for having it in for me. Maybe Nunberg is Zoe's sister or mother. I don't think I'm too far out to expect the unexpected out of these two anomalies. Revelation: Maybe the solution to my present problems lies in the past. And not my own.

I congratulate her again on the sale and send her back to class.

Zoe Koppel: *Two hundred dollars! This is going to really help my get-out-dullsville fund. If I can sell a bunch more I can leave right after graduation. Maybe my life is turning around. One thing's for sure. I am on August's side now. Or at least I'm not going to do anything to fuck him over. . . He's kind of sad these days, pretty intense. I guess life pretty much sucks for him too. He doesn't talk about it, I mean why would he? It's not like we're pals, or anything. . . I wonder why August asked me where I'm from. Not that it's any big secret like some of my life is. But I hope he's not going to go poking around. He may not like what he finds out. Though I guess he has a right to know.*

Outside the rain pounds the windows. A tall figure in an Army poncho passes by bent forward into the wind. Someone familiar. Double take. Jimmy Klein? Rain bouncing off the OD slicker. Hood pulled down over the face. The traveler splashes through the thick puddles and heads towards the superintendent's wing. Klein? Not sure. The blurry image disappears around the corner.

A drop of water starts down the inside of the pane. I make a mental note to report it, though building maintenance is not my problem. Saving my ass is and there's not a lot of time left.

Friday

Give A Man Enough Rope: Don Blake, one of our AP English teachers and the department chairman, asks me if I have a few minutes. He's standing tall over me. Looking down with cordova brown peepholes and thick black eyebrows. His skin is pitted. Beard a kinky gray mess. Calloused hands. Weight a lunch bucket. Former Navy man. Jack-of-all.

- Sure, I say and pull out the chair next to me. I normally enjoy Don's company. At least I did. He was just enough of an iconoclast to be entertaining without jeopardizing his job. But since becoming the English head he's gotten conservative and edgy. Frazzled with the pettiness that comes from dealing with school minutia and being in charge. Administration breaks a few, makes a few, leaves the majority lessened. Today he seems marbled with concern. He plops his wham-o ass down which stretches his plaid sweater vest even tighter. Fashion sense = discount strip mall.

- Mike, are you tutoring Destiny Gibson in AP? he asks over aggressively after waving me to go ahead with my eating.

- Not really, I say taking a bite out of my liverwurst and onion sandwich. I'm mentoring her, though I *have* edited a few of her compositions.

- Does this look familiar to you? he asks and pushes a composition in front of me. Note the sentences I underlined, he says and points at them for emphasis. His paisley shirt, steel wool demi-Afro, and tension glazed eyes make me think of John Lennon. Maybe Seth Rogen. He looks over his retro-readers and asks, Were these on Destiny's original paper?

As soon as I glance at them bells go off. Damn! These are the exact sentences I wrote on her first draft when she asked for some concrete examples for descriptions and an opening. I told her to not use them. That mine were only models. But apparently she ignored that. She might have

244

changed one or two words but that would be the most. . . Plagiarism. Not a dirtier word for an English teacher. And now what to do? I notice that Blake has 2 more compositions.

I chew the sandwich slowly and pretend to really study Destiny's typing. I don't want to sink the wannabe valedictorian. But I shouldn't let her get away with this either. Of course there is no fotching way Blake could nail Destiny. These   sentences don't exist anywhere else but in my head. And in Destiny's cheating little soul. I feel bad. I didn't realize just how much being #1 means to her. And what lengths she'll go to achieve it.

Still, it's on her. Not me. I'll talk to her about it. But for now. . . I've been in enough hot water this year. Do I really need more crapola if Blake decides to make a major issue of it? And he probably will. Fearful of students, or anyone, putting one over on him. One-upping the big kahuna.

- Yes, I say, they were there. What's your problem with them?

- The tone rhythm. The whole syntax isn't in harmony with the rest of her paper. The same thing happens in these other 2 compositions. . . He fans the air as if I cannot see the red ink and underlining from beyond 2 feet. . . If the young lady is cheating, Blake continues, I don't know what her sources are. Couldn't find anything online.

- I know what you mean, I say. Happens all the time with my students too. Look, I'll talk with Destiny and see if I can find out anything. Hopefully it'll at least scare her from repeating whatever it is she's doing.

- I appreciate it, he says and stands to go. By the way, he says, that sandwich of yours. It's so–

- I know, I say. Smelly. But it's as tasty as hell. . . No, he says, I was going to say it's so *you*. See you later. . . He grabs his brief case and is gone in an egress of red ink and the muffled tread of Bean hikers.

So *me*? What the hell does Blake mean by that? That I'm Jewish? Not subtle? Pungent? Fuck him. Number me among the wursts and onions. . . It dawns on me that in covering for Destiny I'm now at her mercy if she entertains telling the truth down the road. Jesus. This two-way street of faith with my mentees is tough. Career ending type now with Destiny and The Kid if anything goes wrong. Taking the bullet. . It doesn't feel good either realizing that the Destiny part of my objective is now gone. At least temporarily. That little Miss Vogue is probably no more improved in writing than I am in avoiding getting shat on by Nunberg. . . Double damn, and kick a freshman.

Saturday

Reflections Of My Life: There's been something utterly devoid and lonely about Saturday since Amanda died. During the week I'm surrounded by people. Even if most of them are teens caught up in their own archipelago lives. Sunday I lunch with Max. But Saturdays. . . People have offered to fix me up. Suggested dating websites. Wanted to sign me up for singles groups. Invited me over for dinner. But I've avoided most of that. . . Last Saturday with Sophia was a big deal. Lots of pressure. My fuckability pretty low. But I acted OK, did fine. Sure didn't with Deirdre after homecoming. It still bothers me. Talk about misreading the signs.

The shadows are lengthening, the sun going down. Light angles in low through the front latticed windows and crosshatches me like a tic-tac-toe board. There is a college football game on but I'm scarcely following it. The book I'm reading is not holding my interest either. The Forsyte Saga by John Galsworthy. Don't know why I grabbed it off the shelf other than maybe I was hoping to get some insight into myself through Soames

Forsyte, a man who lost more than he knew.   A man with only spits of emotion. Pissed off most everyone in his life.

I take a pull on the gin, nibble a jumbo olive.

I need to face it. I'm damaged goods. Not likely to get much better. Don Blake had it right. Liverwurst and onions. Some people just are. . . Maybe there's some higher plan to all this. Be nice to think so. Something beyond teach, correct papers, drink, clean out the litter. . . Speaking of the cat where is she? She usually comes around in the evening when I'm in this chair. The dog is at my feet, but no red tabby. She does what she wants. No ties. Not much interconnectedness. The cat is no Buddhist. No existing only in relation to others. Total lack of engi, dependence. Though she seems to like the dog. And would be pretty fucked if I didn't put out the food and water.

Maybe I need to embrace some truth greater than my life sucks.

Maybe I need a new quest. Something other than trying to move those 6 mentees who are balled and chained to Nunberg and school.

Or maybe people just are not meant to have peace. I don't even know where to look for it. Just a stupid s.o.b. A once-upon-a-kid who licked too much lead-based paint.

The best thing I have going for me tonight is this gin. True as anything.

There's a b&w photograph of Amanda on the end table. It's a good portrait. The photographer wanted her to look up and off to the right. But she wouldn't. Insisted on looking directly into the camera. . . The twilight Amanda is looking at me now. She looks happy, at peace with herself. She usually did. That Julia Roberts smile, the soft Audrey Hepburn eyes. I always had the sense that Amanda had the answers to life's mysterious fucking ways. She usually did. I trusted her sense about things. Leaned heavily on her opinion when in doubt. . . If only pictures could talk. . . What

247

if at the moment of death she had passed something of herself onto me? A bequest of inner fortitude and peace. Would I be any happier in this dim gray room with its ambi-lit tv, dusty furniture, and sagging plants? Would I even be here? And alone?. . . Companionship. I scarcely thought about when I had it. Her physical presence. The arms, lips, breasts, the sex, her husky laugh. The gardenia smell of her shampooed hair. The sight of her rolling over and saying good morning. And it was.

One thing about gin. Especially as a sundowner. It's a real catalyst for introspective slides. The sun goes down. The gin goes down. The past rises up. Surfaces like acid reflex.

I really need to stop drinking for tonight.

But not yet.

Thornton Wilder. Our Town. Does anyone know how good they have it when they have it? I didn't. Though I suspected at the end. Life with Amanda was loving and fun. Most of the time. Life after all is not a fotching laugh track. . .

The wind is picking up outside. It's whistling through windows that are not sealed tightly. Shadows from the front maple weave boney arms across me. The slurry outline of a foked up life. The charcoal room is a hissy fit of running swirls. Drafty. The furnace clicking on-and-off. If it ran on drunken bullshit instead of oil I could save a fortune.

This evening, these thoughts. I'm too much within myself these days. Turning life all inward. Rheumy-eyed, self-pitying. People are right when they say you shouldn't drink alone. Though I do it all the time.

I look at Amanda's picture. And laugh. At first it's just a little haha. Almost forced. Then I spill some drink down my front and laugh harder. Non artificial chortles. I rub the wetness into my shirt to build heat to dry it. And spill more. The stain spreads. I laugh harder. Some field goal kicker goes wide left on a short 3-pointer. I'm laughing from the gut. My riotous mood and laughter build. I laugh, stand, nearly fall over. I throw the glass into the fireplace. The tuxedoed Thin Man. The crystal shatters. The dog jumps. Which keeps the laughing going. . . I laugh until my sides hurt. Till tears run down my face. Till I run out of breath and start to gasp. An emotional purge. The psyche outpouring of pent up stress, overflowing crap. The thought flashes that this would be an excellent time for the big coronary. Drop dead right here. Right now. To die laughing. Who would know, who would care?

But I don't.

The gasps segue to sobs. Then tears.

I sit. Try to stifle the sobs. Cry quietly.

Sunday

Spinning Wheel: I can see the flashing police lights from a block away. The halogen bursts puncture the autumn color. Flashing white light that would be blinding if not filtered by the leaves. About half are still up, clinging to the deciduous hardwoods by increasingly brittle stems. My car crunches through the dead early morning foliage overriding the sound of talk radio and creating twin tire paths. I'm a trailblazer, a barely caffeinated motorist who's mulching and layering the roadway with a fat layer of brown loess.

The call came while I was sleeping. The sun not totally up. The first church goers not yet on the road. Mike, Deirdre said, I think you should come over as soon as you can. . . What's wrong? I asked barely cognizant of anything beyond my bladder needing emptying. Has something happened to Max?. . . Max is OK, Deirdre said, though he's very upset which is bringing Ernie into the picture. Your dad's front yard was vandalized last night. It's pretty much a mess out there. . . I'll be there within half an hour, I told her while massaging my temples and wondering if I was legally sober enough to drive.

I pull up opposite the house. Try not to slam the car door, though I suppose the neighbors who are not staring out their windows are at least out of bed by now. Hard to ignore the ear-splitting volume on the police radio.

Deirdre is in the driveway leaning up against a car that is not her green fungoid Honda. It's a Ford Fiesta I've never seen before. She's talking to the lone policeman while Max is stomping around like some free range chicken. There's a maze of doughnut spirals and straight lines that have ripped up much of the sod and tossed chunks onto the walkway and into the shrubs. Dirt bombs have splattered the clapboard and front door. The exterior is a mottled chocolate chip appearance. Max raking what's left of the lawn and tamping down the larger loose chunks with his slippered feet. He's using an iron rake, then hand sowing grass seed and working it in with a large plastic rake for the finished grade. His wheelbarrow is half full. Bathrobe covered with dirt, wet leaves, dead grass. His face blotted with sweat and earth.

He's keeping a running monologue going with Ernie and does not give me a second glance. I catch snatches of, I'll kill the bastards. Never mind it wasn't much of a lawn anyway. What do you mean calling me Max Brown Thumb?

Max was never overly proud of his greensward and once told me that any man who puts more time and money into yard maintenance than he does into reading, drinking, smoking, and having sex, is a fool. He certainly was not *that* to any registering degree. He used to proudly boast that crabgrass and dandelions would never go extinct as long as he was around. He was the scourge of the block's property values, but because he was so funny and self-critical about it his closest neighbors learned to ignore it. Or at least live with it.

- Mike, can you come here for a second? Deirdre asks breaking into my spectating the Max show.

- Sure, I say and remind myself to act sober, say little, not fall down. I take another sip of coffee and walk over. I become vaguely aware of the wail of a distant siren.

The Da Vinci Code: The policeman stands facing the street while he jots down notes. He's a big guy with a buzz cut, windmill ears, biceps like cantaloupes, and a gut. No hat. Military creases sewn into his shirt. His service belt has a low U sag under the weight of the Glock, extra magazines, baton, flashlight, CS spray, first aid kit, taser, handcuffs, radio, et al. He's a walking commando depot. A tooled panoply not unlike a carpenter except he's not here to do roofing or miter corners.

The cop is taking his time. I haven't the faintest idea what he could be writing. For a second it occurs to me that this could be one of my former students, more likely one of my ex-football players. He glances at me but there's no sign of recognition. I read his name badge and nothing registers with me either. He looks up and asks if I'm the son.

I tell him my name, give my address and phone. He asks if I saw or heard anything last night. I remind him that I don't live around here. I was asleep at home, I say. Ask if maybe we should stop Max from destroying evidence. Evidence? he says. My father is raking out what could be tire tracks, I say. And there could be a lot of rubber residue in there. I point to

Max's wheelbarrow.. . . I have my doubts on the rubber, but the tire tracks seem plausible.

- Sir, he says a bit too smugly, this isn't CSI.   Even if we had the resources we don't have the time to investigate minor Halloween pranks.

- Minor? I say. My father's lawn is ruined!. . . I kick a loose clump of sod and it flips over. I'm tempted to kick it onto his highly polished shoes. The cop's eyes are deep set and dead. Asteroid impacts. He says, Sir, calm down.

- Halloween, I finally say, was last week.

- The tricks sometimes start early and go late, he says pretty goddamn bored. As if it's the kind of conversation he's had many times. Might make a good teacher.

- How many other lawns were vandalized around town last night? Or since the Halloween season started? I ask.

- This is the only one I know of. Property damage like this is only a misdemeanor anyway.

- So that's it? my temper is starting to rise again and I yell to Max, Dad, knock it off! I'll clean this up. Just be patient!

The cop looks from Max to me and doesn't say anything.

Max keeps working and Deirdre walks over and puts her arm around him. He stops, looks at her like she's a stranger. Leans into her and wipes his forehead with a dirt crusted hand. He looks worn out.

An ambulance pulls up curbside. The siren keeps going for a few bars before it's turned off.

- I'll interview the neighbors , the cop says to me and starts walking towards the ambulance. Find out if anyone saw or heard anything. Do *you* know anyone who would do this?

Me? I'm walking alongside him and think of Curt, his father, Jimmy Klein, Madison, Adrianna, Marcus, Jade and her boyfriend. Even that group I saw hanging out down the street. . . I'm a school teacher, I tell him. In this town. There are lots of students who might do this to *me*. But I don't live around here as I already told you. And I doubt any would know that Max is my father. . . There's definite sarcasm in my voice and for a second I wonder why I am being so short-tempered with this cop who seems to just be doing his job. I check it off to school stress, too many tipples last night, and a life that is curdling fast. . . I don't think Max himself has any enemies, I say trying to remember if I heard him complain in recent months about anyone.

- Does he get along with his neighbors? Pay his bills on time? Has he stiffed anyone lately? Gone through a divorce, or had girlfriend problems?

- He's fine with his neighbors. I pay his bills. He's a widower and he doesn't have a girlfriend. The girl with him now is his housekeeper.

Two attendants get out of the ambulance and the policeman nods in Max's direction.

- Who called them? I ask and walk behind the pair of white-coated medics now crossing what's left of the lawn. The policeman follows me. Branches tilt overhead slivering the early morning sunlight. We're walking in-and-out of shadows. It's cold.

- I did, the officer says. Your father has been acting strange. And I couldn't get him to stop and talk with me.

- He's under a doctor's care already, I say and add with palpable agitation. My father is the victim here. Not the criminal!

- Sir, I'm telling you for the last time to calm down.

I notice that a half dozen robins are pecking at the freshly exposed topsoil. One flies off with a worm in its mouth. Another chases off some sparrows who are working the edges. Optimism Bias: One's man ruined yard is another's buffet.

I take a drink of coffee and say to the man in blue, I am calm. It's my father who isn't.

A few feet away the medics have taken Max gently by the elbows while he yells for them to mind their own fucking business. He calls for Ernie to help him and their grips tighten. Deirdre is at Max's side talking soothing honey, wiping his face clean. She might as well be invisible. He's walked to the ambulance and put on a stretcher. I tell the crew that I need a minute with my father.

- Dad, I say, they are just going to take you in for some tests. You'll be home by this afternoon. I'll go with you.

- And I'll clean up your yard, Deirdre states, but I give her a shake of the head and silently mouth, I'll do it later.

I climb into the ambulance. Keep up a steady flow of chatter aimed at Max. Max tells me to close my butthole. Then asks if I'm part of the trauma team.

I'm rearranging deck furniture on the Titanic, locking the door while Vesuvius erupts. If this autumn were any more disastrous I'd qualify for a disability pension. . . I notice something hanging from the bottom of Max's bathrobe. I pull it out. Surprise. Female undies. Deirdre's?

Before the door closes I ask the cop to call me if he finds out anything. He tells me to call *him* in a few days but his tone is not encouraging. It's clear there will not be much followup. The case pretty much closed before the door is.

254

I guess the only good news is that he didn't notice my mismatched plates. Neither did the cop at El America Ecuatoriano when I decked Klein. Win 2, lose 1. The blind, and arbitrary nature of justice.

The early morning light is leaking across the neighborhood, illuminating Max's yard. Turning the brown stained house almost golden. It's sort of pretty. That new-used car in the driveway catches the light and I wonder again who owns it. . . They keep the siren off and the sedative kicks in. Max is quiet. The ride to the hospital without incident.

Rebel Rouser: Late afternoon I cruise Max's neighborhood looking for a dirt splattered car or truck. If I find one I am not sure what I'll do. My cell is charged. I could call the cops. More likely I'll confront the owner. It's the had-it-up-to-here mood. Fairly convinced the damage is school related. It would not be the first time a teacher's house or lawn has been vandalized. Even if Max is not a teacher. Close enough for some of these tottering teens. It's not much of a stretch to imagine someone like Marcus doing this. Or Moseby. Even Jade if she were old enough to drive. Hyped up on drugs or booze. Feeling wronged. Vengeful. Having opportunity. Shadows without a sun.

It is going to take luck and a grand aleatory break to stumble across the right vehicle.

I'm going up and down streets grid-by-grid being as systematic as I can. I'm also checking out driveway surfaces for signs of a recent vehicle washing, streaks of muddy runoff, coagulated dirt or mud.

While I'm cruising I'm sipping vodka. It's not my drink of choice but it's odorless. And was all Max had. . . I asked him about the strange car in his driveway and the panties stuck to his robe. He didn't have a clue.

It's getting dark. I'm feeling the booze. I won't be able to search much longer. Most of the driveways are empty. Cars garaged, or not back from wherever it is people go on a Sunday. As I near the end of a block half a mile from Max's I see a filthy truck sitting in a dimly lit drive. It's riding high on oversized mud-terrain tires and a suspension lift kit. A battery of auxiliary lights on a light bar above the windshield. Yosemite Sam mud flaps. A large rebel flag across the back window. . . Official badass. . . The coating of mud and dirt mask the paint job and run high and long. As if it's been running serious backwoods.

Or ruining lawns.

I know practically nothing about off-roading, but this sure as hell looks like a vehicle that is more than capable of doing Max's lawn. I pull over, take a last drink. Pick up the cell, and start to key 911. Then put it down and get out. Reflective NRA bumper decals catch the streetlight. I reach into the back seat and grab an old softball bat. Think twice and pick up the tire iron. I know that I shouldn't be armed. But I'm angry, nervous. A man of action, I tell myself. I stick the metal bar under my jacket.

There's light coming from the open garage. Voices are loud. Laughing. I start up the driveway. Stop at the truck. The license is in-state, non-commercial. I double check for sod, turf, anything that looks like Max's lawn. There's wet mud in the wheel wells. Wetlands oozes from the bumpers, grill, running boards, lower lights. Sprouts of marsh grass stuck in the fender. Nothing that looks like my father's landscaping.

A lot of empty beer cans line the truck bed. A rack of some sort stands empty against the bulkhead. My impression is Heartland U.S.A. Grand ole boys.

I'm just about to return to my car when I hear a dog bark. It flies out of the garage and bounds down the driveway yapping like this is some sort of hunt. Like maybe I'm the fox. Tally-ho, cheerio! It stops a few feet short and growls. A German Shepherd. Its eyes intense, black death stars. Riveted on my every move. I freeze. Does it sense I'm packing iron? Have a firm grip on it? Am ready to use it?. . . I try to relax. Look nonthreatening. Be nonthreatening. I sway a little.

- Buck! Knock it off!. . . The voice comes from the garage. The tan-black stops barking instantly and sits down. Stares at me. I tighten my hold on the tire iron but keep it undercover. I feel sweat begin to form. The coolness of the late day taking hold, the vodka working its way out. . . Hey buddy, don't worry, the same voice yells. The dog won't hurt you. . . There's more laughter and a, Whattaya want?

I stare into the garage and see 2 men in waders, lined caps with the ear flaps down, and bloodied sweatshirts. They're standing next to a table. Holding knives. For a second I panic and mentally weigh my chances of escaping. Not good. The dog is watching me like a meat display. The smaller man steps out of the garage and stands in a cone of light.

Then the smell hits me.

They're cleaning fish.

- Just looking for an address, I say with as much friendliness as I can muster. . . I give them the name of Max's street and neither man knows where it is. . . The smaller man yells to Buck and the dog bounds back up the asphalt and disappears into the garage. I inhale deeply. Hold it, exhale. I can see my breath.

- There's a gas station a few blocks west, the same man says. . . The other goes back to cleaning fish. The talking one takes a long pull on a silver can. . . How about a brew? he asks across the distance.

- Thanks, but I need to get going. . . I smile though I doubt he can see it in this gloom. Wave him off, belay saying, Yawl take care now, ya hear. . . I take 2 steps backwards, then turn.

I start back to my car.

I can feel the man's eyes on me. I'm tempted to run, sprint. But I don't. Halfway down the incline I stumble over an invisible pothole, my arms fly out for balance, and the tire iron slips. I panic as it spins off into the night. Bounces, clanks on the hard surface like a tolling funeral bell. It rents the Sunday quiet and lands in the street. The neighboring houses are dark. No lights come on.

From behind me a voice yells, Whatthehell was that?

- Nothing! I yell back without turning. I move fast. Just have my hand on it when I hear, Just a minute there bud!

I don't wait but take off running. There's only the width of the street to cross but it looks like an Olympic straightaway. There's an instant command to, Get him, Buck! Followed by a rebel yell. I lift my knees higher and pump my arms.

I'm at my car, the door open, when a shotgun blast rips through the overhead branches and a shower of leaf fragments floats down, twinkling like stardust.

I'm in. The door nearly closed. When Buck arrives. He lunges for the opening, snout leading the way. Large, white, incisors targeting my arm, torso. In warp speed imagination I slam him in the head with the tire iron and he drops to the pavement like a downed piñata. Or is stopped short by my tire iron stiff-arm and does a stagger lee in the street before lunging again.

In reality I'm fast enough to slam the door shut just before that preda-tory muzzle tears flesh. He thuds into the metal adding another dent.

Perfect symmetry with the Jimmy Klein one on the passenger side and the fender crease in back.

Fast And Furious: Before he can recuperate I floor it. Spin the wheels in the mush of gutter leaves. Rocket off swerving down the street. There isn't another shot. I take the corner on practically 2 wheels and for a second think I'm going to lose the rear end. Again. Tumble, flip. Spin like that tire iron did.

I take a few turns that do not lead home. Constantly check my rearview. At one point I think I see the elevated lights of a semi-monster. But after a couple of quick lefts-and-rights they disappear. Whatever they were. . . After a mile and running a few stop signs I settle down. Slow down. Toss out the empty bottle. I drive the speed limit into the shadows and thickening twilight. Thankful I can still run like hell when I have to. Thankful, I guess, I didn't find the culprit. No good was going to come of it.

Monday

Reelin' In The Years: It's on my mind that the police could show up at any time to question or arrest me on my bizarre behavior yesterday. Though I don't think that will happen. One of those suburban yeehaws discharged a firearm within the city limits. Without threat or imminent danger. And drunk. . . Bottom Line: Probably not the complaining-to-police types anyway. Do their own food gathering, take care of their own headaches. And lumped up dog.

I put the shootout behind me. I'm alone in my classroom before first period. My stomach skiddish, unsettled. I pop an aspirin gum and pull long on the coffee. I'm closing my eyes when TJ Sato walks in without knocking. He's unshaven, his hair unkempt, his shirt wrinkled. He has a sad nervous look as if he just incubated from a space egg and stumbled into this world.

- Mr. August, he says talking fast, I thought you should know. I'm dropping out of Grease today. . . He looks crestfallen. As sad as when his former girlfriend broke up with him.

- What? You're quitting Grease? I say scarcely believing my ears. Why? I thought you loved being in the play.

- I did. But I just can't do it.

- Has this got something to do with Audrey?

- No. She wants me to stay. She cried last night when I told her.

- Has it got anything to do with Miss Arbuckle?

- No. She's wonderful.

- I'm clueless, I tell him. Are the kids in the cast giving you a rough time?

- Not them.

- Someone else?

- I really don't want to talk about it. I can't. I thought I should tell you since you're the one who got me in. I owe you.

- If you owe me tell me what the problem is, I say while wondering if I really want to know. I'm up to my psychic armpits in exhaustion and other people's troubles. Between the hospital, repairing Max's lawn, and searching for vandals yesterday, Sunday was a washout. Max is home again but for how long? And at some point within the next few days I need to talk to Destiny about freely using my words. I have no idea how she'll take it and I'm in no rush to find out.

- I just can't Mr. A.

- OK, TJ. I won't push.

TJ looks relieved and I have the sudden impulse to put my hand on his shoulder and tell him that whatever is bothering him will work itself out. But the hand would be physical contact. Plus, it's peppy optimism that I don't feel myself this morning. Maybe TJ's problem *won't* work itself out. They don't always. Tough titty.

There's a crisp metallic chime over the PA, the 5 minute warning before first period starts. TJ needs to get going. There will be students pouring in here soon and I doubt he wants an open air forum.

- Have you told Miss Arbuckle yet? I ask glancing at the wall clock. I can tell by his look that he hasn't. You know, I say, it's not too late to reconsider. I know a little how you feel. I mean, remember, we went to this same school, we're from the same old neighborhood. Homies. . . The thought crosses my mind that I'm being glib and I don't want to be. The same hood. That thought triggers another and with a flash of intuitive insight I ask, TJ, do you know anything about my father's yard being vandalized Saturday night? It happened in your neighborhood.

It strikes a nerve. I might as well have hit him with a 2-by. His face gets red, drops. He looks at his feet. He's shelving something. On another insightful flash I ask, Was Curt Moseby involved? I know he's from that area. You said you used to run in his gang.

- Mr. August, TJ says fast looking at the door, I never said anything a-bout Curt. He'd kill me if he knew we were talking.

- So it was him, I say. OK, don't worry. Your secret is safe with me. . . I stand up, TJ jumps back. He looks nervous, almost sick. He starts for the door and I say, Does Curt have anything to do with why you're dropping out of Grease?. . . I think to myself that it's a long shot, no apparent connection. But the question stops TJ dead in his tracks. . . Mr. August, TJ is talking faster, Curt hates you. He says you have it in for him and his father. He figures what he did to your dad's lawn was part of the payback. Making me drop out of the play some more.

- I don't get why you dropping out of the play is payback. . . I think to myself that I also don't get how I am ever going to meet the TJ Sato part of my objective if he drops.

- Curt heard you got me in and he says it's time for me to man-up. Stop being your butt boy. Sorry, but that's what he said.

There's loud talking. Swift and shallow laughter from the hall. First period students start streaming in.

TJ gives me a quick shrug and leaves.

TJ Sato: *Audrey was really upset when I told her I was dropping out of the play and I had a bad time making her believe I still loved her. It's going to be hard to see her now. We don't even have the same lunch period. I know she's really disappointed, I am too. But I don't know what else to do. Curt said if I didn't quit Grease he'd kick my ass and maybe do something to Audrey too. He laughed and wanted to know why I was dating a retard anyway. Said she was an ass wag. He got me so mad. . . I hate to disappoint Mr. August and Miss Arbuckle. They've been good to me. But what can I do?. . . I hope Audrey will still be my girl. I should see if she's at her locker.*

Chapter 20

November - 6 Days Left and Rising
Atlas Unchained

Tuesday

Scarborough Fair: I have to meet with Nunberg by next Monday. Time grows short. Time to unchain some hell.

I collect the homework, race through the movie introduction, and start The Graduate. Students settle in. Up on the screen Benjamin is asked what he's going to do with his future and the PA clicks on to announce the school is in lockdown until further notice. I pause the movie and lock the door. The blinds are already closed. I inform the class there's nothing to be upset about. There are no crazed militia types roaming the grounds, or rampaging disgruntled municipal workers. It's a drug sweep and to remain quiet. We'll continue the movie.

Of course anything out of the ordinary even for seniors is cause to talk and there's excited chatter now. . . Maybe some are druggies worried that the jig is up. Spread eagled and Miranda-ed right in front of us.

The movie continues. Ben gets the word – Plastics.

The Singleman Party Foxtrot: I drift off thinking about what I did earlier. . . 6:15 a.m. I arrive at school. Go through the usual routines. Five minutes before first period I get The Kid's pot out of my desk drawer. Open up the bag in my pocket. Walk to the entrance. I'm nervous. Try not to make eye contact. Halls clearing fast. Start in the foyer and lay a thin trail of grass right into the main office. Not many people around. No one gives me a second glance. Which helps my nerves and keeps me going.

I check my mail. Note Nunberg's secretary in the distance at the microphone getting the morning's announcements ready. Like always. The other secretaries busy with students and answering phones. The coast clear. Nunberg's office empty. When she's not coming in last minute she's always gone at this time sucking up to the superintendent or working on her coif and makeup.

I do a double check, then continue the marijuana dusting right into her inner sanctum. Sprinkle a generous amount around her desk and shake whatever is left onto the counters, pictures, and personal effects. Only Bad Break: When I'm waving the bag to get out the last remnants my wedding band flies off. Whizzes into space like a whirling space station. No clang, just silence. Stupid not to have foreseen that possibility. Near panic when it happens. Ring might be in the carpet, in a plant, in the couch. No time to search.

Go to the faculty lav. Shake out the pocket, brush the pants, flush the bag, wash the hands. Splash some water on my face. Look at myself in the mirror and force a calm innocent front.

Bridge Over Troubled Water: Not a complicated plan. No fancy Pentagon algorithms to figure the mission odds. No contingency backups. KISS. Smooth as any military operation I was ever on. Except for that damn wedding ring. Anything else that could have gone wrong, such as the K9 unit getting here early and busting my own arse didn't happen. Had to involve a custodian friend but he was happy to do it. Favors owed, no questions asked. . . In the planning stage I debated about leaving a partially filled bag in her desk. But decided no. Setting her up for arrest was not what this was about. I wouldn't want it on my conscience if she were booted. This is about a wicked practical joke, revenge, a lesson in humility, and showcasing the notion that if you feck with August he is going to feck you back. Or at least squeeze your nose, slap your butt, nuzzle your muff.

Why I risked my job for such a nominal gesture I didn't think too long on beforehand. If it was rash and not in my best interest, I can only blame increasing stress. And a sort of floating detachment over consequences.

Nunberg will be a laughing stock for awhile. Fodder for the faculty room pundits who will brutally immolate her and her reputation. There's satisfaction in that. Of course she won't know I'm the one. But of course she *will* know. But never with absolute certainty. George might suspect and maybe I should tell him and trust his sense of omertà. On the other hand some things you just keep to yourself.

That goddamn wedding band. I'll ask my custodian friend to look for it after hours. Probably in the carpet. No sound of it hitting anything. Most likely on the perimeter of the room. Low odds of Nunberg finding it. . . Life is ironic. I got two years of broken glass evaluations because of marriage and taking care of Amanda. And now that ring, the very symbol of our love and commitment threatens to drive in the final spike.

I'll go crazy if I think too much about it. I need to trust the fates and a janitor's 20-20.

I Am A Rock: The film class is quiet, no longer concerned with the scene just beyond the door. I have the volume turned high and if the dogs have any of our own Manuel Noriegas or El Chapo Guzmáns by the throat there's no indication. I wonder how Nunberg is faring?

I look around and see that Marcus's head is down. Cradled in his arms like a Halloween pumpkin. I get up, walk over, stand alongside him.

265

Nothing stirring not even his little mouse-like brain. I bend over and peer into his face at close range. He's out. I could wake him, but no. There are snickers around the room. Most of the class now watching me. I put my finger over my lips and walk lightly back. I enter a zero under his name in my gradebook. He's lucky I am not sprinkling pot on him and calling in the dogs.

Wednesday

Sgt. Pepper's Lonely Hearts Club Band: For the first time since I met with them almost 2 months ago we're all together in the English office. This was a last minute idea. Hopefully one of my better ones.

I push the table aside and form the chairs into a more inter-friendly circle. Destiny, Kaufman, Audrey, TJ, Zoe, Jorge. I have no idea what's going to happen other than I'm going to lay my problem on them and see if we can come up with a solution. Together. Group collaboration.

I have never liked cooperative ventures. Going it alone has always been the way for me. The solitary questing protagonist, the frontier ideal. But that was then, this is now. Now I need to shoehorn these 6 diverse people into one Cinderella objective. And fast. I have not even had time to talk to Destiny privately about her cheating. Time's at a premium and accelerating.

- Thank you all for coming, I say sounding like a game show host. I apologize for pulling most of you out of class, something I said I wouldn't do. I wanted to meet as a group. For each of you to meet the others. And to put a problem before you. See if we can find some solution.

I ask them to introduce themselves and to toss out a mini-bio. Nothing they haven't done before. Group Work 1.0. I share myself, as superficially as they do.

- Thanks for going along with me so far, I say smiling and not sure how to continue. It's not like the teleprompter is loaded. I'm nervous, uncertain. . . You all just expressed a goal you have this year, I finally say. Teachers are required to have one too. I want to share mine. It's important you understand it because each of you is part of it. . . I'm talking slowly, trying to read their eyes, body language. But all I get back is attentiveness. Nothing more, or less.

- You all know about the mentor-mentee program I'm piloting. I told you about it at our first meeting. Probably what you don't know is that I've been tasked by Principal Nunberg this year to improve you academically or behaviorally in some measurable way. It's been my objective. And if I don't meet it. . . I pause. . . I'm probably out of a job.

It feels like a guilty confession more than an admirable goal. And a cry for help. I'm sure the strain shows in my voice.

The news doesn't seem any great shock to them.

- So you're using us to help yourself, The Kid finally says. Don't want Nunberg busting your own hump.

- Not using, I say, though I can see why you might think that. I admit in retrospect I should have involved you all in the process more. Someone told me to do that and I ignored him. Wish I had listened.

- How can we help you, Mr. August? Jorge asks. I personally don't care what your motives are. You helped my family, you're helping me. I don't really need to know more than that.

- I agree, says Destiny, though it would be nice if you really cared about us too. But we're not kindergartners.

267

TJ looks sad, like I just shot his dog. Audrey is in tune with his bio-feedback, her music hall panache bourréeing off.

Only Zoe looks unmoved. . . Not easy to rumple her peasant blouse or twiggy candy cane protrusions of hair.

- You know, I say going off topic, I *do* care about you all. . . I look at Audrey and at each of the others. . . I really do. I want each of you to succeed. I want us *all* to succeed. . . Even as I say it I get moist palms and a dry mouth. I'm parched, choked up. Plumbing an inner desert I haven't visited in years with students. Maybe never. . . I pause and smile nervously. Feel naked. Subject to rejection. Fleetingly wonder about Skyping the rest. . .

I pause longer. Then really level with them. Tell them I have two years of mediocre evaluations. That I am in terrible financial shape after the hospital bills. That I am in real danger of being fired. That meeting my objective is key to keeping my job. And they are ultra-key to that objective, my life, and future.

They are quiet. I don't know how I expected them to react to this meet-and-greet the   real August. TJ and Audrey still look uncomfortable. The other 4 are pensive. Perhaps evaluating the candor of my truth barrage. What I said vs. what they believe. . . Or maybe they just don't really care and are daydreaming. More concerned about getting back to class. Zoe's brown eyes are fixed on the clock.

I say, Maybe I didn't care about you all a lot at first. . . I smile and low key, But you grew on me. Each of you. . . I've been referring to you as Team August and while we are not a formal team you all have more in common than you probably ever guessed. And it's been my pleasure to get to know each of you better.

Jorge asks again what they can do and I tell them I'm not sure. That maybe we could come up with a group plan. But that it will have to be awfully good to satisfy Principal Nunberg, I say . . . No one hops in, and I continue that if we go with the group idea perhaps we could put together an act for the Holiday Talent Show. Harmonize a song, do a skit. I'd be willing to join in if you wanted, I say.

Destiny says that she's not big on any school performance. The group is pondering this when she says, What if we put together a school help line? Sort of a 911 but only for our students. Students helping students like NHS does now. But not academic. Social. Personal. It would be real world. Meaningful.

- That's a great idea Destiny, I say.

We discuss the pluses and minuses and have an excellent roundtable going.

Candle In The Wind: Outside the room there are the usual running and minor hall commotions. One momentary PA distraction. But for the rest of the period we are into it. Only Zoe is quiet. Nonparticipating. I don't push beyond asking her opinion over varying points and getting monosyllabic answers.

We outline a proposal. I don't mention I don't have high hopes. That probably anything I put in front of Nunberg she's going to blackball. I'm upbeat. Try not to let my pessimism show. Hope I'm a better actor than I've been a mentor for everyone's sake. This electronic voice lifeline is something that would be good for them and for all the 9-12 graders. I promise that I'll present their idea to the principal early next week, Monday if possible.

They leave for class. I sit alone. Feel really alive. Wonder to myself if this is what it's like to be born. To burst out of the amniotic fluid and to feel that first real breath. Baby at the tit. Suckling milk. Or is it more akin to being born *again*?   Rebirth. Encountering the holy ghost. Saved. Redeemed. Praise be to. . . Hallelujah!

It doesn't matter. I'm just temporarily outside myself. Doesn't last. I'm back to *me* before I hit the computer. I email Nunberg requesting to meet Monday to finalize my objective. For once we'll have something in common. A mutual desire to get at it. End it one way or the other.

Consensus Soliloquy (one abstention): *We understand that no one is perfect including our teachers. Especially Mr. August. But neither are we, so in that sense we're a perfect match. Some teachers and administrators talk a good game. Like it's all about us students. But they never actually go out of their way to do anything. Talk is cheap as they say. We know Mr. August is not a warm fuzzy kind of guy. But he has a warmer heart than he thinks or lets on. . . We can see that he's hurting emotionally, the pain is there. We'll try to help him. Want to help him with Principal Nunberg. He acts upbeat but there's something in his eyes that says defeat.*

Jumpin' Jack Flash: For a frowsy old bar Hudson's on a Wednesday afternoon fulfills all my delinquent middle-of-the-week needs. The braying is loud, the booze flowing like Prohibition just ended. All the bar stools are taken. SRO souls glad for a spot on the sawdust. Lightness skewers everyone. Young, old. Drunk, sober. Laughter is drowning out the jukebox. The talk loose. Appetites run belly-up to the common soil of good times.

George and I arrive simultaneously and push through to our usual corner.

The first pull is beyond sip. I immediately order another. George is laughing to himself and I ask, What's so funny? You don't know? he says. I thought you'd be the first. Apparently someone thought to have a joke at Nunberg's expense yesterday. Really? I say. I did hear rumors. So what happened?

- Well, while you were vegging out in Film, the dogs no sooner entered the school, George says dramatically, then they picked up the scent of marijuana. The cops know because they found remnants scattered around. The dogs make a beeline, or should it be dogline? for the main office. Cops getting towed like water-skiers. The dogs go immediately into Nunberg's office. They jump paws-up on the counters and desk. Send a whole bunch of pictures and bric-a-brac flying. . . George makes wild flailing motions with his arms. . . It happens so fast it takes the officers by surprise. They gain control but not before there's damage and dog drool everywhere. At least the way I heard it.

Several nearby drinkers are leaning in. Listening intently. Thoroughly enraptured by the story and George's histrionic flair. He toasts them and continues.

- Nunberg is now just outside her door, he says. She's speechless. The secretaries biting their cheeks to keep from laughing. Then the dogs start barking at Nunberg. She must have sat in the pot and it's all the officers can do to restrain the dogs again. Someone said she wet her drawers. Ha. Wish I could have been there. Bet you'd give a kidney to have seen it.

He claps hold of my shoulder and gives it a shake. The eavesdroppers go back to their own conversations.

- Haha, yeah, I say, un-foking-believable. But maybe I will see it, I say. At least the setup. There's a security camera on the lobby. Cops must have some idea of who did it.

- That's the best part, George says. There was a power loss for 5 minutes. But just on that circuit. No video. No evidence. A very clean professional job.

I let a small smile show. Not wanting to be too demonstrative, nor too unmoved. Hoping to deflect any suspicion heading my way. . . Someone will sleep well this week, I say, and it won't be Nunberg. I wonder if the union could be behind it? I ask speculatively. Awful lot of P.O.'d people at the meeting.

- Could be,George says, though I think it's more likely a rogue operation. One person. Maybe two. . . He stirs his whiskey on the rocks. . . Could not have been during the night. There's various security monitoring to include sound. Doors and windows locked. Custodians here till after midnight. Much more likely someone, not a student, who could walk into the office yesterday morning and not be noticed. Someone who can keep his mouth shut. But with motive, cajones, and the calm pose of a military man on a career-ending mission if he's caught. You wouldn't know anyone like that, would you Mike?

George looks at me for long seconds, smiles, and clinks my glass.

- Hell no Tonto, I say. A person like that would have to be totally fucking nuts. An R.P. McMurphy or Hunter S. Thompson, I say making light of it while realizing that not even best friends have to know everything. This is not spill-your-guts social networking. There's absolutely nothing to be gained by telling George. And it would only put his job in jeopardy if it ever got out he knew. I can keep a secret. Live with the little guilt over not confiding in him.

- One's fiction, George deadpans, the other's dead. . . He waves to one of our retired teachers and says, By the way Mike, how are *you* sleeping these days?

I look over the top of my glass at him. Take a drink . . . Not so great, I say. I piss a lot. Get night sweats. . . I briefly wonder if I'm convincing. There's a great temptation to loosen my inner devil, that fuck you maestro that nailed Nunberg. To say something outrageous like, Find D.B. Cooper and you'll have your man. I've used the line before. A signal to George that it was no phantom, but a tough elusive s.o.b.

Me.

But I don't. George lets it drop.

Doctor My Eyes: George has two and leaves for home. I'm watching tv, finishing my third. I'm feeling it, but don't really care. My sugar is probably low.

- Hi Mike, Deirdre says. Crazy today, huh? You should see the kitchen.

- Yeah crazy. Just like in school yesterday, everyday. . . I tap my glass.

- You want another one? . . . She says it like it's not a good idea. Like she might not serve me.

- I'm celebrating. Had a couple of recent victories.

-In school?

- Yeah. But let's not go there. Time to unwind . . . I notice she's a tint flustered and flushed.

- You're right, she says. I could use some down time myself. . . She refills my glass and says it's on-the-house. Pours herself a short one and asks, What should we drink to?. . . World peace, I say thinking of Groundhog Day. . . She laughs, clinks my glass, and says, So how are you unwinding this weekend? If you're not busy, and would like to celebrate

273

some more, stop by Saturday evening. You can dine with Max and me. I'm a good cook.

- So Max tells me. I'm happy he's recovered since Sunday's ordeal. He's lucky to have you. . . I'm looking at her while fighting through a quickly descending fog. There's something I should be asking her. But what?. . . I can't this Saturday, I say. I already have plans. But I'm taking Max out Sunday. Why don't you join us?

- I'm working later Sunday. And there's a paper I have to get done. Are you sure you can't make it Saturday? I'm cooking veal saltimbocca.

- It's tempting. . . I stare at the backbar. Bags of chips, pork rinds, and beer nuts. Jars of pickled eggs and pig knuckles. Packets of beef jerky. For some reason I'm not hungry. . . But I already have plans for Saturday, I repeat.

If we were alone I'd be tempted to level with her. Eighty proof truth. Tell her, I enjoy our friendship and I'm sorry if I lingered a little longer than necessary in front of Max's the other night. Made that pathetic move on you. Rest assured, you have no worries about me in the future. . . Creepy honest and real drunk might get me pontificating, Being physically close to you makes me feel like I'm going back. Not that you look like Amanda, or act like her. But around you I'm back in that time just past college but before mortgages. Preemie adulthood. That in-between shadowland when the future is a big question mark. The glow of student life not quite over. It was great to do once. But I don't want to do it again.

I look at our reflections in the bar mirror. The age difference hits me hard. Probably best not to say any of it. Ever. And to forget any fantasies about the old bump-'n-grind at least until the winky withers, the coochie dries up, and sex is just a boom-de-yada memory. . . The other night my drinking got the best of me. It won't again. Not with Deirdre. There's also the embarrassment factor. No one likes to get shot down. Twice would be in a penis shrinker.

- I can't drink over .08 and drive, I say. Well actually, I can. Do it all the time. But I can't drink and make sense much longer. . . I finish the drink in one long gulp. . . So I need to get going, I say and push a tip forward.

I stand. Turn around. The room spins. I lose my balance. I'm about to test the hardness of the floor when a hand shoots out and grabs me. Come on Mike, Vinnie says, I'll drive you home. . . No, I say, I'm OK. Just my blood pressure dropping when I stood. . . If you say so, Vinnie says.

I put on my jacket and take a step towards the door. Remember what I wanted to ask Deirdre. Accusatory concerns, nasty questions. That car in the driveway. Her panties stuck to Max's bathrobe. Is she fucking the old man? Did he buy her a car? Damn, is she really a gold digger after all?. . . Maybe she found something valuable cleaning out the cellar. Hidden money, letters she could blackmail him with. . .

I turn around and motion for her to come closer. I need 80 proof courage for this, and I have it. . . She leans over the bar and I whisper, Are you screwing Max?. . What? she says. . . Are you fucking Max? I say louder. . . God no, Mike! she says flustered.

She comes around from behind the bar and leads me to a table. What are you talking about? she says. Why would you think that?. . . I tell her about finding the undies. . . She laughs. Says, Mike, did you hear of static cling? I do our laundry together. . . What about the Ford Fiesta? I ask suspiciously. . . It was a loaner, she counters. My Honda blew its transmission. Would you like to see the receipt?. . . When I don't respond she says, You know Mike, you're not the only one with problems. But your biggest ones aren't financial. . . Cheezus Deirdre, I'm sorry. I really am an asshole, I say and squeeze her hand. . . You can be, she says unsmilingly.

275

But let's just forget it. She kisses my cheek and goes back behind the bar. . . I think to myself that I'm lucky George and Deirdre still talk to me. . . It was a nice little cheek peck.

Deirdre Good: *I can't believe Mike accused me of fucking Max. And for personal gain. Guess I thought, and hoped, he knew me better than that. Oh well, he's drunk and I've seen enough in this job that little surprises me. . . I'm disappointed that Mike can't make it Saturday. In another time, in a different world I might hope he'd ask me to stop over his house tonight after I get out. But he's tanked and I'm sure will be sleeping it off. Normally he drinks early, corrects papers, and doesn't make the talk show monologues. Different generations, different hours. . . I wonder if Mike has a date Saturday? He's never said anything about another woman. Or gave any sign. But he could be covering up. Men will be men will be boys. And Mike is definitely part boy. Though it's really none of my business. . . My feet ache. . . I wonder what he was celebrating that caused him to drink so much, so fast?*

Chapter 21

Thursday

The Bottom

Don't Let The Sun Go Down On Me: Marilyn Monroe once said, I have other things but I have no imagination. . . Big tits and a skirt blowing up around her waist aside, even Marilyn could imagine what's behind the hostility and dark piling of Nunberg's email to me this morning. Come to my office during your planning period today, the email says. Don't be late. We need to meet before you leave school. . . No mention of meeting Monday as per my email. . . Not a request to meet at my earliest convenience. A statement. Demand. . . Fuck Nunberg, the sclerotic bitch. . . Marilyn Monroe who gave herself credit for no imagination managed to become the clitoris to the stars. Me, I *have* imagination and where's it getting me? Fired?

It's not taking too much to figure out what this is about.

The wedding band.

The custodian told me he couldn't find it Tuesday after school. Or since. Even vacuumed more thoroughly than normal hoping to catch it. But no silver ring.

I Will Survive: Mid-morning I swing by George's office. He's busy and can't talk. I was going to ask him if he heard anything. Maybe have him assure me I'm a good teacher. Something that corny. Anything positive so I'm not totally callous and down.

I swing into the faculty lav and splash water over my hungover head. Take a good look at myself in the mirror. Definitely thinner. Definitely more worried looking this morning. I force a smile. Try to radiate some positive vibes. The universe is built on frequency. Everything is vibration first, physical matter second. If I can just match the upbeat resonance I want, perhaps I really can change the reality around me. Sow some happy seeds, reap some happy harvest. I smile wider. Go into uni-task brain mode. Try to emanate, become a joyous being.

I wait.

An unseen ceiling fan whirls in its syncopated failing to exhaust lav vapors. A girl in hall shouts something about meeting at her house after school. Plans, I think. People have futures. Do I?. . . Someone flushes a toilet in the female faculty lav next door.

I sigh and let the smile drop. I look hard and deep into that reflection and try to gain toilet room nirvana. I remind myself that all is not lost. Unlike many of my generation I don't need Viagra or Levitra, testosterone patches, penile implants, Upjohn injections, or hair plugs. I do take Vitamin C and aspirin. Occasionally Advil, Preparation H, and Zantac. But I don't use beta blockers, diuretics, ARB's, Lipitor, or any statins. My blood pressure and cholesterol are high. And I can't pass a physical. But I have good genes so I'm not worried. Maybe my balls have shrunk a bit, ejaculatory distance is not what it once was. But I'm not looking to hit the ceiling, so who cares. . . Sex hasn't happen in a long time and if they gave frequent flyer miles for it I couldn't get out of town. But I'm not looking to make babies into my senior years. . . All-in-all I'm a person of worth. In good enough shape to squeeze out a few more years and maybe a few more tits.

I belong in the classroom.

I belong in this school.

I have earned the right to stay.

North To Alaska: I enter and stand in front of Nunberg's desk. She's seated and typing. We say nothing. She hits Print and puts two pages in front of me. I think you know the routine, she says. I glance over the top sheet, take it, sign the other copy and hand it to her without a word.

- I am writing you up for what I can prove, she says. Not monitoring the assembly, your lack of tact in the meeting with the Campbells, your confrontation with Mr. Moseby, and finally your leaving the library in the midst of a crisis.

- Is that all? I say, not at all confident but trying for my best Philip Marlowe steely demeanor. I'm surprised she didn't mention being hungover and falsely accusing Deirdre.

- I want your resignation on my desk Monday morning. . . She's glaring at me and making no pretense of being open-minded. . . If I don't get it I will recommend to the superintendent that you be suspended until I can complete my case against you.

- Which is? I ask suddenly going floaty light-headed.

- You have demonstrated a total lack of professionalism this year. You have now been written up twice over a wide range of incidents, and you will not, I believe, meet your objective. Then, of course, there is this. . . She holds up my wedding band and looks at the engraving. . . Very nice sentiment, she says. Forever yours. And with your initials and wedding date. Don't bother to explain how you lost it during our last meeting in here. I don't think you could have dropped it on the carpet over there in the corner. I found it late Tuesday afternoon, before our janitorial crew gave my room an unusually spotless cleaning. . . I suppose I could now have it tested for marijuana but there was pot in the carpet so I don't suppose there is a case there. There were also traces of pot in the men's faculty lavatory, but. . . Here, she says and hands it back to me. I have a strong case without it.

- And if I don't resign and if the superintendent doesn't suspend me? I'm not inclined towards the former, and I can make a good case against the latter.

- I will make your year a living hell, she says. Your final evaluation will be poor. And based on the likelihood of a reduction-in-force next year you will be let go based on that evaluation and your 2 previous ones.

- If I do resign, would you give me a letter-of-recommendation? I ask barely cognizant of what I'm saying. . . A good one?

- No.

Scientists and historians talk about when worlds and civilizations collapse. The feelings of helplessness, of utter disorientation. There is no pipeline to mercy here. No artery of appeal. I know I need to get out and take the weekend to think it through. I start to turn. I know I should just leave but I cannot help asking, Since you're being brutally honest, I say, I'm going to ask you again. Was it you who sent that OUT OF MANY, FEW letter? Did you have it in for me from the very beginning of the year?

She smiles and says, I did *not* send you any letter.

- Is it personal? I ask. Do you have my license plate?. . . I twist my head and narrow my eyes.

- Your license plate?

- Was your dog killed outside of Woodland Park?

- My dog? No. He was killed in the parking lot of my condo complex. What in the world are you talking about?

I'm out of theories behind her motivation.

- Was finding my wedding band the straw that broke your back? I ask trying to score some final knowledge. Was it, I say, the real catalyst behind this meeting?

Unbelievably my right leg falls asleep and as much as I don't want to, I shake it.

She folds her hands. Pauses still smiling. Leans back, and says, Yes. But you were dead anyway.

Chapter 22

Friday

Over the Woods

The Man Who Shot Liberty Valance: Friday dawns cloudy with a forecast of clearing and afternoon sun. It doesn't feel that way. Does not seem like I stand a prayer at clearing out my own clouds and salvaging my teaching position and future. My life has come down to three days to make a decision that seems to have been made for me.

There's a time to fight. A time to quit. Maybe it's time to quit. Never thought I would say that, at least not before standard retirement. I have fought a lot of administrators over the years. Worked through a lot of arbitrary and meaningless mandates. Had my back and ass up against it many times. A number of which have been documented in my personnel folder in the form of written reprimands. The time when I refused to use a bell curve for a failing class. The time I kept an entire last period class after school on an afternoon when there was no late bus. The book incident when I balked at teaching a new novel that was simple-minded and under grade level. A bunch more.

It does wear on a person. I feel tired. Worse, I feel useless and over-the-hill. There is a saying that there's no ministry in hell, meaning that even god gives up. Maybe I've reached that stage.

Nunberg has been a super-collider of wicked. One of the speakers at the union meeting said he heard Nunberg was nicknamed The Terminator and Hatchet Lady in her last school. It feels right, but I also question why she hasn't been on anyone else's case as much as she's been on mine.

It's a fact that other teachers have been written up. The AP Spanish teacher who called in sick 3 days in a row and was seen at a Salsa concert and a Haitian relief fundraiser. But no teacher except me has been written up more than once. And I doubt anyone received the threat and promise she handed me yesterday.

Could it be I really *am* losing it? That I really *have* become a bad teacher? George says no but he's a close friend. Students are asking me for college recommendations so apparently my word and reputation are good with some of them. . . I've been fighting a lot of demons in-and-out of school these last few years and I have tried to remember Nietzche's advice that whoever fights monsters should see to it that he himself does not become one. Calling myself a monster might be strong. Even Nunberg would probably only label me a professional miscue. A gout of fuckup.

My overwhelming feeling is, and has been, that someone has had it in for me from September. I keep coming back to that anonymous letter. Find the author, find the root of the writeups. . . The force behind the typewriter could be Jimmy Klein. I thumped him hard on the bar the day before school started and bruised more than his head. But it's a far stretch to imagine Nunberg taking orders from anybody outside the power elite, especially a beer and drug sotted creeper like Klein. . . Could be our taxpayers group. They keep a lot of pressure on Hoxley and the board, who in turn trickle down the g-forces to Nunberg. Some real radicals in that bunch including one survivalist with stockpiled foodstuffs and a cyber blog that harps about Armageddon. . . Perhaps the numero uno suspect should be my father-in-law Oliver Phelps. King Prick. Banker, force incognito with the town's finance board and by logical extension behind any upcoming RIF.

Oliver Phelps.

Old money, old prejudices, old grudges.

He has not been in my life since Amanda and I got married and he essentially disowned her for marrying not only a school teacher, but a Jew. He talked to Amanda about it. Never said a word to me, and Amanda begged me not to confront him. Made me promise. He did not come to the wedding, ignored all subsequent invitations. Never wrote or called. Showed up at the funeral but stayed in the background and left before the final, Amen.

As much as I have not wanted to consider the long shot that Oliver Phelps is the marionette master behind Nunberg, it can't be ignored any longer. I'm not going to lose my job because of a long departed promise that had its day. Or any fear of retaliation. Whatever the bastard can do to me, he seems to be doing.

It's time to finally have it out with him.

The House Of Seven Gables: The house sprawls over old farmland in the upscale WASPish DAR community uphill from our factory valley. The Phelps estate has been in the family since the late 1800's and is considered one of the finest examples of high-style shingle architecture in the state. The exterior is based with gray field stone that gives way as it rises to cedar shingle siding topped with a gambrel roof frontispiece and two large projecting side gables. The three story verticalness is brought back to earth by a stone-columned porte-de-cochere that extends out over the circular driveway. Well tended shrubbery, old growth trees, natural bluestone walks and pebbled gardened paths wrap it all in a protective blanket of manicured snobbery.

The weathered cedar is glowing an aureate hue this late afternoon as I ring the doorbell. The impression is warmth, almost homeyness. I don't figure there will be much of that in a few minutes.

284

Dueling Banjos: Oliver Phelps is sitting in the library with a blanket over his legs. The mid-afternoon light coming through the floor-to-ceiling bay window casts him in a spotlit halo of dormant energy. He's in a bathrobe but there's nothing informal about him. White-haired, aquiline, patrician. He is a living reminder of Amanda's looks and the powerful forces I have always been up against.

- What is this supposed to mean? he says in a measured resonating bass. . . He's holding up the OUT OF MANY, FEW letter I sent in with the nurse.

- I was hoping you would tell me, I say leaning on one foot and looking around.

- I have no idea what you're talking about, or what this phrase means. And I would appreciate you getting to your point quickly.

I heard that the old man's time has come down to less than a year, but there's no sense of imminent collapse in his eyes. His voice is Raymond Massey, the kind that reverberates authority.

- Someone mailed me that letter, I say bringing my attention fully on him. At the beginning of the school year. OUT OF MANY, FEW. It echoes the motto on the U.S. seal – Out of many, one. Which is found on U.S. currency. You being a banker, the tie-in to you seems natural. And logical. Especially considering your feelings towards me. An ironic kick in my ass before you kick off yourself.

I think to myself that if I'm being mean-spirited and nasty it's appropriate. Meeting him on his own level. A level which, as death approaches, is probably the only one powerful enough to elicit an honest reaction. . . I quickly explain to him the projected budget cutbacks, likelihood of a reduction-in-force, and the distinct possibility I will be either fired or let go. . . My principal has been writing me up over trivial matters, I say, almost as if she has been ordered to. And I'm guessing that it's the author of that note who's behind it.

- Typical Jewish persecution complex, he says. Has it occurred to you that the note is probably just a joke sent by one of your farcical peers? And that perhaps you really *do* deserve poor evaluations? That perhaps you are not the chosen one destined to save American education?

- I think it's more likely that I'm a target. *The* target of someone looking for delayed retribution. Someone with enough money, power, and influence to make his wishes reality.

- Michael, you overestimate me. I could have you killed, even delete your bank account – if you had one. But for me to get a tenured teacher fired?. . . Phelps takes a drink of some clear liquid and looks out the window. His last line sounded flip, but there's nothing in his lined face that says humor.. . You ceased to exist for me when Amanda died, he says. Before that, I confess, I was tempted to make your life a memorable hell. But I could not do that without impacting Amanda. So I left you alone.

- Fat lot you cared about her, I say. Cutting her off, both from your money and from your person. She deserved to have a father in her life, even a bastard like you.

- Amanda's mother would probably have agreed with you, had she survived Amanda's birth. Neither one was a strong women. And that was always the cornerstone of my resentment of you. Amanda was not brought up to work and to live the life of a school teacher's wife with all the stress and drudgery of that quasi-middle class existence. Nor was she physically strong enough to strive it. I knew that from the beginning. Knew that marriage to you would kill her. Which it did. Her fate was sealed when she said, I do.

- Amanda was a strong lady, much stronger than you ever gave her credit for. She had all of your strength with none of your closed-minded pettiness. We were happy together. Had enough money to indulge our – by your standards – simple pleasures. It wasn't stress, or hobnobbing with the masses that caused her cancer. I honestly don't know what was. It was just a damn tragic break.

- She would be alive today had she married someone of her class, her sensibilities.

- Life isn't a 19th century Grand Tour with summers at Newport.

- It could have been for her.

- That kind of life is narrow, unfulfilling. It was not what Amanda wanted. You have heard, haven't you, that women can now vote, practice birth control, even abort if they want?

- They can also fuck the help and run off to Niagara Falls. None of that is new. A pickup truck marriage. Amanda got what she wanted. And it killed her.

- Has it ever occurred to you that by cutting her off, you yourself added immeasurable stress to her life? Stress she never showed, or talked about. But stress that was there. Deep rooted. Maybe even strong enough to ultimately put her in an early grave.

- Any stress, any sense of loss she felt over me would have been secondary to the strain of an everyday working life with you in the valley.

- You're trying to negate any responsibility. Put it all on me. Did you hate me enough when she was alive that you felt, and still feel, that Amanda was better off dead than living with me, a teacher and Jew?

- I think it would have been better if she never married you. Best if she had never even met you.

That Lucky Old Sun: The wind goes out of me, and the fight. Oliver Phelps is a sad old man stuck in a morass of dark energy. He's about Max's age but without Max's sense of humor about life even in its bleakest times. The world for Phelps turns on a dime and stays turned. Cannot cope with a world in flux. The random, the unscheduled, the unwanted. His nano-world is the annihilation of space by time, that Marx predicted. . . I watch him studying a fly crawling up the outside of his drinking glass. I expect him to shoo it away but instead he just watches it. Mesmerized. He looks back at me as if I am no longer here. Respect for noncerebral insensate insect life, but not for Mike August. Someone once said WASPs love dogs, it's people they can't stand. Phelps never had a dog that I know of, but apparently node-like flying bugs rate high.

- We're getting nowhere, I say. It's futile trying to establish blame. Futile trying to put order into a death that was, and always will be for me, nonsensical and tragic. . . I never told anyone this, but I see Amanda a lot in my dreams. She is always beautiful. Always walking towards me.

The glass begins to shake in his hand and he puts it down.

I turn and start for the door. I pause before opening it and without turning say, I'm only–

I walk out into the sunshine and never look back. I was going to say, Only half Jewish. But why mention it? What would be the point? I leave the letter with him.

Oliver Phelps: *I deal with Jews everyday and have great respect for them. They are hard tough businessmen. Many create jobs, few shirk responsibility. I happen to know Michael is only half Jewish. I know a great deal about him. Perhaps he would have been a better husband for Amanda if he had been all Jewish. Michael is a dreamer, a non-go-getter. He has* *contented himself to teaching literature in a small high school classroom to a handful of students who could scarcely care less about him or what he's saying. From the first he limited himself, his life, and Amanda's. If he had any gumption he would have become a principal, superintendent, and eventually risen to a position of power within the state and national departments of education. I would have helped him. . . I give him credit for confronting me about that letter. It is about the most spunk I have ever seen from him. Of course I did not write it, why would I? You don't warn your enemy you're coming, if indeed you are. I know Michael thinks I'm a bastard, but I am disappointed to learn he thinks I'm a dumb bastard. I always thought he was reasonably intelligent in a street smart sort of way. Apparently he is not even that.*

Chapter 23

Saturday Morning and Afternoon
Desperation Run

Long Day's Journey Into Night: The car window is down and the autumn air is streaming in filling my hungover lungs with crisp frost-scented November air. I have the heater on and the rush of hot air against my feet and legs creates a 2-zone war. Hot-Cold, similar to what Nixon used to do in the summer when he turned the White House AC way down and had the fireplace going. Fire and ice. The end of the world.

I am desperate this Saturday morning. I'm going to a small town about 50 miles from here. A town I have never been to before. A quaint colonial place, according to Wikipedia and George. An early river front outpost against the French and Indians. Yuppie, boutiquey, upscale today. Upriver from the metropolis. Easy rail commuting distance for the professionals who populate it. People who buy local, eat vegan, jog, rock climb, learn Chinese, play the market, read The Times, trust their kids.

Nunberg's hometown.

The secondary road is following a tortuous 2-lane path through the western hills. Houses are few, widely spaced, come at irregular intervals. The road margined by thick woods from a long ago Robert Frost poem. The sunlight is bright but to my back and low. It's making the road into a woodcut of branch lines. I stop to let a rafter of wild turkeys cross. They take their time leaving their wooded world. The poults, the babies, unsure of the macadam, the sound of my auto, follow trustingly. . . Maybe none of us should be leaving home, venturing out, I think. But what choice do we really have? Either we attack life. Or it attacks us. Kicks us right in the ass. . . The turkeys disappear into the far tree line.

It's a beautiful morning. The kind that it's great to be free and on the open road. Or it would be if Bernadette Nunberg and her wanting my resignation were not on my mind, leading me on this cross-state odyssey.

Nunberg. There was nothing of consequence online. Nothing any of the teachers in school knew about her. . . I'm looking for dirt. Something to hold over her head. Coercion, blackmail. Maybe the 2 of us have some tie-in I have forgotten. Maybe she and Zoe do. I need something cheap. Some hushed-up event. Some headline that's tabloid worthy. And I need it by Monday. I have the strong feeling putting the call line in front of her is not going to pass muster. Neither will the work I've done so far with the six. She wants me gone, and she just may get her wish unless I can find some scandalous divertissement.

I take a sip from my stainless travel mug. The homemade Irish cream I dumped on top of the coffee gives it bite. I feel my spirit lifting, which is exactly what I need. I need to be sharp too, but there's not much booze. It'll wear off before long. But for now it's helping the hangover. . . I feel like Fitzgerald driving through the French countryside swilling a bottle of inexpensive red. Rogue motoring, cheap thrills. It helps the miles pass. Makes this gorgeous day even more beautiful. . . Alcoholic prudery be damned. Let the cops enforce it. Catch me if you can.

Mr. Deeds Goes To Town: The river town is everything its homepage pictured. Speed limit is 25 on Main and I am careful to observe it while studying the small restaurants and trattorias with umbrelled tables that line the cobblestone sidewalks. Art galleries, antique shops, clothing stores with mannequins dressed in more money than I make in a week, a month. Street traffic is light, the downtown barely awake. A group of joggers with heads locked to the front, eyes fixated straight ahead run past. Heavy clouds of white breath trail them. A pair of speed walkers and 2 dog handlers give me longer looks.

The local newspaper is right where the internet map said. I pull into a side parking lot, finish the enhanced coffee, and walk purposely into the lobby like maybe I am chasing a Pulitzer. An older woman with gray free flowing hair, half glasses, an elongated Modigliani neck and no makeup asks me in a voice of bell-like clarity if she can help me. I tell her I'm the one who called yesterday about using the morgue and back issues. She escorts me through the empty newsroom, down a dimly lit hall, into a back room. It's stacked with card catalogues and 2 microfilm readers. Take your time, she says. I'll be out front if you need me.

I watch her walk off. A skinny AARP ass but one with a firm little swagger. I am suddenly horny with the mellowed sense of a hangover awash in a slight morning high. Sex, here, now. Right on the old printer's job case. Imprint those buns. . . I force the thought out of my mind and realize I need more coffee. Just coffee.

The card catalogue is in traditional alphabetical order. The 3x5 cards are yellow with age. Most of the entries are typed, later updates handwritten neatly in ink. It doesn't seem that most of the cards have been updated.

I just hope there is plenty here on Bernadette Nunberg that's incriminating.

I pull her card and all the cards that her index cross references. I start grabbing boxes of microfilm. It's going to be slow going to thread each reel and hand crank it to the desired issue, the right page and column. But I have no where else to go, nothing else as remotely as important. I need answers and if they're not here I need to pound the pavement.

After a couple of hours of tedious winding and rewinding I have covered everything that's in the cards. Not much. I learn Nunberg is 20 years out of this local high school, which makes her a little younger than me. She was field hockey captain, basketball manager, president of The Girls' Leader Club. She made a few published honor rolls, won the Rotary scholarship, matriculated at a well known private college. After college she became a teacher here. No way to deduce for how long. . . But no arrests, no accidents. Nothing remotely infamous. A flat life on the public record.

On the other hand her father Sid was arrested for embezzlement. The charges were dropped. Later he was arrested for being a Peeping Tom with a single charge of private place prurient intent. Probation. He died while Bernadette was a junior in high school but not before crashing a car, killing a pedestrian, and being sentenced to 5-10 for vehicular manslaughter. He died in prison. Suicide. There's no recent mention of the mother.

I check Czarina Koppel – nothing. But under Czarina Klein there's a birth notice and later a single line about an art award in middle school. . . I'm surprised, but *not* surprised. The 2 of them, Zoe and Nunberg, *did* live in this same town. Though it's unclear if their time here overlapped. The background information on Zoe was not available back at school. George said Zoe's previous school transcript was missing from her guidance folder.

293

Jimmy Klein. A couple of entries. One pertaining to a bad motorcycle accident that involved DUI and assault. The other for going to court.

I'm not sure what the intersections of these 3 lives are, or if there even is one. But I am more determined than ever to find out.

I finish my note taking and return everything to its proper place. Stop on my way out and ask the senior dame if she ever knew a student or high school teacher named Bernadette Nunberg. Nunberg, she says slowly like maybe that name has gone viral. No, I don't think so, she says. . . She would have been teaching here around 15 years ago, I say. . . You know who would know, she says, Ray Emmet. As a matter of fact, she says and glances at a digital desk clock, he's probably at the coffee shop now having an early lunch.

Waist Deep In The Big Muddy: As I walk into the coffee shop I recognize Ray Emmet right away. The lady tipster said he'd be wearing a flat tweed cap and a pullover sweater. Or maybe a field coat, she hedged. He'll definitely be sitting at the corner window table reading the newspaper. She needlessly added, He's a man of steady habits.

- Ray Emmet? I ask. He looks up, the hat riding low on his eyebrows. I smile and say a little louder, Are you Mr. Emmet? . . . He looks around 70. Might be hard of hearing judging by the way he's tilting his right ear towards me.

- Yes? he acknowledges still holding the newspaper.

- My name is Harry Fines, I lie for no good reason. I was wondering if I could ask you about a teacher you used to work with?. . . I explain that a lady at the newspaper gave me his name. The teacher is our high school principal now, I say and explain that I'm a reporter writing an article about her. He folds the paper, motions to the empty chair, and I sit down.

- Bernadette Nunberg, I say. Explain that she graduated from this high school and later became a teacher.

- Bernadette? he says with no hesitation. I remember her. Not an easy lady to forget. What do you want to know?

- Whatever strikes you as newsworthy. She's doing a great job and I'd like this article to maybe hit the important influences in her life. Explain, or at least hint at, the causes for her success.

I'm facing the window and a red-haired man walking a brindle great dane comes into view. The dog's base coat popping yellow under the late morning sun.

- She's a success as a principal? the old codger says and laughs out loud. Damn, that is newsworthy. Miracles must come easier where you live.

Outside the man is tying the dog to the parking meter. The dog's black mask turns towards me and stares like it knows I'm a phony.

- It's probably a rougher high school than this one, I say. Maybe a better fit.

- I hope for your sake it is, Emmet says. Well, I'm too old to bullshit you so I'll just say Bernadette was not popular when she became a teacher here. Not with the staff. Over achiever, always pushing. She was like that as a student too. But it became more pronounced when she took over the classroom.

He talks, I listen. Tells me she ratted out a couple of teachers to the administration her second year. One for smoking on school grounds, the other for bad mouthing the principal. They both got written reprimands, he says and adds, we always felt we had a spy in our midst. After awhile we stopped talking when she was around. . . No one likes a snitch, I offer. . .

295

Maybe she did it because she wanted to lock in tenure, he speculates. She was no great shakes in the classroom. Maybe to offset all her father's failings. Or her mother's. She probably felt as if she *had* to succeed.

- What about her mother? I ask. What was she like?

- An ordinary enough housewife, I guess. At least until her husband's collapse. After his death she tried working as a clothing store clerk but quit. Talk was that her register was always short. She was a chain smoker. Got lung cancer and died in, I think, Bernadette's final year of teaching here.

Outside the dog has just finished crapping on the sidewalk. He lies down, his great head resting in his paws. Reminds me I'm a little tired myself. And need to drop a deuce. Inside I hear his owner ordering a latte to go.

- Wasn't Bernadette a speech therapist? I ask.

- I heard that she later became one, Emmet follows my eyes outside. But here she taught history. Or didn't teach history depending on your viewpoint.

- Is that why she left? I ask. They denied her tenure?

- Damn that Natasha, Emmet says still looking at the dog. No, she got tenure after her third year. She announced she was leaving for a better paying position. . . He pauses and looks to the counter. Hey Tom, he says roughly, that dog of yours just dropped a load next to my car! Why don't you toilet train that mutt?

Tom looks over his shoulder and says, She's saying what she thinks of your Korean junker. Maybe checking your eyesight too.

Emmet laughs. Says *damn dog* again, and retorts, Just be sure you pooper scoop that load. . . The owner shakes a plastic bag in our direction and replies, You're welcome to go get it Ray if you're in such a hurry. . . Damn dog, Emmet shakes his head.

- Do you know where she went when she left here? I ask.

- No, he says, but I think it was out-of-state.

- Did she own a motorcycle when she was here? Or ride anyone else's? I ask suddenly thinking of the picture on her desk.

- She might have, he says. I have this fuzzy image of her arriving at work one day just before she left. A big bike. No Vespa.

I ask him if he ever knew or heard of Czarina Klein or Jimmy Klein. No, he says, they don't sound like any of my former students. . . Jimmy Klein was a student in my town, I say, but he later lived here. I'm just wondering if he knew Nunberg, maybe dated her. . . Emmet says as far as he knows Nunberg never had a boyfriend. . . She didn't like men? I ask. . . Emmet says he doesn't know about that. There were rumors, he says, that she was seeing both the assistant principal and her department chair on the side. Both married. One male, the other female.

I tell him Klein went to jail for a bad motorcycle accident that involved DUI and assault. Happened here, I say. . . Klein? he scratches the side of his head and says the name again as if repetition might be the mother of memory. No, he says, Klein doesn't ring a bell. But I do vaguely recall a tragic motorcycle accident: 15, 20 years ago. I don't know if it's the same one or not. There are so many crashing drunks that come up here from the city. But there is a pinprick that's telling me Klein was not alone when the accident occurred. That he wasn't even driving, though he took the blame. . . It's coming back slowly. . . Emmet takes a sip of coffee and says, There was bar talk that a woman was driving and that Klein assaulted the other motorist when the guy tried to stop the woman from running off. Not much of a trial. Klein pleaded guilty. No plea bargain. He took the full penalty. The other driver wound up partially disabled. If that's the same accident.

- Sounds like it, I say. Can you remember anything more about it? Anything about the rumored woman?

- Not a thing. You think the woman might be Bernadette Nunberg? he asks reading my mind.

- It's possible, I say. Do you know anyone who would know?

- If it's been kept quiet all these years I doubt it'll come out now. But you never know. You should talk to Marion Radler. She was probably Bernadette's only friend from those years. She still lives here. I don't know if she knows anything, but if she doesn't no one else does. . . He waves at the latte man who's leaving and gets back another plastic bag shake.

Ray Emmet moves the newspaper off the table and says, This must be a helluva article you're writing. I don't know how important it is for you to discover the truth, whatever it is. Or even if there is more. But be careful. Just a word of advice. Bernadette Nunberg will never let anyone beat her. Not without a helluva fight.

He winks. His tuna sandwich and chips arrive. I order a black coffee to go. Emmett pauses before eating and says, Enjoy your day, Harry.

I head for the restroom. By the time I hit the street the sidewalk crap has vanished and there are several lumpy clusters of teens hanging around. Can't escape them even in another state, on a day off.

I walk back to the newspaper office.

Ring Of Fire: Marion Radler. There's little on the microfilm. Active teacher, hometown girl, about Nunberg's age. Another flat public life, as is probably the case with most teachers. I decide to just show up at her doorstep. Might get more information if she is off balance and unprepared.

298

I kill another hour taking a nap in the car, drinking cold water, sucking in lungfuls of mental healing oxygen and planning an approach. If Marion Radler was Nunberg's best friend she's going to be guarded. Unless there was a falling out.

Assuming she knows something that didn't come out with the police investigation or trial, how to get it now? Key problem. . . I could say I'm a cop investigating new evidence about the accident and her name came up. I would claim of course that I cannot reveal the nature of that evidence or my sources. But what if she demands to see a badge or credentials?. . . Maybe pose as an insurance adjuster, a medical claims investigator. But again, if Nunberg were driving that motorcycle that night and Radler knows it, what insurance leverage or medical appeal could get the truth out of her *now*?. . . Maybe a lawyer? Opening a belated liability case on Klein's behalf? He is now suing Nunberg. . . why? And how could he be suing if he confessed? And isn't there a statute of limitations on all this?. . . Maybe I should just offer her a bribe, a really big one. But use *what* for money?

It takes awhile for me to come up with a cover that *might* work. It's far from perfect but this whole undercover chase is a long shot so what have I got to lose? Failure is a real option, I'm not too big to fail. . . I suddenly feel ass-dragging weary with the pressure of this weekend and Monday's approach. I could pray, I guess, but I prayed when Amanda was sick and she died. Deals with god are one-sided. If anyone gives me a penny for my thoughts or prayers they'd be overpaying.

Elusive Butterfly: Home is a riverfront condo. I ring the bell and wait. A sailboat tacks out on the water. The sails go limp as the boat comes about, then billow out in a bulbous explosion of white canvas. I press the doorbell again. From inside I hear a faint, I'm coming. Footsteps are followed by, Who is it? I answer, A friend of Bernadette Nunberg.

When the door swings open the first thing I see is a sleep-lined face. You're a friend of Bernadette's? Marion Radler asks. She is a thin woman who carries her lack of weight with upright brittleness. She looks as if she might fall over.

- Not really a friend, I say. My name's Jeffrey Spaulding. I'm selling a motorcycle. A vintage Harley. Ms. Nunberg gave me your name as a reference.

- I don't understand.

- May I come in, I say. This won't take long but it is cold out here.

She steps back and I enter a living room that's dotted with pieces of Victorian furniture. High in rococo scrolls and curves that look like rosewood and walnut. An ornate bookcase holds sets of matched leather bound books. She switches on a figured table lamp with a shade of pleaded and tousled green. I sit down on a velour settee. She sits across from me in a striped silk arm chair. I feel like I'm in a Big Easy bordello.

- What did you say your name is? she asks politely in that guarded way people do when they do not want to chance offending you but have every right.

- Jeffrey Spaulding, I say again hoping she isn't familiar with Marx Brothers movies.

- And why are you here? You're selling a motorcycle?

- Yes. I am. It's my pride and joy. And I am very fussy to whom I sell it. . . *To whom?* I think. Easy on the formal, I tell myself. Don't want to come off as too phony. It doesn't take a dog like that great dane to spot that.

- I don't blame you, she says. I would feel the same way if I sold my vintage furniture.

300

- Your furniture is lovely, I say in a bit of the old soft sell. She beams and I hope she's getting loose and trusting. . . I want the new owner to be someone who is really deserving of my fine machine, I say. Someone who will take the best care of it. Ms. Nunberg gave me your name as someone who could vouch for her character. And for the fact that she's a good rider.

- I haven't seen or talked to Bernadette in years. I didn't even know she still rides.

- I don't think she has been. But she wants to get back into it.

- I'm surprised. I didn't think after what happened she would ever get back on a motorcycle again. Especially a large one which I assume yours is.

After what happened? I think to myself, then tell myself not to push too fast. As much as I want the truth and am living in a state of emergency, I can't throw the siren on just yet.

- Would you say Ms. Nunberg takes pride in the things she owns?

- She did when I knew her.

- And she is a good rider, a cautious rider? I ask.

- I would say that is the case.

- Did she ever have a 2-wheel accident that you know of? You mentioned something about after-what-happened. Perhaps a fender bender? Or something worse?

Her eyes narrow almost imperceptibly. I said that? she says. I must have been thinking of the accident her father had.

I let it slide and push harder.

- Ms. Nunberg also gave me the name Jack Klein as someone who could vouch for her character and her handling of motorcycles. I tried to contact Mr. Klein but he's apparently out of town. And I would like to close the deal soon.

301

- Jack Klein?

- She said that they used to ride together and that he would even occasionally let her drive his bike with him on the back. Ride tandem.

- Mr. Spaulding, I don't know any Jimmy Klein–

- No, I said *Jack* Klein.

- I don't know *any* Kleins and I'm tired. I think it's time for you to go.

She stands and walks to the door. I stand but don't move. What are you hiding, Mrs. Radler? I ask over dramatically as if this is *A Few Good Men* and I'm Tom Cruise trying to get the colonel to say he ordered the Code Red.

- When she doesn't answer I say, Bernadette Nunberg *was* driving the motorcycle the night Jimmy Klein crashed, *wasn't* she?. . I don't get to say another word. The door swings open and standing there is a tall large stanchion. A living, breathing mountain man. Tangled nest of coppery hair, full beard, an insulated red vest over a wool shirt. He looks at me with traceless ice-blue eyes. His wife swings the door open wider. Is everything OK, honey? he asks while making me into a ceramic figure. Everything is fine, she says. Mr. Spaulding was just leaving.

I tip my baseball cap to them as I walk past. The door slams behind me. I breath a sigh of relief, though I don't know any more about Nunberg and that accident than I did before.

The clock is ticking.

On The Road Again: The ride home takes about an hour. I don't see any more turkeys and feel like I just crossed the road myself for no good reason. If there is anything to my theory that Nunberg was driving the motorcycle the night of the crash, and Klein is now blackmailing her and using that long ago night to get rid of me, I will never be able to prove it.

302

Unless someone confesses. . . Someone. . . The only possibility is that Zoe knows the story and is willing to talk. Seems unlikely she would but there are stranger things between heaven and earth. . .

I'll call her and try to set up a meeting for tomorrow.

Chapter 24

I Hear You Knocking

Saturday Evening

Fingertips Part 2: Sophia and I are sitting on my living room couch watching an old movie on tv. It's the first time she's been here. The first time we've been together outside of school since our date weeks ago. She's been booked, time's been slashed for both of us. . . I thought it would feel strange after nearly a month. It does. But less than I imagined. We're comfortable together. Nothing forced. It flashes through my mind that Amanda and I passed many evenings on these same cushions. Especially later when she was diagnosed. Love and caring never stronger. Mega-candlepower.

Now it's a different woman. No snuggling. We're drinking cognac on-the-rocks. Tossing it down pretty good. Maybe busting a move later. I was feeling tired after doing yard cleanup when I got home. Then she called and suggested a quiet evening here. I was excited at the offer and happy for the distraction from Monday's showdown with Nunberg. . . Sophia drove herself over. Brought the brandy. Basil, tomato, EVOO, and vinegar too. Together we made bruschetta. She even thought of the French bread. This after she asked about snacks and I told her I had plenty of chips and potato sticks.

There's a roaring fire going in the fireplace. The wood aged and dry as kindling from being stored in the basement. I stopped having fires a couple of years ago. The micro-pollutants bothered Amanda's breathing. She was never keen on fires anyway saying they smelled sooty. I'm burning the last of the apple now. The blazing fragrance a mix of autumn, cider, and days growing shorter.

- Your wife was attractive, Sophia says looking at the photo on the end table. I remember her from a few faculty parties. She had style.

- I agree, I say and think of Amanda's request to me near the end. Speak me soft when I'm gone, she said. I will, I told her. Always. . . I really don't want to get into Amanda now and Sophia wisely lets it go. She dips a wedge of bread into the bruschetta and puts it up to my mouth. I nibble, then chomp. Chopped tomato bits spill onto my sweater and we both laugh.

On the screen Gary Cooper playing Howard Roark stares down Patricia Neal as Dominique Francon. Bedroom scene. Stormy night. Opposites giving off lightning bolts. I was never sure if this Fountainhead moment qualified as rape or just carnal predation. Him devouring her. Gladly on her part.

The dog and cat are sleeping on the floor just beyond the fire screen. The cat curled between the mutt's paws.

- I'm not a huge old movie fan, Sophia says suddenly. She slides over and nuzzles my neck.

- Would you rather play cards? I ask. Checkers? Chess? Backgammon? Do yoga?

- How about this? she says opening her pocketbook and pulling out a pre-rolled joint.

I laugh, tell her it's been awhile. She lights it, inhales deeply and passes it to me. We do several rounds of the hit-me-hit-you. Breath holding not something I'm used to. I'm practically winded. . . The dog's head is suddenly up. Listens intently, ears flattened back. I tell him to calm down. Sophia switches the tv to a jazz music channel, stands up and starts dancing in front of me. Slowly at first. Then faster till she's twirling and jumping with a gypsy's unbridled energy. I'm reminded of Nora dancing for Torvald in Ibsen's A Doll House. Sophia leaps, gambols, tosses her braless tits around. Long dark hair down. She's running her thin fingers through it. Whips it around. Wide arcs. Syncopated movement with the tight shift dress over her undulating ass.

I'm as worked up as she is.

She collapses on me. Finds my mouth while her hands work my belt buckle. I pull her sweater up over her head in one fast movement. The dog is barking at the door. Loudly. Frantically. Like being in heat is transferable. I tell him again to calm down, to sit down. I'd remind him he's been fixed, but there's no time.

I give myself over to Sophia. We do it right there on the couch. At one point I get the feeling of being watched. I'm tempted to turn the photo of Amanda face down. But don't. The feeling doesn't leave me.

Sunday Morning

Good Morning Starshine: I sleep late. Dreams of Nunberg and tomorrow mixing haphazardly with Sophia. She went home last night saying she'd sleep better in her own bed and she needed the rest. The dog and cat are downstairs patiently waiting when I finally get going. I let the dog out, feed the cat, put the coffee on, and check my one voice message thinking it could be Sophia. It's Max wondering why I'm late. I call him back and tell him to hold his schwanz. That I'm meeting with someone first and that I'll be there when I'm there.

I am in-and-out of the shower fast and just putting on my shoes when the doorbell rings. Could *this* be Sophia? I smile at the thought of having sex again so soon, and at her initiative. Amanda seldom took the lead but that was OK. And *this* is OK. Then I remember the meeting I scheduled. If it is Sophia I'm going to have make it *really* fast and hope she doesn't fall asleep again.

I open the door all set to say, Good morning lovely – or some other spinning wag. The dog pushes past and standing there is Zoe. I'm surprised and she's looking uncomfortable. We were supposed to meet at a diner for coffee. But here she is. And early. . . It flashes through my mind that this is one reason I don't live in the town where I teach. Pop-ins. Letting her into the house is not an option. I flashback to her flashing me. Fortunately she's in her Sunday best. Gothic church/cathedral.

- Sorry to show up at your house like this, she says, but I decided to go to my brother's cub scout program with my mother. We'll be leaving soon, she says emphatically.

- Sure Zoe, I say, no problem. Tell you what. It's a nice morning. Why don't we sit out here on the front porch and talk? Would you like some coffee?

I go back in. I'm pouring when the phone rings. It's Sophia. Just calling, she says, to see if you want to come over for lunch. . . I'd love to, I say, but I have plans with my father today. Raincheck? Next weekend?. . . Of course, she says. Talk to you in school. . . I'm tempted to say, I might not be there much longer. But I say only, Great!. . .   There's no trace of disappointment in her voice though she does hang up first, and a bit fast. Hope this isn't the start of some new parting-of-the-ways.

I bring the coffees outside and warn Zoe it's hot.

My neighbor across the street is out raking leaves. He gives me a shout and waves his rake. I smile and toss him back a cross-street toast. A couple of cars go by and honk. The dog is scratching at the door. I let him and the cat out. Take a sip of coffee.

It occurs to me in a fleeting way that the women I have the most contact with: Nunberg, Sophia, Deirdre, and Zoe, all seem to be taking the lead in *my* life. That I'm not in charge of squat. That they are cockjuggling all my most important moments. And decisions. Generating the cold fusion that drives much of August. . . It's a tough realization. But there's no time to give it a rope of thought now.

The Girl Can't Help It: So Zoe, I say, do you have any idea why I asked to meet with you? And on a Sunday?. . . I lean back. Relax. Don't want to rush or give her the impression I'm pressing.

- I imagine it has to do with keeping your job, she says. Like you told us about the other day. You probably see me as an obstacle to that. Which I confess I've been. Intentionally too.

I register surprise but not shock. That Zoe has been trying to fuck me over, maybe literally, has been a thought or two. I never did report her.

- My father and Bernadette Nunberg used to fool around, Zoe says without any prompt. I know it's hard to believe but he was a dapper stud. They met at a motorcycle rally. When the booty-pop bitch finally dumped him, he went downhill.

- I suspected they knew each other, I say. I pause and ask, Does this have anything to do with you coming on to me in our conferences? Or was that just my imagination?. . . It's an embarrassing question for both of us. I'm not even sure it's related.

- It wasn't your imagination, she says. My father wanted me to seduce you. Then give him proof so he could get you fired.

What? I think. The slimeball hates me that much? Would pimp his own daughter?

As if reading my mind she says, I'm nothing to him. I always stood up to him.

- If you dislike him so much why would you agree to the seduction?

- He offered me money to get started in New York.

I think about asking why she backed off and stopped the flashing and come-hithers. But I'm sure it's because I wasn't responding. Plus with her paintings selling she doesn't need Klein's money anymore. . . I ask what she and Nunberg are always arguing about.

- Mostly she didn't want me going along with my father's offer.

- So she knew about it.

- Yes.

- Obviously she has some good in her.

- Not much.

The dog comes close and Zoe scratches behind his ear. He sits down on his haunches. She suddenly says, Klein took to hitting my mother after the Nunberg affair and leaving for long periods. There were times we didn't know if we'd ever see him again. And hoped we wouldn't. Any love I had for him was long gone. We hadn't seen him for over a year when he came home this last time. The time you used him for a battering ram at Hudson's.

- I'm so sorry, Zoe. If there's anything I can– . . . She shakes her head. . . With some hesitation I ask, Has Klein been blackmailing Nunberg over a motorcycle accident years ago? One in which Nunberg was driving? Forcing her to fire me? Covering both his bases?. . . Zoe says that Klein was driving that night and that Nunberg was a passenger. There was nothing about it to hold over her head, she says. . . She takes a deep breath and says, I really don't want to talk about this anymore. It's hard. . . She starts to massage the dog under his collar and the dog's head bobs up-and-down with the kneading.

I say, The dog likes you. He senses good people.

The cat hops up on my lap, rolls over, and I pet her tummy. Zoe watches me and says, Trust, there's so little of it in life.

Zoe Koppel: *I had mixed feelings about coming here this morning. Why would any student go to a teacher's home unless it was one of those pathetic May-December romances? Or to work. August was smart not to hire me when he had the chance. . . I stopped short of telling him the whole story. I guess I should have. But it's too much, too soon. It's all part of the shit I'm trying to leave behind when I kick off for New York. Maybe with a little time. Or he can get it on his own. I gave him the opening. . . I almost laugh when he asks how I got his address. Chloroformed generation. Like just because you're unlisted you're off the flat screen. . . I never imagined he had this life. Old colonial. In-town suburbia, Hand Wave Avenue. Nice. Folksy. Right down to the cat and dog.*

Postcards From The Edge: Max is sitting at the kitchen table with his coat on when I walk in. Sorry I'm late Dad, I say, but a problem arose that I had to deal with. . . Hope it's not any problem caused by your schlong rising, or not rising, he says. You're too old for those sorts of dalliances. Remember what George Burns said, Sex at 90 is like trying to shoot pool with a rope. . . Haha, yeah Dad, funny, I say. But I'm not 90. . . You won't make it either if you don't stop fooling around with the help. Ernie says, Screw the help and they'll screw you. . . Dad, forget the Masters and Johnson! I need real advice about a real problem. . . The only real problems involve women and sex, he deadpans and I cannot tell if he's having a good day and screwing around. Or if it's a bad day and things just aren't computing. Zero Google hits. . . Cheezus H, will you knock it off! I practically shout. Dad, I need advice. *Now.* And not from Ernie either. . . OK son, he says, I'm listening.

With some hesitation I tell him the problem I'm faced with in work tomorrow. Explain that my boss is trying to destroy me. That I can grovel and throw myself on her mercy. Hope she has a Damascus Road conversion. Or figure out some way to leverage her off my ass. . . My father listens intently like he's the old Max again solving some engineering problem that has production stymied. Like his intellect is again registering in the optimum EEG range.

- Well, he says when I finish, it's a tough situation. From what you've told me groveling is a long shot. The strong rarely have respect for obsequious behavior. I'd say you need coercion, pure and simple.

- I still think Jimmy Klein is blackmailing her. Though it wasn't over a long ago motorcycle accident. So what then?

Max asks what I think are the key elements of Nunberg's personality. I tell him ambition and biker chick at heart. Sex? he says, and for a second I think he's back screwing around. But he's serious and repeats, The only real problems involve women and sex. . . I definitely think there are juices following under her leather and chains, I say thoughtfully. . . Let's say this fellow Klein knew something about her sex orientation or history, Max suggests. What could it be? And what kind of proof would he have that would be powerful enough, and concrete enough, to make a strong-willed woman like this Nunberg bend? She doesn't seem like the type of wimp pussy to be quietly used.

I think of Jimmy Klein. Everything I know about him. Everything I've ever seen or heard about him. It takes a long few minutes. Then slowly like a dimmer switch being lifted there's illumination. Partial. I explain my theory to Max and he says, You damn well might be onto something.

- I need to make a phone call, I say and leave him with his coat on sitting in the kitchen. . . It doesn't take long. . . When I come back he asks how it went. . . I don't know, I say honestly on edge. No one answered. That in itself might be important. . . He says to stay calm and be patient. . . I remind him I will probably be fired or suspended inside of 24 hours.

He says, Let's say you get some information on this principal. And have to stoop to her level. It's tough. Especially knowing there's mental illness in her family. Some people would tell you that you need to be able to look at yourself in the mirror the next day and like what you see. Not say, There's a real bastard. . . But in this case, no. . . Your role model should be that Italian Michael what's-his-name? The Godfather. . . Corleone, I say. . . That's him, Max says. Damn movie is always on tv. Protect your family. In this case you, and your fellow teachers. . . There are people who have to do the tough jobs in life because there are too many wusses with nerf ball nuts walking around. And at the end of the day if you look in the mirror and say, There's a bastard. Then so be it. Learn to live with it.

Maximilan August: *It feels good hearing Mike ask for advice again and know I'm able to give it coherently. I can't remember the last time he asked my opinion on anything important. Probably when he was a freshman and asked how you know if love is the real thing. I told him when love is not the last word in a telegram it stands a chance of being real. It was wiseass, but* *how the hell would I know how to explain love to a 14-year-old? He never again asked me anything personal till now. Today we worked through a problem. Then I gave him the advice I'd follow myself. I was honest and if the advice was messed up, so what? The only advice my own father ever gave me was, Don't drink too much or you'll get the screaming meemies. He said it with an accent which made it funny. . . I'm disappointed Mike has to run off now. But he said he would be back soon. He hoped.*

Chapter 25

Sunday Afternoon

Secret Agent Man: There is no car in the driveway when I pull up. Would have been surprised if there were. The cape is a piebald mix of pealing lime-green paint, moss-backed shingles, and a badly cracked foundation. Not much of a house. Less of a home from what I know. I knock loudly and press the doorbell. There's an old fashioned buzzer, Bzzzt! Then Sunday stillness. No rustling of feet, no snap of locks being thrown back like the last time I was here.

In his best seller *The Outliers* author Malcolm Galdwell says no one succeeds alone. That even where there is no discernible help, supporting factors come into play to insure the victory. . . It may be a conglomerate of fortuitous breaks that has led to me being here today. But it's only me going in, and only me that'll get arrested if anything goes wrong.

I have no hesitation.

I turn the doorknob and push. The door opens reluctantly. Strike point running in a tight groove in the floor. Stops. I look back and scan the street in both directions. One leaf raker, one gutter cleaner. Both far enough away to be poorly fleshed out. Clouds moving in fast, the day becoming a gloaming cardboard gray. I slide through and push to close it. The warped hollowed panel hitting the frame with a thud. Inside the over aroma is cigarette smoke and pot. Same as before.

I feel it's here. Know it's here. The answer to my year.

What exactly? Incriminating emails. Letters. A scrapbook. Tweets. Video. Receipts. A Diary. Journal. Photographs. What?

Zoe's paintings still fight to give the living room an elegance the place sadly lacks. There are new oils. A portrait that could be me. The face lined, strained against some unknown nemesis. Blue eyes lit with intelligence, pinched with tiredness.

A snap comes from above my head. Radiator pop? I freeze. Outside the wind is picking up. I only hope the deteriorating structure stays up long enough for me to get what I need.

I recon the layout quickly. Two bedrooms down, 2 up, no dining room or family room. Exits front and back first level. Many window shades drawn. I think they were open the day I was in here. . . The house is clean. The painted sheetrock and faded wallpaper fronted in many spots with Zoe's artwork and Jimmy Klein's photographs. Some of the blowups framed, most just thumb-tacked to the drywall.

I concentrate my search in Klein's flop off the kitchen first. Doesn't take long. No desk, nightstand, or bookshelves. Bureau drawers stuffed with nothing but stale smelling clothes. I pull the drawers all the way out, but nothing hidden. Closet short on clothes, long on camera equipment. Nikon and Leica mainly. An old Kinaflex. Assortment of lenses, filters. Light stands. Small canisters of film with varying ISO's. Nothing digital.

I open the cameras. Two have film that's been partially shot. I take the rolls, though exposing them to sunlight has already neutralized them. I think. I'm just about to move to Zoe's room when I decide to check between the mattress and box spring. Surprisingly there are two plywood bed boards. Is Jimmy Klein's back that bad?

I Can See Clearly Now: At the foot of the bed I lift the top board and sandwiched between the 4x8's is a bulky manila envelope. Jackpot? My heart accelerates. I look over my shoulder in a reflex action. Pull out the

315

envelope and almost drop it. I move into the kitchen, sit down at the table, spread out the contents. Bingo! This has to be it.

I go upstairs to Zoe's bedroom. On a small cheap trestle desk is the only computer in the house. I take it out of Sleep mode and check iPhoto. Not a single picture. Open Safari and check the internet History. No file sharing sites that I see. No photo sites or social networking groups bookmarked. I'm a little surprised Zoe's computer isn't password protected when she's not around. Surprised, but not too much. Not today. She did let me know they would be out of the house. Rather emphatically.

Her single bookcase has no journals, diaries, scrapbooks. Nothing nostalgic or self-revealing about the room.

I have all I need anyway with this envelope. I can check the names and dates online when I get home. I'm already anticipating what the Google searches will show.

Before leaving I decide to check the basement. The stairs are steep, the handrail loose. One section under the first floor bathroom has been partitioned off. Without hesitation I open the door. Inside all the accoutrements you would expect to find in a darkroom. Various sized processing trays, sink, an expensive looking enlarger with timer, paper safe, cutter, adequate venting. The drying line is draped with photos hanging like festooned pennants. Black and whites. All of Sophia and me. Last night. Smoking that joint. Later in various stages of undress and lovemaking. I take the prints and negatives and make a mental note to kick Klein's ass when I get the chance.

It's My Party: The stairs seem even steeper going up. I'm careful with the skewed sense of balance that bad knees give you. I'm halfway to the top when the front door scrapes against the overhead floor. I freeze. Someone enters. Pushes the door closed. Stumbles around. Crashes into a wall. Swearing. More shambling steps. Feet dragging. I'm watching the underside of the pine flooring following the progress. Living room. Bathroom. Pissing. Kitchen. Bedroom. Flop.

I wait. Silence. Then snoring. I ease myself into the living room and start for the front door. I should be nervous but I'm not. Maybe because I'm more pissed than anything. I stop, turn, and walk into the kitchen. Look into the bedroom. Klein is sprawled across the bed on his stomach. Head to the side, arms straight out as in a crucifix. Mouth open, drool running.

I take the exposed film out of my pocket. Pull it totally out of the canisters and drape it all over Klein's prostrate figure. Curlicued streamers for the drunken reveler. He stirs, rolls over. Knocks the ribbons of celluloid off. Curls up like a chambered nautilus. Resumes snoring.

I put the twisted rolls back on him. Wrap on around his head like a sweatband. Leave him arabesqued in a deep slumber.

Chapter 26

Monday - Zero Hour
The Shell Road

As Time Goes By: In Yates' Revolutionary Road Mrs. Givings wonders why things always have to change. Why, when all you ever wanted, you had. Why, when all you ever asked of god was for the world *not* take an evolutionary flop. For the status quo to remain static. For a spinning planet made for motion to accept that many of its inhabitants prefer stationary.

And now it's my place to ask the same question. Why should a world I was perfectly content with have to change, crack in the Matrix?. . . First my mother dies, then Amanda. Then Max shifts in-and-out.

And now Nunberg.

Life should be simple for me. But the shoulds are not my life. Financially I *should* be in good shape, but I am not. I *should* be a well respected veteran teacher, but because of a 2 year lapse I'm not. There *should* be many fruitful years till retirement with this a banner year. But Suddenly Nunberg. She balls up everything. Transforms wine into water, gold into base elements. Unbalances the equation.

I'm feeling restless. Combative. Like I should be applying camo and undergoing the ritualistic arming. Natty Bumpo a.k.a. Hawkeye a.k.a. the Pathfinder in Cooper's *Leatherstocking Tales* ready to charge the frontier whooping and bloodletting.

C'est Moi: It's Monday. Flashpoint. Time for the August family to settle accounts.

318

I shave close, comb my hair, press a shirt, put on my best dark suit and tie. I polish my finest pair of dress shoes, use a teeth-whitening kit on my yellowing ivories for a little extra glint. I splash on some designer scent Amanda gave me.

I go into the living room and pick up Amanda's picture. Take a long look at it. Touch the glass. Ask her out loud to be with me this morning. To guide me. . . I wait, half expecting some rush. As if her spirit or the holy ghost of fuck overs will lend me strength.

But there is nothing.

The Shape Of Things To Come: I email Nunberg that I will be in after this period with my answer to her demand. There's no reply back. Students want to know why I'm dressed up but seem satisfied with my answer that I'm going for a job interview. An important one.

The Film class is quietly watching 2001: A Space Odyssey. It's a puzzling movie for them and I'm a necessary voice-over. Clarity out of ambiguity, order out of chaos. It starts here and will finish in Nunberg's office next period. I'm trying to split my attention between the movie and the upcoming conference. Mentally going over the anticipated conversation while verbally trying to bring sense to the class of ape-like humans for the first-time-ever beating in each other's brains with leg bones and skeletal remains. Even as I explain that the bones represent the dawn of the tool age and that this is a watershed moment in our evolution, I'm wondering if next period will be a watershed moment in my own evolution.

- Mr. August, Giselle turns around, why did the movie just jump from a spinning bone to a spinning space station? I mean, didn't they just skip like what, a million years? Maybe a billion?

319

I smile. Trust Giselle to lighten my mood. I need to make a reasonable attempt now at explaining the segue and the related theme. I covered themes in the lead-in, but what teen remembers anything past the school doors? Not Giselle. I'm already X-ing out bringing lucidity to the hallucinogenic ending. Giselle will understand the closing when I understand collateralized swaps and financial arbitrage instruments. And maybe all the shit that has come my way this year. And not a foking moment sooner.

I pause the movie and tell her that the movie did indeed just jump millions of years. Congratulate her on her keen observation. She beams and we are back to Tom Shadyac's one-planet one-humanity. Mooshy times.

I start explaining the segue. Old educational model, teacher the answer machine. There's noise in the back and I see Marcus talking to Madison. . . Marcus, I say, report to the detention supervisor tomorrow afternoon. . . What! he howls. Why?. . . Because you were talking when I was. Only one teacher per class. . . But I was paying attention too, he protests. . . Really? Explain the segue. . . What's a segue? he asks. . . A segue is what's going to fill the time between now and your detention tomorrow afternoon. . . That's not fair, he wails. Don't I get a warning?. . . No, I say, no warning. . . I wasn't the only one talking, he whines in that thin reedy voice of his. . . You were the only one I saw, I say and think to myself, The account settling starts now. . . He protests more. Says I gave him a detention just the other day. Accuses me of not liking him. Of having it in for him. . . I smile and tell him to come back after school if he wants any more discussion. Madison is consoling him now, no doubt feeling lucky that she doesn't have a detention too. And maybe a little P.O.'d he even brought up the fact of others talking. In any case she draws a bye.

The movie resumes. Goes for another 20 minutes and ends.

The class files out.

Nunberg. She's in a regular day now checking email. Barking out orders. Pulling the creeping undies out of her crack. . . I hope I'll be reversing the flow. Taking her on an east-west journey against the planet's rotation and off the edge of a stupefyingly flat earth.

Dead Skunk In The Middle Of The Road: Her secretary waves me on. Nunberg's door is open. I walk in without knocking and take a long glance at the re-arranged pictures and assorted paraphernalia. All seems returned to normal after the K9 romp. I scarcely noticed the interior decorating or anything else last week when I was in here. Nunberg sees me looking and she smiles as if to say, Take a good last look.

- So, she says, you have made your decision?

My answer is to place a typed form in front of her and sit down. She eyeballs it fast like a laser scanner. I notice she's wearing a silky scarlet dress with black waist sash and scarf. Very appropriate. . . This is not an answer, she says. This is only your objective. Basically the same one you told me about in the library.

- I've decided not to resign, I say.

- You're wasting my time. I told you this was not acceptable.

- I've added the call line proposal, I say . . . I lean over and point to it on the typed form. . . It's something my students want, I say calmly. . . I quickly outline the particulars, reiterate their enthusiasm for it.

- A student-to-student call line will never do, she finally says. It would not be happening within school boundaries, hours, or common sense parameters. We cannot be letting students give serious emotional advice to other students even with the backups and safeguards you cite. Do you have anything else? I can see you want to play this the hard way.

I ignore her last and say, I believe it should be given the go ahead. There is nothing wrong with any of it.

- Mr. August, she says eyeing my suit suspiciously and talking patiently like a parent to an unruly child, are you being stubborn or just difficult?

- Professional, I say. If you won't approve this I'm going over your head. To the superintendent if necessary. . . My voice is unemotional. My face registers nothing. Even as my metabolism kicks into overdrive.

- That is your contracted right, she says. You will be seeing the superintendent soon enough anyway. But I assure you he will support me in this. And will be receptive to firing you.

There's no reading her voice or body language. I'm reminded of Alex in Anthony Burgess's A Clockwork Orange. A thug who could talk sweetly of Beethoven and beauty while practicing rape and violence. Maybe an extreme comparison but all year she's had me in the crosshairs like some zodiac principal. And I'm not feeling generous.

- Just so I'm clear. You won't endorse my paperwork? I ask. And you want me to resign or I will be fired?

- Correct, she says and for a brief second, her voice falters. It seems she might be on the verge of relenting. Of saying, OK this is much better, I approve. . . But the hesitancy I thought I saw is gone. Her lioness eyes focusing hard on me. If she's fighting an internal battle over this, the predatory side has won.

I pause. Realized coming in that the chances of the call line putting my paperwork over were practically nil. Like scanning the skies for ET signals that just aren't there. Still, there's always hope. With any rational person. Trouble is Nunberg is more into self-preservation than being rational.

I need to take this all the way.

In a starburst flash it all plays out in my mind.

The Ride Of The Valkyries: I will put Jimmy Klein's stuffed manila envelope on top of Nunberg's desk. Take out the photos, names and dates on the back. Nunberg's face, body, and name on every single one. Span around 15 years. The others in the photos are various bosses she's had over the years. Department chairs, assistant principals, superintendents, BOE members. Even a curriculum director. Intersecting her career with these higher-ups was time consuming. Couldn't vary them all online. But enough. Lots of naked people. Lots of raunchy sex.

I turn the top photo towards her. Then slowly show the rest. One-by-one. . . Nunberg stares but there's no stunned reaction like I expect. She did not get this far by overreacting. . . But I'm cool too. Knowing that my year and career have come down to this moment has chilled me.

- You know what these are, I say as I flip through them.

- I have absolutely no idea what you're talking about, she says. And I would appreciate you putting those things away.

- You had sex with virtually every boss you ever had. Screwed your way to the top, so to speak. Men, women. Married, single. Do I need to go on?

There's rapid blinking. Hand rubbing from her.

- You have some photos, she finally says. I'm not denying that.

- Take a better look at them . . . I place the pile squarely in front of her. She glances quickly at the top few, then neatly restacks. . . You have noted, I say, that there are names and dates.

When she pushes the photos and typed forms back, it's with a cold look. Reptilian. If she were a snake I'd be crapping in my pants now and reaching for the anti-venom.

As bluffs go it's pretty damn good. She's got the sang-froid of an archetypal Agatha Christie murderer. The type that can nonchalantly dump arsenic into your tea and breezily ask you if you want a crumpet or watercress sandwich with that. . . I've left Nunberg's presence more than once this year with my ass in my hand.

But that's not going to happen today.

- And you're not bothered by these photos, I ask, because—

- Such things are easily photoshopped. As these obviously were. I don't even recognize most of these people. And if I ever see these photographs again, or hear about them. . .

I think to myself that this conference is going like a Japanese Noh play. Serene introduction, extended middle narrative, and an ending that is swift and surprisingly sudden. The three part jo-ha-kyū pace is natural. Parallels the birdsong outside. It's time to end it. Let the kyū descend.

- Maybe you should look at this one, I say and hand her a photo of Superintendent Hoxley and her. Bare-ass naked. Humping on what looks like the sofa. In his school office.

Frantic chirping turns my head. A singing group of brown speckled finches in the rhododendrons has been startled by a crow. I almost smile.

- Another obvious photoshop, she says and for a second I think she's going to tear it up. Instead she says, I'm warning you buster. If you don't want your ass hit with a libel—

- Ahh, I say, the real Nunberg . Biker chick at heart. But allow me to finish. Jimmy Klein was, and apparently still is, a helluva photographer when he wants to be. A pro at one time. Including investigative work. I've

324

seen his photos at his house. Very impressive. In all sorts of light. He peeks in a lot of windows. Stalker type. . . If these photos ever get out it will be public humiliation. Even if you've done nothing technically against the law. You're lucky they don't stone adulterers anymore.

I settle back. Her face is blank. Wonder what she's thinking? No sign now that the nympho-for-promotion accusation with photos has gotten to her. Maybe she's shored up by the almost certainty that even if she's terminated she'll still get a nice severance package. Six figures plus, for sure. . . I have no doubt she's mentally played through all this what-if-I'm-accused scenario many times. Sexual users are sneaky bastards.

- So there's been no serial sex? I ask when she remains quiet.

- I won't even dignify that accusation with a denial. And I am telling you for the last time to leave. And if you ever repeat what you just said to me. . .

Corriger la fortune – a French expression meaning to correct one's fortune through denial of the past. Nunberg does it well, Cannes award quality.

I take a deep breath. I could show these photos to the superintendent now, and hope he realizes on what side of the August-Nunberg his best interest lies. But I think a photo forensics lab is the way to go first. Have these photo verified. I believe that photoshopping can be detected with the right equipment. Color saturations, compression, other anomalies. Later Hoxley. The press if necessary.

Sending Out An S.O.S.: That's how it plays out in my mind. In reality we're just sitting staring at each other. Again. Interminably. Quietly. Not even the birds singing.

Suddenly from just outside the door there's a loud commotion. Followed by my 6 mentees walking in. Nunberg's secretary right behind them. I tried to stop them, she says, but–

- We're here to support Mr. August, Jack Kaufman says leading the charge. The others nod. Destiny steps forward. He's done a great job tutoring me for AP. He's helped all of us. . . TJ says, He got me in the play. . . Audrey says, Me too. . . Jorge says, If it wasn't for Mr. A, my future as a teacher would be– . . . They all talk at once. Even Zoe seems to be mouthing something. Nunberg listens for 30 seconds then stands up. Thank you for coming, she says. I understand your points. But it's time for you all to. . . The students reluctantly leave. TJ hesitates at the door and says, Good luck Mr. August.

When we're alone Nunberg says, That was impressive, I have to admit.

- I knew nothing about it, I say.

She's silent. Then says, But it changes nothing.

Is she sad? I sense an effusive transfer of emotion.

While trying to read her face I think of those 6. Know now that whatever happens I will be all right. The cornfields have gone to stump. The pastures surrounding the town are rolling brown, soon to be covered in white. But I will be OK. Those 6 have stockpiled me for the winter. No longer a lone pioneer weathering the years. Buffeted, battered, surrounded only by the markers of those who have gone before.

I have support. Maybe even affection.

I am ready. I know what I have to do. Even if it costs me my job.

She Lets Her Hair Hang Down: I say, Listen Ms. Nunberg I'm in possession of something I think you should have. . . I take the manila envelope from my briefcase and pull out the photos. . . I say, Jimmy Klein had these photographs. Now I do. I don't want anything to do with blackmail or all the trouble these shots could bring. To a lot of lives. . . I put the photos back into the manila envelope and lay it in front of her. . . They are yours to keep. To destroy. Whatever you want to do. The negatives are in there too. Nothing has been digitalized. Jimmy Klein is out of your life. For good.

She pulls the photos partially out. Eyes them fast. Pushes them back in, and closes the clasp. I can see her mind racing. Are these really the originals? Are there really no copies? Why is August being so nice to me, especially after all the grief I've given him? Nunberg's face shifts through a range of pictorial thumbnails. . . I say to her, Trust, there's so little of it in life. Those were Zoe's words to me yesterday. Maybe we can start here. And now.

Tight on Nunberg. Her face starts to brighten, skepticism and distrust giving way.

- The only thing I'm asking for, I say, is a fair shake at meeting my objective and keeping my job. If I really have become a bad teacher, I don't deserve the right or honor of staying on as a classroom teacher. It's your call.

I sound really noble. The sincerity legit.

This blind generosity and guileless probity were unplanned. I was fully prepared to push the accusation and all it entails. To include even continuing the blackmail. Goal: To force a good evaluation for me, Becky, and anyone else Nunberg's been trying to ax. But the harmonizing appearance of my 6 changed all that. And now I'm hoping now that my magnanimity will lead to her own. I know I'm making myself into a sacrificial lamb if she doesn't cave. Giving the photos to her with no stipulations, no duplicates. But it's just the right, and the good thing to do.

Trust.

327

A massive headache is rising.

- You know Mike, she finally says, I never wanted to terminate your employment. But Jimmy Klein told me that unless I. . . Maybe I deserved you stringing me along just now. Making me squirm before you gave me these – she taps the envelope. . . Can we put all this behind us? Never mention any of it again? Let me sign your paperwork. And we can both get back to the business of educating the young.

There is no trace of principal invectiveness.

She signs with a flourish. We shake. I take the signed form. Feel my heart rate coming down. The headache ebbing.

Ticket To Ride: As I'm leaving the main office School Nurse Betty stops me and wants to know if I changed my mind about the field trip this year. It would be a good thing to do Mike, she says, the right thing. . . She no sooner asks, then I notice my 6 standing off to the side. Waiting. The Kid says, How did it go? The faces around him tense. . . I shoot them all a thumbs up. There's cheering. Like they're ready to hoist me up onto their shoulders and parade me around the school. . . I was already smiling, now I start laughing. What's so funny? Nurse Betty asks. . . Field trips, I say as the 6 surround me and arms reach out for hugs. I am up with those. Just took a helluva one.

Chapter 27

June - Graduation

Pomp and Circumstance

River Deep - Mountain High: It's a beautiful sun-splashed evening. A denim sky. Warm and dry. Shadows from the trees lying soft over lawn chairs and blankets. Many family members and friends in attendance. Including the parents of my 6 novitiates. Commencement speakers on the outdoor dais. Didactic swathes of advice. Pursed-lipped wisdom. Mylar balloons bobbing above the seated heads.

Introspection - Is That All There Is?: Soon after my conference with Nunberg life returned to a comfortable script devoid of big surprises and unrecognizable patterns. Actor Rob Lowe called such a period after you reach a goal The Peggy Lee Syndrome. Said he experienced it when he achieved success early in *The Outsiders*. For him it was a letdown feeling. For me and the entire school it was a much appreciated and needed hairpin turnabout.

The last speaker is Destiny Gibson with the valedictory address. She talks about the years that bind, and the incommunicable past. Mentions specific school watershed events. Refers to a dozen classmates and faculty who made a difference. Says, Mr. August, a teacher who lives poetry. . . She finishes to a thick round of applause and hoots and hollers. . . The graduating class is presented to Superintendent Hoxley and the BOE. The first rows of the class rise and move as a line to stage right.

The alphabetical roll begins with Higham saying, Julie Abraham. Nunberg handing out diplomas.

Introspection - High Heel Sneakers: Nunberg. She's been a new person since November. No longer the meshuganah shiksa. Not quite bubbly. Not a bitch-cumbered wet rag either. Everyone's noticed the difference but I never took credit. To do that I would have had to reveal her sordid past. And I'm not into character assassination. Guess she did what she thought she had to do to get ahead. Coming from those years with a low glass ceiling. In any case I'm no one to judge. . . Rumor has it that she's up for assistant superintendent.

The cap-and-gowned seniors are crossing the stage one-by-one. Accepting their diplomas. Shaking hands. Moving the tassel. One girl does a cartwheel, another   flashes the peace sign. A boy pantomimes sailing his cap. Nunberg wearing a tight smile when an air horn blasts. School administrators around her forcing good-natured tolerance.

Introspection - We're In The Money: The financial pressure came off admin and the school budget in mid-November. Somehow the town's finance board reshuffled monies and came up with at least a one year fix. Rumor had it that it was my father-in-law's doing. But if Oliver Phelps was involved he never said. No commented a reporter. Of course never contacted me.

Two colorful beach balls are now being batted around in the student section. One floats into the parent seats and they keep it going. I look at

Nunberg and she's looking less strained. Getting used to the idea that this celebration is about the students. Let the good times roll. Or float.

Introspection - Jeepers Creepers: Nunberg. I have to confess that there was satisfaction in making her squirm 7 months ago. Ian McEwan in Atonement says that when people take revenge the same reward centers are activated in the brain that are associated with satisfying hunger, thirst, and sexual appetite. . . I'm eating much better since our conference. Have gained weight. My ring stays on.

Audrey Clover! Higham's miked voice rings out. She walks across the stage like it's a jump house and shakes Nunberg's hand like she's pumping a well dry. Small private college next year.

Jorge Espinoza. Full athletic scholarship. Took Destiny to the prom. Restaurant building a steady and loyal clientele. He gives me a wave.

Destiny Gibson. Ivy bound. Summer internship at the state's biggest daily. We never did get her call-line idea past the board.

Jack Kaufman. New York University next year. We took second at Beatnik Now!. Performed twice more including the Talent Show here. Now he's a solo act.

Zoe Koppel. She leaves for NYC tomorrow. With money to burn. And a few connections. Had an offer from The Art Institute but is opting instead to work.

Introspection - Pandora's Box: Zoe. Quite a girl. Never said she set up Jimmy Klein's fall. And I never asked. . . I still don't know for certain who wrote that letter, though given how it's all played out it was probably him. But who knows or cares. He's left town again. His means of employment temporarily gone . . Similarly I never found out what that damn Do You Have Hot Lips contest was all about. Nunberg cancelled it after our conference. It'll always be Fitzgerald's Dr. T. J. Eckleburg billboard to me. A subliminal lesson that so much of our lives and motivations center on sex. But not all. Brave new worlds.

Giselle Martin, Higham sings out. All smiles as she crosses the stage. Going to a beauty academy next year to become a cosmetologist. She gives a generic wave and forgets to move her tassel.

Curt Moseby. Delayed enlistment with The Marine Corps. I never did deal with him for ruining Max's lawn. I thought of siccing Jorge on him, but vigilante justice was not the answer. Maybe The Corps is. He struts across the stage like he's already an NCO.

Madison Murphy. Never apologized. Did ask me for a recommendation which I gave. Tore her ACL playing softball. Limping now. Soccer future at a small Catholic college questionable.

TJ Sato. Off to basic training within a few days. The Basic Military Food Service Training School after that. He and Audrey are still friends but no longer hand holding. I told him I would write. I wave now.

Marcus Schmidt. Fouled up the final film project. Barely graduating. Working for a landscaper who specializes in curtain drains and sewer line excavation. Sees me and for a second I think he's going to flash the bird. Instead he stumbles on the stairs.

Introspection - Clap Your Hands: My twisty-twiny ensemble of six did well this year. What the future will bring who knows. But I'm optimistic. The German-Jewish philosopher Walter Benjamin wrote about an angel of history who flew backwards, hands to his face, appalled by the devastation behind him.

But that didn't happen here.

X,Y,Z. The last graduate crosses the stage and the cheering rises to the level of a title game. Caps spin into the air. Huzzahs rise to the heavens. I'd hug Sophia but she's not close enough. George says, Another year. He laughs.

The orchestra and chorus start the recessional, Graduation (Friends Forever). We march out and the faculty form a reception line near the gate. Over the heads of the first diploma holders to walk the gauntlet and get congratulated, I see the parents of my six. Thank you so much, Mr. Espinoza shouts. His wife moves in and gives me a hug.

There's still Project Graduation. A long night of party ahead. But it's over for now.

Epilogue

The Time Of My Life: It was an interesting and rewarding year for me. For the most part I avoided what James Hilton in Goodbye, Mr. Chips called the creeping dry rot of pedagogy. The dreaded sameness that kills the profession for many veteran teachers. I varied my lessons and the students were challenging. I have Nunberg to thank for that. At least partly.

Of course she was also the reason that my life for the first 9 weeks of this school year was hell. Dominated by reaching a school objective that proved to be a big con. It was draining. On the other hand without it I would not have met my 6 mentees. And my life would have been definitely shallower for their absence.

All's well that ends well. Simplistic. But I'm feeling the truth of it.

Among some who know me peripherally the perception is that I'm now veined with Zen-like contentment. Since November they've occasionally said, August, you look happier. You've changed. . . But that's a false positive. I don't feel different. I'm still the same Mike. Still tired. Still drinking too much. Still can't pass a physical. Still worried about Max who's gotten worse. Still seeing Sophia occasionally. Still friends with Deirdre. Still missing Amanda.

Still up-to-here with the Gibraltar-like cragginess.

If there's been any personal change it's that I know that through it all we teachers *do* make a difference. Sometimes when we least think.

Homeward Bound: Max never asked about my conference with Nunberg. I was at his house later that watershed day and played the guitar for him. He hummed along, then closed his eyes. As I rose he asked in a sleepy voice what I saw in the mirror. I looked at my hazy reflection in the framed portrait of Bernice and him hanging on the wall and said, I see a bastard. But he's on the rise. The descent is over.

He smiled.

I kissed him on the head, and softly closed the door behind me.

Made in the USA
Charleston, SC
18 June 2013